RIPPED OFF

RIPPED OFF

AN IAN CONNAH THRILLER

VAUGHN C. HARDACKER

Encircle Publications
Farmington, Maine U.S.A.

Cover design by Christopher Wait
Cover images © Getty Images

Published by:

Encircle Publications
PO Box 187
Farmington, ME 04938

info@encirclepub.com
http://encirclepub.com

To: my grandson, Nickolas Kaad
Jane, Skipper, and Ginger
Dana M. Hardacker

All my brother and sister Marines,
especially those in harm's way

In Memory of

Constance Lee (Harris) Hardacker (1951 – 2006)
Lorraine Jean (Virgin) Hardacker (1929 – 1991)
Beecher Norman Hardacker (1918 – 1998)
Norman Carl Hardacker (1942 – 2006)
Dana M. Hardacker (1951 – 2022)
Marvin Earl Hartley (1924 – 1986)
Margaret Frances (McGuire) Hartley (1925 – 1975)
Marvin E. (Skip) Hartley Jr. (1945 – 2019)
Kathryn Donna Hartley (1947 – 1963)
Shirley Dawn (Harris) Bokun (1936 – 2019)
Richard Franklin Harris (1939 – 2012
James Louis Harris (1941 – 2021)
Ryan Kaad (1994 – 2017)

War is the statesman's game,
the priest's delight,
the lawyer's jest,
the hired assassin's trade.
—Percy Bysshe Shelley

PART I

RETURN TO THE GAME

1

For the fourth time, Ian Connah walked out of the courthouse a free man. Four marriages and four divorces, in baseball jargon, he was O-for-four. His disposition, which was usually surly at best, was especially foul. He'd disliked paying his former wives to live with him; now, the court was forcing him to pay them *not* to live with him… and that really pissed him off.

He couldn't help but think that it was enough to cause his return to his former profession. He immediately realized that his thinking was truly screwed up. Going back to that life was a *bad* idea. He was not a religious man by any definition of the phrase. Still, he thanked God that during the ten years he had been a hitman for Paddy O'Reilly's South Boston mob, he'd stashed away enough money to last him the rest of his life. In his former profession, when someone retired, it meant they were either in prison, or their spouse was filing a claim with their life insurance company.

He chuckled, thinking what the divorce settlement would have been if the judge knew his true worth. He'd been smart with his money. Since high school, he had invested it with Harry Sandberg, his younger brother's friend, and a reputed financial wizard. Thanks to Harry, that nest egg had grown substantially. As much as he hated doing it, the court's judgment was going to force him to dip into that money.

On the other hand, a simple investment in the price of four hollow-point bullets would remove all of his financial burdens. He immediately dismissed that idea as lunacy. Everyone knew that whenever the cops arrived at a murder scene, they immediately listed the victim's spouse as a suspect. An ex-spouse who was paying multiple former wives—in his case, all of whom refused to move on and find new suckers to marry—would immediately send him past the status of "person of interest" to that of the "prime suspect."

He settled back in his four-by-four truck and looked at the half-horse town where he had been living incognito since he had given up "The Life." So, here he was. If ever a place was in its death throes, it was Prefontain Station, Maine. He once proposed that the city council shorten the name by dropping the Station part. After all, he stated, the railroad station had closed more than forty years ago—in fact, no railroads even ran through there anymore. The councilman to whom he spoke looked at him in such a way that Connah knew what he was thinking—something along the line of him being a friggin' idiot from *away*. Nevertheless, the hick town did have one thing in its favor: none of his former colleagues in Boston had a clue about its existence.

$ $ $ $ $

Connah turned into his drive on Lake Osprey and saw his bank manager, Herbert Harvey, standing on his deck, staring at the lake. He walked to the deck and knew from the look on Harvey's face that this was not a social call. Harvey was the only person, along with Harry Sandberg and Glenn Ouellette, Connah's personal accountant, who knew about Connah's turbulent past, and how much money he currently had in his portfolio. "You don't look happy, Herb."

"If you think *I'm* unhappy, wait until I tell you what I learned this morning."

"Why do I suddenly get the feeling that what has so far been a very crappy day is about to blow up into a full-fledged shit-storm?" Connah walked past Harvey and leaned forward, resting his forearms on the deck railing. He studied the unusually calm lake surface and said, "Okay, lay it on me."

"You're broke. Not quite to the point of insolvency, but broke just the same."

Connah slowly turned his head, and his eyes narrowed. "*Broke?*"

"Broke."

"What about the investments that Sandberg made for me?"

"There never were any investments."

"I had three million dollars, not to mention that stock in that solar panel company he told me was going great guns."

"Over the past five years, Sandberg and Ouellette sold all your shares in Sun Power, Incorporated, and bit-by-bit, withdrew what money you had in my bank."

"How the hell could they do that without my knowing it?"

"You may recall that—against my advice, by the way—you signed a Power of Attorney giving them full authority to make any and all financial transactions for you. My people knew that you'd done so and thought nothing of it. To cut to the chase, by the time you send out this month's alimony checks, you'll need a co-signer to buy a pack of gum."

Connah turned from the railing, crossed the deck, and unlocked the sliding glass door that overlooked the lake. "I think I need a drink. You want to join me?"

2

Connah sat in his favorite chair, staring at the moon's reflection on the lake surface. He slowly twirled bourbon around the inside of his glass. He picked up the phone and called Glenn Ouellette. After making several unsuccessful attempts to reach him, he tried calling Harry Sandberg. That phone rang once, and he got a message stating the number was no longer in service. He broke the connection and called his brother in New Hampshire. Someone answered on the second ring.

"Hello."

"Mandy?"

"Yes, who's this?"

"Ian… is Tom there?"

There were a few moments of silence, and Connah knew what was happening. His brother's wife, Amanda, suffered from manic depression and dealt with it by self-medicating. Under normal circumstances, Mandy was an attractive, intelligent woman. However, during a manic episode, she could be in one of two states. If she was on a high, she'd be in constant motion, talking incessantly. On a low, she could barely function, usually sitting in a semi-comatose state. When she spoke again, she said, "Tom?"

"Tom, my brother."

"Oh, that Tom! I'll go look."

After a minute of listening to "Dancing with the Stars," a male voice came on the line. "This is Tom. Who is this?"

"Didn't she tell you that your brother was on the phone?"

"She's having a bad day."

"Yeah, that's goin' around. Forget about Amanda. I need to get in touch with Sandberg."

"Gee, Ian, I haven't heard from Harry in over six months."

"That makes two of us."

"I believe that his sister lives in Portland, though. You want her number?"

"Yeah, my business with him is urgent. I'm hoping that his sister knows where he is."

"Hold on," Tom said. "I'll only be a minute." When he set the phone down, the loud clunk almost busted Ian's eardrum.

Tom was back in no more than two minutes. "His sister's name is Pergamos."

"Are you shitting me?"

"Pardon?"

"Who in their right mind would give a kid a name like Pergamos?"

"All I can tell you is that it wasn't me. Now you want this number or not?"

"Yeah, give it to me." Connah reached across the table beside his chair and pulled a small notepad to him. He grabbed a pencil and said, "I'm ready."

"The area code is 207—"

"Every area code in Maine is 207."

"Boy, you have a hair across your ass today. The number is 353-5353. Damn, I should have remembered that huh? This number is a couple years old, so I don't know if it's still good."

"What about an address?"

Tom read off an address in Portland and then asked, "So, how you doing, brother?"

"Jeanie just took my ass to the cleaners." He got a sudden thought and chuckled.

"I say something funny?" Tom inquired.

"I left the courthouse and found out that my accountant, Glenn Ouellette, and your old buddy Harry took a powder with every penny I had set aside."

"No?"

"The reason I chuckled is that neither the judge nor Jeanie know that I'm so friggin' broke I can't pay attention, let alone alimony. So, you can see that, like Amanda, I'm having a bad day."

"Don't go there, Ian."

"You're right. If she had any say in the matter, I doubt she would choose depression. I have to go. Talk to you later." Connah broke the connection and threw the cordless phone at the couch. He flopped into his chair, a worn leather recliner, and thought about his plight. Going after Harry Sandberg and recouping whatever was left of his stolen money was a given. There was a significant debt to be collected. His dilemma was twofold: First, where would

Sandberg run? A place where they wouldn't ask questions—many Caribbean islands and several Asian and European countries would fit the bill. The second problem was the kicker. Where would he get the money to finance his pursuit of Sandberg? Tom had been out of work for the past year, losing his six-figure salary since the hi-tech company he worked for outsourced his position. Possibly hiring some Hindi who worked for four figures a year... if that. So, he doubted he could borrow from him.

That really only left him with one option, Padraig (Paddy) O'Reilly, his old boss in the Boston mob. Connah got up and poured himself another drink. Showing up at Paddy's door, after two years of hiding, might possibly take care of all of his problems... especially if the Irish mobster held a grudge. There was a high probability that he would. When it came to having a grudge, Paddy was like an elephant. He would carry it to the grave.

Connah drained his glass and resolved to drive south first thing in the morning. He would go to Tom's and decide what he would do from there.

3

Harry Sandberg's sister lived in a 200-year-old two-story house sub-divided into apartments in the Munjoy Hill neighborhood. Connah wondered what the rent must be, given the view of the Casco Bay they offered. He also played with the thought that maybe Pergamos Sandberg was a financial whiz like her brother, possibly an embezzler too. He always believed that apples don't fall far from the tree.

The panel on the porch showed her apartment listed as 2-B. He pressed the buzzer and, after a few moments, a husky female voice said, "Yes?"

"Miz Sandberg?"

"Who's askin'?"

"My name is Ian Connah. I need to get in touch with your brother, Harry."

"Come up, the door at the top of the stairs. On the right."

The door buzzed, giving him access. He climbed the stairs and saw a woman standing on the threshold of the door on the right. Pergamos Sandberg looked nothing like her brother. Harry was short, dark, obese, and just plain ugly; his sister was tall, blonde, shapely, and attractive.

"Miz Sandberg?" he asked.

She nodded. "Call me Perrie. Come in."

"I'm Ian."

Connah followed her into her apartment and noted how neat it was. His first impression was that everything had its place in Perrie Sandberg's world. She seemed to be the most organized person he'd ever encountered.

Once inside, she closed the door and asked, "Would you care for something to drink?"

"No, thank you. I don't want to impose on you any more than I already have."

"So, you're looking for my brother."

"I am. I have some business with Harry."

"Your name is familiar. Are you by any chance related to Tom Connah?"

"Yes, I am. Tom's my brother."

"I dated him back in high school. He was quite popular back then. I don't recall you, though."

"I'm five years older. I was out of high school before Tom went in."

"I've often wondered what became of him."

"He's living in New Hampshire now, married, and working for some computer company."

"Well, if you see him, tell him I said, hi. Now, what's Harry done, stole something of yours?"

"Nothing that serious. I just need some financial advice."

"If you want my advice, you'll take your money to Foxwoods and play blackjack. You'll have a better chance of coming out ahead. My brother is a get-rich-quick-schemer and is always on the lookout for people who want to get poor quick. As for your question, I really don't know where he is. He and I haven't spoken in over ten years. If he took off with enough of your money, you might try the Caribbean. He always hated the cold weather."

Connah studied her body language and saw none of the tell-tale signs of prefabrication. "Well. I'm sorry to have bothered you."

As he turned toward the door, she said, "Ian, if you do find him, don't tell him we talked. I don't want him within 500 miles of me. You may have figured out that there's no love lost between us."

Connah acknowledged her request by nodding his head once and left.

$ $ $ $ $

Ainsley is a small town nestled in the Merrimack Valley of southern New Hampshire. The majority of the residents are hi-tech workers employed in neighboring Massachusetts. Longtime residents, who had lived there before the high technology boom of the 1970s and 80s, believed that everything below Concord was no longer New Hampshire. It was a suburb of Boston and could be annexed by Massachusetts any day. Connah studied the subdivision as he followed the winding road through the trees. The homes that lined the thoroughfare were all in the half-million-plus range and sported large yards, many of them so new that the landscaping was treeless and immature.

He came up to Tom's house and turned into the drive. His brother stood in the yard, leaning on a lawn rake. Connah stepped from his car and stood beside it. "Leaves haven't started turning yet."

"I know, but I need to get some of this thatch up." A small pile of brown grass lay by his feet.

"Wait until spring, and then burn it. That's what the old man always did."

"Times have changed, Ian. You strike a match to light a cigarette, and some environmentalist will start screaming air pollution. And then throw a bucket of water on it and you. What do you think will happen if I start a fire on the lawn?"

Connah shrugged. "That's why I live where I do. Not so many idiots up there."

Tom turned toward the garage and motioned for Connah to follow him. Once inside, Tom hung the rake on one of the many holders lining the wall. Always fastidious, Tom's garage was as neat and possibly more organized than some people's houses, with the exception of maybe Perrie Sandberg's apartment.

"How's Amanda doing?" Connah asked.

"She's having what I call a *tween day*."

"Okay, I give up. What's a *tween day*?"

Tom looked like a lost child. It was evident that his wife's burden was also his. "She's neither up nor down—she's just here. Do you know what I mean? It's like she's lost in a limbo where she's the only occupant."

"I don't want to be in the way. I'll head on to Boston."

"You're more than welcome to stay for as long as you like, but if she seems distant, it isn't about you. Okay?"

"I can deal with that. If I forget and become frustrated with her, you set me straight. Is that a deal?"

"You can count on it. Now, come on in."

Connah knew why Amanda chose to battle her bipolar disorder by self-medication; her prescribed medication bottomed her out, and she felt like a zombie. Therefore he did not reply, nodded agreement, and followed his brother into the house.

The interior of Tom and Amanda's home was as neat as the garage. Not a single thing was out of place. "This place looks terrific," Ian remarked.

"Yesterday, Mandy was in one of her moods where she can't sit still. When she gets that way, she cleans."

Connah gritted his teeth and thought: Great, she'll be dusting me off if I sit for ten seconds.

Amanda exploded into the room, pushing a dust mop across the hardwood floor. She saw her brother-in-law and abruptly stopped. "When did you get here?"

"About five minutes ago."

"How long are you staying?"

"That depends."

She began dust mopping the floor again. "Okay."

Tom led him into the kitchen and opened the refrigerator. He took two beers out, handed one to his brother, and motioned Ian to follow him. He opened the sliding glass door that led to the deck, walked out, and flopped in one of the chairs surrounding a large glass-topped table. An umbrella kept the sun off them as they sat. "So," Tom said, "what brings you back here? I thought you said that you would never leave Maine again."

"I need to find Harry."

"I knew that as soon as you told me that he'd embezzled your money."

"How well do you really know him?"

Tom took a drink of his beer. "We hung out back in high school. We were never really close, though. However, he always struck me as being honest and trustworthy."

"Tom, that was thirty years ago, we're older, and times are different."

"I know, better than anyone I know." Tom leaned back. "I'm a forty-plus-year-old man in high-tech, a thirty-something's industry. Do you have any idea of how many resumes I've sent out this past year? Hundreds, out of which I got three interviews, one company even flew me to Dallas. But the minute you sit down across the desk from a twenty or thirty-something, you know the interview is over, and you won't be getting a second."

"Yeah, getting old does suck. The thing that irritates me about it is that I haven't done a single thing to get old—I just hung around long enough."

"All that aside," Tom said, "how much did Harry steal from you?"

"The truth?"

"Yeah, that would be nice."

"All I had."

"How much?"

"More than three million."

Tom leaned forward. "Holy shit, Ian. I worked for big money for years, and I haven't gotten anything close to that. In fact, I'm thinking of putting this place up for sale. We're at the point where we can't afford it anymore." Tom was the better looking of the two brothers, six feet two inches tall, with dark hair and a mustache (both of which were now turning gray). His face was starting to show worry lines, and Ian realized how hard the past few years had been on him. "Do you know that in the last ten years, I've had seven jobs, and I didn't leave one of them voluntarily? Every one of which has been outsourced to some third-world shit-hole."

"I had no idea, Tommy. To me, you were always the one whose life was stable."

"Well, until the millennium it was, since then it's been one year of work followed by a year and a half of unemployment. We won't even mention the beating we took on retirement."

Ian gave him a questioning look. "You have no retirement?"

"The majority of high-tech companies didn't have pension funds. They dangled a carrot called the *stock option*, which by the way is of no value if the price of a share falls below the option price or if the company has been bought out or gone away."

"That sucks…"

"That's enough about my troubles. How about you? I've never known what you did for a living. The last job you had that I knew about was the Marines. What did you do that paid enough for you to stash away three million?"

"You remember what I did in the Corps?"

Tom took a drink. "If I remember correctly, the old man raved for a week when he learned you'd become a sniper rather than learn some type of trade."

"Yeah, not a lot of jobs for a shooter…"

Tom's head snapped up. "No, way… There's no way that you earned a living from shooting contests."

"You're right about that."

"We were pretty good with firearms. You still haven't told me what you did to make that much money."

"Tom, I killed people."

"A mercenary?"

"An assassin, although I guess one could say they are one and the same. I worked for the O'Reilly mob in Boston."

"You got to be shitting me."

4

The Connahs dined out at a local steak house. Ian's reservations about Amanda were soon put to rest. Rather than being hyperactive, she sat quietly, almost like a zombie.

Tom had made a point of asking the hostess to seat them at a secluded table, and Ian was impatient for their main course to arrive. His occupation had taught him that it was best to remain as invisible as possible when in public. Two men seated at a table with a woman who acted like a live corpse was not a formula for anonymity. He was thankful when dinner was complete, and they were back in Tom's car. "How long," Tom asked, "would it take to train us?"

Ian knew what his brother was asking but opted to play dumb. "Train you to do what?"

"Train Mandy and me to do what you do? I'm tired of working my ass off to make someone else rich."

"Tom, you do realize that you only get paid for completing the tasks you're given?"

"No problem there. I've done that for years."

"The difference is that in this case, completion is usually someone's death."

"No big deal, is it, Babe?"

Amanda didn't reply. She was in the backseat, looking through the window and staring into the primordial darkness.

Ian leaned back, closing his eyes. He envisioned being on a two-day stakeout in a confined space with Amanda and never knowing what her frame of mind would be from moment to moment. "I don't know, Tom. It takes a certain type of person to be able to squeeze a trigger, take someone's life, then sleep at night."

"We can do it, can't we, Babe?"

There was no reply from the backseat.

Tom made his case the rest of the evening, and Ian tried to evade making a decision. Finally, Ian gave what he hoped was an answer that would move them away from the topic without committing to anything. "I have to drive to Boston tomorrow. Let me think on it, and I'll give you an answer when I get back in a couple of days."

$ $ $ $ $

Boston had not changed much since Connah had last been there. But then, except for the Big Dig, the city had not changed much in over a hundred years, buildings would come and go, but the streets and neighborhoods remained basically the same.

As he drove through South Boston, Connah noticed the residents sitting on their porches. They eyed every strange vehicle that traversed the narrow streets, and Connah knew that they were sensors in an early warning system. Within minutes of an unknown vehicle entering the neighborhood, Paddy O'Reilly had the vehicle's make, the number of occupants, and their race.

He found a parking spot near Paddy's Pub. As he walked toward the bar's entrance, a homeless drunk staggered out of the alley. He extended his hand, and Connah saw dirt caked to his skin and packed under his fingernails. "I haven't eaten in two days," the transient said.

Connah reached into his pocket and took out a money clip. He peeled a five-dollar bill from it and gave it to the derelict. "Buy something to eat. No booze," Connah said, although he was sure that booze or drugs were what it would be used for. He passed the beggar and entered the bar.

He stood inside the door allowing his eyes to adjust to the transition from the bright sunshine to the tavern's dim interior.

When he regained full vision, he saw that the pub had not undergone renovation since he last was there. The bar was still circular and centered, and booths lined the walls. In the middle of the back wall was a door leading to the dining room. On the back wall of that room was yet another entrance. This one led to Paddy O'Reilly's office. Connah knew that no one could approach the inner sanctum without checking in with the guard. Today that guard was the bartender, Rich Kelly. Connah slid onto an empty barstool.

Kelly was only adequate as a security guard but a terrific bartender. He could recall the name of a customer who had paid a single visit to the bar six months earlier. If you were considered a regular, which Connah had been, Kelly knew what your favorite drink was. He slid a bottle of Samuel Adams and a frosted glass across the bar. "Hey, Ian, what brings you back? We haven't seen you in over a year... heard you were up in Cow Hampshire or some other butt-hole place." He poured the cold beer into the glass.

"Maine, I moved to Maine."

"Like I said, we knew you went to some backwater shit-hole. Although I was up to Maine once, there're some nice parts."

"Yeah, that there are." Connah raised his beer and toasted Kelly. "The boss in?"

"Yeah, she is."

"She?"

"You've been gone a while. Paddy's dead."

"Dead? Someone hit him?"

Kelly's broad grin showed all of his nicotine and caffeine-stained teeth. "You might say he went out taking his last shot."

"Really?"

"You recall that ex-stripper he took up with?"

"If she's the one I remember, her professional name was Lotta Bangen. Who could forget a woman who wears a 54 triple-D?"

"Her real name was Bridgette Schwartz. Well, Paddy just finished riding her hard and putting her away wet when his heart fucking blew up like a roman candle..."

"Paddy always said that he wanted to die at ninety-nine, being shot by a jealous husband as he climbed out the wife's bedroom window. I guess going the way he did was pretty close."

"You ask me," Kelly said in a conspiratorial tone, "he either sobered up or took the fucking bag off her head, and that's what really done it."

"So, who's running the business now?"

"Billie."

"Like in Paddy's daughter, Billie?"

"Same person, only a lot tougher than when you and she were an item." Kelly looked up, then turned away and began wiping glasses.

The air around Connah smelled of Chanel No. 5, and he turned to see who was wearing it. Billie Jean O'Reilly stood directly behind him. She was as alluring as ever and still wore her red hair so that it fell to her shoulders in soft waves and her brilliant green eyes seemed to flash. She wore tight jeans, fashionable high-heeled shoes, and a snug white blouse with the top three buttons open, allowing him to see the swell of her perfect breasts. "Long time no see, Ian."

"That it has been, Billie. Looks as if you're doing okay for yourself."

"Well, after Dad died, I inherited the business."

"All of it?"

"*ALL* of it. In fact, your showing up is rather fortuitous. You looking for work?"

Ian picked up his beer and said, "Maybe we ought to talk someplace private."

She laughed. "I'm not the impressionable youngster anymore, Ian Connah. It's going to take a lot to... well, you get my drift. Follow me."

5

As he followed Billie O'Reilly, Connah sipped from his glass of beer and could not help but smile at the exaggerated sway of her hips. She must want me to do something nasty, he thought. The question is whether it's dangerous, risky, or both. Knowing Billie, he was confident of one thing. Whatever it was, she was desperate to get it. She opened the door and stood on the threshold so that he could not avoid brushing her breasts as he entered the office. She closed the door and locked it.

Connah walked to one of the two chairs facing her desk, but she sat on the couch that lined one wall. She patted the seat beside her and said, "Sit here."

He stood facing her and said, "Billie, you and I go back a long way. You only turn on the charm like this when you want something—something that's either very big or very unpleasant."

"Sit beside me, and we'll talk about it."

Connah gave in and sat on the couch, making a point of maintaining a foot of separation between them. She crossed her shapely legs and then said, "Why are you here, Ian? I thought you were done with... well, retired."

"I've had a recent financial setback and need some money fast."

"You here to borrow money?"

"No, I can't abide with the usual interest rate that comes with borrowing from the O'Reillys. I'll work for it."

"Doing what?"

"You know my skill set."

Billie stood and walked over to her desk, picked up a pack of cigarettes, and lit one. She offered the box to Connah. "Cigarette?"

"I quit a year ago," he said.

"My, but you have changed."

"Look, Billie, about my leaving—"

She waved her hand as if she were shooing a fly. "I'm over that. Besides, I'm too busy for fooling around like I used to. It just so happens that I can use you right now."

"Doing what?"

"The same thing you did for my father."

"My rates have gone up, Billie."

"Not a problem. The risks have also gone up considerably."

Connah shifted as she returned to the couch and sat down in the same spot she had vacated. He was unsure, but he believed that another button in her blouse had become undone. This job, he thought, must be a real ball-buster. "Who you want me to hit?"

"Bimbo Spinelli."

"What? Let me get this straight—you want me to hit Bobbi Spinelli? I know you two have been rivals since junior high school, but has it reached the point that you want to have her killed?"

"A lot has happened since you left. Like my father, Mario Spinelli is dead. Like me, Bimbo has inherited the family business. However, unlike me, she's been encroaching on some of my interests. I want it stopped, and I want her gone."

"Billie, never in my professional life have I knowingly hit a woman. I'm not going to start now."

She slid closer. Now there was no doubt that another button had come undone, and the lacy fabric of her bra was visible. She butted the cigarette, leaned forward, and kissed him passionately. Connah's resistance collapsed, and he returned the kiss. His hands moved to her breast, and he felt her hand press against his crotch.

"Once we settle the Bimbo issue," she whispered, "we'll discuss Jiggs Wark."

Connah pulled back. "Jiggs Wark? Billie, are you trying to take over the entire city?"

She deftly unhooked his belt, and he felt her hand slide inside his trousers. "Oh my," she said. "You did bring your gun with you."

6

Harry Sandberg rolled onto his back and relaxed as the Puerto Rican sun warmed his body. The lithe masseuse kneaded oil into his flesh, and he felt himself respond. She gave him a coy smile. "I see you're fully awake."

He looked over his ample stomach and could not see his erect penis. He then looked at the Hispanic lovely who worked on him. The young woman's big breasts swayed as she stroked. God, he thought, why did I wait so long to make my investments pay off? When you have a couple million bucks, you could have the face of a Saint Bernard, and good-looking women will crawl all over you.

As if on cue, the masseuse slid her bikini bottoms off and straddled his legs, moving up until she was able to mount him. Harry suppressed a smile as she leaned over his stomach and kissed him. "*Señor* likes Margarita, no?"

"The *señor* likes Margarita, *yes*."

As Harry approached release, his satellite phone rang. Margarita reached over, picked it up, and answered. "Señor Sander's residence." She handed the phone to Harry.

"Yes."

"Harry, it's Glenn Ouellette."

"I told you to never contact me—"

"He knows."

Harry's erection died, and he pushed the masseuse away. She stood beside the table, and he ignored her pouty look. "When did he find out?"

"Three days ago. I was told that he went back to Boston. Probably trying to raise money to come after you."

"Shit." Harry paused for a second, letting Ouellette's words sink in. "After me? Are you saying that he has no idea that you're in on this too?"

"I don't know. He's too smart to not have suspicions. Either way, I've left Maine. That should help confuse the issue. He'll have to look in two directions."

"What's the probability he'll find out where I am?"

"He has a lot of contacts in the mob. How strong those contacts are, I can't say? However, I'd assume the worst."

"Okay, I'll take steps to protect myself."

"It's been nice doing business. If all goes well, we shouldn't have to talk again." Ouellette broke the connection.

Margarita returned to the massaging table and tried to revive his shrunken manhood. "*Señor* has bad news?"

Harry got up, picked up a terry-cloth robe, took a roll of money from the pocket, and handed it to her.

"Margarita come same time tomorrow?"

"Sure, sure." In a show of disgust and worry, he tossed the robe on a chair and stared out at sea, still nude.

$ $ $ $ $

Margarita crossed the patio and entered the cabana, wiggling her naked buttocks at the human toad as she pranced. Once inside, she closed the sliding glass door and pulled the drapes closed. Confident that the fat pig could not see her, Margarita slipped into cutoff jeans and a tank top. Reaching up with her hands, she removed several hairpins and, with a nod of her head, freed her long ebony hair and slipped her feet into an expensive pair of sandals. She walked to the sliding glass door and parted the drapes just enough for her to see out. The *americano* was visibly upset by the phone call and paced back and forth. As she studied his massive belly drooping so low that his manhood was hidden, she tried to recall if she had remembered to take her pill that morning. If she were to have a child from this man, it would be a freak. People would come from miles around to see if it was a human or a giant toad… there was too much ugliness in the world already—she did not want to bring this one's child into it. She took a cell phone from her bag and made a call.

She kept her voice low and spoke in rapid Spanish. "Felipe? It is Juanita. I think this one is about to run."

"What happened?" Felipe Rojas asked.

"I don't know. There was a phone call from up north, I think. After that, he was upset and angry."

"We will have to move quickly then."

19

7

Connah sat up and watched Billie as she leaned against her desk and lit a cigarette. "So," he quipped, "you still smoke after sex."

She slid her panties up over her hips and reached for her jeans. "During too," she replied. "Now that we got that out of the way, are you ready to get down to business?"

"I haven't agreed to anything yet."

Billie held her jeans in her hand. "Are we going to have to renegotiate this?" She ground the cigarette out in an ashtray and dropped her jeans. As she neared the couch, she slid her underwear down again. "You drive a hard bargain, Connah."

He grinned at her. "And you love it."

$ $ $ $ $

Billie sat on one end of the couch, and Connah sat on the other. He almost laughed at her when she said, "I'm not getting up until we have an agreement."

"Billie, are you serious about hitting Bobbi Spinelli and Jiggs Wark?"

"As serious as what just happened on this couch."

"All right, let's get dressed. I never talk business while I'm naked." He slid on his jeans.

"Even when you talked with my father?" She smiled an impish smile.

"Especially when I talked to him. Christ, if I walked in here naked, he would have had my body dumped in the marshes."

Once again, Billie slid her underwear on and then slipped into her bra. She hooked the clasp in front, slid the garment around her torso, bounced her breasts until they rested comfortably in the cups, and slipped her arms through the straps. "I don't want that."

"You don't want my body in the marshes?"

"Of course not. I don't want Bimbo and Jiggs's carcasses there either. I want them out in the open where the entire city can see them."

"I won't take a contract on Bobbi, but I will consider taking a job ensuring that no one hits you."

"At what price?"

"Two hundred-fifty thousand a year. As far as going after either Bobbi or Jiggs, my recommendation as your security consultant is that you forget about it. It would blow the lid off this city and start the gang war to end all gang wars. It might even be the end of all of you."

Billie pulled on her jeans, walked to him, and bent over. She playfully slipped her tongue in and out of his ear. "I would be willing to pay twice that, provided you throw in stud service."

"Want to negotiate that?"

She laughed. "I don't think you have much negotiation left in you—not for a few hours anyhow."

Now that they were fully dressed, Billie turned somber, her frivolity gone. "Ian, I don't expect you to do this alone. If I recall correctly, you always worked with... what was it you called Stoney? A spotter, that's it."

"I haven't heard from Stoney in over a year."

"I may be able to reach him; I'll add a hundred thou for Stoney. Or, I can give you Sean Sutton."

"Sutton's still around? I was sure that someone would have killed him long ago."

"He's still around. However, there is one problem."

"What's that?"

"He's another interested party. Like you, he's always wanted to get inside these jeans." She stuck her thumbs into her waistband and pulled outward. "Unlike you, he hasn't gotten there yet. Should he find out about our negotiation sessions, he may become a problem. I'll expect you to deal with that *pro bono*."

"What else? I know you, Billie, there's always an 'oh, by the way.'"

"There are two other things, actually. First, there's Dick O'Schaunessey."

"How is he a problem? O'Schaunessey was always the dirtiest cop on the Boston Police Department—both physically and ethically."

"Well, Dick is a captain now, and he has the same issue with me as Sutton.

He isn't able to negotiate as well as you."

"You didn't sleep with that asshole, did you?"

"Hell, no. If word ever got out that I did, it would mean that when it came to men, my taste is all in my mouth."

"All right. So, what is the second thing?"

"Bimbo has wanted your scalp on her belt since we were in school. I want to be sure that if you do get the opportunity to shoot her, you use the gun that shoots lead bullets."

8

Donald Stone stood on the bank of the slow-moving river, casting a dry fly onto the surface of an eddy fed by the current. He worked the lure across the clear, clean water, holding it below the rippling water. A brook trout broke the surface, and Stone set the hook. "Gotcha," he exclaimed.

Before he could net the fish, he heard footsteps behind him. Old behaviors sprang into action. He dropped the fly rod and spun around, reaching for the pistol he wore beneath his fishing vest. He recognized Ian Connah and relaxed. "You cost me a fish, Ian."

Connah grinned. "Maybe a fishing rig, too." He pointed toward the river.

Stone spun and cursed, "Shit!" He scrambled after the one hundred-fifty-dollar rod and reel, grabbing it just as it was about to enter the water. He felt the fish fighting to get free and began to play it.

Connah walked to the shore and picked up Stone's net from the ground where he had dropped it. He reached out and dipped the net, scooping the fish out of the water.

"Thanks," Stone grunted. He took the net from Connah and walked away from the shore. He squatted, retrieved the trout from the net, and held it against a measure. "Twelve inches, nice fish," he said before returning to the water and releasing it.

"I never understood the concept of catching a fish so you can let it loose," Connah said.

"The way I look at it, it's the closest most men get to be God. I have all the power and the control. Whether that fish lives or dies is entirely up to me."

"Kind of like being a sniper."

"But," Stone interjected, "a hell of a lot less risky." He wiped his hands on his pants and grabbed Connah in a bear hug. "How you been, bro?"

"I have been okay, taking it easy."

"How's the wife… this one's name is Lucinda, isn't it?"

"Jeanie, Lucinda was two years ago. Like her, Jeanie is an ex-wife too."

"Ouch. That's what, three?"

"Four, but who's counting."

"I would imagine your lawyer and your accountant."

"You have a point there. As a matter of fact, that's why I'm here. I need a spotter."

"You're back in the game?"

"I have no choice in the matter. I went to pay the lawyer and Jeanie, only to learn that my financial team is out of town."

"And?"

"And they took all my money with them."

"So, that's who you're going after?"

"Eventually, before I can set my sights on them, though, I got to accrue funds for the hunt."

"So, who are you working for in the interim?"

"Billie O'Reilly."

Stone raised his eyebrows. "Be careful with that one, man. Who's the target?"

"She wanted me to hit Bobbi Spinelli, I refused. Despite my refusal, Billie hired me… us, if you want a job… as a security consultant."

"What? Since when do mob bosses hire consultants? They usually use their own muscle."

"Yeah, I know what you mean. I think it's a matter of insurance. It appears that they are about to start one helluva gang war."

"They?"

"Billie, Bobbi, and Jiggs Wark, too."

Stone whistled. "Even her ball-buster father didn't have enough brass to try and take on both Spinelli and Wark at the same time. After that, what's she goin' to do, send us after the Russians?" Stone gathered up his fishing tackle, and he and Connah strolled along the short tree-lined road to his pick-up. He dropped his gear into the truck bed and then looked Connah in the eye. "It isn't like you to get in the middle of a war. Did Billie screw your brains out to get you to agree to this?"

"Hey, the spirit resisted—"

"Yeah, yeah, I know, but the flesh is weak. I will admit that if Billie ever got me in a leg lock, I'd probably agree to hit my own dear mother." He opened the door to his truck. "Where you staying?"

"With my brother."

"Where and when do we meet?"

"Paddy's Pub in Southie. Day after tomorrow at ten in the morning."

9

The Hispanic man sat quiet, staring across the desk at the fat man using Harry Sanders as an alias. The English translation of the Spanish logo painted on the glass office door said: *Felipe Rojas, Private Investigator and Security Expert.* Rojas leaned back in his swiveling office chair, his hands forming a steeple in front of his face, and he stared at the ugly *gringo* who sat before him.

Rojas spoke slowly, ensuring that he always referred to his sister, Juanita, as Margarita... the name by which this fat *comilón* (greedy pig) knew her. "*Señor*, for me to be able to guarantee your safety, you must remain in Puerto Rico. I have no resources in either Mexico or South America."

"I repeat, how much will it cost for you to arrange for me to get to Mexico or South America under the radar?"

It was evident to Rojas that this over-weight, sweaty American would not trust him, no matter how stellar the endorsement given by Juanita, aka Margarita. The man reminded him of Sydney Greenstreet. The actor who played Kasper Gutman, the villain in *The Maltese Falcon* movie he'd seen on television.

"I am uncertain what it is you mean by under the radar."

Rojas slowly slid open his top right-hand drawer and reached inside. He remained seated when the gringo struggled to his feet. He thought it was humorous to see the obese man attempting to look imposing and threatening. It was not an easy task when you carried around a stomach so large that you only saw your feet when you sat down. "I am afraid, that I must say *buenos días*, Señor Rojas."

Rojas removed his hand from the desk drawer holding a nine-millimeter pistol pointed at the fat man. He almost laughed when the American's face paled, and he backed up several steps as if he thought he was about to be attacked. Rojas refrained from allowing his anger to show. Instead, he turned on the charm. He was well aware that the smile on his face was sugary, so much so that it was enough to put the person it was intended for into a diabetic coma. Still, he knew that he could not allow this mark to walk away.

Sandberg's face dropped when Rojas dropped the pretense that he was helpful. "Sit down, *señor, por favor.* The only place you will be going is to take us to the *dinero.* You see, I have done my homework, as you *americanos* like to say. I checked into it when Margarita told me that she had a wealthy client from up north. I have many friends in the Boston area—Lawrence, to be exact. It seems that the dinero in your possession is *negro dinero.* If you are not familiar with the term, it means 'black money,' *illegally* obtained money."

Sandberg fell rather than sat into the chair he had recently vacated.

When Sandberg was settled, Rojas placed the handgun on his desk and said, "That is better. Now let us get to the heart of the matter, shall we?"

Sandberg swallowed, and Rojas saw the sheen of sweat cover the man's face, dripping from his triple chins and soaking his shirt. "My people in New England have reported that there is a financial adviser from Maine who has gone missing. Also missing is three million U.S. dollars. Dollars that once belonged to another man—a man you should never have fucked with. This man was retired, but now he has reappeared, back in his former profession. The word is that his return from retirement is not voluntary. He is earning money to find the financial adviser who stole his money and balance the books. I believe, Mr. Sanders—I also know that that is not your true name, which by the way, is Sandberg. You're really not very good at this embezzlement stuff, are you?"

"This is preposterous—"

"Rule number one, when you assume a false name, never choose one that is so close to that of your true name. It is too easy to guess. It's not unlike using your wife's name and birth year as a password on your computer. Do you understand?"

Sandberg swallowed hard again, all the response that Rojas needed.

"Again, my question for you is this, how badly do you want to disappear, and how willing are you to take on one, maybe two, partners? I hope that you didn't split the take with someone else because three million dollars doesn't go as far as it did twenty years ago."

10

Over the years, Roberta Spinelli had been known by two nicknames: Bobbi, which she didn't mind, and now, thanks to that red-headed mick bitch Billie O'Reilly, *Bimbo*, which she hated. Bobbi had been her father's idea. When he realized that his wife would not bless him with a son, he knew that his daughter would have to follow in his footsteps if he wanted to keep the business in the family's hands. He began calling her Bobbi because he felt the name would not immediately identify her gender.

She sat at a corner table in the North End Social Club, smiling as she watched some of her father's old goombahs playing cards and drinking. There was no doubt in her mind that the old Sicilian mobsters hated the fact that she was *Capo,* and as such, they could not exclude her from the all-male social club. Before taking charge of the family, the only women allowed into their inner sanctum were prostitutes and strippers. And they were only allowed in on special occasions. She puffed on her cigarette and sipped her gin and tonic. It had been a good week; they had successfully taken over another neighborhood business from that stupid mick-bitch.

The front door opened and a silhouette entered the club. A flash of brilliant sun briefly lit the dim interior. When the door blocked out the brightness, Bobbi could discern Anthony D'Altrui (Tony D.), one of her capo regimes. She ground her cigarette in an ashtray and watched him approach. She pointed at the chair across from her as he neared and waited until he was seated. "You don't look happy, Tony."

"That's because what I gotta tell you ain't gonna make you happy, Boss."

"Really, then suppose you lay it on me?"

"Now, you got to remember that this is just what I heard—"

"Tony, stop shitting your pants and tell me."

"I was havin' a beer at Chandler's when a couple of O'Reilly's goons came

28

in and sat at the bar. You know me when I want a couple of beers, I don't like being disturbed. So, I was sitting off by myself. Chandler's ain't well-lit, and there's a seat on the end of the bar that ain't got no light. You can sit, listen, and not be seen."

"Damn it, Tony, get to the point!"

"Okay. These goombahs gets to talkin', and next thing I know, I hear that the bitch has brought in a couple of guns."

"Really?"

"That ain't all. O'Reilly hired them full-time."

"Sounds like she's getting ready for a war with me."

"And Jiggs Wark."

"So, my old rival is going to try and take over the entire city. Well, let her come. It isn't the first time that she's tried to beat me. She hasn't won yet."

"There's one other thing," Tony said.

"What?"

"The guns she hired are that Irish asshole, Ian Connah, and his shithead buddy, Don Stone."

"Welsh."

"Huh?"

"Ian's Welsh, not Irish. You call him a mick, and he'll blow your head off, although not as quick as he would if you called him an Englishman, but he'd do it just the same." She lit another cigarette and said, "I heard that Ian was out of it now, retired to some backwater town in Maine."

"Word around town is that he needs some cash fast and has thrown his hat back into the ring."

"Now that," Bobbi said, "is a coincidence."

11

Ian Connah sat on the deck contemplating ways to stop his brother from pursuing a second career as a hitman. Since he arrived, Amanda had been in a manic state, and he remembered what Tom had said. He did his best to act as if everything was normal. Now, he thought, if I only knew what normal was.

His brother came through the glass slider carrying two beers. "Thought you might be ready for a refill," he said. He placed a beer on the table and flopped into the vacant chair beside Ian.

"You want to do what I do for a living. You got to cut back on the sauce… way back."

"What? Now you're accusing me of being an alcoholic?"

Ian pointed toward the house. "If I was married to her, I'd dive into a bottle and never come up."

"You know, brother, I don't think it's considered proper for someone to walk into a man's house and call him an alcoholic and his wife a nut-case."

"You know me, Tom. I always tell it like I see it."

"Ian, there are times when you run your mouth before you engage your brain."

"No argument there."

Tom took a long drink from the frosty can of beer. "Ahhhh. There isn't anything better on a hot day than a cold beer."

Connah stared at his brother for a few seconds, finding his rejection of his warning to cut back on his alcohol consumption hard to believe, and then stood up. "I'll be heading back to Boston for a couple of days."

"Oh?"

Connah maintained piercing eye contact with his brother, "I got a job there."

Tom placed his beer on the table. "Let me come with you."

"I don't have time to deal with an inexperienced person. This will be a tricky job."

"Who are you hitting, a drug dealer?"

"It's not a hit. I've been hired to protect a mob boss, a *female* mob boss."

"Wow, Ian, that's way cool."

"If I make one little mistake, she'll be wearing my testicles for earrings."

"She sounds vicious. Do I know her?"

"You remember Roberta Spinelli?"

"Yeah, I think I do. Little ball of fire, beautiful eyes, long legs that ran from her ass to the ground, and long coal-black hair. I seem to recall that her old man was in the Italian mob. Hey! You don't mean that she's your target?"

"Not a target. Billie O'Reilly hired me to protect her from Bobbi."

"Billie, now that one I remember. She'd scratch your eyes out just to make sure her nails were sharp enough." Tom took a sip of his beer. "If I remember accurately, you had a thing with both of them back in high school."

"Yeah, I was the piece of meat the two tigresses fought over."

"Refresh my memory, which one won?"

"All I'm going to say is that I got the worst of it."

"Seems to me that you could use some help on this."

"I have a partner, and we've worked together before."

Tom's face dropped, and he looked wounded. "I meant that you could use the help of someone who knows the target."

"Tom, these women are not the teenage girls you remember. They are now two of the three top mob bosses in Boston. They'll order a person's death with all the emotion they display, touching up their make-up. Like I said earlier, this catfight is between two big cats. I promise you that I'll let you help me and I'll train you, but not on this job. It's going to take all my concentration to keep from being the main course on their menu."

"You haven't had much luck with women, have you?"

"What makes you say that? The fact that I've been divorced four times?"

"That's one indicator. You seem to have an attraction for women who can't, or won't, put up with your lifestyle."

"What in hell are you talking about?"

"You're like a tumbleweed, Ian. You can't stay put for long. You blow into town on a gust of wind, and on the next gust, you blow out again. Yet, you're attracted to women who are oak trees. Their roots are deep in the ground. The only way you'll ever be happy is if you pair up with another tumbleweed. The problem is that, as of yet, you haven't come across a single female tumbleweed. Most women have a problem living out of a suitcase… or in your situation, a gun case."

"When did you become a shrink? I don't have any problems with women."

Tom chuckled. "Of course, you don't. As soon as you got divorced for the fourth time, you got involved with two women, both of whom would love to put a ring through your nose and lead you around like a trophy bull. Getting back to the original subject, what happened between you and Jeanie? I thought you were getting along fine."

"She divorced me for reckless driving."

"What?"

"Yeah, I drove past her with a red-head in my truck. As for Billie and Bobbi, you got your facts screwed up, Tom. Hell, we've known these two since we were in grade school."

"Yes, we have. Nevertheless, you're the only one who seems to keep getting involved with them."

"Well, Billie is great in bed. I don't know about Bobbi—yet."

Tom shook his head. "You aren't going to stop with these two until one or the other has you singing soprano."

Ian grinned and then sang, "AHHHHHHHH!" in falsetto.

"What have I missed?" Amanda walked out of the house and sat beside her husband.

"Nothing," Ian said. "Just me and Tom discussing old times."

"Well, don't let me stop you."

Ian studied his sister-in-law for a few seconds. She seemed calm and collected, an obvious sign that she was over her latest manic episode. The problem was that she could have another at any moment. She could be in constant motion, physically and verbally, or sitting alone, talking to herself in a low voice. It drove Connah crazy when she was like that. However, what bothered him the most was when his sister-in-law was not in a manic episode. He actually liked her. Unfortunately, before this time, he'd seldom seen her in that state.

Amanda sipped on the only thing Ian had ever seen her drink, warm water with a slice of lemon. Somewhere along the line, she'd either read or heard that warm water was the healthiest thing one could drink. It was a belief that Ian did not share. She set the glass next to Tom's beer and turned her attention to her brother-in-law. "So, Ian, Tom told me that you've suffered a financial setback."

Ian glanced at his brother, not entirely happy that Tom had shared a confidential conversation with his wife. He said, "My financial adviser and my accountant raked me over the coals. They took off with all of my savings."

"Tom told me that. He also told me how you made so much money."

Ian cast another look at his brother and then looked at Amanda. "What was I? The subject of your pillow talk?"

"Don't be so sensitive, Ian," Amanda said. "We *are* family, after all."

"I hope that you haven't discussed this with anyone outside of the family."

Amanda gave him a solemn look. "I know that you don't understand what I deal with every day, Ian. Nevertheless, I am family, and I know when to keep my mouth shut about something."

Ian was surprised, and he tried to deny how he felt about her. "It isn't that I don't understand, it's just that when you—"

"Have an episode?" she filled in.

"I don't know how to deal with it," he replied.

"That's easy enough, do what Tom does."

"What's that?"

"He either ignores me or throws my butt in bed and jumps my bones."

Ian had a mouthful of beer, and her comment surprised him. He swallowed, hoping he wouldn't choke while doing so. He placed the can on the table and laughed. "I guess my only recourse is to ignore you."

Tom gave him a tap on his bicep. "What's wrong, brother? Did she shock you?"

Ian nodded.

"If you stick around long enough, you'll learn that she's full of surprises."

"No shit," Ian commented.

"So," Amanda said, turning serious, "what's your game plan?"

"Don't really have one. My old boss, Paddy O'Reilly, has died and gone where dead Irish mobsters go. His daughter is now running things, and she's hired me as a security consultant. So, I guess I'll just have to see where that takes me."

"Security consultant," Amanda said. "I like that. It sounds much better than hitman or hired gun."

"I thought so, too."

"I also know that Tom approached you about training us to do the same work."

"Amanda, I have to be honest. I've got some reservations."

"Like my condition?"

"Yeah, like your condition."

"Well, maybe we should start the training and, like you, see where that takes us."

As hard as he tried, Ian couldn't come up with an argument.

12

Billie O'Reilly was playing solitaire and drinking a margarita when Bobbi (aka Bimbo) Spinelli exploded through the door of Paddy's Pub, ruining the afternoon's serenity. The crazy bitch stormed across the room, walking to Billie's table like she was the Queen of Sicily... if there was such a thing.

Spinelli stood beside the table, waiting for Billie to acknowledge her and offer her a seat. Billie turned a card, looked at it, and placed it correctly on the table. "Nice jeans, Bimbo," Billie said without looking up. "A bit too tight, though. The quarter in your back pocket shows heads."

Spinelli realized that she looked stupid standing by the table like a humble peasant and sat down. "I see you've changed hair-dressers; I can hardly see the gray."

"What do you want, Bimbo? Whatever it is, get it out, and then you get out. Spending time with you is as stimulating as visiting a graveyard on a wet Sunday."

"I have been hearing things."

"Get new hearing aids, did we?" Billie turned another card.

"I heard that you put Ian Connah on your payroll. You plan on putting a hit on me?"

"Listen, Bimbo—"

"My name is Roberta or Bobbi."

"Like I give a damn. As for me hitting on you. You aren't my type."

"Well, I just wanted to inform you that I know about it, and anything you can do, I can do."

"Sounds like a great song lyric. You should write it. Of course, you'd have to go back to school to learn how to write."

Spinelli bent across the table and said, "You haven't changed a bit, you know that?" She stood up so fast that her chair tipped over, hitting the floor with a loud bang. She spun around and started walking away.

"Hey, Spinelli…"

Bobbi turned her head.

"I've already got a couple of jobs lined up for Ian."

13

Ian Connah parked his car in a small privately-operated parking lot and walked through Boston's north end. He knew that Bobbi Spinelli ran her operation from the social club her father owned on Prince Street, in the heart of Italian-dominated North Boston. However, Bobbi Spinelli lived in a million-dollar home in Wellesley.

He approached a homeless guy sitting against the building. Connah noted that despite his dirty clothes and shabby appearance, the vagrant's eyes were clear, not bloodshot as those of most transients. Even sitting against the wall, he had about him an aura of authority. Connah tagged him as a cop.

When Connah closed with the bum, he smelled the stench of clothes that hadn't been laundered in months. "Can I get a buck for a sandwich?" the vagrant asked.

"Depends on the sandwich. Let me see it."

The bum stared at him as if he could not believe what he had just heard. He started to retort, but Connah cut him off before saying a word.

He spoke to the undercover cop in the same manner that he'd talk to any derelict. He said, "Buddy, don't let your alligator mouth overrun your hummingbird brain. It could mess up the rest of your life." He turned and started walking away. However, he could not resist giving the *bum* another verbal shot. "You should work the Esplanade, better class of people there and, while you're at it, you should jump in the Charles. You fucking stink."

Connah knocked on the door of The North End Social Club and waited for someone to open it. The door opened inward, and a burly man with a five o'clock shadow said, "Yeah?"

"Ian Connah to see Bobbi."

"Wait here." The mug closed the door and disappeared. He returned in no more than two minutes and opened the door wide. "Boss says it's alright for you to come in."

"Now, isn't that nice of her."

After the bright sun, the club's interior was as dark as a bear's den. Ian stood inside the door for a few moments, allowing his eyes to adjust to the lack of light. When his vision improved, he saw Bobbi sitting at the back of the club's main room with several men clustered around her. He turned in that direction.

The hood guarding the door stopped Connah by placing his hand on his chest. "Hold on, I gotta make sure you ain't carrying."

Connah raised his arms and let the doorman pat him down.

When the mug was satisfied that Connah was not carrying a weapon, he stepped back and said, "Okay."

Connah walked to the table, and when Bobbi saw him, she sent her men away with a flick of her wrist. "Well," she said, "look at what the cat dragged in, and the dog wouldn't take back out."

Connah smiled and sat at the table. "How you been, Bobbi?"

"What you want, Connah?"

"Hey, come on now, we're old friends, Bobbi. We go back a long way."

"Not as far back as you and Buffalo Billie."

"I don't think I've ever heard her called that before."

"What else would you call a woman with early American looks—she looks like an American buffalo."

Connah, who was not a person to overlook a chance to make a wisecrack, said, "That's strange. Just yesterday, she told me that you were living proof that the American Indians screwed buffalo."

Spinelli slapped the table. "How much you want to take that bitch out? Name your price, and you got it."

"Take her out?" Connah pretended to be confused. "Is she available? I figured a woman with her looks would have a steady guy."

Bobbi wasn't buying his act and said, "Don't fuck with me, Ian. I know she paid you to hit me."

"What? If that were true, I'd be nuts to walk in here. Besides, I've never hit a woman in any way, shape, or form as of this date. I'm not going to start now. I do have some ethics. One or two, anyway. Shit, it's been rumored that I even have a few morals."

"As for you walking in here, we both know that isn't your style," Spinelli gave him a stern look. "You don't like close up. You'd rather snipe someone at 300 or 500 yards."

"Actually, I prefer 600 or more. You got to admit, it keeps from messing up your clothes, doesn't it?" Connah sat back in his chair and flashed his most charming and disarming smile.

Bobbi saw the smile and became as suspicious as she would be when talking to a used car salesman. "You still ain't told me why you're here."

"To say hello to an old friend."

"Okay, hello. Now that we've put all the bullshit aside, how much would it cost me for you to do O'Reilly?"

"Haven't you gotten over her beating you out for the cheerleading team?"

"I got over that a long time ago. Hell, I saw more of the football team than O'Reilly ever did."

Connah got up and chuckled. "I'll bet you did." He walked toward the exit, stopped after five paces, turned his head, and said, "Five million—half upfront."

"That's a bit steep. Tempting, but steep."

"Well, she and I are old friends—then there are those ethical and moral issues I mentioned."

Bobbi got up, walked over to him, and wrapped her arms around him. "You know, Ian. I always liked you. How come you never came on to me?"

"Come on, Bobbi. Little old me against the entire football team. I wouldn't have had a chance."

"I recall that you were a hockey player."

He bared his teeth. "Best implants money can buy."

She ran her finger across his chin, touching a jagged scar. The result of being hit in the face with the blade of a stick. "Hockey is a rough game; the players are tough."

Connah smiled at her and pushed out of her arms. "Compared to the games you and Billie play, hockey is for cream puffs."

"Then you became a Marine sniper."

"That only means I'm good at closing relationships from a long distance."

She handed him a card. "That's my home address. Come over after ten tonight. I may have something for you."

He glanced at the card and put it in his shirt pocket. "How long has the undercover surveillance been out there?"

"You mean the fake bum? They've had him out there for a week. If it ain't him, it's someone else."

"What was your first clue that they're cops?"

"No self-respecting bum would waste their time hanging out in that alley. There ain't no food dumpsters."

14

Connah walked out into the mid-day sun, blinking against the sudden onslaught of daylight. He almost walked into the side of a four-door sedan with black-walled tires. The car may as well have had Boston Police stenciled all over it. The door opened, and he heard a familiar voice say, "Need a lift?"

"Nah, I'm parked a couple blocks away."

"Don't play wise with me, Connah. Get the fuck in the car."

Connah slid into the passenger seat, used his feet to clear away the fast-food bags and wrappers that covered the floor, and looked at the driver. Whereas many people thought that Captain Dick O'Schaunessey was an imposing man, Connah thought he was nothing but a fat bully. He was also a person who would pat you on the back with his left hand while he was punching you in the face with his right. O'Schaunessey was as crooked as the Kancamangas Highway through New Hampshire's White Mountains. That in itself made him an impressive enemy. But what made him truly dangerous was that if he were to have his conscience taken out, it would be done in outpatient surgery.

"Heard you were back and that Billie hired you."

Connah studied the cop's craggy face. Remnants of a half-dozen Dunkin' Donuts clung from his mustache, and coffee stains and cigar burns covered his shirt. Connah felt sorry for the buttons on the cop's shirt; each was working as hard as Atlas holding the world on his shoulders.

"Well, you heard correct."

"What you doing consorting with the enemy?"

"What are you talking about?"

"Don't play games with me, shithead." O'Schaunessey smiled; it was a malevolent, evil smile that exposed his coffee and tobacco-stained teeth.

One of his canines was black with rot, and a greenish coat of something ran along his gum line. "Me and Billie got this thing going. She tells me everything. For instance, she told me that you're back in the business, and she paid you to handle her security in case Bimbo tries to have her whacked."

"Well, since you know so god damned much, you also know that a sniper always does a preliminary scout of the area before selecting a hide."

"Even when I was in the army, you back-shooting sniper bastards always pissed me off. Ain't none of you got the balls to face a man one-on-one."

"I didn't know they used snipers in the War of 1812, and as far as I'm concerned, one-on-one is a basketball game played by trash-talking kids. Speaking of which, how much more trash-talk are you going to subject me to?"

"I don't like you, Connah. I never have. You're a fucking snake of the worst kind."

"At least I'm out in the open about it. It's you dirty cops who expect the public to pay them a salary for twenty years and then a pension for who knows how long. All while you get paid by the very people that you're supposed to protect good citizens from. That gives me a major case of the ass. You were born under a fucking rock, O'Schaunessey. Although around here, the only rock big enough for you to hide under is Mount Washington. You have one hell of a nice day, okay?"

Connah got out of the car and leaned back in before closing the door. "You better call Jenny Craig. A target as big as you would be a piece of cake at 600 meters." He slammed the door.

15

Don Stone sat at the bar when Connah walked into Paddy's Pub. He and Billie discussed something that must have been of international importance because neither paid attention to him as he approached.

Connah flopped into a vacant bar stool and motioned to Rich Kelly. "Bring a cold draft, will you, Rich?"

The bartender acknowledged him with a two-fingered salute, picked up a clean glass, and turned to the tap.

"Where you been?" Billie asked.

"Went to see your competition."

"Which one? Jiggs or Neigh?"

"Neigh?"

"Yeah, back in high school, it was evident that Bimbo had no horse sense, and those monstrous chompers made her look like an old nag, so we called her Neigh."

"The way you two snipe at each other, I'm surprised you need me at all."

"Now that I think about it," Billie said, "it might be fun to scratch her eyes out personally."

"I also had a talk with your paid cop friend."

"Dick's not so bad."

Stone started laughing.

"What's so funny?"

"That obese piece of shit only sees his dick when he stands in front of a mirror," Stone said.

"He serves his purpose," Billie replied.

"You ought to give him a referral," Connah said.

"To who?"

"An oral surgeon. Any dentist worth their salt would take a single look in his mouth and know that it was a good time to buy that yacht they wanted."

"Let's get back to Bimbo," Billie said. "When are you gonna put a bullet through her tits?"

"We already covered that—I won't," Connah said. "Bobbi knows I'm working for you now. She'll know that it'll be best if she lets things settle down a bit. At this point, she's as wary as a tomcat in a neutering clinic."

"Just so you don't let her get me." Billie lit a cigarette and blew smoke into the air.

"I thought it was illegal to smoke in a public establishment," Connah commented.

"So, call the goddamned P.C. police. See if I give a shit."

Kelly placed a frosted glass of beer in front of Connah.

"Put it on my account… on account of our boss hasn't paid me yet."

Kelly shook his head and said, "There must be a million comedians out of work… and look at who we get." He turned away and walked down the bar to check on other customers.

Billie got up, ground her cigarette out and said, "My office, before you leave."

"This a private party, or can I bring Don?"

"Screw you, Ian." She spun on her heel and disappeared into the dim interior of the pub.

"I heard something that you might find interesting," Don said.

"Such as?"

"I did a job in Lawrence, where I worked with a Puerto Rican who owed me some cash."

"You get it?"

"I got more than that. Seems this guy has relatives down in P.R. One of them rented a cabana to an American."

"So?"

"A rich, obese American, he said the man's name was Harry Sanders…"

"That," Connah replied, "is the best news I've had all day." He belted down a large mouthful of beer, placed the empty mug on the bar, and said, "Be back in a minute. Duty calls."

"You going to get some money from her?"

"Yup, you better go pack a bag and get us a couple of seats to San Juan."

Stone tossed two airline tickets on the bar. "My bag is in the truck. We leave at seven in the morning."

Connah gave a two-fingered salute and walked toward the boss's office.

16

Wellesley, Massachusetts, is upper-middle-class, possibly even lower upper class. The homes are in the high six figures, some into seven figures. A Wellesley home is to the Boston mob what a Long Island estate is to New York's Cosa Nostra. He was sure that the neighbors were not overly pleased when the Spinelli clan had bought their estate and moved in. Bobbi and Billie were South Boston or Charlestown type of people. Connah felt that he stood out like a pair of fire-engine red shoes. It was not a place where he felt at home.

When he turned off Route 9, he followed Washington Street until he turned into the Spinelli drive and confronted an imposing and manned front gate. The security guard made the Jolly Green Giant look like a dwarf, and he bent low as he peered through the open window of Connah's truck. "Watcha want?" he asked.

Connah almost laughed in his face. Bobbi may own a home in one of the most exclusive suburbs in Boston, but she still surrounded herself with morons. "Ian Connah, Ms. Spinelli is expecting me."

The giant straightened without saying anything and walked into a booth that seemed at least three sizes too small for his bulk. In seconds, the iron gates opened, and Connah was allowed access to Bobbi Spinelli's castle.

He followed a tree-lined drive until it looped in front of an impressive house. Looking at the Gothic design of the stone building, Connah thought that things were going well in Spinelli's kingdom. He parked in front of the steps leading to the front door and got out of the truck. Before climbing, he turned and looked back at the four-by-four and wondered if it felt as out of place as he did. It sure as hell looked like it did.

The door opened, and an honest to God butler stood on the threshold. If his earlier notion made him feel out of place, the feeling of alienation he felt now was yet stronger. Connah felt like he had cut a loud fart in a quiet church. "Good evening, sir." The man sounded and looked like the poster boy for anal retention. "Miss Spinelli has been expecting you."

Connah studied the vast room in which he stood. He was sure that if his Prefontain Station home was dropped in here, it wouldn't touch any of the walls. The marble floors shone so brightly that they looked like a skating rink with a surface so pristine any hockey team would love to skate on it. The walls were lined with trophies, not cups and plaques, but animal heads. Connah wondered if there was another trophy room in the house, one where they mounted the skulls of vanquished foes. If so, he asked himself if he would be there in the future? He had second thoughts about the scam he was trying to work for a brief moment. How would these two tigresses react if they knew that he had no intention of shooting either of them? They were going to be pissed big-time once they realized he had used them to finance his true quest; the search for Harry Sandberg.

"If you will follow me, sir."

Connah followed the butler's stiff back down a hallway lined with expensive artwork, walking on a carpet so plush it felt as if he were walking on a soft mattress. The butler stopped before a door and opened it. Connah thought it was odd that the servant stepped aside and announced him without entering the room. He motioned for Connah to enter.

Connah stepped out of the hall into a massive boudoir. A colossal fireplace took up three-quarters of the wall directly across from the door and, even though it was a warm August evening, a robust fire burned in it. The flickering flames were the room's only source of light.

"Come in, Ian."

In the ambient light of the fire, the masculine sound of her name was at odds with her feminine appearance. She was every inch a Roberta and stood beside a sofa that was so large a Roman orgy could take place upon it. The reason the butler had not entered the room became immediately apparent. Her negligee covered all the key areas but hid nothing. Despite her Sunday-school smile, it was obvious that she was dressed for a sultry Saturday night date. Hell, he thought, looking at her through the sheer material, I didn't dress for the occasion. Although he wore jeans and a black T-shirt that fit tightly on his muscular torso, he knew that he was grossly over-dressed for what Bobbi seemed to have on her mind.

"I was beginning to wonder if you were coming, Ian."

"You always dress like that to spend an evening alone?"

"A girl always has to be ready." She gave a coy smile. "You never know when a good thing might come along."

"Look, Bobbi, I don't know what you have planned, but I've always found it to be trouble when I mix business with pleasure."

"Pleasure? This could just as easily be a part of the business." She closed with him and wrapped her arms around his neck. She stood five feet, nine inches, and had to stretch onto tip-toes to rise up enough to match his six-foot height.

The scent of Mademoiselle filled the air around her, and Connah responded exactly as he knew she wanted him to. Connah thought, what the hell? After all, she is a beautiful woman. He had an earth-shaking epiphany: he finally became aware of what his dilemma in dealing with Billie and Bobbi had always been. They were both beautiful, sensual women, and he was a mere man. He circled her waist with his arms. "Just what part of the business might this be?"

She nuzzled against his chest. "If you play your cards right, you could own half of all the Spinelli empire."

He stepped back and held her, his eyes dropping to her ample breasts, which looked different than he remembered them when they were kids. He thought she must have had them enhanced, and whoever did it must have billed her a bunch. From his vantage point, they obviously did a terrific job. "We both know that would never happen. The Italians would put a hit on me so fast it would make your head spin."

She turned, freed herself from his arms, and walked to the sofa. Once there, she spun around to face him, the sheer gown fanned out, and allowed the fire to reveal all of her charms. She popped the cork on a bottle of champagne. "Something to drink?"

"You got a cold beer? That stuff tickles my nose."

She smiled. "You never were very romantic, Connah."

"Okay, Bobbi, you've revealed all of your weapons, so let's get to the chase." He motioned to the room. "It's blatantly obvious that you've set this little trap to entice me to take a contract on Billie."

"Maybe I just want a romantic evening to remember old times. Then again, I could just want to get laid."

Connah laughed. "Either way, it looks like I'll be getting screwed."

17

San Juan blistered under the fiery mid-day sun. The beachside hotels benefited from a cooling breeze off the Caribbean, and Connah and Stoney made the most of it. They sat on the patio outside Connah's room, smoking cigars and drinking Cuba Libre, the unofficial cocktail of the island—Bacardi Superior Rum mixed with cola and served with lime wedges.

"So, what's our plan?" Stone asked.

"We go visit this…" he pulled a crumpled slip of paper from his pocket and read from it "…Ivany Padrón Hurtado, that your man in Lawrence said has a line on Sandberg."

"Well, we aren't going to find him sitting here."

"Whoa, Stoney. This isn't New England. This place is like India, and you know what they say in India."

"No, but a little bird just landed on my shoulder and whispered that I'm about to learn."

"The people in India say that only mad dogs and Englishmen go out in the midday sun. I am neither a mad dog nor am I English. Although I've been called a son of a bitch more than once."

"By your exes, I'll bet."

"Actually, they all seemed to favor no-good bastard."

"In our line of business, being that may not be a bad thing," Stone said.

"You ever get tired of it?"

"Tired of what?"

"Our line of business. All the bodies are piling up… some of them visit me in my sleep."

"We've been lucky, Ian. All the guys we hit were shit birds. Hell, I was surprised when people showed up for their funerals."

Connah took a drink. "Most of those mourners had no idea who those assholes were. I can't think of anything old people like better than a good viewing. Ever go to a funeral home and watch them? They hate a closed coffin. One time I saw an old bird open the lid when she thought no one was looking. When we shoot some mug in the head and really mess 'em up, we're actually doing the old farts a favor. We provide entertainment that costs less than pay-for-view."

Stoney chuckled. "I can identify with them. I love going to the funeral home when some douche bag I hate has died. I stand over the coffin just to gloat that I out-lived them."

"Yeah, remember when we were kids? The first thing we read in the morning paper was the sports, then the comics? In our twenties, it was sports and the headlines. Right now, it's the headlines, then the sports pages. Old farts read the obits and then read about the murders. The bloodier and more horrific the killing, the better they like it."

Stone stared at his friend for a moment and then said, "Now *that* gives me something to look forward to."

18

Ivany Hurtado was small, thin, and wrinkled as a sun-dried raisin. He looked like his diet consisted of road-kill. The Puerto Rican was also one of the greediest old men Connah had ever encountered. He struck him as being a person who would steal the ashes from a crematorium and sell them to cannibals as Instant People. Still, he was the sort with whom Connah enjoyed doing business. There was no illusion of honesty in Hurtado. You knew from the outset that he was out to beat you.

"*Señors*, please, sit."

The table at which they sat was centered in a homemade patio. The ground was hard-pan dirt, and the enclosure's borders were defined by a string of cheap Chinese paper lanterns. The roof was a trellis topped with some sort of vine that was taking over bit-by-bit. It was interwoven and entwined like a pit of vipers. Connah eyed it suspiciously. Who knew what might be slithering around up there.

The old man disappeared into the house's interior, returning several minutes later carrying a tray on which sat a bottle and three glasses. He placed the platter in the center of the table and then sat down. When he distributed the glasses, his hands shook as if he had Parkinson's disease; booze spilled over the sides of Connah's glass as the old man filled it.

Once the drinks had been poured, the old man sat back and said, "¡*Salud!*"

Connah and Stone raised their glasses and downed the fiery liquor. Stone gasped and said, "What is this stuff?"

The old man smiled; his toothless mouth resembled the maw of a bottomless pit. "It is called *pitorro*."

"Which is?"

"It is my own special rum. I make it."

Stone held up his glass and stared into it. "Puerto Rican moonshine."

"I am not sure what moonshine is."

"It's homemade liquor," Stone answered.

Connah poured another shot and turned to Hurtado. "My friend was told by your nephew in the states that you have news of Harry Sandberg?"

The old man looked as if he had no idea what he was talking about. Connah took a fifty-dollar bill from his wallet and placed it on the table. The old man snatched it faster than a lizard catching a fly.

"He is calling himself Sanders," Connah added.

"I was told you knew where can we find him?" Stone said.

"He was renting my cabana in Añasco. They make wonderful *pitorro* there."

"Where is this Añasco?" Connah asked.

"To the west, just north of Mayagüez."

Connah stood. "Thank you for the drinks and the information."

"There is more, *señor*. He has fallen under the influence of an evil man, Felipe Rojas. Whatever it is that you seek from this gringo may be gone. Rojas and his sister Juanita are known to prey on *americanos fugitivos*. Your friend has lost all his money if they are up to their old tricks. Also, there is the problem of lost income. The man rented my cabana for three months but only paid for one. Now I believe that he has fled. Perhaps word of your arrival precedes you?"

"How much a month?"

"Six hundred dollars."

Connah threw six one-hundred-dollar bills on the table. "We'll split it... I'm sure you'll find another renter."

"That will be fine," the old man said.

When Hurtado smiled and snatched the money up without arguing about the remainder, Connah knew he had been had. The old shyster probably had a waiting list of potential renters. "In that eventuality, where can this Rojas and his sister be found?"

"Mayagüez. I can give you the address of his office."

"If there's anything I like," Stone said, "it's a one-stop-shop."

19

Sean Sutton sat before his boss. "I can't believe that you brought Connah in on this. I could take care of Bimbo and Jiggs and not break into a sweat."

"I don't doubt that, Sean. Nevertheless, no sooner would you pull the trigger than the entire city would know who put the hit on them. Connah's reputation for being independent adds an element of doubt."

"I don't like that guy. He hits from hidden locations. It ain't manly."

Billie ground out her cigarette. "Maybe so, but he's damned effective. When word gets around that Connah is on the hunt, everyone gets scared, for the very reason you just mentioned. You never know where or when he's going to hit you."

"I still don't like it."

"Sean, life is full of things we don't like. Now, will you go find something constructive to do?"

Sutton stood and walked to the office door. "Mark my words, Billie, this is going to come back to bite our ass. People won't like it."

"You know, Sean, I learned a long time ago that it's impossible to please everyone, but pissing them all off is easy. Therefore, I don't worry about it anymore."

Sutton grinned at her. "You're pretty good at pissing people off, Boss. I got to hand that to you."

"I do have a job for you."

"Name it."

"I want to know what Spinelli is up to. The last I heard, she was sniffing around Louie Roubideaux's place. I wouldn't be surprised if she's trying to turn him. The action from his place is lucrative, and I don't want to lose it."

Sutton saluted her with a two-fingered parody of the Boy Scout salute. "I'm on it."

$ $ $ $ $

Louie Roubideaux was a drug dealer and a grifter. His reputation was that he could swim in shark-infested waters, and the sharks would leave him alone out of professional courtesy. He was also a mercenary. His allegiance was to whoever was paying him the most at any given second. He was possibly the most hated man in Boston, and he was also doing everything he could to become one of the richest. Sutton found Roubideaux in a bar near the TD Bank Garden, which Sutton still thought of as The Boston Garden—old habits die hard.

The Frenchman sat at the bar nursing a cup of coffee. It was evident to Sutton that he awaited his couriers to deliver the proceeds from various drug pushers around the city. Close to the junction of the MBTA Orange, Blue, and Red Lines, the bar was in a perfect location for his minions to make their drops.

Sutton slid onto the barstool to Roubideaux's immediate left. The pusher stared at him in the mirror behind the bar. "What brings you here, Sean?"

"Billie sent me."

"I figured that. Every time I see you and O'Reilly together, you're sniffing around her ass like a dog in heat."

Sutton stiffened, tempted to shoot the Frenchman right then.

Roubideaux started laughing. "She's got you by the curly hairs, you know that?"

"Ain't none of your business what she does or doesn't have."

"You ever going to wake up, Sutton? That crazy mick broad is never going to let you into her hive. She's the queen bee, and all you'll ever be to her is a drone."

"Well, if I'm going to be a drone, I'd rather be Billie's drone than Bimbo Spinelli's."

"Careful where you say that, Sean. Bobbi has ears all over town. She's got as many lapdogs sniffing after her as your bitch does. Most of them would love nothing better than to neuter one of O'Reilly's mutts."

"Billie's been hearing a noise that you and Spinelli may be closer than she'd like."

"Ain't any of her business who I talk to."

"When you're under her protection, it is."

"Yeah, for twenty-five percent of my business. Bobbi's willing to protect my people and me for twenty."

"I'll let Billie know that you want to renegotiate your deal."

Roubideaux took a drink of coffee. "You do that."

Sutton stood up and said, "I guess you heard that Billie rehired an old employee?"

"Nope, ain't heard nothing. Anyone, I know?"

"Ian Connah."

Roubideaux's face turned ashen.

"You might want to reconsider that desire to renegotiate your deal. You get my drift?"

20

It took less than two hours for Connah and Stone to drive from San Juan to Mayagüez, the eighth largest city on the island with more than 90,000 people. It took even less time to find the office of Felipe Rojas. The Americans settled down at a sidewalk table of a small cafe across the street from the strip mall. The private investigator had his headquarters in the central office. They drank coffee, watched, and waited, confident that it would not be long until someone entered Rojas's office.

It was just before ten in the morning when a small man in a business suit unlocked the door and entered the suite. "There's our man," he said to Stone.

Stone studied their target for several moments and said, "Does he remind you of that guy in the movies... Gomez Addams?"

Connah chuckled. "Now that you mention it, he does."

They allowed the man five minutes to settle in, and then Connah stood up. "Time to roll."

They crossed the street, already feeling the heat of mid-morning on their backs. As was his custom, Connah wore a black T-shirt and light windbreaker. The jacket only served one purpose; it hid the nine-millimeter pistol he wore in a holster on his back. Stone took a position near Rojas' office window before reaching the entrance. He removed a laser pointer and grinned at Connah.

The difference in temperature between the outside and the interior of the boutique-sized office was sufficient to raise goosebumps on Connah's arms. The Hispanic they had observed enter the building sat behind a metal desk of the sort Connah had not seen since he was in the military. The guy had a thin mustache similar to that popular with male actors in the film noir movies of the 1940s. He wore a cheap suit that Connah was sure he thought looked expensive. If Harry Sandberg was involved with Rojas, he was not as bright as Connah had previously thought. This character looked like the type who would murder his parents and beg the court for mercy because he was an orphan.

The man stood and said, "May I help you, *señor*?"

Connah sat in the sole chair that fronted the heavy metal desk without waiting for an invitation. "I believe that you can."

"I am Felipe Rojas." Rojas bent forward and offered his hand.

Connah ignored the hand, making sure he kept his eyes narrowed and locked on those of the Puerto Rican. "Ian."

Rojas sat down and asked, "Well, Señor Ian, what service can I perform for you?"

"I'm here to recover some stolen money."

Rojas sat up and inclined his torso forward, signifying that he was interested. "Where and from whom was this money stolen?"

"It was stolen from me."

"I see."

"It was embezzled by a man named Harry Sandberg." Rojas's facial expression remained fixed. Connah was impressed. This guy was an accomplished grifter. "You possibly know him as Harry Sanders."

"I know of no person by that name."

"I beg to differ, and my companion is of the same frame of mind."

Rojas looked past Ian and, with a smug look, said, "Companion? I see no one."

The so-called security expert's eyes were drawn to a red light that flashed across them.

"I assume a highly-skilled investigator such as yourself knows a laser sight when he sees one?" Ian said.

Rojas leaned back in his chair. He placed his hands on the chair's armrests as if he were ready to get up.

"I'd stay put if I were you," Ian said. "Moving could be detrimental to your health."

Rojas dropped his hands and asked, "What do you want?"

"Two things. One, however much of my money that you stole from Sanders and what he stole from me."

"I stole nothing from you."

"Sandberg, or, as you know him, Sanders, stole his money from me. Therefore, anything you took from him is rightfully mine."

"And if I don't see it your way?"

"You have contacts in the states, call them and ask if they've heard of Ian Connah. Go ahead, get a character reference. I'll wait."

It took less than ten minutes for Rojas to learn all he needed about the man in front of his desk and his companion. His face blanched when he said, "What is the second thing you want?"

"I want to know where *Sandberg* ran to, what alias he may be using, and how long it's been since he ran."

Rojas picked up his phone.

"May I ask who you're calling?"

"My sister, she will bring your money."

21

Dick O'Schaunessey walked into Paddy's Pub and asked Kelly if Billie was in. The bartender gave the cop a dirty look, filled with loathing, and nodded toward the back. "In her office."

O'Schaunessey removed the smelly, extinguished cigar butt from his mouth and dropped it into a glass that had about an eighth of an inch of liquid in it. Kelly eyed the loathsome tobacco and said, "Smells like it was soaked in piss and then dried."

"Nothin' but the best for me," O'Schaunessey said, exposing his gross dental work.

Kelley stared at the fat man's back as he waddled toward the rear of the pub. He turned the water tap on in the bar sink, spit into the basin, and said to no one in particular, "Talking with that son of a bitch always leaves a bad taste in my mouth…"

As O'Schaunessey passed through the dining room, early diners smelled the aura of stale tobacco and unwashed clothes that hung around him like a noxious shroud and looked on with distaste. He was so used to being looked at in that manner that he had become oblivious to it and ignored them as he walked past. Nevertheless, one woman did attract his attention when she grunted in disgust and threw her fork in her plate. He grinned at her, and seeing his discolored and rotted teeth destroyed any trace of appetite she had left.

He passed through the back door and found himself in front of Billie O'Reilly's office. He opened the door and stepped inside unannounced—or so he thought. He immediately halted, his hand still on the knob when he was confronted by the mob boss, holding a revolver that was pointed at his ample belly.

"I thought I told you to never come in here during my busy hours…"

O'Schaunessey felt his face heat with a mixture of anger and embarrassment. "I got somethin' to tell ya and thought that it shouldn't wait."

Billie pointed to the corner of her desk. "See that black thing? It's called a telephone. You could have called. It isn't smart for you to be seen coming and going around here. If the internal affairs people investigate you, you'll be about as useful to me as a knife is in a gunfight."

"Yeah, yeah." He closed the door behind him and entered the room. He saw Billie's nose wrinkle with disgust and stopped advancing toward her. "You got problems," he said.

"Don't we all?"

"No, real problems. Jiggs Wark has put a bounty out on you and Spinelli."

"I hope he's offering more for me than Bimbo."

"Billie, this ain't no laughin' matter. Harvey Westin is in town."

Her face paled. "I thought Westin never left the west coast."

"Shit, if the amount of money I hear Jiggs is offering is accurate, they'll be coming from goddamned China for this one."

"What do you mean?"

"The way I hear it, numbers in the neighborhood of one million dollars are being thrown around. You better take this seriously, Billie. For that kind of jack, you can't trust anyone. Even your most trusted people are gonna be looking for any opportunity to cash in."

"That sonuvabitch."

"If you're talking about our mutual friend, Jiggs, what did you expect? He's old school. Jiggs thinks there's no way a couple of broads can run a business."

Billie lit a cigarette. "We'll see about that. Get out of here. I got work to do."

22

Juanita arrived a little after eleven. She wore faded cut-off jeans, a strappy top with no bra beneath, and she carried a metallic silver briefcase. She barged through the door and into the office and abruptly halted when she saw Connah off to her left, leaning against the wall. "Are you okay, Felipe?"

"I'm fine. Did you bring the money?"

"*Si*, why is it that you wanted me to bring it here?" She gave Connah a wary look.

"Because," Connah said, "if you didn't, I was going to kill him."

"Who are you?"

"If my money is not in that case, I'm about to be the most horrible thing that has ever happened to you. I'll make you regret the day your screaming mother brought you into this world."

She gave her brother a questioning look.

"Place the briefcase on my desk, Juanita. He will do what he says. His name is Ian Connah. In certain areas of the world, he has quite a reputation as an assassin for hire."

She placed the case on the desk, and Connah remained where he was. "Make sure that you don't get between ol' Felipe here and the window." Turning to Rojas, Connah said, "I'm certain you got a piece somewhere in your desk. You will not be able to reach it before I put a nine-millimeter slug in your gut." He motioned to Rojas, who opened it, and said, "Now, turn it so that I can see what's inside."

Rojas flipped the catches and opened the case. He rotated it, making its contents visible.

"Take everything out of it and put it on the desk."

When Juanita looked at Connah, he knew that she would kill him if given half a chance. Obviously, she and Felipe were planning on using the money to live in style. The old Cuban had told him that Juanita was a whore disguised as a masseuse. Without the money, she would have to continue doing so, and it was apparent that it was a career she had hoped to leave behind.

Connah took a cloth laundry bag from his back pocket and threw it on the desk. "I'm feeling benevolent today," he said, "count out one thousand for each of you and then put the rest of the fifty thousand in the bag." Before either Juanita or Felipe got any ideas, he removed the nine-millimeter pistol from the holster he wore on his back, which was hidden by the windbreaker. "You make one false move, and I'll kill you both."

Felipe counted out twenty one-hundred-dollar bills and placed them in two even stacks. He picked up one, folded the bills, and put them into his pocket. He handed the remaining ten to his sister and then put the remainder of the money into the sack.

Connah held his free hand out, palm up, and moved his fingers in a motion indicating the bag should be thrown to him. He caught it and walked toward the door. "If anyone interferes with me between now and when I leave this island, I'll come after you. You'll never know where or when, but I'll put a bullet in both of your heads. *¿Entendido?*"

Juanita and Felipe stood rigidly in place. Their only movement was to nod affirmation that they understood.

$ $ $ $ $

Connah departed the office and walked across the street to the rental car. When he was halfway across the thoroughfare, Connah saw Stone put away the high-power laser device that he had aimed at Felipe Rojas. Once Connah settled into the passenger seat, Stone drove away.

"Well," Connah said, "that worked out pretty good."

"They come up with the money?"

"Yeah, I gave them each a grand for inconveniencing them."

"Sounds more than fair to me."

Connah's satellite phone rang. "Who in hell can that be?" He took the phone from the holder on his right hip and hit the talk button.

"Where the hell are you?" inquired an anxious and obviously upset Billie O'Reilly.

"Taking care of some personal business. What's up?"

"What's up is that that rotten asshole Jiggs Wark has brought in some out-of-town talent, and Bimbo and I are number one and two on their hit list. I need you back here—yesterday!"

"All right, calm down. I'll be there tomorrow—"

"TOMORROW! Where the hell are you?"

"Puerto Rico. I'll be on the next flight out."

"What about Stone? Where the hell is he?"

"Right now, he's sitting about three feet to my left."

"Ian, I'm paying you two a shit load of cash. I expect you to be here in Boston, not on a frigging vacation in the tropics. Get your ass back here ASAP. Jiggs has brought in Harvey Westin, and who knows who else."

The connection went dead.

Connah turned to Stone. "You heard?"

"I heard loud and clear. Billie sounds upset, not to mention scared."

"What gave you that idea—the fact that I was not on speaker?"

"That and the fact that she mentioned Harvey Westin. He's one of the best. If he was hired to kill her, she's as good as dead."

"Westin is probably the third-best sniper I know of."

Stone said, "Who are one and two?"

"You and me."

"You sound convinced."

"If we aren't the best, we'll know soon enough."

Stone pressed the accelerator, and they sped toward San Juan.

"What about Sandberg?"

"According to Rojas, he's somewhere in Brazil. Once we clean things up in Boston, we'll worry about him."

"In the meantime, he's living it up on your fucking money."

"Can't be helped. However, we should be able to recoup some of my cash in Boston."

"Oh?"

"Billie is paying us to cover her ass. I don't see any reason why Bobbi shouldn't throw some cash into the pot. After all, she and Billie are up against the same enemy."

Stone said, "This is starting to sound like that old Clint Eastwood spaghetti western, *A Fistful of Dollars*. Two groups of hoods who hate each other and the lone gun-for-hire playing one off against the other."

"Only I'm not alone."

"If you keep getting me involved in these shooting wars, you damned well could be."

Connah playfully punched Stone on the arm. "You love it. If it wasn't for all these shooting wars, you'd be bored as hell."

Stone said, "We're getting old in a young man's business, Ian. Believe me when I tell you that I was content standing next to that trout stream with my fly rod."

23

Harvey Westin hated the East Coast. As a matter of fact, it was his firm belief that once you traveled east of the deserts and hills of California, there was no intelligent life to be found. He loathed the old brick buildings along Boston's waterfront. He thought that the only way to salvage them was to blow them up and rebuild the whole place in stucco, Spanish-American decor.

He walked past the newly-renovated TD Garden, home of the hated Celtics. He fantasized about attending a game between them and the Lakers. In his mind, he was on the catwalks high above the playing court at the Staples Center or the TD Garden with his beloved sniper rifle. From that lofty perch, he could shoot any players who were not wearing purple and yellow uniforms.

He shook off the pleasing mental images of the mayhem he would cause on the disgusting parquet floor below the platforms and waved down a cab. There was no way in hell he was going to rub elbows with the two-legged vermin who patronized the MBTA rail system. A yellow taxi stopped, and he got in. The interior reeked of cigarette smoke, and Westin glared at the back of the driver's head. "Where may I take you?" a middle-eastern voice asked.

Westin got out of the cab. "No place. Your cab stinks. Isn't there a law against smoking in a cab in Boston?"

The driver raised his right hand and elevated the middle finger. When Westin slammed the car door, the cabbie sped off. He flagged down three cabs before one meeting his environmental standards stopped. He gave the cabbie the address to where he wanted to go and then slid the transparent shield closed, cutting off any opportunity for the driver to engage him in conversation.

Westin studied the interior of the passenger compartment and decided that there was no way to determine if it was sanitary enough for him to remove his gloves. He watched the rundown buildings pass by one by one.

Harvey Westin was one of the most successful, sought-after, and highest-paid assassins in the United States. However, he suffered severely with obsessive-compulsive disorder. His compulsion with cleanliness did aid him in his work. It required an immaculate shooting hide that always left a crime scene devoid of any evidence that could lead to him. He believed that only a stupid dog shits in its own back yard and only stupid hitmen worked in their home city. He only worked outside of Los Angeles.

The cab passed through City Square, crossed over the Charles River, and took Rutherford Avenue through Charlestown. On his right, Westin watched the Bunker Hill Monument pass by. The dirt and chaos of the never-ending highway construction in the area repelled him. The landscape did not change much when the cab sped through Sullivan Square and entered Somerville. It would take, Westin decided, a nuclear holocaust to clean up this city.

The cab stopped beside a rundown, seedy-looking auto body shop on a back street so narrow that Westin would be surprised if they worked on anything larger than an ATV. The cabbie studied him in the rear-view mirror, obviously wondering what a man in a $2,000 suit would want in this place. Westin opened his briefcase, waited until the driver slid the Plexiglas barrier open, and handed him a twenty-dollar bill that had never been folded. The driver, in turn, flipped through a wad of bills that had been crumpled and smoothed. Westin thought that they looked as if they had been slept on. The man peeled off a five-dollar bill and two ones and held them through the opening. Westin stared at the filthy, loathsome money for a few seconds and then said, "Keep it." He got out of the car.

He studied the dilapidated appearance of the building. He wondered if he had spent a lot of money chasing a rumor. This place didn't look like the office of someone capable of offering a million dollars for a hitter. He straightened his tie and approached the door. He heard the whine of pneumatic tools and the loud hiss of pressurized air. He entered the building, saw the dust and debris that drifted in the air, removed a handkerchief from his pocket, and held it over his nose and mouth. The interior of the garage belied the tiny appearance of its outside. The building ran back a good hundred feet. Several vehicles in various stages of repair were parked diagonally along the walls. The back wall was another garage door, which was open, giving Westin a view of the busy street that ran past the back of the building.

A man wearing coveralls and a cloth cap with visor pointed to the rear, goggles, and a painting mask was sanding and smoothing an area on the rocker panel of a car. Although not a car and truck buff, Westin knew at a glance that it was a classic Chevrolet Corvette, pre-Stingray, from the early 1960s. He realized that the substance in the air was some form of filler and resin used to repair fiberglass car bodies, and he pressed the handkerchief tighter. The auto body technician saw him and straightened up. He raised his goggles and lowered the breathing apparatus he wore. He studied Westin for several seconds and then said, "I don't do work for the public." He pointed to the Corvette that he had been repairing. "Restoring these old classics is my avocation."

"I am looking for Joshua George Wark."

The man held out a dirty, fiberglass-coated hand. "I'm Jiggs Wark. What can I do for you?"

Westin stared at the obviously unclean hand. He knew it was impolite to shake a man's hand wearing a glove. Nevertheless, there was no way that he could touch that filthy paw. After several seconds, Wark dropped his hand and gave him an intense look.

"I'm Harvey Westin."

"Ah, the hitter who never gets his hands dirty."

He removed his cap, revealing a bald head, then took off the goggles and mask that filtered the fine fiberglass dust from reaching his lungs. "Let's talk in the office," he said.

Westin studied the man as he followed him down a narrow corridor. He believed Wark was in his fifties or sixties. He stopped before an interior door and motioned for the gun for hire to follow him through. The threshold revealed a large office that was immaculate compared to the auto body shop. Wark indicated to one of two chairs that were positioned along the wall. Between the chairs was an elegant table and pole lamp combination.

Westin settled into the table's left chair and stoically watched as Wark slid out of his coveralls. Beneath the canvas jumpsuit, Wark was dressed like a Wall Street executive, wearing a tasteful shirt, tie and suit pants. He sat behind the desk, removed his dusty, paint-stained work boots, and put on a pair of highly-polished wing-tip business shoes. He crossed the room and sat in the vacant chair to Westin's left. "I assume," Wark said, "you're here about the, shall we call it a reward?"

"Call it whatever you like. I'm here about the million-dollar hit."

Wark nodded in agreement. "Actually, it is hits, plural. Multiple targets, up to a total of one million dollars." Westin noticed how he unconsciously patted the top of his bald head as if he still had a full head of hair. He wondered if Wark usually wore a hairpiece. "What do you know about my requirements?" Wark asked.

"All I know is I received a letter announcing the million-dollar reward and that if interested, I should contact one Joshua George Wark. I must say I find your nickname rather odd."

"I used to go by Jay-Gee, but as a kid, my friends began calling me Jiggs, and it's stuck. Let me fill you in on what's going on."

"Please do."

There was a knock at the door, and Wark said, "Come in."

A dapper young man appeared through the portal. He stopped when he saw Westin. "Sorry, Boss, I didn't realize that you were busy."

"Not a problem, Wayne. Stick around for a bit." Wark turned toward Westin and said, "This is Wayne Archer. He's as close to being the number two man around here as I got. Wayne, this is Harvey Westin."

"The Harvey Westin?"

"In the flesh," Westin said.

Archer took a seat on the couch that lined the wall to the right of where Wark and Westin sat. "Please," he said, continue your discussion."

"Actually," Wark said, "we were just starting." He turned his attention to Westin. "I got a couple of competitors."

"So, I've been told, William O'Reilly and Robert Spinelli."

"Well," Wark said, "you got it partly right. It's Billie Jean O'Reilly and Roberta, aka Bobbi, Spinelli. Their fathers, Paddy and Mario, respectively, died without leaving an heir with balls, so their daughters took over."

"You want me to hit them?"

"If not you, anyone. This is not an exclusive contract. It's an open reward of half a million each for their demise. In short, I want those bitches dead."

"Okay, how many other shooters have taken you up on your offer?"

"Counting you, three."

"Who are the other two? Anybody, I might know?"

"Possibly."

"So, this is first-come, first paid."

"Basically." Wark handed a manila folder to him. "That's an organizational chart of their respective operations."

"What is the payment schedule?"

"No payment schedule, five hundred thou each, up to the agreed-upon million bucks, payable as soon as I see definitive proof that the contract was fulfilled."

"What if I have to, shall we say, deal with some of their flunkies to reach the women?"

"I don't really care. You do what you have to do. I'm only paying for the women. I think you should know that getting to O'Reilly may be tough."

"Why would she be any tougher than Spinelli?"

"She's brought Ian Connah in as her security."

"Connah, I've heard of him. That's a challenge worth taking on. In fact, I'll gladly do him gratis. The publicity alone will make me millions more."

Westin stood and walked to the door. When he had covered half the distance, he paused. "You still haven't told me who else you've spoken to about this?"

"Two people, Alonzo Diaz and some former IRA mick named Tegan Hale."

"Tegan, what a strange name."

"Maybe so, but she's as ruthless as the two she's after. I wouldn't put it past any of these three women to cut off a man's balls and keep them in a jar of embalming fluid so they could recall the fun they had collecting them."

"If I have to take these other two shooters out, who pays?"

"Not me. But it'll cut down on your competition."

"Just thought I'd ask." Westin left without another word.

Westin closed the door behind him, pressed his ear against it, and listened to the conversation inside.

"That fucker is weird," Archer said. "Just looking at him gave me the creeps. He doesn't even have eyebrows."

"I've checked him out," Wark responded. "He has some hang-ups about cleanliness and hair, but the bastard is as cold-blooded a killer as Connah."

Westin smiled. As he left the building, he wondered how long it would be before Wark found out that the one reason why he had never been caught. Like his targets, some of his employers had not survived the experience.

24

At 2:30 a.m., Sean Sutton waited as Kelly closed down the bar and carried the day's cash and receipts back to Billie's office. When Kelly returned from the back, he grabbed his jacket and said, "Boss says we can take off," as he slipped into it.

"I think I'll hang around and see that she gets home okay."

Kelly shrugged and walked to the door. "I got to hand it to you, Sean. You don't give up easy."

Sutton grinned. "Can't give up. There's too much to lose if I do."

"She isn't ever gonna be happy with anyone but Connah. If you ask me, they ain't ever going to marry, at least not to each other."

"I'll take my chances."

"G'night." Kelly walked into the night.

A rifle shot broke the quiet early morning, and Kelly tumbled back through the door. Sutton rushed over and caught him. He held the bartender by his underarms and saw the bullet hole in his forehead. Warm liquid ran down the front of Sutton's shirt and pants. There was another flash, then Sutton's head exploded, and he toppled backward, landing on the floor with Kelly laying on his legs.

$ $ $ $ $

Billie heard two shots, bolted out of her office, raced through the dining room and into the bar. Sutton and Kelly lay on the threshold of the entrance. If it wasn't for the pool of blood Sutton's head laid in, they would have looked like the parody of a couple of bobsledders on the run. She reached up on the wall and turned off the bank of wall switches, plunging the bar into darkness. She crouched low and scurried behind the bar, where she fumbled around until she found the revolver that Kelly always kept there. She sat against the bar, feeling her slacks absorb water from the floor.

She rose and peered over the bar toward the front entrance. Whoever the shooter or shooters were, they seemed content to take what they had and not enter the pub. Billie grabbed the cordless phone from the end of the bar and dialed in a preprogrammed number.

The phone was answered on the third ring. "Yeah."

"O'Schaunessey, get your ass over here—quick!"

"Billie, it's two-thirty in the morning—"

"No shit, and I got two bodies in the threshold of my door. Now, get your fat ass out of bed and get here ten minutes ago!"

She broke the connection and dialed a second speed-dial. This call was answered on the second ring. "Where the fuck are you?"

"Miami International, waiting to board a 6:40 a.m. flight to Boston. What's up?"

"Some asshole sniper just took out Kelly and Sutton, that's what. Don't even go home from the airport. You come directly to the pub, understand?"

"Yeah, I should be there by ten."

"You should have been here now! I don't know what in hell was so important that you had to run off to the Caribbean, but it better not happen again."

"All right, Billie, I got your point. Now call in some of your boys, keep your ass low, and call 9-1-1."

"O'Schaunessey's on his way—"

"Like I said, call some of your boys. I don't trust that slimy bastard as far as a toddler could throw him. For all you know, he's working with the goddamn shooter."

She took a deep breath. "You're right, Connah. He's greedy enough to go after that bounty."

$ $ $ $ $

"Billie?"

"That you, O'Schaunessey?"

"Yeah, are you okay?" The BPD captain was outside on the sidewalk.

"You gonna come in?" Billie asked.

"It's better that I don't. The last thing we need is for any trace of me to show up inside."

She heard sirens and stood up from her hiding place on the floor behind the bar. Connah's last words were in her head, and she still held the revolver, hiding it behind her back. "Do you have any idea who did this?" she asked.

"My informants tell me there are at least three heavy-hitters in town. Alonzo Diaz, a former female IRA hitter, named Tegan Hale, and Harvey Westin from the left coast. He looked at the bodies and added, "This looks like Tegan's work. She's a cold one, that's certain. They must be here for Wark's bounty on you."

The sirens sounded louder and closer as Billie rounded the bar. She forced back her desire to pace the room, smoking one cigarette after another.

O'Schaunessey watched her for several seconds and then said, "Billie, I got to get out of here. It will look suspicious if a captain arrives on the scene before the patrol people."

Billie dismissed him with an abrupt flick of her right hand. "Go, I'll handle this my own way."

"Billie, a bloodbath ain't gonna solve nothing."

"I'm going biblical on this. The Bible says an eye for an eye... well, I'm going a shooter for a shooter."

"What are you talking about?"

"If these assholes can hunt me, then I can hunt them. I'm giving this job to my security consultants."

O'Schaunessey stepped to the threshold. "This could blow the lid off everything. It could be the end of all three of you."

"Connah told me that, too. If that's the case—so, be it."

25

Connah sat at the bar, sipping from a frosty glass of beer. He inhaled the heady scent of Billie's perfume. The television above the bar was tuned to a local cable news channel. The picture was of the front of Paddy's Pub, and Billie asked Fiona McBrietty to turn up the volume.

Fiona was Kelly's replacement and had worked twenty hours a week as a part-time bartender until today. Now, or until Billie could make other arrangements, Fiona was the interim head mixologist. She stepped up onto a small stool and turned the sound up, giving Connah an unimpeded view of the back of her shapely legs, from the hem of her short plaid skirt to her ankles as well as her butt.

"Why don't you use the remote?" Billie asked.

"I can't find it."

"Well, find it, I hired you to tend bar, not moon the customers."

Fiona cast an impish look in Connah's direction and said, "Yes, ma'am."

"And stop calling me ma'am. I'm only a couple of years older than you."

"Yes, ma'am." She darted down to the far end of the bar, where another customer needed a refill.

Billie stood up and beckoned for Connah to follow her to her office.

He leaned over the bar, picked up the remote control, and muted the TV. He set the controller on the bar and followed Billie. "Nice looking young woman," he commented.

"Yeah, I guess you could say that she knows how to raise a hem to get a man. It wouldn't surprise me if you knew what color underwear she has on."

"Do I detect a bit of jealousy?"

"I just wish she was as good a bartender as she is a flirt."

Once they were in Billie's office, she got to the point. "Ian, you have to get them before they get me."

"I know that. It may be more effective if I just took out the source of all this."

"Do you truly believe that Jiggs Wark is behind this?"

"You and I know damned well he is. If you hadn't been so blinded by your hatred for Bobbi Spinelli, you would have seen that he's been playing you two against each other since you took over from your fathers. Let you ladies blow each other up, and all he has to do is walk in and clean up the rubble."

"Paddy always said that Jiggs was a rotten backstabber."

"No argument there. Jiggs has definitely set things up in what he believes is a no-lose situation." Connah flopped on the couch. "He's brought in some real heavy hitters. As a matter of fact, he may have turned Boston into a modern-day Tombstone. The money he's dangling out there will attract every idiot in the hemisphere who has fantasies of being an assassin."

For the first time since he had returned to the field, Connah saw that Billie was afraid. She looked as if she had just realized that this situation was something that she was not equipped to handle. "So," she asked, "what do we do?"

"Go on the offensive. In fact, it may not hurt for you and Bobbi to set your differences aside and become allies in this matter."

As if on cue, the phone rang. Billie answered it and listened for several seconds. "We'll be there." She hung up. "Speak about coincidences. Bimbo wants to meet later tonight."

Connah stood and turned to the door. He stopped just before exiting the office and said, "Yellow."

"What's yellow?"

"Fiona's underwear."

$ $ $ $ $

"I've never been here before," Billie said as she and Connah walked inside the North End Social Club. "I hope I've dressed appropriately."

"Don't worry," Connah commented, "you're dressed fine. All this place is is a bar with folding tables and chairs. Hell, the food probably sucks, too."

Billie abruptly stopped and inspected the interior. Connah was correct; there was nothing fancy about the place. It was nothing more than a beat-up bar and a back room furnished with card tables. Local smoking laws did not apply to private clubs, and cigarette and cigar smoke hung heavy in the air. All conversation ended when Connah and Billie walked across the room to the table in the rear, where Bobbi Spinelli sat with her number one goon, Anthony (Tony D) D'Altrui.

"I see they haven't hit you yet," Billie said when she and Connah stood beside the table.

"Sit," Bobbi said. "We got too many other problems to be bitching at each other."

When Connah and Billie were settled across from Bobbi and her bodyguard, Billie opened her purse and lit a cigarette. She offered one to Bobbi.

"No thanks, I got my own."

Billie inhaled and said, "Suit yourself. You called me. What's on your mind?"

"An alliance, at least until we put an end to this bullshit that Jiggs dreamed up."

Billie looked at Connah. "Jiggs won't be a problem for long. Once he's gone, they'll take off—those of them that are left. I owe one of them."

"So, I hear. Talk around town is that the Hale bitch struck you," Bobbi said.

Connah stared at D'Altrui. "Tony, if I was you, I'd keep my eyes open and my ass low," he said.

Connah knew the man was a fool as soon as the Italian thug answered, "I can handle myself."

"So could Kelly and Sutton. They were two of the best," Connah said. "When there's a timber rattler after you, the only way to ensure that you're safe is to stay out of the woods—and you don't have that option."

"Like I said, I can take care of myself. Besides, by taking out Kelly and Sutton, the shooter gave me a warning."

Connah chuckled. "I hope you understand what you're up against. I'm familiar with all three of these shooters. Diaz will hit you like a pile-driver when you least expect it. Hale, she'll use a car bomb if the opportunity avails itself. Harvey Westin, now there's an entirely different breed of snake."

"And you?" D'Altrui asked.

"I can take you out anytime and anyplace I want."

"That," Bobbi said, "is why I asked you both here." She reached beside her chair, placed a briefcase on the table, and slid it forward until it was in front of Connah. "Two hundred fifty thousand dollars. I've heard that's your fee for security consulting." She turned her head slightly to look at her rival. "I wanted to be upfront about this." She turned back to Connah. "With what I heard she's paying, that makes a half million."

Connah grinned. "That's only half what I can make if I throw my hat into the ring with Jiggs and his hired guns."

"This way, you keep it all," Bobbi said. "You were always loyal, Ian. Not to mention, the word is that for one of them to get the million, they need to hit both of us, and you only need to take Jiggs out."

Connah placed the briefcase on the floor beside his chair. "You got any problem with this?" he asked Billie.

Without taking her eyes off Bobbi, she shook her head. "Just so long as you're working on the problem."

"And if I don't get them before they get you?"

Bobbi broke away from the staring contest that she and Billie held. "Then there won't be anyone to demand a refund, will there?"

"Okay, now we come to the tough part."

"What," Bobbi asked, "is the tough part?"

"Yeah," Billie mimicked, "*what* is the tough part?"

"If I'm going to protect the two of you, you can't be on different ends of the city."

"Are you saying that..." the women said in unison.

"I'm saying that you need to stay together. I would prefer someplace outside of Boston. A location where I know the turf and Westin, Hale, and Diaz do not."

The mob leaders stared at each other. Their eyes narrowed and looked venomous. Connah was reminded of a film he had once seen of a mongoose fighting a cobra. For a brief second, he tried to figure out which was the snake and which was the viverrid. Either way, he knew that he needed help keeping them safe from each other as well as from Hale, Diaz, and Westin. He stood, picked up the briefcase, and said, "I'd better get to work on the arrangements." He looked at Billie. "You coming, or are you two going to have a girl's night out?"

Billie got to her feet, glared at Bobbi for a second, and said, "Fuck you, Ian. Don't forget, you're still only hired help."

Connah nodded to D'Altrui. "It looks as if you and I got something in common. Like I said, keep your ass low and don't skyline yourself. These are three of the best shooters in the country. Fortunately, you people have *THE* best working for you."

26

Harvey Westin carried a backpack and a rectangular case as he climbed the stairs. He took care to keep his weight where the steps abutted the wall, thereby minimizing the tell-tale squeaks and groans that would give away his presence. Once the assassin reached the roof, Westin squatted and duck-walked to the abutment that faced the North Side Social Club. He dropped his backpack, swapped his leather gloves for a pair of latex ones, and removed a blue tarpaulin. One edge of the tarp was fastened to the short wall, creating a clean backing against which he'd sit while making the rest of his preparations. He removed his suit coat, folded it neatly, and then took a dark jumpsuit from the pack and put it on.

He removed a Barrett M95 fifty caliber rifle from its customized case and caressed it with love as he wiped the metal parts with a light coat of oil. He actuated the bolt and loaded the rifle with five .50 BMG rounds. He carefully wiped each one with the oily rag to remove any dirty debris and fingerprints that may be on the cartridge's surface. He lowered the bipedal legs and set the weapon on the tarp.

His weapon ready, he removed a range-finder from the pack and put his eye against the viewer. He swept the street, noting various distances as they appeared in the reticulated lens. The front door of the North End Social Club was 525 meters away, an easy shot for one of the best sniper rifles in the world. He placed the instrument next to the rifle. He looked around for a flag or any device that would allow him to estimate the wind speed and direction. He spotted an American flag on the top of a building behind him and saw that the wind blew toward the target. Westin was pleased, the quarry would be downwind, and his bullet would have the added advantage of an aiding wind. It would have little if any, effect on the projectile's flight. He picked up the rifle and, with great care, adjusted the scope for the best shot at his target.

He removed the last items from the pack, a small folding stool and a Thermos of tea. He set up the small, folding seat. Assured that it was far enough away from the building's precipice to make him unseeable from below, sat on it, removed the cap from the Thermos, and poured a cup of tea. Satisfied that everything was in order, he sat back to wait.

$ $ $ $ $

After midnight, Westin had been in position for over fourteen hours. He fought against his body's desire for sleep and, for a second, wondered if, for the first time, he should have used a spotter to assist him on the hours spent observing the kill zone. He poured the last of the tea. It had long since ceased being hot and was, at best tepid. He raised the cup to his lips and saw movement halfway between his hide and the social club on a rooftop. He slid off the stool and settled into a prone shooting position. He placed the rifle against his shoulder and slowly moved it along the rooftops while searching the area through the scope.

I hope it's Connah, he thought. Best to get him out of the way as soon as possible. He spotted the dark figure and settled the cross-hairs on it. Westin studied the shadowy shape. If he was going to take a shot, he wanted to be sure that it was one of his competitors before shooting. There was no incentive in shooting some horny, pimple-faced teenager trying to score with his equally acne-laden girlfriend.

He lay immobile, his attention riveted on the black shape. He saw a brief flash of light when a streetlight's glow hit the lens of a rifle scope. The shooter rose, and Westin saw shoulder-length hair pulled back in a ponytail and an unmistakable female figure. "Hello, Tegan," he whispered.

The door to the social club opened, and a man walked out onto the sidewalk. He looked both ways and crossed the street, stopping beside a Cadillac. He fumbled in his pockets, probably looking for his keys.

Westin turned his attention back to Hale and saw that she aimed at the man. Returning his attention to her target, Westin focused his scope until he could clearly see his face. He ran Spinelli's people through his mind and recognized Tony D'Altrui—second in line to become boss.

Hale's rifle cracked, and he heard the familiar thud of the round hitting home. D'Altrui did a half-turn, fell forward, and landed face down on the concrete sidewalk with a loud SMACK. The lights in the social club immediately turned off, and those in neighboring buildings came on.

"Well," Westin muttered, "looks as if the festivities are over for tonight." He looked to see if Hale was still around and saw that she'd disappeared, leaving no sign that she'd ever been there. He knew that the area would be crawling with cops in minutes and, with haste, gathered his equipment. In ten minutes, he had everything packed and exited the hide using the fire escape at the rear of the building.

27

Connah found his target eating breakfast in the Bristol Lounge of the Four Seasons Hotel. Harvey Westin sat at a table beside the window, staring out at the view—a panoramic vista of the Public Gardens and the swans on the pond.

Connah pulled out one of the empty chairs across from Westin and sat in it without waiting for the hitman to acknowledge him. Westin peered at the intruder, obviously shocked that anyone would have the unmitigated gall to disturb him at breakfast. Connah nodded, picked up the carafe, turned the cup from a new setup, and poured coffee. He took a sip and said, "Good coffee." He held his hand out and said, "How are you, Harvey?"

Westin stared at the hand but made no effort to grasp it.

Connah grinned. "What's the matter? I washed it this morning." He settled in the chair, pulled his hand back, and said, "I don't think we've ever crossed paths before. I've heard you pretty much stay on the left coast, and I've always worked on the right."

"I've heard of the great feats performed by Ian Connah, whom I assume you are. What can I do for you?" Westin inquired.

Connah studied the face of his competition. Westin reminded him of some type of reptile—totally hairless, square head, flat nose, and eyes that seemed bereft of lids. He looked like a pale version of the gecko in the television commercials. "Nothing, I always like to know what I'm up against. You see, I know why you're here, and I've been hired to stop you. Was that you last night? Whoever hit D'Altrui was one hell of a shot. It was stupid, though. Now Spinelli's people know the threat is real and will be extra careful."

Westin stared at Connah; his reptilian eyes didn't blink. "It wasn't me."

"Then it was either Hale or Diaz."

"Who are they?"

"Harvey, my eyes may sparkle, and my teeth may glitter. But when you shit me, you're shitting a shitter. You know your competition, the same as I do."

"I'm told that you have your share of hang-ups, too," Westin countered.

"True. I don't have many, but shooting women is one of them. That's a problem that we obviously don't have in common." He took a final drink of coffee and stood up. "From now on, I think you'll find the going a bit harder. Now, if you'll excuse me, I have a message to deliver to Jiggs Wark."

"Connah."

"Yeah?"

"I'm looking forward to this."

"I am too. I want to see if you're half as good as the hype."

"Coming here like this and letting me know who and what I'm up against is as stupid as what Hale did last night."

"So, you do know who the northside shooter was. Maybe my coming here *was* stupid, but I'm trying to cover all the bases. I've always believed that the devil doesn't like it when you get to hell and tell him you don't know who sent you." Connah gave Westin a mock salute and left.

$ $ $ $ $

Connah arrived at his brother's house and left the motor running when he went inside. Tom met him as he walked through the door. "You know you left your motor running?"

"Yeah, I can't stay. I stopped by to offer you a job. It pays a hundred grand."

"What? A hundred thousand! Who do I have to kill?"

"Actually, the job is the opposite. I've been hired to protect some people from a couple of hitmen."

"I'm getting a strange feeling about this. Who are you protecting?"

"Billie and Bobbi."

"Who wasted money on hitmen to get them? All you have to do is kidnap them and put them in a room together. In less than an hour, they'll have killed each other."

"That's where you come in. While I'm trying to bring down the shooters, you need to keep them from doing just that."

"Can I bring Mandy?"

"Sure." Connah thought about the consequences of Amanda being involved. On the other hand, she could be the one thing that could keep Billie and Bobbi from killing each other. She would drive them so crazy they'd be too busy trying to find ways to kill her to even think about harming each other. "Now, all I need to do is find a place."

"What about something up your way? It's 400 miles from Boston, and I doubt that the hitmen you're up against know of it."

"That might work. As a matter of fact, I know a couple of realtors who specialize in renting remote camps up there."

28

The small caravan of sport utility vehicles navigated the narrow ruts, tree branches, and bushes that scraped the sides of the trucks. They topped the rise, and through the trees, they got their first glimpse of the lake below.

"Is that it?" Billie asked Connah.

"That's Lake Saint-Basile."

She studied the area surrounding the body of water. "I don't see anything remotely resembling civilization."

"This is the wilderness, and for the most part, it's uninhabited."

"I hope there is at least a house of some sort?" Billie sounded like a little girl who'd moved and left all of her friends behind.

"I rented an old hunting and fishing lodge. It has all the amenities." He chuckled. "Providing the generator doesn't break down."

"How long will we be here?"

"That depends on how long it takes for me to square things with Jiggs Wark."

"How do you expect to do that from here?"

"I don't. Once you guys are settled in, I'm going back to Boston. It's time I had a *Come-to-Jesus* Meeting with Wark."

$ $ $ $ $

"You live way up here in the willy-wags?" Bobbi asked. She was obviously not impressed with the lodge. "Looks like something out of a rerun of *Bonanza*."

"This is rented to anyone who wants a get-away. It belongs to a guy from New York and twenty years ago was a hunting and fishing lodge. I live about fifty miles away, in Prefontain Station."

"What's around here?"

"Not much. This lake is too remote for most people who want a get-away place. There are a few cottages on the far side." Connah pointed to a mountain on the opposite side of the lake, "That's Starvation Mountain. In the early 1800s, there was a family that lived there. Nobody saw them for an entire winter, and when a couple of people went up to check on them in the spring, they found that the guy had murdered his wife and kids…then, he cut his own throat with a straight razor."

"Are you serious?" Billie said. "He cut his own throat?"

"That's the story,"

Bobbi stared off into the dense woods on the side of the road west of the lake. "What's over that way?"

"Hundred, maybe a hundred and fifty miles of woods," Connah replied.

"Where in hell have you brought us?" Bobbi asked.

"Officially, it's the North Maine Woods. The direction you're facing is west. You will come to the nearest paved road if you trek over that ridge and walk for thirty or forty miles. That road runs north to Fort Kent and south to Patten. If you continue west for about another hundred miles, you'll be in Quebec, Canada. The province, not the city."

"What," Billie asked, "are we supposed to do? How far to the nearest mall?"

"About sixty miles, by road to Presque Isle. Although I doubt you would consider it a mall, not like the ones you're used to—the food court is one full-service restaurant and a Chinese take-out."

"How many stores?" Bobbi inquired.

"If you counted them on your fingers, you would run out of stores before fingers." Connah could not help but smile at the shocked expressions on their faces.

Amanda walked onto the deck. She was so intent on the soliloquy she had with herself that she ignored Connah and the women.

"Surely there are some stores up here," Billie said.

"There's a JCPenny in Presque Isle. There was a Sears store and a Kmart in the Presque Isle mall, but they shut down about a year ago."

"Are there any that are not currently on the brink of bankruptcy, like Neiman-Marcus?"

"There's a Walmart not far from the mall."

"Do people actually shop in those places?" Billie asked.

"You make do with what you have, or you drive one hundred and fifty miles to Bangor."

Bobbi stared at Amanda, who was ambivalent to their presence and still mumbling to herself. "Who is she talking to?"

"Beats me," Connah said. He picked up a couple of the many suitcases they had brought and walked onto the wooden walk that surrounded the log building. He led them to the rear of the lodge and climbed a flight of stairs that led to a large deck. He stopped before a set of heavy glass sliding doors, set the luggage down, and took a ring of keys from his pocket. He used one to unlock the door. He placed the bags inside and turned to retrieve more. He was surprised to see Bobbi and Billie standing side-by-side. They leaned against the deck's railing and stared at the lake.

"It is tranquil," Bobbi commented as Amanda walked by once more, still muttering in a low voice.

Billie gave Amanda a quick look and said, "If you can ignore the background noise."

Connah pulled the drapes across the glass doors and walked onto the deck. The women looked over their shoulders at him.

"Stay off the deck as much as possible and always keep the drapes closed. The light makes you an ideal target for a sniper with a high-power scope."

Neither of the women said anything, making him believe that maybe, for the first time, they truly understood the danger they were in. He turned and walked inside, leaving them to ponder the reality of their situation.

29

Connah walked into the body shop and was met by Wayne Archer, whom he knew to be one of Jiggs Wark's gunsels. "Where's Jiggs?"

Archer pointed over his shoulder with his right thumb. "In the back. You're Connah, aren't you?"

"Yeah, I'm Connah."

"Wayne Archer, I've heard of you."

"And I of you." Connah stepped past Archer and glared at him when the thug grabbed his arm. "If you don't take your paw off me, I'll break the fucking thing," Connah warned.

"I doubt that. However, it may be fun to see you try. Either way, you don't go back there until I let the boss know you're here."

"Then, by all means, let him know."

Archer dropped his hand and disappeared through a door. Connah occupied himself with looking at the classic cars parked in the garage. He walked over to a 1965 Pontiac GTO and admired the car when Archer reappeared. "You into *goats*?" he asked.

"As a kid, I always wanted one of these."

"You don't look that old."

"I'm not, but my father's younger brother had one."

"Which engine?"

"The 400 cubic inch, 6.6 liters. It was a fire-engine red, four-on-the-floor convertible."

"Sounds sweet. What happened to it?"

"He got married."

"Enough said. You can go back. You carrying?"

Connah removed a nine-millimeter pistol from his jacket and placed it on a workbench. "Keep an eye on it for me, will you?"

Archer saluted him with two fingers. "It'll be right there when you get back."

Connah nodded and walked through the door into Jiggs Wark's office. Wark sat behind a desk covered with papers, most of which appeared to be invoices of one sort or another. "How's it hanging, Jiggs?"

"What you want, Connah?"

"To talk." Connah sat in one of the chairs that fronted the desk and settled back. The atmosphere was heavy with the odors of cigarette smoke and stale coffee.

Wark dropped the paper he had been reading and leaned forward. "Talk about what?"

"Who should we discuss first? Harvey Westin, Alonzo Diaz, or Tegan Hale? I'll bet Westin."

"What are you rambling on about?"

"Competition, Jiggs, it's the stuff that makes America great. In fact, it's against the law to try and set up a monopoly."

"Connah, I got shit to do. Are you about finished with the frigging economics lesson?"

"Almost. You know the economy stinks, and jobs are hard to come by. As a matter of fact, one should do everything in their power to stay employed— even if a competitor is determined to put your company out of business."

Wark maintained eye contact with Connah but remained stoic as if he had no idea where he was going with this rambling discourse.

"I know you put out a bounty of a half-million bucks each on Billie O'Reilly and Bobbi Spinelli. So, they've hired me to make sure no one collects it. I take pride in my work, Jiggs. I make it a point to always meet my objectives."

"Get the fuck out of here. You're crazier than a bat at an indoor rock concert."

Connah stood up, walked to the door, and turned to Wark. "One last thing, Jiggs. The key to success in anything you endeavor is ensuring that you are working on the problem. Not the symptoms, but the source of the problem. Now Westin, Hale, and Diaz are symptoms, and I will take care of them. You, Jiggs, are the source. If you take away the money, you take away the shooters."

"Are you threatening me?"

"Nope, just quoting a basic law of physics, so you'll know how I see things."

Wark sat transfixed; his eyes bulged, and his complexion turned red. "The next time I see you—"

"You know my reputation, Jiggs. You won't see me, and that's your main problem. Now that all of that has been said. You have one helluva nice day." Connah walked out, closing the door behind him. Passing through the garage, he picked up his pistol from the workbench.

Archer was under the hood of the GTO and straightened up when he saw Connah. "You outta here?"

"Yeah, if I were you, I'd give your boss some time to himself. He seemed a bit put out when I left him." Connah stopped before he exited the building. "You wouldn't know where I can find Alonzo Diaz. Would you?"

"Never heard of him."

"You will before long. See you around."

$ $ $ $ $

The limo pulled alongside the curb in front of Paddy's Pub. "I won't be long," Westin said, and he exited the car. He stopped before entering the pub. Attempted to study the interior through a window. There was a film of urban grime coating the portal and the dark interior, so there wasn't much visible.

Nevertheless, he saw several local lushes sitting at the bar with beer mugs and shot glasses before them. Westin shook his head; it was a poor specimen of humanity that would be in a bar, drinking this early in the morning. He sighed, and a shudder ran through his body. He tugged on his gloves to ensure they were snug and opened the door.

Once inside, he walked to the bar, stopped beside an empty stool, and removed a packet of sanitary wipes from his inside jacket pocket. Westin extracted a wipe and used it to wipe the seat and back. When he was satisfied that the stool had been decontaminated as much as he could get it, he sat. The bartender, a young woman, walked down the bar and stopped before him. She wore a black skirt and white blouse with FIONA written on a nameplate. "What'll ya have?" she asked.

"Do you have Dewar's Signature?"

"No way, that stuff costs over $300.00 a bottle. I got a twelve-year-old, double-aged, though."

"I'll settle for the double-aged." Westin bent forward and looked both ways at the bar back. "Sterilize the glass if you would please."

Fiona gave him a stern look. "You some kind of wise guy? I clean all my glasses in hot water—very, hot water."

"I meant no insult. It's just that I'm rather particular. Would you please run some of that boiling water over my glass for me?"

Fiona stared at him for a few seconds and then said, "Sure." She turned away and walked along the bar, took a glass from the stack, and turned on the water in the sink. Westin visibly relaxed when she used a pair of large tongs to hold the glass in the steaming water. She allowed the glass to cool before using the same pair of pincers to drop in two ice cubes before pouring the scotch whiskey.

She placed the drink in front of Westin, and he put a crisp, new twenty-dollar bill on the bar. He noticed her staring at the white cloth gloves he wore and said, "I have a skin condition."

She shrugged as if to say: We all got our troubles.

"Doesn't this establishment belong to Paddy O'Reilly?"

"Paddy's been gone for two years. His daughter owns it now."

"Really? I haven't seen Billie in years. Is she in?"

"No, she's away for a while."

"That's too bad," he said. "I really needed to speak with Paddy. However, now that he's gone, I need to speak with her. Do you know where she is?"

"Nope, I only work for her. I'm not her confidante."

"Surely, you must have some way of getting in touch with her. What if there's an emergency?"

Fiona shrugged. "She calls here every day. Billie says it's no different than going to the bathroom. It isn't an emergency until it's running down your leg, and by then, the emergency is over."

"What if there was... I don't know... a death in the family?"

"It's always been Billie's and my belief that dead people don't think anything is urgent."

Fiona scooped the twenty from the top of the bar and walked toward the cash register.

Westin watched her walk away, and his eyes narrowed. Her brash attitude confirmed his belief that everyone on the east coast took great pride in being a pain in the ass. Which added fuel to his already strong dislike of everything related to it. He left his untouched drink on the bar and exited the pub without waiting for his change. Evidently, all of O'Reilly's employees either knew nothing or were extremely tight-mouthed. He wondered if the same was true of Spinelli's people.

$ $ $ $ $

When Fiona returned with his change, the creep was gone. When no one was watching, she picked up the drink, removed the ice, and returned the whiskey to its bottle. Within seconds all she could remember of him was that she thought he resembled an albino lizard but was an excellent tipper.

30

Connah was in one of his favorite bars, eating lunch and watching the local news when he learned that there had been another gangland sniper killing. He saw the aerial shots of a rooftop and called to the bartender. "Justin, you want to give me some volume on the television?"

He sipped his draft and concentrated on the newscaster's voice. "The police have identified the victim as Louis G. Costello. Costello, a member of the North End's Spinelli mob, has been suspected of being an assassin for hire. He has been indicted several times but released when no evidence or witnesses to his crimes were found. This is the third sniper-like attack this week. One must wonder if what we're seeing are the opening acts of a war between Boston's organized crime factions. A spokesperson for the Boston police met with reporters this morning…"

The picture switched, and Connah almost choked on his beer when the obese figure of Captain Dick O'Schaunessey appeared. He stood on the sidewalk beside an unmarked police car. The car's door was open, and the usual wrappers from fast-food franchises were visible on the floor. The least the overweight bastard could have done is put on a clean shirt, Connah thought. He listened closely to the TV. "…there is no evidence of a gang war taking place on the streets of Boston. At this time, we are investigating these shootings as unrelated crimes."

A reporter stuck a microphone, on which the station's call sign and channel were mounted, into O'Schaunessey's face. "Captain, do you have any suspects?"

"Not at this time."

"Is it true that Ian Connah, the reputed enforcer for the O'Reilly mob, has been seen in town?"

"I have no knowledge of Connah's whereabouts."

"In fact," the reporter said, "my sources tell me, where it was thought that he was retired and had left Boston, he is in fact once again in the employ of the O'Reilly mob."

O'Schaunessey glared at the reporter. His bulbous red nose seemed to fill the sixty-five-inch high-definition screen. "Now that's the biggest alkie nose I've seen all week," the bartender commented. "You'd think the cops would want to keep that guy away from the cameras. He looks like a walking bowl of soup."

"A bowl of cream of cesspool." Connah turned back to the TV.

"As I said, I wouldn't know where Ian Connah is or what he's been up to…" O'Schaunessey said.

The reporter was not to be outdone and said, "Aren't these types of hits Connah's M.O.?"

"There are similarities," O'Schaunessey answered. Connah thought the asshole looked uncomfortable and grinned.

"It sounds as if you know him quite well." The reporter shoved the mike back in the captain's face.

O'Schaunessey ignored the question and ended his fifteen seconds of fame. "That is all we are at liberty to say at this time. It ain't proper for me to comment on an open investigation, let alone three of them." He got into his car and slid across the seat. Connah saw the fast-food trash roll into a wave as O'Schaunessey's fat ass acted like a bulldozer in a landfill.

"I heard enough," Connah told the barkeeper. "You can turn the volume down."

While the bartender turned down the volume, Connah turned over his check, reviewed the amount, and then took a twenty-dollar bill from his pocket. He tossed the money on the bar and said, "Keep the change."

The barman scooped the check and the money and said, "Thanks, Ian. It's been good seeing you again."

"You too."

Connah stood on the sidewalk, basking in the warm early afternoon sun. Wark's hired guns had been busy. They were whittling down the senior members of the two organizations—it wouldn't be long before they would be looking for him, Billie, and Bobbi. He decided to take steps to protect himself and his employers.

31

Billie and Bobbi had not agreed on anything since they were in junior high school and first discovered the love of their lives—Ian Connah. However, they now had a common cause—they wanted to kill Amanda Connah. They stood on the deck overlooking the lake and watched as Amanda dashed inside.

"I think," Bobbi commented, "she just had a brainstorm."

"A drizzle is more like it," Billie replied. "I'll bet it takes her an hour to cook Minute Rice." She stretched her arms and looked at the setting sun. The sky on the western horizon was a fiery red. The trees had taken on a blue look that accentuated its brilliance. "I don't think I've ever before seen sunsets like that."

Bobbi glanced at the western sky. "No big deal. If you've seen one sunset, you've seen them all." She walked past Billie, heading for the cabin's interior. "Christ, I need a goddamned drink."

Tom Connah passed Bobbi and stepped outside the sliding glass door. "Your friend has quite the attitude problem."

"The only way Bimbo Spinelli will ever have a friend is if she gets a dog—and it'll probably bite her. Knowing her, she'll bite it first."

"You know, this situation is hard on all of us. As difficult as my wife can be, she's nowhere near as irritating as when you two are hissing and spitting at each other. Your acting like a pair of rabid wolves is not making things any easier."

Billie stood in place, uncertain as to what she should say.

"I'm not asking you to like each other, but to be quite frank. You two have to be two of the most spoiled brats I've ever encountered."

Billie was shocked. She couldn't recall the last time anyone had spoken to her in such a manner. She felt her face flush. Her ire was not directed at Tom but at herself. She swallowed and held her hand out. "You're right, Tom. We've been making everyone here miserable. Bim—Bobbi—and I need to declare a truce until this situation is resolved."

"I can't tell you how appreciated that will be. But if you can't come to an agreement, stay the hell away from one another."

"You know, Tom. Sometimes we forget that the people who patronize us and say what we want to hear are not our friends. Our true friends tell us what we need to hear. I can't speak for Spinelli, but I'll do my best to make things a bit easier on you."

"While we're baring our souls, I know that when Mandy is in a manic state, she can make a cockroach crawl up a wall backward. But please believe me when I say she can't help herself. She knows that medication can control her episodes, but the drugs make her feel like a zombie, the walking dead, if you will. Please, try to understand that. I'll do my best to keep her away from you until she levels out."

Billie placed her hand on Tom's arm. "It must be terrible for her to live like that."

"It is." His face broke into a conspiratorial smile. "For what it's worth, there are days when I think it would be better to eat a bullet than to deal with what she copes with every day."

"She's lucky to have you," Billie said. "If I ever get really sick, I hope I have someone like you around."

Tom said, "I don't think standing out here like this is very smart. The people looking for us are professional snipers, and we make enticing targets."

32

There was nothing to be gained by talking with Harvey Westin again, so Connah drove north. He wanted to draw the three shooters out of the city and into an environment more favorable. Connah knew that Westin was an urban sniper who suffered from obsessive-compulsive disorder. To him, going into the wilderness was going to be a terrorizing experience.

He arrived at the lakeside cabin an hour after the sun had set and heard the argument before he was halfway to the door. He stood on the deck for a moment listening to Bobbi shouting, "If exercise eliminates fat, how the fuck did she get that double chin?"

He opened the door and walked inside. He saw Bobbi pointing at Amanda, who appeared oblivious to what was going on, as she glared at Tom. Billie sat at the counter, inspecting her nails as if nothing was happening. "What is going on?" he asked.

Bobbi spun around and attacked him. "I can't spend another damned minute locked up out here in the middle of nothing with A. T. and T. over there!"

"A. T. and T.?"

"She's Always Talking and Talking!"

"Tell me, Bobbi, has it ever dawned on you that people get tired of hearing you yap and bitch all the time?"

Bobbi's eyes blinked rapidly, and her head snapped back.

"All right, calm down. We got important things to discuss."

Bobbi opened her mouth to retort, then thought better of it, and flopped into a chair. She folded her arms across her chest and reminded Connah of a teenage girl who had been told she had lost the use of her cell phone for a month.

Amanda ceased talking and looked like a confused puppy.

Billie stopped inspecting her nails and studied him intently. "I get the feeling that something has happened in Boston," Billie said.

"As you know, there are three shooters looking to collect Jiggs's bounty." Connah paused for a few seconds. "That number is still firm. Our best hope is that they stay competitors and don't decide that one-third of a million tax-free dollars isn't a bad payday and team up. Tegan Hale and Alonzo Diaz worry me more than Westin. I don't mean to sell him short, but he's severely OCD, and for him to come to a place like this will drive him nuts.

"On the other hand, Hale and Diaz have no major hang-ups." He walked to the small bar, opened the refrigerator, and took a cola from inside. He opened it and took a drink. He placed the can on the bar and said, "Hale is former Irish Republican Army. She fought the Brits for years, and all anyone knows about her is that she's probably killed more people than anyone will ever know. Her reputation is that she will crawl through fifty meters of broken glass and slide down a banister made by Gillette to accomplish her mission. She prefers to use a long gun but will also wire a bomb to the handle of your toilet, so it detonates when you flush.

"Alonzo came up through the Sinaloa Cartel. He'll kill you from a thousand meters or from a millimeter—it's all the same to him. He's good with firearms but loves to use knives." He looked at Bobbi. "Since you two have been gone, they're concentrating on your people… Costello was killed yesterday."

Bobbi paled visibly. "The bastards."

"I don't know anything about their lineage, but these are three bad sons of bitches. If we're going to keep you two alive, you're gonna have to help us and stop all the infantile arguing."

Ian picked up his soft drink and waited to see who would be the first to break the silence that had taken over. To his surprise, it was Tom who asked, "Now that we've gotten past that, what do we need do to do?"

Ian took the floor: "Don Stone will be here tomorrow afternoon. Early the following morning, we begin making preparations. I don't know about you people, but I've been on the road all day and need to get some rest." He walked out onto the deck. He settled into a chair and stared at the moon's reflection on the smooth water as he sipped the drink. When Tom sat beside him and took a sip of his beer, Connah said, "Make that your last one until this is over."

"Give me a break, Ian. I've only had a couple tonight."

"How many this afternoon?"

When Tom averted his eyes, Connah knew that his brother had been drinking most of the day. "Tom, when Stoney gets here, we're going to train you on defensive tactics and weapons. I will have my hands full dealing with three highly proficient killers. The last thing I need do is worry about your state of sobriety."

Tom put the beer down and said, "C'mon, Ian, I only had a couple."

Ian gave his brother a stern look. "Do you know who you just sounded like?"

Tom hesitated for a moment and then said, "Yeah, I never thought that I'd talk like her."

"You remember what it was like when we were kids? We stayed out all night until we were sure that she'd passed out before we'd go home. Having no milk for our breakfast cereal, but there was always a six-pack of beer in the fridge."

Tom laughed a cynical laugh. "Remember the time we drank milk in one of her beer glasses, and she flipped. She screamed at us that it made the beer taste flat."

"Remember the whipping I got when I told her she should wash them before she used them?"

Tom became solemn. "Yeah, Ma beat you so bad I thought she was gonna kill you."

Ian, too, switched the topic. "Well, she's dead and gone now."

"Yeah, she drank so much of their product, you'd have thought the least the brewery could have done was send those big horses and wagon to carry her coffin to the graveyard."

They burst out in laughter that echoed across the lake.

33

Harvey Westin finished his coffee and placed the cup precisely in the center of its saucer with great care. He dabbed his lips with one of his personal napkins and then set it in his pocket, then glanced at his watch and stood up. He removed a pair of white cloth gloves from his jacket and put them on; it was time to go to work.

On his way out, he stopped by the front desk and waited for the clerk to finish cashing out another guest. She thanked the elderly couple and then turned to him. "How may I be of assistance, Mr. Westin?"

Westin removed a plastic bag from his hip pocket, opened it, and extracted his wallet. He drew a twenty-dollar bill, which looked like it had recently been washed and ironed and slid it across the counter. "Would it be possible for housekeeping to change the spread as well as the linen on my bed each morning?"

She slipped the twenty in her pocket and said, "Of course, I'll have the head of housekeeping ensure that it happens."

"Oh, and have them vacuum everywhere, even under the bed. I have allergies and cannot abide dust. Thank you."

Before he exited through the automatic revolving door, Westin crossed the lobby and placed a black pork pie hat on his shaved head. He adjusted his dark sunglasses and walked outside. A black stretch limousine sat by the curb, and the doorman held the rear door open. "Your ride, sir."

Westin slid into the back seat and said, "Driver, would you give him five dollars? I'll add it to the bill."

"Of course, sir." He slid his arm out the window and waved to the doorman. The doorman quickly grabbed the five and nodded to Westin. "Thank you, sir."

Westin dismissed him with a wave of his hand and said, "Go to South Boston."

"Where in Southie would you like to go, sir?"

"Paddy's Pub."

"Not a place I'd expect someone of your class to frequent. A tough element hangs out there."

"I hired you to drive me, not give me advice."

The driver straightened in his seat. "Of course, sir."

As the limo pulled away from the curb, Westin slid his gloved right index finger along the car's interior and inspected the white fingertip for dust.

34

Harry Sandberg hung up the phone. The call had disturbed him. He realized that was understating how he truly felt. The call had actually scared him shitless. Ouellette had sounded extremely scared when he told him that Connah was raising money to come after them and had gone back to being a gun for hire. In his most recent call, Ouellette had told Sandberg that he needn't panic because Connah was engaged in a gang war. One that could change the power structure of organized crime in Boston.

He paced back and forth in his São Paulo hotel room. He was beginning to believe that coming here was a mistake. The economy was like a yo-yo, and one never knew how much they were worth. The fiscal state of the country was a significant concern. The Brazilians argued about it in their congress, or whatever the hell they had down here, and no one seemed capable of fixing the cluster-fuck.

He left his room and took the elevator to the lobby. There was a travel agency office there, and the false travel documents Rojas had obtained for him were top-line. A cute, buxom young woman smiled at him when he entered the agency. "May I be of assistance, *señhor*?"

"I'd like to arrange for a flight to Manaus."

"Will you need a hotel there?"

"Yes."

$ $ $ $ $

Connah stood behind his sister-in-law and watched her load the thirty-eight-caliber revolver. He had fully expected to have to explain each and every step to her but was surprised when she handled the handgun as if she had been around weapons her entire life. "You seem familiar with weapons," he said to her.

Amanda had a manic-free moment and could carry on an intelligent conversation. "I grew up with six brothers, all of whom hunt and fish. The nearest girl lived seven miles away, so if I didn't want to grow up a hermit, I learned to do the things my brothers did."

"Can you hit what you shoot at?"

Amanda squared her body to the target and spread her feet until they were shoulder-width. She placed her firing side foot slightly behind her support foot—she was in as perfect a fighting stance as he'd ever seen. She held the revolver with both hands, pulled the trigger, and fired three times—all in one smooth motion. Connah looked downrange and saw three holes tightly grouped in the bull's eye. Okay, he thought, that answers that question, but can she hit a live target that is on the move, or better yet, shooting back. Even the greatest of marksmen found it much more challenging to shoot at another human being.

Amanda placed the revolver on the stump beside her and turned to Connah. "I can shoot."

"I see that. What if the target is four or five hundred meters away on a day in which the wind is blowing with gusts to fifty miles per hour?"

"Four or five hundred meters is not handgun range. You'd need a long gun for that."

"Exactly. The guy who will be hunting us is an expert. He's adept at hitting targets at six hundred meters and more."

Amanda looked at her husband. "Tom could. As a matter of fact, this whole training thing is a waste of time."

Connah knew that his brother was nowhere close to possessing that level of proficiency. Rather than disagree with Amanda, he said, "Even I need to refresh my skills periodically."

35

Amanda was right about one thing; Tom was a much better shot than Connah had ever imagined. Both were very proficient with short and long guns. Connah decided to concentrate the training on tactics rather than firearms. They spent the remainder of the day in the lodge, discussing camouflage, selecting a hide, and how to move through a given terrain without being detected.

After two hours, their session was interrupted by Billie and Bobbi arguing.

Connah left Amanda and Tom and stormed into the common area where the two protagonists stood face-to-face. Both of their faces were flushed with anger, and he immediately knew the situation was volatile. He stepped between the combatants and pushed them apart. "What the hell is going on here?"

"I'm gonna kill her," Bobbi said. "Slowly."

"You better bring food because it's gonna take you more time than you got left!" Billie countered.

"Shut up! Both of you, shut up and sit down!" Connah felt that he'd scored a small victory when they both backed up a step, sat on opposite ends of the sofa, and stared at him. He sat between them. "I got enough to do without being a referee for a couple of stupid schoolgirls. In the event it has slipped your minds, there's a team of professional killers out there, and you're their list of targets." He dropped his hands in frustration. "Shit, if I didn't need money so goddamned bad, I'd let them have both of you."

Both women looked shocked. Connah's outburst seemed to take them by surprise. "We're paying you well to protect us," Billie protested.

"Yes, you are." Connah sat down between them. "That's the only reason I don't let you two go at each other until you kill one another."

"Westin is looking for you, and I've heard that he's like a fuckin' bloodhound.

Once he gets the scent, there's no holding him back. It's only a matter of time before he finds this place, and we need to be ready for him. That will not happen if you two don't set aside your junior high school grievances and help us."

"What can we do?" Bobbi asked.

"Stop acting like two fisher cats fighting over a carcass. If you can't get along, then stay the hell away from each other." He glared at each of them in turn. "Is that clear?"

They both nodded. The women sat with their arms folded across their chests, faces down, and jaws clenched. Body language did nothing to convince him that they'd gotten his message.

"I said, *IS THAT CLEAR?*"

They each nodded.

"I want to hear you say it—both of you."

"Yes," Billie said in a hushed voice.

"Bobbi?" Connah inquired.

"Yeah."

"Okay, now I got to get back to what I was doing. Can I trust you two to act like a couple of adults?"

Their petulant nods told him that the chances of them getting along were between slim and none, and slim had already left town. Connah shook his head in frustration and turned toward the den where Tom and Amanda were waiting for him.

"Ian?"

"What, Billie?"

"What's a fisher cat?"

"A weasel on steroids."

36

Harvey Westin entered Jiggs Wark's office and sat in one of the chairs fronting the mobster's desk. "I got your message."

"Which message was that? I recall sending you several."

"The one saying that you have information about the whereabouts of O'Reilly and Spinelli."

"Well," Wark said, as he sat back and lit a cigarette (he noticed Westin's look of disdain but ignored it), "you'll have to wait a bit—until the others get here."

"You invited us all?"

"You're damned right I did. The last thing I want is for any one of you to get pissed at me because you think I'm playing favorites. What I tell to one, I tell to all."

There was a knock at the door. Wark maintained eye contact with Westin and said, "Come."

The door opened, and Tegan Hale entered the office with Alonzo Diaz. She wore black jeans, a black blouse, and black boots. Her long black hair was pulled back into a ponytail and pulled through the opening in the back of her adjustable black baseball cap. Her complexion was tan, and there were creases at the corners of her eyes; obviously, she spent a great deal of time out in the harsh sun.

Diaz was short, no taller than five feet three inches. He wore a thick black mustache, and his hair was long enough that it curled around his ears, which protruded straight out from his head. Westin thought he looked like a Cadillac going down the road with its doors open or the wings of a radar antenna. His Mexican heritage was evident in his facial features, which did nothing to hide his *mestizo* ancestry.

"You sent for us?" Hale said.

"Yes," Wark answered. He motioned toward Westin with his right hand. "You guys know each other?"

"Only by reputation," Hale replied.

"Have a seat, and I'll get to the point so you can do what you will with the information I have. Before I start, does anyone want something to drink?"

"Nothing for me," Hale said.

"Nor me," Westin added.

Rather than sit as Hale had done, Diaz leaned against the wall beside the office door. He gave a quick nod of his head and settled back.

"You don't say a helluva lot do you?" Wark asked him.

Diaz shrugged his shoulders.

"You can speak, can't you?"

"Only when I have something to say." The Mexican's voice was deep, his accent heavy.

"I called you here because I have some information that may interest you—I know it did me. I have been told that Connah has them staying in a friggin' cabin in the Maine woods."

"That's it? A cabin in the woods." Westin said.

"That's all I know. Hey, it's a start." Wark sucked on his cigarette and blew smoke in Westin's direction. "You guys stand to make a lot of money from this, and now you want me to do all the work for you? Get your asses out on the street and narrow it down. Someone in Boston has to know where in hell they are. Fuck, try the real estate offices, especially those who specialize in renting vacation places."

Westin got to his feet and made a point of coughing so that Wark was aware of how he hated smoking. When the gun-for-hire was at the door, Wark said, "I will tell you that Connah lives on a lake up there, way up in Aroostook County."

"I suppose asking the name of the lake would be presumptuous of me?"

"Not at all. My source in the O'Reilly camp told me that he lives in a hick town called Prefontain Station and is near Lake Osprey. Personally, I don't think he's stupid enough to take them there. Ian Connah may be a lot of things, but being an imbecile ain't one of them."

"That remains to be seen," Westin said. He took a clean handkerchief out of his suit coat inside pocket, draped it around the doorknob before opening it, and left.

Hale sat in her chair for several moments, and Diaz leaned against the wall. Finally, Hale stood up. "Well, I hate to break up this interesting little get-together, but I got people to see, places to go, and things to do when I get to where ever in Maine it is." She stood and walked out of the office.

After a few seconds, Diaz grunted, straightened up, and followed her out.

$ $ $ $ $

Westin walked into the small realty office and surveyed the dusty interior with disdain. He pulled his gloves tighter and looked at the old man sitting behind the desk. The sun glistened off the man's semi-bald pate, and sweat covered his face. Westin glared at the disgusting specimen of humanity and waited for the realtor to speak first.

"Can I help you?"

Westin thought that the old man's breath would knock a buzzard off a gut wagon. "Joshua Wark sent me here."

"Joshua Wark?" For several seconds, the realtor seemed confused, and then his face lit up as he appeared to have an epiphany. "Oh, you mean Jiggs Wark."

"I believe he uses that unfortunate *nom de plume*."

"I'm Willum Charrette. I own this agency. Please, have a seat." Charrette scrambled around his cluttered desk and grabbed a pile of brochures and fliers that sat on the only guest chair in the room.

Westin removed a handkerchief from his pocket and dusted the chair seat and back before sitting. "Mr. Wark informed me that you may be able to assist me in a matter of his and my concern."

"I'll do my best. Ji… Mr. Wark is a valued customer."

Westin sat stoically. He doubted that Wark had much to do with a small-time scumbag who rented inferior dwellings in North Scrotum, Maine. "Do you have access to certain databases?"

Westin noticed that Charrette's eyes seemed to widen, and a greedy leer came to his face. "I do have sources of information. However, some are quite expensive."

Westin remained emotionless and said, "We can discuss the financial aspects once you get me the information I require."

"Of course. What might the nature of this information be?"

"I'm seeking someone who recently, within the last couple of weeks, has rented lodging, possibly on a remote lake in the state of Maine."

"That covers a lot of ground. Could you possibly narrow the field for me?"

"It would have to be a large building, capable of housing five, maybe more, people comfortably. I've been told it is most likely in the northern part of the state."

"Sounds like Aroostook, Penobscot, and Piscataquis counties." Charrette turned sideways to Westin and scrolled the mouse pointer across his computer monitor. "There are a lot of possibilities up there. So, I can't guarantee anything. There's also the possibility that arrangements were made without the assistance of a realtor."

"I understand all that, do what you can."

"Do you have any idea which part of those counties we're looking at?"

Westin studied the room and spied a map of the state of Maine on the wall. He walked to it and looked at it for several seconds before touching it with a gloved finger. "Here. Within a 100-mile radius of Prefontain Station."

Charrette glanced at the map and said, "Ahhh, Aroostook County—a lot of remote lakes up there."

"How long will it take you to obtain the information I require?"

Charrette glanced at his wall clock. "If I don't have something by three this afternoon, I'm never going to."

"I'll see you then."

37

Connah walked along the wooded lane with Tom and Amanda. They had been training for the better part of a week, and he had to admit, albeit grudgingly, that they had picked up many of the critical concepts very fast. The morning was crisp. There were already traces of color in the leaves of the deciduous trees, a sign that fall foliage season was only a few weeks away.

Tom lit a cigarette, and Connah said, "If you're serious about working with me, you'll have to give that up. The smoke could be a give-away to your location, not to mention the smell will carry for miles. On a dark night, the glow of a cigarette can be seen up to fifteen miles away."

"Well, on a job, I won't smoke."

"Sure, you won't. Nicotine addiction is stronger than heroin addiction. When a junkie goes cold turkey, they're usually beyond the worst of the withdrawal symptoms in three or four days. A smoker will crave nicotine for years after they quit."

Tom stared at his cigarette.

"See," Connah said, "right now, you're wondering if you can quit. Or, if you want to go through with this."

"I can do it. I *will* do it. But since I have to give up drinking and now smoking, I have to wonder what's next... sex?"

"Only if you're sharing a hide with me. I'm serious about smoking, though. The last thing you need is to have a coughing fit while you're concealed."

"I've been after him to quit for years," Amanda said.

"That brings us to your problem," Connah said. "How do you propose to deal with your mood swings?"

"I'll be all right," she replied, with a sharp edge to her tone.

"Amanda, you go off on tangents. There are times you start talking and go on and on for hours. If that's not bad enough, you become oblivious to whether or not anyone is listening."

"I have my regimen."

"You need to take some form of medication."

"The meds they give me bottom me out so that I don't even feel alive. It's as if I'm a zombie or something."

"Then you only have two options. One forget about all of this. Or two, get the doctor to prescribe a drug that doesn't affect you so much." Connah stopped and studied his brother and sister-in-law for a few seconds. "Now we come to the hard question. Do you guys think you can look through a telescopic sight and kill another human being?"

There was doubt written on their faces which, strangely enough, he saw as a positive sign.

"I—I don't know," Amanda answered. "And I probably never will until I try it."

"That," Connah said, "is the best answer you could have given me. What about you, Tom? And, I don't want any macho bullshit. I want a truthful answer."

"Truthfully, I'd have to give you the same answer."

"I can accept that. Nobody knows how they'll react until the time comes. Unfortunately, there's only one way to find out."

"Try to do it," Amanda said.

"Yup, and we can't arbitrarily go out and shoot someone."

"I have an idea," Amanda said.

"Which is?" Connah asked.

"How about the next time that Bimbo and the Irish bitch start fighting, we each shoot one?"

Connah couldn't suppress a smile. "Don't tempt me."

$ $ $ $ $

When the Connahs arrived back at the cabin, Don Stone was sitting on the deck drinking a cup of coffee. Tom and Amanda greeted him and went inside. Stone looked over the rim of his cup. "How's the training going?"

"Better than I thought. I think they're at the point where they can be dangerous—to themselves if nobody else. As for whether or not they can do it, we won't know that until the time arrives."

"Well, we may find out sooner than you'd like."

"Really."

"Yup, my sources tell me that Wark's hired guns have been checking into real estate transactions around the state."

"Shit, that should keep them busy for months," Connah said.

"Maybe, maybe not. You and I both know that it's impossible to completely cover your tracks."

"We've known all along that eventually, they're going to show up."

"We could go after them," Stone said.

"All in good time, of the three, Westin is the biggest threat. Still, he's severely obsessive-compulsive. He can't stand dirt of any kind. Let him come up here and tramp around the woods for a while. That will drive him so friggin' crazy he might screw up."

"And the others?"

"I'm working on that. It's possible we may deal with Westin and go after the others before they know where we are. While we're talking," Connah said, "from now on, this deck is off-limits for all of us."

The peaceful afternoon was abruptly destroyed by the sound of a loud argument inside the cabin. "Oh yeah," Stone said, "I forgot to tell you that it looks as if the truce is over."

Connah opened the sliding glass door and stepped inside. "WHAT IS GOING ON?" he bellowed.

Bobbi spun around, obviously ready to take on a new threat, and pointed behind her at Billie. "I can't handle that bitch no more!"

"Screw you and the Italian stallion you rode in on!" Billie, too, was in attack mode.

Once again, Connah stepped between them and held his arms out, his right pointing at Spinelli, the left at O'Reilly. "I told you two that if I'm going to keep you alive, the fighting and bickering has to stop!"

"She started it," Bobbi shouted.

"I don't give a shit who or what started it. I'm going to finish it. If you two don't stop your infantile bullshit, I'll take you both back to Boston and let you deal with Jiggs Wark using the incompetent goons who work for you!"

The two combatants remained in their aggressive postures, their faces red with anger.

Connah waited for a few seconds, letting things settle down, and then said,

"Sit, both of you." When neither woman moved, he asserted himself, "I said, SIT!"

Once they were seated, he stood before them and said, "We're coming into a critical part of this thing. I have no doubts that Diaz, Hale, and Westin are using everything and everyone at their disposal to locate you two. I want you to keep in mind that *YOU ARE THEIR TARGETS*. Not me, not Stoney, and definitely not Tom and Amanda. All we are is an obstacle they have to overcome to get at you guys. If they can, they'll sit out there and wait for a clear shot at you. They won't shoot at us because they'll lose the element of surprise if they do. Am I clear about this?"

Both Billie and Bobbi sat still, looking like chastised children. "Neither of you," Connah continued, "is making this easy for us, and if it keeps up, I'll gather up my team and leave you two here to see who kills who first. My money is on you killing each other before Westin and company get off a single shot. One more of these childish outbursts, and I'll lock you in your rooms and only let you out in shifts. Do you understand?"

When he received no response, he elevated his voice. "*DO YOU UNDERSTAND?*"

They each, in turn, nodded their heads.

"Good." He walked toward the kitchen and stopped before entering. When he saw their murderous looks, he shook his head in disgust. He looked toward the ceiling and muttered, "Give me strength," and he left them alone.

38

Harvey Westin stared at the rundown general store. He hated the thought of having to walk into such an unsanitary-looking building. The outside consisted of logs, so old they had turned gray. He saw spider webs running from the eaves to the side of the structure, and he saw the web occupants, some bigger than his thumb, lurking in wait of the next captive. A rusty soft drink sign hung at a forty-five-degree angle supported by a single chain and squealed as it swung in the breeze. That the owners had let the exterior become so filthy made him wonder what the inside of the building looked like. He shuddered, swiveled in his seat, and placed his feet on the dusty, unpaved dooryard. When his shoes touched the ground, dirt and dusty grit drifted up, covering them. Westin flinched and made up his mind that he would have to disinfect everything when this job was finished.

He thought back to the phone call he had received from Willum Charrette. Informing him that he had narrowed down the possible places where Connah could be hiding the women to two lakes in far northern Maine. The trail led Westin to a bump in the road called Pedigumpus Center. If one could call it that, this town consisted of a seldom-used railroad track and a single crossroads. On one corner stood the general store. Westin stood, stretched, and dropped his hands from his back. An old man came out of the store. He limped toward a rusted Chevy pickup truck. The vehicle looked like it would take a hefty bribe to pass even the most rudimentary annual vehicle inspection.

"Excuse me," Westin called to the man.

The old man stopped and stared at the source of interruption. He squinted at Westin as if he needed glasses he could not afford. He stood with one hand on the truck's door handle. But made no move to either approach Westin or enter the Chevrolet.

"Can you tell me how I can get to Pedigumpus Center?" Westin asked him.

The old man continued to look at him as if they were from different worlds, which Westin was sure they were, then said. "You must be from away?"

"I am."

"If I was you, I wouldn't move a God damned inch." The rusted truck door screeched in protest when the local pulled the door open and entered. He leaned out of the open window and added: "Cause you're standin' in the middle of it." He started the motor which, like the door, protested as it turned over.

Westin watched the truck disappear down the road leaving a trail of white smoke behind. He wondered if everything here squawked when it moved. Approaching the store, Westin shook his head in disgust.

As he feared, the interior was as bad as the outside. His shoes squeaked, and the worn, faded linoleum was sticky. As he walked, the effort of lifting his feet was like he was crossing a metal deck while wearing magnetic shoes. The back wall was covered by two large coolers, and he heard the compressors wheezing as they tried to keep the contents cool. A single fan was centered in the ceiling. It wobbled as the out-of-balance blades rotated. The ceiling's surface was constructed from some antiquated ornate metal material. Rust-colored stains from numerous roof leaks showed through the faded white paint. Another old man, who looked older than the man he'd encountered in the parking lot, stood behind a counter. On the counter sat an NCR cash register that appeared so old that its serial number could be 000001. The storekeeper eyed Westin with the same level of suspicion he gave all strangers. "Kin I he'p yuh?"

Westin gave the store another visual search and said, "How can I get to Lake Saint-Basile?"

The old man turned his head and sent a stream of brown saliva flying toward the floor behind the counter. Westin heard the noxious liquid splatter against what he believed was a metal spittoon or bucket and shuddered.

"Yuh go back out this road and turn left. After about two miles as the crow flies, yuh'll come to the old brown barn that's painted yella now. Take a left there. You follow that road for two or three miles until you come to another four corners and take a left. Yuh foller that road fer two miles until you come to the T intersection, go left. Yuh can't miss it."

Westin stared at the store owner for several seconds. "Let me repeat that." He recounted the old man's directions and then said, "It seems to me that will lead me right back here."

The old man's wrinkled face cracked into a toothless smile. "'Twill. Ain't nothin' that pisses me off more than givin' d'rections to someone who can't foller 'em." He chuckled to himself. "What you drivin'?"

"A Ford Focus."

"That one a them gas-propelled roller skates?"

"It's a compact car, yes."

"Then you ain't going to Saint-Basile by road. You'll never make it in no compact. You need a four-by-four to travel them tote roads. Fact is you need one with high road clearance, as high as you can git. You'd sink that thing yowah drivin' so deep it'd disappeah from sight."

"I can get another vehicle. How do I get there?"

The old storekeeper reached under the counter and retrieved an atlas of the state. He flipped through the pages until he came to the one that depicted the appropriate section of the state. "We're heah." The old man pointed to a crossroad where route 11 intersected with Grand Lake and Saint-Basile Roads. He slid his finger along the line indicating Saint-Basile Road and then southeast until it came to a small lake. "The lake, which is more of a pond, is only nine feet deep at its deepest point, is heah."

Beside the lake was a tiny dot that said Goddard Village. "Is that a town?" Westin asked.

"Depends on what you considah a town. Back in the sixties, the loggin' companies was fightin' one of them infestations, somethin' called the Spruce Bud Woahm. They set up Goddard Village. In those days, the B and A." The old man realized that Westin didn't know B and A, so he clarified. "That was the Bangor and Aroostook Railroad. It's been out of business for twenty or twenty-one years now. Anyways, the B and A line from Oakfield to Fort Kent ran beside the lake, and the loggin' cump'nees built a general store and a hotel, complete with a restaurant theah. Once they had harvested all the trees they wanted b'fore the budworm got to them, they just took their buildings down, put it on rail cars, and hauled it up the line. All's left of Goddard Village now is five or six camps, a fair-to-middlin' trout stream, a shallow mud bottom lake that breeds more leeches than fish, and a whole lotta nothin' else."

Westin twisted his head rather than touch the atlas and said, "But the roads still go in there?"

"Yup, but like I said, you're gonna need a four-by-four or an ATV. I don't know why anyone would want to go in there. Unless they's lookin' for a place to get away from it all. Come to think of it, I heard that they may be some folks in there rentin' Cody Levesque's old sportsman lodge." The old man grew pensive. "Cody never made it with that lodge. The lake ain't somethin' anyone with half a brain would travel any distance to see. In fact, there's nothin' theah to attract anyone."

"Really? I'm intrigued. I have this hobby of visiting and photographing out-of-the-way places. Where can I rent a truck?"

"Nearest place I can think of is Presque Isle. Although Houlton's closer as the crow flies, Presque Isle is closer by road."

"How do I get to Presque Isle?"

"Take Route 11 north to Ashland, then follow the signs."

$ $ $ $ $

Tegan Hale and Alonzo Diaz were sitting in their rented mud and dirt splattered pickup truck. They were parked on an unpaved woods lane to observe the general store. "You think he's on to something?" Hale asked.

Diaz watched Westin get into his rental and pull out of the parking lot. He consulted the DeLorme *The Maine Atlas and Gazeteer* that sat on his lap and commented: "Don't know, but he's headed north. According to this map, the nearest town of any size is Presque Isle."

"Well, let's see if we can learn anything in the store."

A beat-up one-ton truck with several red and blue fuel containers tied against the headboard of the flatbed pulled into the store. Two men, who appeared to be in their twenties, got out, and one went inside while the other began removing the gas cans from the truck's bed. He lined them up beside the gas pump and began filling them.

Hale drove up behind the one-ton and parked. She looked at her partner. "Let's see if these yokels know anything."

Diaz said, "Be with you in a minute.

$ $ $ $ $

Carl Hafford had run the Four Corners Variety at the crossroad in Pedigumpus Junction for over fifty years. He watched the woman bounce her way through the door and gave her petite but buxom figure a once-over. "Howdy, young lady," he greeted her.

114

The smile she gave him was enough to make an old man wish he was forty years younger.

"You sell wine?" she asked.

"Sure do, ain't got nothin' fancy though, mostly Boone's Fahm, stuff like that. Not many champagne drinkers in these pahts." He pronounced champagne 'cham-pag-nee' and pointed to the back corner of the store. "Come to think of it," he added, "I think I may have a couple of bottles of Gallo or even Manischewitz, too."

The woman smiled at him. "I'm sure I'll find something that will do me."

Hafford admired the view as she walked to the back of the store.

Billy Moran placed a twelve-pack of the cheapest beer in the cooler on the counter and looked in the same direction as Hafford. "You an ass-man too, Carl?" he asked in a low voice.

"Billy, at my age, I'm an anything man."

Moran laughed and walked to the snack display and grabbed two bags of beef jerky, which he threw on the counter beside the beer.

"That everything?" Hafford asked.

"Other than the gas that Whit's pumpin'." Moran turned and looked at the young woman bent over, studying the various bottles of wine. "I'd give a month's pay for an hour with her in my bed."

Hafford's brow furled when he looked at Moran. "Billy, you got yourself a problem or two."

Moran laughed. "You think?"

"I think."

Moran's cousin Whitney walked inside and said, "Got sixty bucks in gas, Carl."

Carl grabbed a brown bag and used a pencil to write the different prices on the bag's side. He totaled their bill and wrote that on the bag.

"You ever gonna get one of them new cash registers that does all that addin' for yuh, Carl?" Billy asked.

"What fer? I can add it just as good. When I went to school, we had none of them calculators and had to learn a bunch of stuff, like our 'times tables' and how to add, subtract, multiply, and divide. Now take your generation. If you ever lose 'lectrity, you wouldn't know whether you should shit or go blind." He looked up and said, "All together, that'll be seventy-nine fifty-four."

Moran handed him four twenty-dollar bills. "Ate the hell out of that, didn't it?"

The woman walked to the counter and placed two bottles of Australian wine on the counter. "You lied to me," she said with a smile. "You actually have a fairly good selection."

Hafford smiled, exposing the gaps where his canine teeth had once resided. "Truth be known, they's a whole bunch of winos around these pahts."

The Moran boys grabbed their items and stood still, admiring her figure.

The door opened, and a short Mexican-looking man walked in. "You find what you wanted, Tegan?"

"Yes." She turned to the Morans. "You fellows wouldn't know of a guy and a couple of women who're renting a place on some lake near here, would you?"

"I ain't heard of no one. How 'bout you, Whit?" Billy replied.

"Nope. But we get a lot of people from *away* this time of year. There's lots of places over on Squapan and up at Portage Lake for rent."

"There is that old lodge over on Saint-Basile, but no one's used that for years," Billy replied. "Lake's too shallow and ain't worth a bucket of spit for water sports. Cain't even swim in it. The bottom is all mud, and the water's full of leeches."

The woman paid for her wine and handed the bag to the Mexican. "We're supposed to meet some friends for the weekend."

"Local folk?" Hafford asked.

"No, one of them is a funny lookin' sort," the Hispanic added. "He's got no hair and is as pale as an albino deer. Always wears black."

"You just missed that fellow. Now that you mention it, he was looking for Goddard Village too."

"Ain't never heard of it," Whitney said.

"You're too young to know about it. About fifty years ago, it was a whistle-stop along the Bangor and Aroostook Railroad. Come to think of it, it was on the shore of Lake Saint-Basile."

The woman seemed to get interested. "That sounds like Harvey. Do you know where he went?"

"Yup, Presque Isle. He was drivin' one of them gas-propelled roller skates, and I told him there was no way he'd get into that lake without a higher road clearance—it wouldn't hurt none to have four-wheel drive either. Ain't no one maintained the road in there since the lodge shut down."

"Where's the rental agency?" the woman asked.

"Near the airport on the corner of State and Parsons Streets, that's where five streets all come together," Billy answered.

"Thanks," she said, "you guys have been a great help."

Hafford and the Morans watched the couple jump in their dirty four-by-four and drive off in the direction of Presque Isle. "Must be one hell of a pahty planned someplace," Carl said. "I ain't had so many customers from away—ever."

39

Westin drove along Presque Isle's Main Street. It was evident that the city was dying. He laughed at the thought that a place this small would ever consider itself a city. By California standards, it was barely a small town. Almost half the buildings in the business district were vacant and appeared to have been so for a long time.

Unfamiliar with the area, he followed the main flow of traffic and passed into a part of town that showed some promise. He noted several fast-food restaurants, one of the more economical hotels in a national chain, a mall with a mostly empty parking lot, and two national brand stores: a nationwide discount retailer and a big-box hardware chain store.

He turned into the mall, hoping to locate a travel agency that might be able to direct him to a place where he could rent a four-wheel-drive vehicle. He saw an area of the lot where most of the cars were parked and slipped into an open spot.

Entering the building, Westin found himself in what passed for a food court but consisted of a single chain restaurant and a Chinese take-out. Again, he laughed under his breath. How any place with two restaurants could be considered a food court baffled him.

Westin noted several people sitting at small tables near the Chinese place and walked toward it. He stopped beside a young woman who was drinking an energy drink and asked, "Pardon my intrusion. Could you tell me if there's a travel agency or information booth in the mall?"

She looked at him as if he were a visitor from another dimension, which he was starting to feel like. She had a spacey look when she shrugged her shoulders and said, "I don't know." She sipped on the energy drink, and he thought she looked as if the concept was utterly alien to her.

"How about a phone booth? Is there one in the mall?"

Her only response was a blank look.

An elderly man sat two tables away and overheard them, and Westin heard him laugh. "Mister, I doubt she's ever seen a public phone, let alone a phone booth. Nearest one I know of is over in Caribou, about fifteen miles north on Route 1. Them cell phones pretty much put the git to them."

Westin walked to the man's table. The old guy wore a woolen plaid shirt, faded blue jeans, and a John Deere cap from which locks of white hair poked out. "Well, maybe you can help me? I need to rent a four-wheel-drive truck or SUV. Is there a rental place in town?"

"There's a place on Parsons Street, but your best bet is the south side of town. Go out here to the light and turn left on Main Street. Keep goin' 'til you pass the college. There's a Rent-A-Wreck on the left, just past the inn and convention center."

"I was thinking more along the lines of something like Hertz or Avis."

"Then just keep on drivin' south 'til you get to Bangor—although there might be something at the airport."

"I don't think I've ever heard of a rent-a-wreck."

"They're all over the place. What they really are is body shops that rebuild stuff that the insurance companies have written off as bein' totaled, they fix 'em up, and what don't sell they rent."

"You say there's one going south?"

The old man repeated the directions, and Westin asked, "Where might I purchase some clothing?"

"Here in the mall, you got JCPenny. I expect Penny's to be the next one to haul ass outta here. Most days, they got more workers than customers in that store. Wally World has pretty much driven out every other business around here." He took a drink from a foam cup of coffee and said, "What kind of clothes you lookin' for?"

"Something suitable for walking in the woods."

"Your best bet is Wally World. If you want some good boots, I'd go over to the Trading Post—they specialize in that sort of thing."

Westin thanked the man and exited the mall, wondering at which point of the drive up here he'd passed the line of demarcation between intelligent life and these people. He decided to rent a suitable vehicle, get a room, and clean up. Buying a wardrobe could wait until later. He shuddered at the thought of the type of lodging he'd find in this place.

$ $ $ $ $

Westin made arrangements to leave the small rental car at the airport. The woman at the counter said that people were always looking for a rental. They had an agreement with the national rental company he'd rented from in Bangor to have them picked up. He then arranged for a taxi to pick him up. In a small town, he couldn't be fussy about the condition of the cab. Every nerve in his body was on high alert during the short ride to the locally owned rental agency. He rented an SUV and then drove south on U.S.1 and obtained a room for the night at a small hotel that was narcissistic enough to call itself a Convention Center. Like everything else he'd encountered since he arrived in this backwater town, it was nowhere near to what he was accustomed to. Still, at least it appeared to be clean. Without seeing his room, he asked the desk clerk to send someone from housekeeping to his room with a complete set of bed linen, including a newly cleaned spread. The clerk gave him a hurt look and said, "Sir, our linen is changed every day."

"I don't doubt that," he countered. "But you don't change the spreads, and who knows what has taken place on top of them. I want a fresh *complete* set of bedding on my bed."

The clerk said, "I'll get right on it, sir," and picked up her phone.

"Which way is the restaurant?"

"Through the double doors and to the left."

Westin entered the restaurant and waited for the hostess to seat him. While standing at the reception desk, he saw two familiar people sitting at a table in the center of the room. Tegan Hale motioned to him.

The hostess approached, and Westin said, "I see my party, thank you." He then walked to the table and greeted the occupants. "Tegan, Alonzo, I have to admit that I'm surprised to see you here."

Tegan Hale offered him a seat to her right. "Sit here, Harvey."

Westin pulled out the chair, removed a handkerchief from his back pocket, and wiped the seat and back with it. When he was finished, he held the cloth between his index finger and thumb as if it were a loathsome implement of death. He scanned the room, looking for a place where he could dispose of it. He saw a busboy clearing a table, walked over to him, and placed the handkerchief on his tray, taking great care not to come into contact with the dirty dishes. "Dispose of that if you would, please." He ignored the busboy's astonished look; he was used to being looked at as if he was from some as-yet-undiscovered planet.

He returned to the table where Hale and Diaz watched him and pointed to the chair he'd recently wiped down. He asked, "May I?"

Hale gestured with her hand and said, "Be our guest."

Westin sat down and said, "*Be our guest* could be interpreted to mean that my meal is at your expense."

"Why not?" Hale responded.

A server appeared, filled Westin's glass with water, and placed a menu in front of him. He noticed her glance at the white cotton gloves he wore. "I have a skin condition," Westin said. He looked at her name tag and then pointed to the glass she'd filled with ice water. "I wonder, Sharon, if I might have you bring me a freshly washed glass—I have no idea how long that one has been on the table or what it may have been exposed to."

She stared at him, and he knew that she was trying to determine whether or not he was serious or was pulling her chain. "What," she asked, "you OCD or some shit?"

Westin felt his face heat with ire but didn't give in to his desire to put this foul-mouthed person in her place. "Just bring me a fresh, clean glass, please."

She shrugged and left.

Westin watched her depart and then turned to his companions. "Do you think I should have warned her about how close she is to blowing her tip?"

"Nah," Hale said, "she probably wouldn't understand anyhow."

Westin acknowledged her with a slight nod. "Well, I must say that this is a pleasant coincidence—or is it not a coincidence?"

"It isn't," Hale replied.

Westin turned to face Diaz. "You don't say a lot, do you?"

"I speak when I need to. So far, I ain't heard nothing that I need to respond to."

Westin waited for a few moments and, when he realized that nothing more was forthcoming from the Mexican, turned back to Hale. "Must have made for a long trip up here. So, tell me, if this isn't a coincidence, what is it?"

"An attempt to create a pact," Hale answered.

"A pact?"

The server returned and placed a glass in front of Westin. He held it up so he could look through it at the ceiling light. Slowly rotating the glass, he detected a water spot. "I thought I was clear when I asked for a *clean* glass."

He placed particular emphasis on the word clean.

"It's clean," the server replied, sounding defensive.

Westin showed her the water spot. "Do you see that goddamn spot? This glass is not clean. Now, if it's not too much trouble, get me a fucking clean one. Do you understand the concept of clean? You know, no spots, no smears, no fingerprints?"

The server snatched the *dirty* glass from his hand and made a hasty exit. Westin turned to Hale and said, "I guess it's as hard to get good help up here in the northeast territory as it is in the United States."

Diaz looked confused. "We are in the United States."

"He's making a joke," Hale replied. "One that's not funny."

Westin turned his attention to the menu. "So, let's talk about this pact you're proposing?"

40

Connah walked into the store and took a twelve-pack of beer from the cooler. He paused, recalled his warning to Tom about alcohol, and returned it to the cooler. He moved down to the soft drinks, took a twelve-pack of cola, and approached the counter. The old man rang the purchase in his antiquated cash register, and as he made change, he said, "You're new hereabouts, ain't cha?"

Connah stared at the man for a second, wondering why he wanted to know. He dismissed it as just local curiosity. "Some friends and I are staying near Goddard Village."

"Ah, I heard someone was stayin' at Cody Levesque's old sportsman lodge. Did your friend find you?"

"What?"

"Just yestidee they was a weahd lookin' feller in here askin' about how he could get to your place."

The old man spoke in a heavy Maine accent, and it took a few seconds for Connah to understand what he'd said. "A weird-looking fellow?"

"Yup, all dressed up like he was goin' to church or a funeral. Wore white cloth gloves the entire time he was here. Wanted to know all sorts of stuff about the lake and Goddard Village. I told him they was no way he was goin' in there with that gas-propelled roller skate he was drivin'. I guess he went to Houlton or Presque Isle to rent a four-by-four or ATV. He kinda looked like one a them ninja turtles I seen in a movie, only white."

Connah took his change and the soda and left. As he turned onto Saint-Basile Road, he knew without a doubt that if Harvey Westin hadn't already found them, he was damned close.

$ $ $ $ $

As soon as he arrived back at the cabin, Connah gathered everyone into the common area. "It appears that Harvey Westin may know where we are, and if he knows, it won't be long before the other two do, too. So, it's time for us to go tactical. From this point forward, we need to be alert."

Bobbi Spinelli leaped to her feet. "Be alert! Why in the hell don't you go after him? I don't think I can take another minute being cooped up…" She looked at Billie O'Reilly's angry face, paused, and then obviously amended what she was about to say. "…here."

"You can leave anytime you're ready," Connah shot back. "In fact, it might be considered a favor by the rest of us."

Bobbi's face fell at his harsh words, and she looked like a child who had been caught playing with matches.

"On the other hand," Connah said in a calmer voice, "if you stay with the program, this might be over in a couple of days."

"I have to agree with Bobbi about one thing," Billie said. "Why don't you go after him?"

"There are several reasons why it makes more sense to make him come after me. First, I'm unfamiliar with the terrain and want to set up a hide. Second, neither is Westin, and he suffers from OCD, and for him to have to stalk us through the woods will drive his compulsions wild. Third, I know he's been asking about this place, but I don't know where he is now. So, we'll set up some outposts and watch for him. Once I know he's definitely close, then I'll go after him."

"It sounds as if you're concerned about finding him," Billie said.

"To a degree I am. He's an unknown entity to me. We've only dealt with each other for a few days, and, if he's anything close to his reputation, he's a formidable foe."

"What?" Bobbi and Billie exclaimed in unison.

"For him to have survived as long as he has and run up the score I've heard. He's got to be damned good." Connah slowly made eye contact with everyone in the room. "That's why I've been riding everyone's ass so hard. I've been in this line of work for a long time. Like Harvey, I've had to be good to avoid looking at the grass from the brown side up. To get to the point, I know better than anyone else what we're up against."

"But," Billie interjected, "you've also heard about his weaknesses."

"Other than the OCD, none of his targets have survived to tell of any technical or tactical weaknesses. I believe the best strategy is to make him come here. If I can chase him through the woods, it will drive him nuts."

"Wait a minute," Bobbi said. "I think I heard you say chase *him* through the woods. We're paying you to stay here with us."

"Unfortunately, the only way I can confront him is to be out there. If I stay with you, he has no incentive to deal with me."

"So," Billie snapped, "we're to be bait?"

Connah bore a sheepish grin when he said, "That surprises you? You've been bait since Wark put the bounty on you."

41

Connah entered the living area and immediately knew that any truce between Billie and Bobbi was history. The two women sat on opposite sides of the room, and they looked like a set of bookends. Both of them sat with their arms folded across their chests and their heads inclined forward, foreheads tipped down. They glared at each other through narrow slits where their eyes should have been.

He made a point of ignoring them as he crossed the room and poured a cup of coffee from the carafe that sat on the bar. He perched himself on a stool in front of the bar and swiveled the seat until he could see both of them. He sipped from the cup of coffee and said, "Okay, what's going on? The silence is deafening."

The combatants remained silent, obviously content to glower at each other. Connah finished his coffee in silence then placed the mug on the countertop with a loud bang. He stood and walked to the center of the room. "Right about now, I've half a mind to kill you two myself and collect Jiggs's bounty."

Billie was the first to end their staring contest. "You wouldn't dare—"

"Hell, there's no way any court would convict me. I believe that they would consider it a mercy killing."

"*She* started it," Bobbi said in a pouting tone.

"I did not," Billie protested.

"How old are you two? You act like a couple of twelve-year-old girls fighting over a boy." Connah paused and then added: "Come to think of it, that's all you two have done since you were twelve. Isn't it time you got over the infantile desire for each of you to have what the other has?"

"She has nothing that I want," Bobbi dissented.

"Who are you trying to convince of that—you or me?" Connah held up a hand, muting the women before one or the other could protest any further.

126

"All you're doing is making things easier for Westin. He knows we're in this area and is reputed to be like a bloodhound on a scent. We need to be on top of our game to eliminate any and all distractions so we can concentrate on getting him before he gets you.

"I think it's necessary to remind you once again that *you* are the targets, not me, not Stoney, not Tom, nor Amanda. That doesn't mean he won't kill us, but he'll only do it if we're between him and either of you."

Billie and Bobbi were both red-faced, and they reminded him of two chastised children. He opted to leave things that way. "Now," he said, "to put an end to this crap. I've one more thing to say. If there are any more of these immature arguments, I'm walking out of here, and you'll be on your own. Is that understood?"

Neither woman spoke.

"I'll interpret your silence as agreement." He left the room.

When Connah stepped onto the deck, he saw Tom, Amanda, and Stone sitting there. "What's up?" he asked.

"Have you," Stone said, "given any thought to shooting those two idiots and collecting Jiggs's bounty for us? It'd be a hell of a lot easier, not to mention more profitable, than what you're putting up with."

Connah leaned against the railing and folded his arms. "There isn't a second that goes by that I don't think about it."

"Only," Stone replied, "you got this idiotic idea about honor, and you gave your word."

"Plus, I took their money. Without us, Billie and Bobbi will be dead within twenty-four hours."

"Most likely by their own hands," Tom added.

Amanda said, "You might as well stop threatening to leave or kill them. They know you won't do that."

All Connah could do was nod his head in agreement. "It's time that we got our shit together, too. This deck is definitely off-limits from now on. It's too exposed, and this lake is no more than half a mile wide, and that's well within the range of a decent sniper, and our enemies are a helluva lot better than decent."

42

Harvey Westin listened to mud from the unpaved surface rattling against the undercarriage of his rental. As he drove down the remote dirt road, the four-wheel-drive truck rocked from side to side as its wheels fought to stay in the deep ruts. Westin assumed they were formed by the over-loaded logging trucks that periodically passed him. Muddy water and bugs had coated the truck's hood and windshield, and each time Westin splashed through one of the scores of deep pools of water that submerged the thoroughfare, he cringed. The ever-present trees scraped the sides of the rental and coated the wet windows and windshield with tree debris. Each time Westin turned on the wipers, smearing the window, he vowed to make Connah pay for forcing him to venture into such a God-forsaken place. He glanced in his rear-view mirror to see if Hale and Diaz were still behind him. Their truck was about one hundred yards back, weaving from side to side as they made vain efforts to avoid the mud that his tires threw into the air behind him.

He rounded a bend in the road and saw a sign warning of a narrow wooden bridge ahead. Westin's hands tightened into death grips on the steering wheel as he entered the bridge. From the corners of his eyes, he continuously cast wary glances at the guard rails while keeping his eyes on the road ahead. He saw the deep eddy of the stream; the tannin level of the water was so high that it was a shade of brown so dark it appeared to be black. He snapped his head to the front, afraid that he would veer off the path in the direction that he looked. He involuntarily held his breath until his front tires dropped off the wooden structure and back into the ruts in the hard-panned dirt road. He exhaled explosively and ventured a glance at the GPS sitting on the dash. It told him that even though he'd just crossed over the Saint-Basile River, he still had a twenty-mile drive to the lake bearing the same name. He determined that if he had any control over the method of Connah's death, it would not be fast.

$ $ $ $ $

A sign saying Main Street appeared out of nowhere. The road did a ninety-degree turn along an elevated bed of railroad tracks. A white sign with *GODDARD VILLAGE* written in black block letters appeared, and Westin stopped. He rode the brake and crept forward until the nose of his truck was past the trees enough for him to look to his right into the settlement. No signs of life were detected. He turned and slowly followed the dirt lane. He paused before a small stream that ran across the *street* and was alarmed when he realized that he was driving along the crest of a beaver dam. His stomach lurched when he broke out of a coppice of brush and saw several buildings. He stopped and studied the village. Three rudimentary cabins were built along a slope on his right, and there appeared to be two newer structures, large enough to be called homes, across the tracks to his left. He saw no vehicles, no power lines, and no telephone lines. Never in his life had Westin been in a *village* so remote and isolated from civilization.

The absence of any signs of another human being encouraged him. Unless Connah had placed lookouts in the area, there was no one or thing to warn of their arrival in the area. Westin fought back his inner demons as he argued with himself about the necessity of leaving the safe cocoon of the truck to do the foot search that he knew was required. He picked up his Barrett M95 rifle and exited the vehicle. Once outside, Westin loaded a five-round magazine into the weapon, worked the bolt, loaded a cartridge into the chamber, and shut the truck's door. When he saw the thick layer of dirt and mud that coated the vehicle, he took great care not to touch the sides when he got out.

The mud was at least one-half-inch deep, and he heard splashes with each step he took, and an involuntary shudder ran through him. He quickly crossed the muddy road and stopped on the gravel bed that held the railroad tracks and, while awaiting the arrival of his partners, pondered where to start the search for their targets. He determined that his first step was to double-check the immediate area to see if anyone else was around.

He avoided the muddy road surface by walking on the railroad tracks until he reached a wooden crossing. He stood there studying the road and saw that while it was wet, it was hard-pan. He overcame his natural tendency to avoid anything that was not paved and stepped onto the roadway. When he felt the hard, packed clay surface, he sighed in relief and walked toward the houses that sat on the side of the road facing the lakeshore.

He checked out the first house. He stepped onto the porch and peered into the windows. He saw no visible signs of recent occupancy—in fact, the furniture was covered with white cloths. He circled to the back and encountered a small shed with what looked like a heavy cable leading into the rear corner of the building. Again, he looked through a window and saw that the shed contained what he thought was a large generator. That, he thought, answers the power question. He looked toward the lake and estimated the shore to be about fifty feet from the back of the house. He spied a narrow path that led to the water and cautiously followed it, keeping his firearm at the ready position if he was to encounter some wild animal. Westin followed the footpath to the lake and found an area where the grass and brush had been cleared away. He stared down into the water and saw the lake bottom was mud rather than sand or rocks like most glacial lakes. Westin decided that this was a man-made lake created by a dam. He recalled what he'd learned from the desk clerk at the hotel. The clerk at the hotel was a fisherman and had spent time on this lake. He told Westin that it was shallow, no more than nine feet at its deepest point. "Nice fish in there, just the same." He went on to add, "I don't recommend wading though, not unless you got a pair of chest-waders. The shallow water gets warm, and the leeches love it. I even caught a couple of trout with leeches stuck on them like those fish that attach themselves to sharks."

"Remora," Westin had answered.

"What?"

"Remora, the fish that attach to sharks, are called Remora."

"Well, there ain't none of them in Saint-Basile, but like I said, lots of leeches."

Westin shuddered at the thought of having a leech on his skin and turned away from the lake. When he arrived back at the house, he noted that Hale and Diaz had parked behind his truck and stood on the railroad crossing. He walked toward them, and they met him halfway.

"See anything?" Hale asked.

"I haven't had time to check all the buildings, but it doesn't appear that anyone is here."

Diaz studied the settlement and said, "Won't hurt for us to check them out."

Westin couldn't help but show surprise that the Hispanic assassin had spoken without being directly asked a question.

"We'll check out the ones on the other side of the tracks," Hale said, "why don't you finish checking the ones by the lake?"

$ $ $ $ $

It took less than a half-hour for the three to check all the buildings. They met back at the trucks and moved them to where the ground was firmer. Once settled, Westin produced a topographical map of the area. "I bought it at some hunting and fishing store called The Trading Post," he said. "He took a towel from his SUV and handed it to Hale, who used it to clean mud off the hood of her truck.

Hale spread the map out and revealed a detailed map of the lake and surrounding area. "Looks like a lot of swamp and bog, except for here." Her finger pointed to a ridge that looked down on the lake from the north shore. They looked in that direction to get their bearings.

"What's this?" Diaz asked, pointing to a road that skirted the south side.

"Some sort of access road," Hale guessed.

"Access to what? I'll bet there's something down there. Everyone says there's a bunch of people staying here, but they ain't in this village," Diaz replied.

"You may have a point there," Hale said. "One of us should check it out."

"If they are staying down there someplace, this ridge would be a great place for one or two of us to set up," Westin said.

Both Diaz and Hale looked at him. He immediately detected their suspicion of his motivation, knowing that their feelings were justified. Once on the high ground, all advantage would be his. He tried to assuage their doubt. "Nobody said it would be me. Look, if this is going to work, we need to have a little trust in one another."

"Okay, I'll give you the benefit of the doubt," Diaz said. "I'll check out that road, see where it goes, and what's on it."

"Harvey and I will check out that ridge," Hale said. "For all we know, Connah decided that it's too strategic a position to be left unoccupied. Either he or Stone could have a sniper hide up there."

"It's a big ridge," Westin agreed, "it'll take at least two of us to check it out."

43

Bobbi stormed into the room and confronted Connah. "I want to leave."

"You do." Connah placed the coffee he was drinking on the table. "How long do you think you'll last with Westin looking for you?"

"My people will protect me."

"If we were looking for a drug pusher or gang leader, I might believe that. But we aren't. We're dealing with a highly skilled, if somewhat fucked up, assassin. One who can strike at long distances and has no reservation about who he kills, so long as he eventually gets the target or targets he's after. Then there's the other consideration."

"Which is?"

"You probably won't get out of here alive."

Bobbi began pacing the room. "I need to go home! I can't stand living like Mrs. Daniel fucking Boone no longer."

Connah stood up and stepped toward her. "Bobbi—"

"Don't you friggin' Bobbi me! I'm outta here."

He stopped approaching her and said, "Fine, go."

"Who'll be driving me?"

"No one. We still have an obligation to Billie. You want to leave, go ahead and leave, but you walk."

They were interrupted when Billie walked into the room. "What's going on?" she asked.

"Bobbi's changed her mind about being here."

"I hope the new mind works better than the old one did."

Bobbi clenched her fists and started toward Billie. "I've had all I can stand of you, bitch!"

Connah stood between them, and his cell phone rang as he held them apart. He pressed the talk button and listened. "Okay, I'll be there in a minute." He turned the phone off and placed it in his pocket. "Ladies, I don't think you should think about anything but keeping your asses low. That was Stoney. He said there are a couple of strange trucks in the village. I think we can assume that Harvey Westin and company are either here or on their way."

"Do either of you have a weapon?" He gave each of them a stern look. "Other than your mouths."

"I have a pistol," Billie answered.

"Me too."

"If they aren't loaded, load them and keep them with you everywhere you go… even to the bathroom. Keep away from the windows, and don't go out on the deck." He walked over to the glass slider and pulled the drapes together. "I'm shutting down the generator, it makes a hell of a racket, and it'll be safer if there are no lights. I'll send Tom and Amanda in here. Please don't shoot them."

"Where are you going to be?" Billie inquired.

Connah pointed toward the closed drapes. "Out there. While Westin is hunting you, I'll be hunting him."

44

Connah stood in the brush, studying the four-by-four SUV that sat off to the side of Main Street in Goddard Brook Village. A smile spread across his face when he saw the dried mud coating the truck. He had no doubt that wherever Harvey Westin and his colleagues were, Westin's OCD was, more likely than not, running amok. He turned away from the truck and slid further back into the cover of the alder bushes. It was time to make a decision. Should he stay here and wait for them to return, they would have to do that eventually. His other options were to return to the cabin or patrol the forest until he found their hide. The prudent decision would be to wait where he was, but Westin's return would mean that he had accomplished his mission and Billie and/or Bobbi were dead. Against his better judgment, Connah began to make his way back to the cabin.

Connah didn't know about Diaz and Hale, but Harvey Westin was by any means not an outdoorsman. He was city-born and bred. To the best of Connah's knowledge, Westin's exposure to the wilderness was limited at best. On the other hand, Connah enjoyed being in the great outdoors and the north Maine woods in particular… advantage him.

Connah circumnavigated the lake, taking great care to move slow and quiet. Lake Saint-Basile was not significant as lakes went. It only covered four hundred nineteen acres. Of the numerous game fish indigenous to Maine, only brook trout inhabited it. Still, at a sniper's pace, it could take several days to circle the lake's perimeter. Connah's hyper-keen level of attentiveness caused him to tense every muscle in his body, braced against the shock of a bullet hitting him at any second.

Suddenly, Connah heard a vehicle approaching the turn-off to the lodge. He darted into the trees, squatted beneath the hanging branches of a large pine tree, and watched as a four-by-four pickup truck slowly passed by. It was a warm afternoon, and the driver had the windows down, making him easily identifiable. His mind raced, trying to decide what he should do. If it was Westin or the other guns that Jiggs had imported, that was one thing. On the other hand, it could be anyone from a game warden to a forester marking trees for cutting. When the truck was abreast of him, he recognized Alonzo Diaz.

The truck's brake lights lit up, and after a second, the door opened, and Diaz got out. Connah crept forward on his stomach, trying to get to a place where he'd have a clear line of fire. He got within twenty-five meters of the truck and saw Diaz urinating in the ditch alongside the road.

If Diaz was checking out this road, where were Hale and Westin? The ridge across from the lodge came to mind. The building would be easily visible to anyone on it—and it was well within the range of many high-powered rifles.

What to do? He had two choices: take Diaz out, which would tell the others that Connah was hiding the women here without a doubt. He could let things go and hope that Diaz wouldn't see the turnoff.

Diaz got back in the truck and started forward. He continued his slow patrol, and when he was past the turnoff, he backed up and stopped.

Connah ran through the woods in a crouch, ignoring the heavy thuds of his boots hitting the debris-covered ground. Deadfall from the trees snapped and cracked under his feet as he leaped over a large, downed tree and found himself on the edge of the road.

Diaz carried a rifle when he got out of the truck. He circled around behind it and stood at the mouth of the narrow tree-lined access road that led to the lodge. Suddenly he turned, saw Connah, and raised his weapon.

Connah dropped to one knee, placed his firearm into his shoulder, turned off the safety, and fired.

The full-metal jacketed .308 caliber bullet hit Diaz in the chest, and he staggered back, bumping into the back of the truck. He sat down on the bumper, looked at his chest, then at Connah, and then tumbled sideways to the road's surface.

Connah rose to his feet and slowly advanced toward Diaz. He kept a close watch on him until he stood beside him. He bent down and placed two fingers on his carotid, feeling no pulse. He heard a noise and spun toward the drive to the lodge.

Don Stone's voice came from the shadows. "Connah?"

"Over here."

"Was that your shot?"

"Yeah, we got one less shooter to worry about. Give me a hand, will you?"

Stone appeared out of the brush alongside the road, took a pair of leather gloves from his pocket, and put them on. He and Connah dropped the tailgate and lifted the Velcro strips that secured the bed cover to the vehicle. They picked up Diaz's body and rolled it into the back of the truck. They closed the gate, fastened the bed cover, and then Connah got in the cab. "You want a lift?" he asked Stone.

"Naw, it ain't far."

"I never knew that you were squeamish about dead bodies."

"I ain't. In case the cops find that body, I don't want anything that might identify me on it."

$ $ $ $ $

Harvey Westin felt the sharp sting of a mosquito's bite, reached back and pressed his hand against his neck. Westin cursed and wondered why anyone would want to live in such primitive conditions. He took a bottle of DEET formula insect repellent from his pocket, squirted some into his hand, and shuddered with disgust when he applied it to his neck. An oily film covered his hand, and Westin stopped short of wiping it on his trousers. He scanned the immediate area and snarled when he saw that he'd have to use some plant that harbored who knew what varieties of insect. He vowed that as soon as he finished this job, he would take a bath in scalding water, and never again would he take an assignment in a place without a five-star hotel. He ripped a broad-leafed plant from the ground and wiped his hand before continuing the climb to the summit of the ridge.

As he climbed, he looked up at Hale's backside and had to admit that she did have a great shape. A shot was fired across the lake, and both he and Hale stopped and looked in that direction.

"You think Diaz got one of them?"

"Well, there's one thing we know… either he got one of them, or one of them got him."

"You got that right. Looks as if we lost the element of surprise."

"If Connah's as good as I've heard, we never had the element of surprise," Hale said. "More than likely, he's been preparing for us from the minute he got here."

"Well, let's finish this climb."

They crested the ridge and saw no clear firing lane due to the heavy density of trees and brush. Westin said, "We should head down and check out the lakeshore. Maybe there's something there."

Hale nodded her agreement, and she turned and headed down on a narrow, heavily overgrown path. After a few seconds, Westin followed her.

Unbeknownst to Westin, they were on a game trail and, in a short time, broke out of the trees and walked onto the narrow sandy strip that circled the lake. He scanned his position, paying close attention to the bushes lining the water. He still saw no signs of human life. He turned his attention to the far side of the lake and saw a single building. Of all the structures they'd seen on the lakeshore, it was by far the largest. If Connah was hiding the women here, he was doing it alone, and that was the only place large enough to comfortably shelter more than two or three people. He removed a pair of high-powered binoculars from the case suspended from his shoulder by a strap and looked around for someplace where he could settle in and observe the place. He found a tree stump that looked big enough to serve as a chair, took a handkerchief from his pocket, and cleaned it as best he could. He wiped at the stump for several minutes, saw that his labor was in vain, spread the handkerchief, and sat. He made up his mind that his only recourse was to suffer in silence and, with a sigh of resignation, settled in to observe the building on the opposite shore. He raised the field glasses to his eyes, estimated the distance across the lake slightly more than three hundred yards, and settled in to observe the structure across the lake.

He heard a noise behind him and looked over his shoulder. Hale stood beneath a massive oak tree and motioned for him to join her. He returned his field glasses to their case and followed her into the woods.

$ $ $ $ $

Connah knew without a doubt that Westin and Hale were in the area. Since the other camps and buildings in Goddard Village were usually unoccupied during the week, it was a given that Westin was someplace close where he could observe their cabin. His first action was to ensure all the drapes and blinds were still closed, and no one had violated his rule that the deck was off-limits. His second was for Stoney and him to begin a slow, foot-by-foot search of the area around the lake.

He had been sitting in the trees beside the cabin for several hours, watching the perimeter of the lake, hoping to detect a flash of light reflecting off a lens. The afternoon had turned unseasonably warm. Sweat ran down the back of Connah's neck, tickling as it made its way across his shoulders and down his back before it was absorbed by his T-shirt. He needed to locate precisely where Westin—and possibly Hale—was on the other side of the lake. At this point, the lake was less than half a kilometer across, an easy shot for a sniper with even rudimentary skills.

Connah slowly panned the trees on the far side with his tripod-mounted Leupold GR20-60x80mm Boone and Crockett HD spotting scope. The high-powered optics made an object one-thousand yards away appear as if it were only forty-six feet from him. He adjusted the focus by turning the wheel on the side of the scope and moved it ever so slightly to the left. The sun reflected from the lake surface, and a stiff breeze rippled through the trees, pushing the warm air around. Connah looked to the west and saw the towering shape of cumulonimbus clouds, a sure sign of a late afternoon thunderstorm. He laughed and thought: That's all Westin needs to drive him completely out of his mind. Maybe things will work out in our favor yet.

Out of the corner of his eye, Connah detected abnormal motion. He bent over the spotter scope and turned it to the source of the movement. It took several seconds for him to see the basis of the movement that had drawn his attention. A magnificent whitetail buck drank from the lake. Its majestic rack of antlers curved forward. He estimated the deer to be a twelve-pointer—it was a trophy animal. Suddenly, it looked to its left, peered at something for several seconds, and then bolted into the woods. Connah panned in the direction that the buck had looked, and there, standing beneath a giant pine, were Tegan Hale and Harvey Westin.

They seemed to be looking directly at him. To determine whether or not he'd been seen, Connah slowly raised his right arm, and Hale waved back. Through his high-powered lens, Connah saw the smiles on their faces before they turned and disappeared into the forest.

"Well, that seals it," Connah said. "Now that they know where we are, the hunt begins."

45

Westin crept through an area of dense brush and noted that the day had gone dark all of a sudden. He jumped when a bolt of lightning hit a tree further up the ridge, followed by a sharp CRACK-BOOM! The acrid smell of ozone filled the air around him, and the wind increased, making the lake look like a pot of boiling water. A sudden deluge of rain hit him like a 100-foot wave slamming into a cliff. The wind escalated, and he was assailed by bits of debris and broken branches. He quickly looked for shelter and another flash of light, followed by an immediate earth-shaking boom, sent an old dead tree tumbling down mere feet in front of him. Panicked, Westin remembered that you should never seek shelter under a tree in a thunderstorm, and he was surrounded by thousands of them—each one a natural lightning rod! A bolt hit another dead tree, which exploded, and its base burst into flames. *Forest Fire!* A gust of wind pushed a surge of heavy rain, soaking him and the tree. The deluge was so intense that the fire immediately sputtered and died.

The wind raged. Gusting to levels that Westin had never experienced. Deadwood fell all around him—it was what he'd imagined it would be like to be caught in an intense artillery barrage. The area lit up, and another lightning-thunder sequence shook the ground.

Westin heard something close and spun around in time to see a black bear, terrified by the storm, lumber within a few yards of him. Its eyes were hyper-extended in fear, and it ignored the two cubs that ran behind it. Westin knew he had to find shelter before being killed by either a falling tree or a panicked animal. He looked to his left and saw Hale staring at the bears. However, unlike him, she had her rifle in her shoulder, ready to fire, and her weapon followed the bears as they charged up the ridge. Westin was amazed by the speed of the wild animals and watched them until they disappeared from sight.

He hollered to be heard over the sounds of wind, falling and creaking trees, and thunder, "We got to find shelter!"

When Hale nodded in agreement, he turned and frantically scanned their immediate area for a hide.

$ $ $ $ $

Connah noted the sudden decrease in the day's brightness and gathered his equipment. He entered the cabin and pulled the slider closed. Just then, the sky seemed to explode with a flash of blinding light, immediately followed by a deafening boom. The storm was on top of them, and within seconds a thick sheet of rain raced across the lake; pea-sized hailstones slammed against the glass door and then bounced off the deck's flooring. He couldn't help but grin. Westin and Hale are in for quite a go of it, he thought.

He sensed a presence behind him and turned. Tom stood in the kitchen, a nine-millimeter pistol in his hand. "All things considered," Tom said, "you shouldn't come busting in that way."

"Well—" A flash of lightning and simultaneous crash of thunder so loud that it shook the building as if they'd just had an earthquake interrupted him. Billie and Bobbi came rushing into the room.

"I've never been in a storm this fierce," Billie exclaimed.

As if on cue, the hailstones changed to the size of ping pong balls. They hit the building, roof, and deck with loud bangs. The ice balls hit the glass slider; the banging of their impact was deafening. Suddenly, the glass broke, and a jagged crack raced from top to bottom. "Holy crap!" Bobbi yelled.

$ $ $ $ $

As fast as it had descended upon them, the ferocious storm abated, Westin crawled out of the water-filled depression below the fallen maple where he and Hale had sought cover. A chilling wind followed the frontal passage, and violent shaking wracked his body. He stared at the mud that coated his hands and clothes, felt his heart rate increase and terror take over his self-control. Water still dripped from the trees, soaking him further, white hailstones littered the ground. His heart was hammering so fast he believed he was on the verge of having a heart attack, and his mental state altered from terror to absolute paranoia. His mind became consumed by a single thought: If I don't get out of here, I'll die!

Westin turned and began trotting toward the small cluster of camps and his rented SUV. He completely forgot his mission. All he wanted to do was drive back to his hotel room (the very thought of the fifty-mile drive in filthy clothes panicked him further), and clean up. He called to Hale, "I'm going back to the hotel—this is too much."

Hale's muddy face and matted hair showed out from the water-filled depression where she'd sought refuge from the storm. Her voice escalated to compensate for the loss of hearing brought on by the thunderclaps. "What? I can't hear shit… that thunder was too fucking close."

Westin repeated his plan to return to Presque Isle and clean up. "Are you coming?"

She gave him a look that said he was pathetic and said, "One of us has to stay and keep an eye on things—what if Alonzo is still out there? Maybe he's hurt and needs help?"

"Screw him," Westin replied. "If the situation was reversed, he'd leave us in a heartbeat."

Hale was inspecting her rifle. Her hair was stuck to her forehead, and the area around her eyes was white, and mud and bits of dead leaves and twigs covered her face and matted her hair. Westin thought that she looked like a mutant raccoon.

"You do what you got to," she said, "but if I get them while you're giving in to your OCD, I'm keeping all the bounty."

"I'll only be a few hours."

"Yeah," she said, her voice stern, "but a lot can happen in a few hours."

"Have it your way, but I'm going back to civilization to clean myself."

"Like I said, you do what you got to do." She held her hand out to him. "Just leave me the surveillance gear so I can keep an eye on them."

Westin handed her his expensive high-power binoculars. "Don't get them dirty."

Hale stared at him for a few seconds. Her look told Westin that she thought he was disgusting. Then she said, "Get the hell outta here." She turned and started up the ridge in the direction the bears had run.

$ $ $ $ $

141

Westin followed the lakeshore, headed toward the siding in Goddard Brook Village, where he'd left his truck. Each time a raindrop fell from the trees and hit the ground with a thud, he spun in that direction; on a couple of occasions, his finger tensed on the rifle's trigger. He was super-vigilant and turned in circles as he moved through the brush and weeds that lined the lake.

He almost cried with relief when he came to the clearing that delineated the village from the woods. He broke into a run as he closed with his rented truck, stripping off his soaked, muddy shirt as he approached. Westin removed all of his outer clothing and footgear and wore only his underwear. He reached into the pocket of his black jeans to get his keys. He shuddered when his hand came in contact with the heavy, wet grime that coated the inside. He fumbled with the keys until he got the door open, threw his soiled clothes into the back, and placed his weapon butt down on the floor before the passenger seat. His hands were shaking convulsively when he slid into the driver's seat, fought with the key until it finally slid into the ignition, and actuated the starter.

Once the motor started, Westin sat back, rested his head against the headrest, and waited for the heater to kick in. It took an eternally long five minutes for the fan to blow warm air, and he felt his heartbeat slow down. Bit by bit, he began to get control of his runaway emotions. In a short time, his panic abated, only to be replaced by a deadly resolve—for the first time in his life, a job had turned into a personal vendetta. He placed the truck in drive and began a U-turn. Suddenly the front end dropped down and to the right. "What the fuck?"

Westin cringed when he stepped from the truck and placed his bare feet onto the road, and thick mud filled the gaps between his toes. He began trembling in response to the continuous waves of revulsion that racked his body. He circled to the passenger side and stopped abruptly when he saw the front right wheel lying on the ground.

$ $ $ $ $

Stone and Amanda had joined Billie, Bobbi, and Connah in the living room. "What's going on?" Stone asked.

"I saw Westin and Hale. They were across the lake watching this place. Right about now, Westin's most certainly having major doubts about this job.

This storm may drive him away, but he'll be back. Hale, on the other hand, will probably stay. I believe that she's the more lethal of the two."

"I don't think Westin will be going anywhere," Stone said. He reached into his pocket and showed Connah what he had—in his hand were six lug nuts. "If he tries, he ain't going far."

46

Jiggs Wark walked into the garage and motioned Wayne Archer to join him. "You heard anything from Westin?" he asked when Archer stood beside him.

"Nope, not since he called and said that he'd located them on that lake."

"You know when I started this, I had no idea that it was going to be a long-term project." Wark was quiet for a few seconds as he thought over the situation. "Pack some shit. We're going there."

"To Maine?"

"If that's where Westin is, that's where we're going. Hell, I may save myself a million bucks."

"Okay, you're the boss."

$ $ $ $ $

Westin inspected the truck's wheel and saw that someone had removed the lug nuts—to make matters worse, they had either taken them or thrown them into the woods or, even worse, the lake. He cursed and slapped the hood of his truck. He stomped his right foot in anger, and the cold, soupy sludge splashed his inner legs and groin. He stood barefooted in the middle of the unpaved road and howled in rage.

Once again, he lost control and gave in to his compulsion. He had no concept of time, and when he stopped screaming profanities at no one or thing, in particular, he didn't know how long he'd been raving like a mad man. Anger overcame his panic, and he became determined to kill everyone who had put him in this predicament. But first, he was going to clean up as best he could. He reached into the back of the truck, taking care not to touch the filthy clothes any more than necessary, gathered his clothes together, and walked to the lake. He shuddered with revulsion and waded out into the water until he was up to his knees and began rinsing the mud and grime off his clothes and his body. When he finished *washing* the clothes, he began rubbing the dirt off the submerged portion of his right leg. He felt several bumps that had not been there before. He lifted his foot out of the water and saw what he thought were two black worms on his right calf. He brushed at them several times before realizing that the worms were attached to his skin and wouldn't fall off! Although he'd never before seen one, he guessed what the parasites were—leeches! His shout of anger and disgust echoed across the lake.

$ $ $ $ $

Connah carried his bolt-action .308 rifle when he exited the lodge by the door opposite the lake. He turned back and said, "I want all of you to stay inside. I'm going to put an end to this right now."

"You want me along?" Stone asked.

"I need you here, keeping things secure, more than I need you with me."

"If it was me," Stone added, "I'd start at Goddard Brook Village."

"My thoughts exactly."

They heard a loud string of curse words echoing across the lake.

"Either Harvey has tried driving his truck, or something else has set him off." Stone laughed. "He probably took a leak and found a tick on his dick."

Bobbi laughed. "Have to be something small, I'll bet. Probably not much there for a tick to latch onto."

Connah walked out of the door, entered the woods, and began circumnavigating the lake without comment.

$ $ $ $ $

Connah came to the railroad tracks and stayed back in the trees while walking parallel to the railbed into Goddard Village. When he reached the road that led from the woods to the small cluster of buildings, he saw a disabled four-by-four SUV. Stoney's trick with the lug nuts had obviously been an unmitigated success. The only thing left for him to do was to find Westin.

Connah cautiously crept out of the protection offered by the pine and deciduous trees that bordered the railroad bed and bolted across the tracks. He re-entered the woods and dropped to his stomach, expecting to hear a rifle shot at any moment. He lay quiet and listened to the wind rustling through the trees, water falling from leaves and branches, and the squawk of birds as they recovered from the storm. He began crawling toward the disabled truck and then heard someone screaming obscenities. He recognized Harvey Westin's voice. He rose up and dashed for the cover offered by the SUV.

Peering across the truck's hood, Connah saw Westin. The hitman stood in the lake, his legs submerged to his knees. He wore a T-shirt and boxer shorts and was bent over, staring at his legs and talking to himself, the words a mixture of anger and tears. Connah couldn't suppress his smile as he thought: Looks as if Westin's OCD has kicked into high gear. Westin still held a pistol in his right hand despite his scant clothing. Connah released the safety from his rifle and left the security of the pickup. He jogged into the trees that lined the lake.

Connah found concealment in a coppice of alder bushes hidden from Westin's sight but with a clear lane of fire. Westin was so enmeshed in inspecting his legs that he was oblivious to Connah's approach. Connah heard Westin cursing and threatening to kill everyone within a fifty-mile radius. Connah crept to another advantageous position less than twenty feet from Westin. He stepped into the open and said, "You gonna make it, Harvey?"

Westin raised his head and, while still bent over, angled his torso and stared into the trees from which Connah's voice had come. When the killer-for-hire straightened up, Connah almost laughed out loud when he saw that Westin's disdain of hair was complete, and he shaved everywhere.

"Human Beings don't live in shit holes like this," Westin shouted.

"Really? People hereabouts consider this God's Country."

"Who can believe in a God that would create something as vile as a leech?"

"That your problem? Don't worry. They don't drink much and, once they drink their fill, they'll fall off. Of course, there's always the chance you'll get infected from the bacteria they regurgitate. Who knows what other kinds of animals they've sucked blood from? I wouldn't be surprised to learn that they spread rabies."

Westin's eyes widened in alarm. "*What?*"

"Nasty little buggers. They have been known to get into the body. I heard about a guy who got one inside his dick, but that was in Vietnam."

Westin said, "You're shitting me, right?"

"I wouldn't shit you, Harvey. You're my bas-turd. Believe it or not, they'll even enter through your ass and attach to your guts."

"How do you get these things off?" Westin asked.

"Well, if you'd thought to bring insect repellent, you might have avoided them altogether."

"I have repellent. It didn't work."

"Did you check to see if the repellent wouldn't wash off in the water?"

Westin swiped at the parasites again.

"I was you, I'd be careful not to squeeze them. They might puke some of the bacteria-infested blood into you. You need something like a credit card."

Westin glared. "A credit card! You can't be serious."

"You got to use something thin. You need to get under the mouth and break the suction. If your fingernails are long enough, you can use them. However, I don't think that will work in your case. If I recall, you keep your nails cut really short. I imagine that you don't want to get dirt under them. Some people touch them with a lit cigarette. Nah, that won't work either. You don't smoke. Either way, Harvey, you got to get them off you. I read that in Egypt, some of Napoleon's soldiers drank leech-infested water. Some of them suffocated to death when the leeches in their throats sucked enough blood to become bloated and blocked their airways. So, rather than chatting with me, you need to get them off, or you'll have real problems."

Westin started toward the shore, trying to run through the water. As he closed with him, Connah raised his rifle until the cross-hairs of his scope were centered on Westin's chest.

Westin saw Connah, stopped his advance, and asked, "I don't suppose you're going to let me walk away from this, are you?"

"That depends on you. If you're anywhere close to being as smart as I've been told, you'll stay put right where you are. One more step, and this conversation will come to an abrupt stop."

Westin stopped still standing in water that came to the center of his shins. "You haven't answered my question: Are you going to let me walk away?"

"Are you going to walk away—all the way?"

Westin sighed. "Probably not. A million bucks are too big a prize."

"That's what I thought, too. If the situation was reversed, would you let me walk away?"

"No. Not me anyway," Westin said. "Are you going to at least give me a chance?"

"What, you think this is a western movie? You know they're far from reality."

Westin ignored the question and said, "You know Hale and Diaz are around here someplace."

"Diaz is out of it."

"You kill him?"

"Yeah."

"So, it's just Hale and me."

"All the more reason to cut down on the odds."

Westin raised his handgun and pointed it in Connah's direction.

Connah fired his rifle and shot Westin through the chest. The bullet's impact made him back up a step.

The assassin's eyes widened as if he could not believe what had happened, and then he fell forward. Connah watched the corpse settle in the water and then start bobbing up and down in the wind-swept swells.

Connah walked to the lake's edge and looked at the body. Blood flowed into the water surrounding Westin, enveloping him in a red cocoon. Nearby a floating bunch of black clothing bobbed in the windblown ripples. He shook his head and said, "That was a stupid fucking move, Harvey."

$ $ $ $ $

Hale heard the shot and turned toward the direction it had come from. The gunshot wasn't what she expected to hear from a fifty-caliber Barrett. Still, she was unsure if Westin had fired it. She was sure of one thing; she needed to know what had happened.

She took her time circumventing the lake. If the shot had been fired by someone other than Westin, she didn't want to expose herself. The ground was boggy, and her clothes were covered with some sort of prickly stuff, and cattail fluff coated her from head to foot. She stepped into a deep mud hole that wrenched her right knee and threatened to suck the boot off her foot. Hale massaged at the pain in her knee for a moment and then continued walking. She knew she should take extra caution and stay alert. Her knee throbbed so severely that she could not resist watching the ground beneath her when placing her feet on what she assumed to be firm ground.

Hale took the better part of an hour to reach the settlement, and what she found there confused her. Westin's truck sat in front of the railroad crossing, and she immediately saw that one of the front wheels was off the SUV and lying on the muddy road. Every internal alarm developed over ten years as a terrorist and gun-for-hire went off. She scanned the area looking for any sign of Westin but saw none.

She approached the rental truck and peered in the backseat. There was a spot on the seat. She touched it, and it was damp; the open area in the rear of the SUV was empty. She turned her attention to the front. A brief look revealed Westin's Barrett M95 propped against the passenger seat, butt on the floor. Had there been a klaxon hooked to Hale's warning systems, it would have been wailing. She dropped into a crouch and ran to the nearest house on the lakeside of the tracks.

She crept along the side of the house, studying the ground. She saw bootprints; water in the indentations left by the treads told her they were made recently. She saw a narrow path running from her location to the lake and followed it. Arriving at the lakeshore, she saw Westin's black shirt and jeans, more tracks, one set of footprints, and a pair of grooves that could be drag marks. It was evident that something… or *someone* had been pulled out of the water. She followed the deeper tracks, indicating that the person who'd left them was carrying a heavy load. The trail led to the railroad tracks, and she followed them until she saw where someone had slid down the embankment to the woods below.

She followed the trail until it dead-ended at a pile of broken branches and deadfall. She moved a couple of pine boughs and found Westin. "So, that's what happened to Harvey." She squatted beside the pile and studied the woods surrounding the area until she was sure that Westin's killer was no longer in the area.

47

Archer passed through the EZ-Pass Lane and accelerated up the Maine Turnpike. "Looks like we got about five or six hours ahead of us."

"What in hell made Connah take them so far?"

"Maybe he figured that if they bitched at each other as much as usual, he could kill them while they were distracted, and no one would ever find the bodies."

Wark laughed. "Wouldn't put it past the son of a bitch to try and collect the bounty from me."

"Well, you didn't put any conditions on who could do the job. Hell, that's how Westin got involved. That fuckin' guy is goofy as hell."

"Yeah, he's all of that. I'll bet if he had known that Connah was going to lead him into the friggin' willy-wags, he'd have never gotten involved in this."

"You know, boss, all you had to do was ask, and I'd have taken those idiot broads out for you."

"What? And risk losing the best body-work guy I've ever had?"

$ $ $ $ $

Connah arrived back at the cabin at dusk. When Stone saw him walk out of the woods, he met him on the deck. "Is it over?"

"It is for Westin. We still got Hale to deal with. She won't give up. Not so long as Jiggs keeps the bounty on them. It wouldn't surprise me if he didn't try to do the job with his own people."

"Like Archer?"

"Like Archer, who scares the shit out of me. He's way too quiet and comes across as being as harmless as a baby."

150

"I'll see what I can learn about him," Stone said. "We headed back to the city now?"

"We'll give it a couple of days. Who knows, if Hale learns that she's the only one left, she may bug out too. Maybe, if she still wants to collect that bounty, she'll try to do it in Boston."

"What'd you do with…?"

"Westin? I hauled him up the tracks about a half-mile or so, then dragged him into the woods and covered him up with deadfall. I'm certain that if Hale wants to certify that he's dead, she'll have no problem following the trail I left. Otherwise, by the time the insects, coyotes, and other predators get done with him, it'll take DNA from his bone marrow to ID him. About now, he's standing in Hell, and for once, his OCD isn't driving him nuts."

"You think anyone will come looking for him?"

"Other than whoever he rented that truck from? Who knows? Even if they do find him, they'll never find out who killed him." Connah reached into his pocket, retrieved a brass cartridge, and held it up for Stone to see. "I was close enough when I shot him that the round passed through him and is at the bottom of the lake." He turned and threw the brass as far out into the lake as possible. "That ought to do it." He walked inside the cabin.

$ $ $ $ $

Connah walked into the general store and nodded at the old storekeeper. Pumping the handle several times, he poured a cup of coffee from the urn, walked over to the tables that formed a small coffee area, and sat. "Where's everyone?" he asked the old man.

"They'll be along. Most o' them don't get about like they used to."

Connah glanced at his watch. "It's a bit early, only seven-thirty."

The old man looked at Connah in a manner that made him feel that the old-timer thought he was crazy. "I thought you was talkin' 'bout the lunch crowd. Mornin' folks was in hours ago."

Connah laughed. "You had me going there, old man."

"Now, you're one pop'lar fella. There was two more of them, city folks, from away, in here last night. Wanted to know about that fancy-dan that was in here earlier in the week. When I told them that I ain't seen no sign o' him, they ast about you—leastways I thought it was you they ast about."

"What they look like."

"One was older, maybe fifty or so, the other was young, but then everyone looks young to me. The older guy was tall, maybe six-one, skinny fella, didn't have no more meat on him than a pahtridge leg. The young one was maybe two inches shortah, but big, you know. He looked like he could lift the back-end of a car and hold it while you changed the tires."

The descriptions fit Jiggs Wark and Wayne Archer. Connah thought: Maybe I can put an end to this once and for all. He stood, paid for his coffee, and said, "Didn't happen to mention where they were staying, did they?"

"Matter of fact, they did. Told me that if I learned anything, they had rooms in Patten."

"They say where?"

"Didn't have to. There's only one place there, the Hartley House. It's one a them bed and breakfast places."

"Easy to find?"

"Ain't bin to Patten, have you?" The old man gave Connah a toothless smile. "This here road is Route 11. It runs right through the center of Patten. Hartley House is the biggest building that ain't a bahn. If you come to a cluster of buildings, you're in the middle of town, and you went too far."

Connah thanked him and left the store. Once he was in his truck, he called Stone on his cell phone. "I'll be gone most of the day."

"Trouble?"

"I just heard that Jiggs and Archer are in the area."

"Let me guess, the old guy at the store."

"I'm starting to think that he's 4-1-1 for the entire state."

"You need me?"

"I don't think so, but if I do, I'll call you."

"Good enough."

Before Stone broke the connection, Connah said, "Can you keep Billie and Bobbi from killing each other until I get back?"

"Don't know. But if there's anything I like, it's a challenge."

48

Patten, Maine, is a lumber town. Its location was strategic to several rivers and streams used in the nineteenth and twentieth centuries to transport lumber to the Penobscot River and float it to the mills in Bangor and Millinocket. However, the last log drive to the Penobscot River took place in 1976; trucks now carry the lumber. Leaving the town as yet another example of the proverbial one-horse town after the one horse has left for greener pastures. The sign Connah passed on route 11 listed the population as 1,017. From what he saw as he entered the town limits, he wondered where they were hiding.

Finding the Hartley House was no problem. He came to a sign stating that it, along with the rest of the buildings on the Hartley Farm, was listed in the national register of historic places. The B&B was a remodeled farmhouse with an attached barn for a parking garage. The atmosphere was cozy, almost too much so. In a conventional hotel, isolating Wark would be a whole lot easier than it was going to be in a converted private home. Connah cruised through the parking lot and saw no cars with Massachusetts plates. Either Wark was not here yet, or he was out.

Connah decided to take a chance, and he parked in front of the entrance and walked inside. As soon as he walked through the front door, he found himself in a foyer-like room that had been remodeled into a reception area. To his left was the desk, and to his right, a pair of French doors led to a large sitting room complete with a working fireplace. He assumed what led up to the guest rooms to the left of the sitting-room door was a solitary stairway. There was no way for anybody to enter or leave the B&B without the young woman who sat behind the desk observing them.

The desk clerk smiled a professional but mechanical smile and asked, "May I be of assistance?"

"Yes, I'm supposed to meet someone here. Has a Mr. Claude Balls from Chicago checked in today?"

She paused for a moment and then said, "No one from Chicago has checked in today."

"You're sure?"

"Yes, the only people who've checked in in the past twenty-four hours were from Boston. I'm absolutely positive that no one named Balls is a guest here."

"I wonder where he could be. I'm sure you'd remember him. He's a retired tiger trainer... he has scars down the side of his face where a cat he'd abused got its revenge."

"That must have been horrible," the desk clerk said.

"Yeah, it was. A book was written about his life. You may have read it. *Tiger's Revenge* by Claude Balls."

"I haven't read it. But it sounds interesting."

"You can get it from most book stores. Your local library may have it." Connah glanced at his watch. It was just past six. "Where can I get something to eat in this town?"

"The only place local is the Dew Drop Inn. It's on the corner of Shin Pond Road and North Road."

Connah smiled and said, "Thank you. You've been a great help."

As he stepped out onto the porch that ran around the building, he heard her say, "You're welcome. Please revisit us."

"I might do just that," he said. "Check out that book. It's a page-turner."

It took Connah less than five minutes to locate the Dew Drop Inn, a task made easy since it was the only place open in what passed for downtown Patten. He parked across the street and saw Jiggs Wark and Wayne Archer sitting in a booth by a front window. Connah shook his head. It would be so easy to just pop them both and finish this once and for all. He shrugged off the thought, got out of his truck, and watched his targets as he pondered how he would get to Jiggs without a gunfight developing. After five minutes, Archer stood, walked down a short corridor, and disappeared.

Connah crossed the street and entered the restaurant. Without waiting for an invitation, he walked to the table. He stood so that his nine-millimeter pistol was visible only to Wark. Jiggs's eyes widened when he saw who stood beside him. "Get up, Jiggs."

Wark stayed seated.

"I know you're waiting for Wayne. If he walks out of that door, I'll have no recourse but to kill him—you, too."

Wark stood, and Connah stepped back. "Walk outside and don't think about doing anything stupid."

"If you're going to kill me, it may as well be here as anywhere."

"I'll only kill you if you push the issue. Now walk."

Connah led Wark across the street, and when they reached his truck they stepped onto the sidewalk, keeping the pickup between them and the restaurant. Connah opened the door and said, "Get in."

When Wark was seated, Connah said, "Open the glove box."

Wark complied.

"Hand me one of those tie wraps."

Wark removed a white plastic tie-wrap and handed it to Connah.

Connah secured Wark's hands behind his back.

Wark glanced toward the restaurant.

"Jiggs, I hope you aren't thinking about doing something stupid, like shouting. If you do, I'll pop you right here."

Wark sat back in the passenger seat, his hands held secure by the plastic restraint. Connah grabbed the seat belt and then reached across and fastened it. When he was satisfied that Wark couldn't move, he rounded the truck and got in. He started the motor and drove forward to an abandoned gas station, where he turned around. When they went past the Dew Drop Inn, Connah saw Archer standing beside the booth, looking confused.

"Wayne doesn't look happy," Connah said. "What did you do? Stick him with the bill?"

Wark looked at Connah but said nothing.

Once they had passed through the congested area of town, Connah increased his speed to sixty miles per hour, five over the posted fifty-five mile per hour limit. Neither he nor Wark had spoken since they left the town, and as far as Connah was concerned, that was fine. Wark broke the silence. "I take it that Westin is dead."

Without taking his eyes from the road, Connah said, "You can forget about Westin. He's done his last hit."

"Hmmm, I thought he was good."

"He was good, but this time he was out of his element. We won't mention the obvious fact that I'm better."

"What about the others?"

"Diaz has made his last hit, and Hale is still running loose."

"So," Wark said, "what are you going to do with me?"

"You and I are going to take a ride through the woods."

"Should I start confessing my sins to God?"

"Jiggs, we're only going to be driving for an hour. You won't have enough time."

When Wark laughed, there was an angry tone to it. "I never thought I'd get it up here in the middle of nowhere."

"Who said anything about you getting it?"

"Ain't that what this is about?"

"Hell, no. This is about you, Billie, and Bobbi sitting down and coming to some sort of compromise and putting an end to all this stupid bullshit between the three of you."

"On a scale of one to ten, the chance of that happening is zilch-point-shit."

"I'll settle for you pulling the bounty and letting Hale know about it."

"What's the matter, Connah? You afraid you may have to hit a woman?"

"Thus far, I've been able to avoid doing that—but if it comes down to her or me, the one who walks away is gonna be me."

49

"When you get away from it, you really get away," Wark said when Connah turned into the tree-sheltered drive. He looked at the encroaching trees and brush and chuckled. "Now I know what you meant when you said Westin was out of his element. He must have gone nuts out here."

"His compulsions got him killed in the long run," Connah replied.

Connah stopped the truck, got out, and walked to the passenger side. He opened the door, released Wark's seat belt, and cut the tie-wrap, freeing his hands.

Wark said, "Just what is it that I'm supposed to do here?"

"I already told you. You, Billie, and Bobbi are going to iron out your differences. This stupidity between the three of you stops here—one way or the other."

Wark laughed. "Who you shitting?"

"Jiggs, you're in no position to get cynical. Keep in mind that I have a thing about shooting women—but, you ain't a woman."

Wark seemed pensive for a moment, looked at the remote surroundings, and then laughed. "No. I sure as hell ain't."

"Follow me," Connah said.

Wark rubbed his wrists, trying to regain feeling in his hands. "So, this is where you hid them? I'd've never found this place in a thousand years."

"That was the idea."

"Frankly," Wark said, "I'm surprised that Westin and the others found you."

"Would'a been better for two of them if they hadn't."

Connah led Wark across the deck and inside the cabin. Billie and Bobbi were standing in the middle of the room, squared off as if they'd been at each other's throat again. Connah shook his head in frustration and said, "We have a guest."

The two rivals paused and, if it was biologically possible, Connah would have expected to see claws appear from the tips of their fingers. He turned to Wark and said, "You know Jiggs, it may be a good thing I saved you from having to pay out a million bucks—you may need it to pay for a nice funeral."

"What," Bobbi said, her words fraught with malice, "is that son of a bitch doing here?"

"Hey," Connah said, "don't be casting aspersions on an animal that isn't here to defend itself." He pushed Wark into a chair. "Now," he continued in what he hoped was a good, calming voice, "you three are going to stay here until you come to some sort of workable agreement."

"The only workable solution I'll accept will be both of them dead," Billie said.

Bobbi folded her arms across her chest and nodded in agreement. "I won't be happy until I send flowers to their viewings—both of them."

"Shut up, all of you," Connah said. "Here's the plan. I'm giving you three days to reach a compromise. If by then you haven't, I'll take the money that you owe me and leave."

"After you get us back to Boston," Billie added.

"No, you can get yourselves back. Or kill each other up here where there's minimal chance of a bunch of innocent bystanders being gunned down in the process."

Amanda walked through the room, muttering and talking to herself in a subdued tone. She was oblivious to anyone and walked out onto the deck. There was no doubt that she was in a severely manic state. Within seconds Tom came rushing into their midst. "Anyone seen Mandy?" He looked as if he was at his wit's end.

Connah, Billie, and Bobbi all pointed toward the deck in unison. Tom rushed out in pursuit of his wife.

"What the fuck was that?" Wark asked.

"Over the next three days, you'll find out," Billie said. "Christ, I need a drink." She spun and walked toward the kitchen. "You want something, Bimbo?"

"You call me that again, and I'll give *you* something."

"Whatever, come on, I need a shot of whiskey, or two, or three."

50

Hale located the keys to Westin's rental truck and realized that the keys were useless unless she found a stash of lug nuts. She stood in the middle of the road and tried to figure out a way out of the wilderness. She was almost sure that Diaz had driven their truck down the road that ran along the lake's south shore. But how far?

She estimated at least ten miles, possibly even fifteen, to the store, and she didn't feel like hiking that distance through the wilderness. She looked at the sky and saw that it was dusk, and in minutes the area was going to be pitch black. She tried to recall the last time she'd been in a place with no street lights. More likely than not, it was back in the old country, some pissant village in central Ireland... so remote they needed a generator to get daylight. The truck Diaz had rented was the best option. Besides, who knew what would meander across the road once it was dark. Hale checked her rifle to ensure there was ammunition in the magazine and a live round in the chamber; then started walking down the road.

$ $ $ $ $

The truck sat off to the right-hand side of the road. Hale bent forward as she tried to determine if anyone was keeping watch on it. She crept forward and stood beside the vehicle. She opened the door, thankful that Diaz had remembered to remove the interior light, and felt along the right side of the steering column. Her hands came in contact with the keys. They were still in the ignition, and that disturbed her. No one would leave the keys unless... suddenly she dropped into a crouch as she finished her thought... unless they were using the truck as bait to lure her into a trap.

She sat on the ground with her back against the truck door, listening for the telltale sign of someone in the area. She heard the nocturnal clatter of the woods at night, crickets chirping, and the croaking of frogs. Mosquitoes and some demonic creature from hell called the black fly (which she was told by some local people she'd met was as close to a vampire as they had in these parts) swarmed around her. She felt them feasting on her blood.

After several long minutes, she decided to take a chance on getting away in the truck. She opened the door as quietly as she could and slipped beneath the steering wheel. She turned the key, and the pickup immediately started. The vehicle's nose was pointed in the wrong direction, so she pulled the gear shift lever into reverse. The tires spun as she turned and looked over her right shoulder to keep the pickup on the road.

$ $ $ $ $

Stone was sitting in the sunroom when he heard the motor start. He grabbed his handgun, ran out onto the deck, jumped over the railing, and ran down the drive toward the road. He reached the thoroughfare and saw the truck do a K-turn and race away. He raised his pistol to fire a shot.

"Let her go."

Stone turned and saw Connah standing off to one side of the drive.

"How in Christ's name did she start it so quickly? I didn't hear a sound."

"I put the key in the ignition this afternoon."

"What?"

Connah approached his partner and stood beside him. They watched the truck disappear into the night. He draped his arm around Stone's shoulders and said, "I don't know how you feel, Don. But I've about had it with killing people."

Stone slid his pistol into his belt and said, "Let's hope that she keeps going and doesn't make us regret letting her get away."

"Unfortunately, she still thinks there are a million bucks at stake. Unless somebody tells her that the bounty has been removed, we'll be seeing Miss Tegan again." Connah turned Stone toward the lodge. "Come on, let's go see how the negotiations are progressing."

"You know, Ian, it'd make our lives easier if the three of them killed each other."

"I agree, but we have to keep them alive, at least until we get paid."

51

It was still dark at 5:00 a.m. Tegan Hale followed route 11 to Patten. She saw a diner and decided to stop for breakfast before heading back to Boston. She had finished her meal and was drinking the last of her coffee when Wayne Archer walked in.

He was as surprised to see her as she was to see him. He walked to the booth she occupied and asked, "Want some company?"

Hale dipped her head, indicating that he should sit across from her. He hesitated for a second, and she realized that he had the same aversion to sitting with his back to a door as she. "Don't worry," she said, "I'll watch your back."

Archer slid into the booth and grabbed a menu from the condiment rack to his right. He looked at her plate and saw the remnants of egg yolk and some sort of white sauce. "What did you have?"

"Eggs Benedict."

"Any good?"

"I've had better, but then I've had worse too."

The waitress arrived, and he ordered one of the numerous breakfast specials listed on the menu and coffee, which was included with the meal. When she walked back to place his order, he turned to Hale. "What brings you here?"

"I could ask the same question of you."

"Jiggs and I came here for supper last night. He disappeared while I was in the restroom, and I haven't seen him since."

"Well, I can help you with that. The chances are that Ian Connah has him."

The waitress placed a cup of coffee in front of Archer and dumped several plastic containers of half-and-half beside it. Turning to Hale, she asked, "Anything else for you, Hon?"

"I'm fine," Hale said. When the server left, she turned her attention back to

Archer. "Connah has been holed up in some shit hole northeast of here with the women."

Archer stared intently at the female assassin. "Do you know where Diaz is?"

"I don't know where Diaz is, but I'm pretty sure it was Connah who took out Westin. I wouldn't be surprised to learn that he's got your boss up there right now."

$$\$ \quad \$ \quad \$ \quad \$ \quad \$$$

Connah brought the three competitors into the living room. He knew his job as mediator was not going to be easy. The angry look on each of their faces was all he needed to prove that none of them was a morning person.

"Just what are we supposed to do?" Billie asked. "Kiss, make up, and sing 'Kumbaya' around the campfire?"

Connah replied, "Well, Jiggs could remove that bounty on you two, for starters. Remember, Tegan Hale, is still out there."

Billie and Bobbi turned toward Wark.

"Well," Bobbi asked, "what about it, Jiggs?

Connah smiled at Wark. "Keep in mind that Stone and I are still under her employ. Not coming to some sort of working agreement could result in some severe repercussions."

Billie said nothing for a few moments and then added, "If he doesn't, we could just put a bounty on his head, and our shooters are here."

Wark began to fidget in his seat. "I don't have a way to contact her, or I would."

Connah threw a cell phone at him. "Call Archer. I'll bet he can get the word out. Put it on speaker."

Wark punched a number into the cell, and after a few seconds, Archer answered.

Wark said, "Wayne?"

"Yeah, Jiggs. Where are you?"

"Right now, that doesn't matter. I need a favor."

"Sure, what is it?"

"Have you been in contact with Hale?"

"I just finished eating breakfast with her. She figured that like Westin and Diaz, you were dead, and there was no one to pay the bounty, so she hauled ass."

"Gone?"

"That was the opinion I got."

"Okay," Wark said. "Call around and put out the word that the hit is off. I'm in negotiations with O'Reilly and Spinelli—we're going to resolve things."

"You got it. When are you gonna be done?"

Wark looked at the assembled group. "Head back to Boston. This may take some time, maybe a few days."

Wark closed the call and tossed the phone to Connah. "That good enough?"

"You better hope it is—if anything happens to either of these women, and I think you're behind it, I'm gonna come for you."

"My word is my bond," Wark said. "What about them?"

"You won't have to worry about them—they'll be too busy trying to kill each other to worry about you."

$ $ $ $ $

Hale left Archer at the diner and drove to Interstate 95. She accelerated down the ramp, and barely missed hitting a car. Immediately after she passed it, bright blue lights flashed on and strobed through the predawn darkness.

She pulled over onto the breakdown lane and stopped. She watched the side mirror and saw a Maine State Police officer exit his car, holding a lit flashlight. He shined the light on the truck's license plate, paused for a moment, and then walked back to his cruiser.

Hale muttered under her breath. Chastising herself for being careless.

The cop exited his vehicle and stood near the back of Hale's truck. He stood there for several minutes, and then another police car arrived with its lights flashing. The second cruiser parked in front of her truck, and the driver disembarked. He checked the highway for traffic and then walked toward her. She watched the second cop until he stopped his approach and stood near the left front of the truck, his hand on his still holstered sidearm. Suddenly there was a tapping on her window. She saw cop number one and rolled down the window. Hale smiled at the cop, hoping he'd go easy on a solitary woman.

"Do you know why I stopped you, ma'am?"

"Because I didn't see you and cut you off?"

"That was the main reason."

"Why two of you for a traffic stop?" she asked.

"We can never be too cautious when making a stop in the dark. Not to mention we were on our way to having breakfast together at the diner in Patten."

Hale looked over her shoulder. While distracted, she saw that the second officer had circled around and held a Glock alongside his right leg.

"Do you have any other weapons in this vehicle?" cop number one asked.

Hale's rifle was propped up against the passenger seat in plain sight. She exhaled and nodded.

"Please step out of the vehicle and keep your hands in plain sight while you do."

Hale slid out of the truck. She wondered if there was any way she could talk her way out of this.

The cop standing near the back of the truck said, "Do you want to open the tailgate, please."

Hale walked to the back of the truck, dropped the gate, saw Diaz's body, and said, "Fuck me."

Cop number two shined his flashlight into the covered bed, pointed his pistol at her, and asked, "Anyone you know?"

$ $ $ $ $

Archer passed two state police cars at the end of the ramp to I-95 south. He saw Tegan Hale standing behind the truck she had driven earlier in the strobing blue lights. Her hands were secured behind her back. Several weapons lay on the bed cover, and one of the cops was unloading more from the truck. He slowly passed them and set his cruise control to the speed limit.

PART II

THE HUNT FOR HARRY SANDBERG

52

Connah stood on the deck of his home, staring out at the lake. He heard Don Stone open the sliding door and turned. Stone held two mugs of coffee in his hand. He handed one to Connah and stood beside him.

Connah looked at his partner and said, "This sitting around waiting for word about Sandberg is driving me nuts."

"Ian, have you considered that maybe Sandberg didn't pull this off alone?"

Connah's brow dipped, and he scrutinized his friend. "Yeah, I been thinking about that."

"From the moment you learned that Sandberg had ripped you off, you've had him, and only him, in your sights. How was he able to hide the embezzlement? Someone else, someone with an accounting background, had to know what was happening."

Connah sat deep in thought for several minutes and then said, "I came to that conclusion a couple weeks ago. There's only one other person who could have known, Glenn Ouellette."

"And who is Glenn Ouellette?"

"He is, *was* is a better choice of words, my accountant."

Stone stood up and said, "Maybe we ought to pay your accountant a visit?"

Connah pushed away from the railing and said, "Yeah, maybe it's time that the accountant gave me an accounting of what the fuck he does for his money."

$ $ $ $ $

Stone and Connah stood on the sidewalk in front of the closed office of Glenn Ouellette, CPA. "It's after ten o'clock in the morning," Stone commented. "He should be here."

"C'mon," Connah said. He led Stone across the street to the only restaurant in town that was not a fast-food franchise.

They entered the small diner and sat at the counter. Mary Rousseau, the waitress/owner, walked over and stopped before them. "Morning, Ian, who's your friend?"

"This is Don Stone. Don, meet Mary. She owns this dive."

Rousseau playfully tapped Connah on the head with her pencil. "Don't you be calling this fine establishment a dive, Ian Connah."

Connah laughed.

"You want breakfast or just coffee?" Rousseau asked.

"Coffee is enough for me," Connah answered.

"Me, too," Stone added.

"Have you seen Glenn lately?" Connah asked her.

"Now that you mention it, it's been a while."

"Any idea where he might be?" Connah asked.

"Beats the hell out of me. No one seems to know. He's been gone for a month or more. Come to think of it, we ain't seen much of you in a while either."

"I had some business to take care of down-state," Connah answered. "It ain't like Glenn to just take off without a word."

"Maybe Claire knows where he is." Rousseau turned and poured two mugs of coffee. "You sure you don't want a muffin or something to go with that?"

$ $ $ $ $

Connah turned off the highway and parked in front of a neat set of farm buildings.

"Nice setup," Stone commented.

Connah glanced at the immaculate white farmhouse and the giant red barn. "Yeah, one thing about French-Canadians, they keep up their buildings and cars." He glanced up the road at Claire Tardiff's neighbor's yard, which was full of rusted machines and trash and a barn that was collapsing in on itself. "Then there are others," he left the comment hanging.

An attractive woman in her forties came out of the door and onto the farmer's porch that circumvented two sides of the house. She stopped at the top of the stairs. When Connah exited his truck, she said, "That you, Ian?"

168

"Yeah, how you doing, Claire?"

"Fine, just fine." She stepped aside and said, "Who's your friend?"

Connah introduced Stone, and Tardiff said, "C'mon in, got fresh coffee on the stove." Before she reentered the house, she said, "Ain't seen you in a while. What brings you by?"

"I've been trying to locate Glenn. Nobody seems to have seen him in a while," Connah answered.

The temperature inside the house was cool regardless of the August mid-day heat outside. Connah inhaled a scent that took him back to his early childhood. "Do I smell homemade doughnuts?" Stone asked.

"Set yerselves down," Claire said. "How do you like your coffee?"

"Black," Connah and Stone said in unison.

She placed two mugs on the table and then brought a pot of coffee and filled them. She returned the pot to the stove and then sat across from Connah and said, "Why you lookin' for Glenn?"

"I need some accounting information."

"I ain't seen him in a couple of months or more. He did call, though. I think he was chasin' that useless ex-wife of his."

"Oh? Does she live close?" Connah asked.

"Out in Chicago. The caller ID showed a '630' area code the last time he called. The number should still be in the phone. Let me check."

When Claire left the room, Stone said, "It can't be this easy."

"Don't get your hopes up. The phone used may have been a burner. But then, I'm sure Mensa hasn't been beating on Glenn's door to get him to join."

Claire returned with a slip of paper and handed it to Connah. "That's the number he called from."

Connah glanced at the paper and saw a number and an address. "What's the address?" he asked as he shoved the piece of paper into his shirt pocket.

"That's the address his ex-wife, Gwen, put on the Christmas card she sent me."

53

Naperville, Illinois, is thirty-five miles southwest of Chicago. Forty years ago, it was nothing more than a minor crossroad surrounded by cornfields. However, due to the explosive growth of Chicago's western suburbs, the town has grown, the population has quadrupled, and the cornfields have given way to subdivisions and malls.

They found Gwen Ouellette's last known address on the southwest side of town. They parked three houses away, on the opposite side of the street, and watched the house for any signs of activity.

"You really think he's stupid enough to come here?" Stone asked. "Any idiot would think to come here first."

"Glenn Ouellette's next criminal thought will be his first."

"You don't consider ripping you off a criminal act?"

"I do. However, unless I've completely misread Glenn, I'd bet dollars against donuts that was Sandberg's doing. Glenn has been two steps away from bankruptcy for as long as I've known him. All Harry had to do was dangle some cash in front of his nose. Glenn would have gone after it like a salmon after a smelt."

"We can't sit here all day," Stone said. "This is a pretty upscale neighborhood, and someone is bound to report a couple of men sitting in a strange car."

"You're right. We should move."

Before Connah could put the transmission in drive, a compact car approached and turned into the driveway. Connah watched the Ford Escape park and Glenn Ouellette get out.

"Well," Connah said, "look who's just arrived."

"There is a god," Stone said.

Connah grinned. "Considering what you and I do for a living, I hope that you're wrong. Either that or he's as all-forgiving as the preachers say."

Connah drove forward and turned in behind the Ford.

Ouellette was standing on the front porch when he noticed them turn in. His face was evidence of his initial surprise, immediately followed by a look of fear.

Connah got out of the car and said, "Let's talk, Glenn."

"I-Ian, what brings you here?"

"I'm certain you know damned well what brought me here. Do you want to talk here or inside?"

Ouellette walked off the porch and slowly approached his former client. "Ian, I know what I did was stupid, but I had my reasons."

Connah folded his arms and said, "Enlighten me."

"I was way behind on my maintenance payments—"

"Maintenance? You ripped me off to get something fixed?"

"In an Illinois divorce, there is no alimony. The court will assess a monthly maintenance payment, so the spouse can go to school to learn a trade or get retrained in one... then there were the house payments."

"How much?"

"I only got $500,000. Sandberg took the rest."

"How much was the maintenance and house payoff?"

Ouellette shuffled his feet. "Twenty thou in maintenance and one-hundred-fifty thousand to pay off the house."

Connah approached Ouellette and grasped the back of his neck. "You know what I should do, don't you?"

"Ian, I was desperate... please don't kill me."

"There was a time when I'd have dropped you already. How much is left?"

"Three-hundred-thirty."

"You're going to give me the three-hundred grand. You keep the thirty. In return, I want two thousand a month. At three percent interest, you should pay me off in thirteen years. You're the accountant. Figure it out."

"Thanks, Ian. I don't deserve this."

"You miss one payment, though, and I'll come for you, and there won't be no amicable arrangement. I'll be looking for the money on the first of every month." He turned back to the car, pausing before he got in. "All you had to do was ask, and I'd have helped you out."

"Thanks, man."

"Like I said, two grand due on the first of the month, or either me or someone I send, will come for you. Where's the money?"

"In a checking account."

"In a checking account? I would have expected an accountant to have invested it."

"I figured that, in case I had to run, I needed it to be liquid."

"Where's the bank?"

"Here in town."

"Here's what's going to happen. You and I are gonna drive to that bank in your car. Stoney will follow in ours. You're going to get a cashier check for two hundred and seventy-five thousand and twenty-five grand in cash. All of which you will give to me."

"Sure."

Connah motioned for Stone to back out of the drive and then got into the Ford compact with Ouellette.

Forty-five minutes later, Connah and Stone were driving toward the airport.

"Never known you to be so understanding," Stone said.

"This way, I get some of my money back. I kill him. I get nothing."

Stone chuckled. "I thought he was gonna shit his pants when we pulled in."

Connah grinned. "If I'd stolen half a million from me, I would have."

54

Connah and Stone exited customs at the Guarulhos International Airport in *São Paulo, Brazil.* "This place is friggin' huge!" Stone exclaimed.

"Fourth largest city in the world, based on population. New York isn't even in the top twenty. However, based on area, New York is the largest."

"How in hell are we ever going to find him?"

"Our first stop is to find this…" Connah took a business card from his shirt pocket and referred to the back, "…Eduardo Ferreira."

"Just who might that be?"

"The guy to whom Rojas sent Sandberg. He's some kind of *fixer.*"

"Fixer? Connah, where do you come up with this crap?"

"For a price, he fixes shit. He can get you anything from new identity papers to a ranch in the middle of nowhere." Connah grew pensive. "At the goddamned rate Harry is throwing my money around, there won't be any left when we find him."

They followed a corridor that led them to baggage claim and customs, carrying on a discussion as they walked. "Speaking of that," Stone said, "what do you plan on doing to him when we do catch up with him?"

"I haven't thought much about that."

They arrived at baggage claim and saw a carousel with a monitor showing their flight number. They stood next to the conveyor, waiting for their luggage to appear.

Stone glanced around, ensuring there was nobody within hearing range, and said, "You gonna whack him?"

"I should, but I'm gonna try to think up a way to make him wish I had whacked him. I want something long-term. Killing him is too quick. I want the son of a bitch to suffer. Leave him too broke to get back to the United States—you know, make him have to live the life of a homeless peasant."

Connah pondered for a moment and said, "I guess we'll just have to leave him so fuckin' poor that even if he lives in the world's poorest country, he'll still be a pauper."

"What is the world's poorest country?"

"I think," Connah answered, "it's someplace in Africa."

"And in the Americas?"

"Haiti."

"We taking him there?" Stone asked.

"Nah, I don't care where you are. If you're broke, life sucks."

$ $ $ $ $

The cab dropped Connah and Stone in front of a glass and concrete high-rise. "A lot more impressive than Rojas's office."

"All it means is that Señhor Eduardo Ferreira is a more expensive scumbag."

They entered the building through a revolving door, and Stone stopped. "You feel that?" he asked.

"What?"

"Heat. It's warmer in here than outside. We forgot about the seasons being the opposite down here. It's the middle of winter, and we're dressed for summer."

"If all goes well, we won't be here all that long. Besides, we're so close to the Equator that the seasons don't really change," Connah said.

"What if he's here somewhere? This place is big, and we don't know our way around."

"Let's talk with Ferreira. Our next step depends on what he tells us."

They entered the lobby and found a directory mounted on the wall near the elevators. Stone studied it for a few seconds and said, "Friggin' thing is in Spanish."

"Portuguese," Connah said.

"What?"

"In Brazil, they speak Portuguese, not Spanish, although there isn't much difference."

Connah studied the directory and found what he sought. "Ferreira is on the tenth floor."

They exited the elevator on the desired floor and found suite 1015 with no problem. The signage on the door said: EDUARDO FERREIRA, ADVOGADO. They entered and found themselves in a reception room—Connah guessed it to be twenty feet wide and ten feet in length. There was a desk centered beside a door on the far wall. An attractive young woman sat behind the desk, typing on the keyboard of a computer. She looked up and said something that neither of them could understand.

Connah knew that most Brazilians are bi-lingual and asked in English. "Is Señhor Ferreira available?"

She said in English, "Is he expecting you?"

"I hope not," Stone said.

Connah saw her questioning look and gave Stone a look that said, *Ease up on the comedy stuff.*

"No," Connah said, "we have only now arrived in São Paulo."

"What is the nature of your business?"

"It's a personal matter that I would like to keep confidential."

Her brows went up, and he knew she took his comment as an indication that he did not trust her and had affronted her professionalism. She picked up the phone, pressed a single digit, and spoke in rapid Portuguese. After a few seconds, she said, "Señhor Ferreira is busy, but if you can wait a few minutes, he may have some time to meet with you."

Connah and Stone took seats in the row of chairs in the far corner of the room. A small table that was covered with magazines sat between them. Stone moved the periodicals around and then sat back. "Not a single copy of *Field and Stream* or *Outdoor Life*."

"Makes no matter," Connah said, "they would most likely be in Portuguese, and you can't read it."

"No, but I could look at the pictures."

The door beside the receptionist desk opened, and a man who could have been a double for Cesar Romero entered the room. He nodded at Connah and Stone and said, "Señhor Connah?"

"Yes. Señhor Ferreira, I presume."

"*Sim*, please come in."

He led them into an opulent office with a breathtaking view of São Paulo's skyline. Ferreira noticed Connah studying the view through his window, and he said, "Magnificent is it not?"

"Yes, this is my first visit to Brazil. I had no idea that São Paulo was this impressive."

"That is a sentiment shared with most of your countrymen when they visit for the first time. For some reason, Americans find it hard to accept the fact that your New York and Los Angeles are smaller." He motioned to a couple of leather easy-chairs. "Please be seated."

When they were settled, Ferreira pressed a button on the side of his desk, and the receptionist appeared. "Lara," Ferreira said, "bring us refreshments, please." He turned to Connah and Stone. "You wish something?"

"Coffee would be nice… black," Connah replied

"The same," Stone added.

Without saying a word, Lara left the room.

"Now," Ferreira said, "what is it you Americans say? Ah, yes, how may I help you?"

"A couple of months ago, it was brought to my attention that my financial adviser embezzled—stole if you wish—all of my cash reserves."

The door opened, and Lara reentered the room carrying a tray with three sets of cups and saucers, spoons, and a pot of coffee. She placed it on the small table against the wall to the left of Ferreira's desk and left the room.

"While I find this very interesting, I fail to see how it involves me." Ferreira poured three cups of coffee and handed one each to Connah and Stone.

"We followed this man, Harry Sandberg, also known as Harry Sanders, from Boston to Puerto Rico. He hired a man named Felipe Rojas—a man of dubious reputation," Connah explained.

"I still fail to see why I should be involved."

"I had a talk with Señhor Rojas, and he told me that he'd referred Sandberg to you."

"If this Señhor Sandberg were to be a client of mine, I could not tell you of it."

"Do you have any idea of who Stone and I are?"

"No."

Connah reached over and took a message pad from Ferreira's desk. He wrote a phone number on it and placed it in front of the lawyer. "Call that number and ask for Rodolfo Barros Ribeiro. He'll go over my resume for you. We'll wait in your office."

Connah stood up, and he and Stone placed their coffee cups on Ferreira's desk. They turned to the door and stopped short when Ferreira asked, "Just what is it that you do?"

"We're hitmen," Connah said. "'Assassin' in your language, check us out."

$ $ $ $ $

When Connah and Stone returned to Ferreira's office, the receptionist ushered them directly into the inner office.

"I assume you have checked our references?"

"Señhor Ribeiro speaks well of you."

"We've done a couple of jobs for him. He is also a close friend."

"It will take me some time to locate this man."

"So, you do know him?" Connah said.

Ferreira shrugged his shoulders. "I, too, have a reputation to protect. What will you do to this Sandberg or Sanders if you find him?"

"You're better off not knowing the details. I want as much of my money back as possible. The rest will be up to Sandberg."

"You will not kill him?"

"It's hard to get money from a corpse," Connah answered.

"Please leave the address of your hotel with my receptionist. When I know something, I will send someone to you."

"How will we know this person is from you?"

"He will say: My Uncle Eduardo sent me."

55

Connah and Stone were a quarter way through a bottle of scotch whiskey when someone knocked on their door. "I got it," Connah said.

When he opened the door, Connah saw a tall, slender man who appeared to be in his late twenties. He wore a three-piece suit, and his shoes were shined to a high gloss. He smiled, and Connah wondered if he was a fan of 1930 and '40s movies, which would explain the thin mustache that rested on his top lip.

The young man thrust his hand toward Connah and said, "I am Diego López Sousa, my Uncle Eduardo sent me."

Connah stepped aside. "Come in."

The Brazilian walked into the room and said, "How is it you say *boa noite*? Ah, yes, good evening." His English, though heavily accented, was understandable.

"Good evening to you," Connah replied. "I'm Ian Connah, and this is my partner, Don Stone. Would you care for a drink?"

Sousa saw the bottle of scotch whiskey and said, "*Sim* (yes), no ice, please."

Stone took a glass from the stand that held the room's coffee maker and ice bucket, poured a healthy three fingers into it, and handed it to Sousa.

Sousa sipped from the glass and nodded with satisfaction. "*Obrigado...* thank you. Before you leave my country, you must try *caipirinha*. Brazil's national cocktail is made with *cachaça*, a hard liquor made from sugarcane, sugar, and lime."

"Sounds sweeter than my girlfriend's ass," Stone said. "Personally, I don't trust booze that doesn't taste like booze."

Sousa got down to business. "My uncle told me that you are looking for an American."

"Yes, he's most likely using a different name. He's a fat bastard and always sweaty," Connah said.

"A man who fits that description was here. He left last month."

"Do you have any idea where he went?" Connah asked.

"Manaus, if he left there, I have no information." Sousa took another sip of the whiskey.

"How far is Manaus?" Stone asked.

"By plane, four hours, by car or bus, fifty-four hours."

"Where the hell is this place?" Stone asked.

"North, Amazonas State."

"The Amazon Jungle?" Connah asked.

"Yes, please remember that Brazil is larger than your United States and the Amazon alone is larger than India."

"How far is it?" Stone asked.

"By air, 3,885 kilometers or 2,400 of your miles. By bus, 4,000 kilometers or 2,529 miles."

"The same distance as Boston to Los Angeles," Connah said.

"I hope," Stone commented, "you aren't even considering the bus."

"What's the matter? You afraid of spending four or five days on a bus?"

"Possibly more," Sousa said. "Once you leave the main cities, the roads are not dependable and are often flooded or washed out."

"Book us two seats to Manaus by plane," Connah said.

"I hope this isn't a puddle-jumper plane," Stone said.

Sousa laughed. "It will be an airliner. Manaus has a population of two and a half million. It is a modern city, originally a major source of rubber. There are many old plantations with their mansions still inhabitable."

"Can you arrange a guide for us?"

"My wife's brother, Otávio Rodrigues Correia, is a guide. He also owns a four-wheel-drive Range Rover. I will call and see if he is available for hire."

$ $ $ $ $

Much to Stone's relief, the flight from *São Paulo* was uneventful, and the airport in Manaus was modern. They had no checked baggage and walked outside of the Arrivals Terminal. A tan Range Rover stood beside the curb, and a short, lean man wearing tan cargo pants and a matching short sleeve shirt waved to get their attention and then held up a sign that said CONNAH. "I think our ride's here," Connah said.

The little man trotted toward them. He smiled a broad smile that showed he was in dire need of some dental treatment. "Señhores Connah and Stone, I am Otávio Rodrigues Correia, the brother-in-law of Diego López Sousa." He handed each of them a business card, then reached for the Americans' carry-on luggage and led them to the Range Rover.

The ride into town astonished Connah and Stone. Manaus was as modern as any mid-size city in the United States; it even had a skyline. Correia gave them a tour guide version of the city's history as he drove. "Manaus was first settled in 1669 as The Fort of São José do Rio Negro. It was not until 1832 that the fort became a town with the name of Manaus. In 1848 it became a city with the name Cidade da Barra do Rio Negro, which is Portuguese for 'city of the margins of the Black River'."

Connah half-listened to Correia's lecture and stared out the window. When they passed a colossal stadium, he asked what it was.

Correia said, "That is Arena da Amazônia, where they played some games in the 2014 World Cup."

The Range Rover turned off the boulevard and stopped before a modern high-rise building. "This is the Caesar Business Manaus, the highest-rated hotel in the city. I will pick you up here at 8 o'clock in the morning. Tonight, I must see someone who can find your Señhor Sandberg or Sanders. If you need me, my *telefone* number is on the card I gave you."

"We'll meet you here tomorrow morning."

$ $ $ $ $

After leaving his clients at the hotel, Otávio Rodrigues Correia drove to the city's southern boundary with the Rio Negro. He parked in front of an unscrupulous-looking building with a neon sign of a curved anaconda snake. Below the snake, the words "CLUBE SUCURI" flashed on and off.

He entered the club, taking care to give a wide berth to the glass tank in which an anaconda stared out at him. He knew the serpent was ten feet long and his cousin's pet. It was wrapped around a capybara, the largest living rodent and a cousin to the guinea pig. The snake's muscles rippled as it crushed the life out of its meal. He weaved his way through the tables, walking toward the back corner. Two tables were pushed together, and his cousin, Fábio Correia Goncalves, sat with a young woman on his lap.

Goncalves spotted his cousin as he crossed the area, where the nightly sex shows were performed. He yelled loud enough to be heard over the cacophony of the late afternoon customers shouting to be heard over the bellowing jukebox. "Otávio! Come and drink with me, cousin." He pushed the woman off his lap, and she landed on her butt. She leaped to her feet, gave Goncalves an angry look, spun around, and began patrolling the room for potential customers.

Correia made his way to the table and sat beside his cousin. No sooner was he settled into his seat when a young woman in a skimpy skirt appeared at the table.

"*Caipirinha* for my cousin and for me," Goncalves shouted.

The woman did a one-hundred-eighty degree turn and trotted to the bar.

"What brings you to my club, Otávio?"

Goncalves was the head of one of the largest criminal enterprises in Manaus. It was affiliated with the PCC (*Primeiro Commando da Capital*), Brazil's most prominent criminal organization. He controlled prostitution in four of the city's seven regions, loan sharking in three, and ran a drug network that took in cash from all seven. He carried on like an overweight buffoon but was a ruthless gang lord. People who missed a loan payment or intruded on his territory were often discovered floating in the Rio Negro or the Rio Solimões. He was not a man to be trifled with.

"I have a contract with two men from the north. They are looking for a man—one who has stolen a lot of money from them. He calls himself Sandberg or possibly Sanders. He is a fat man who sweats a lot and has perhaps been in this area only a month. There is reason to believe he intends to settle here."

"What is in it for us, cousin?"

"The Americans are *assassinos*. I think it may not be a bad thing for them to owe you a favor."

Goncalves slapped his cousin on the back. "You are always looking for an angle. What is in this for you?"

"Connah, the leader, had a large amount stolen, around three million U.S. dollars. I think it's only fair that we get a quarter share."

Goncalves's brow furrowed as he did the math in his head. "That would be seven-hundred-fifty-thousand U.S. dollars. At the current rate of exchange…" He accessed the calculator on his cellular phone and keyed in the numbers. "…Almost two-and-a-half-million *reais*."

Correia touched his glass to his cousin's. "Not bad for a week's work, eh?"

56

Correia did the tour guide thing for two days with Connah and Stone. They were having a late lunch when Correia's phone rang. He spoke Portuguese to the caller for several moments and then shut off his phone. "That was my cousin, Fábio. He has some information for us."

"Has he found Sandberg?"

"Fábio would not have called if he didn't learn something of interest. He will meet us at his club in two hours."

$ $ $ $ $

Correia took so many turns that Connah and Stone were thoroughly lost. The vast expanse of the Rio Negro could be seen behind the unimposing building in front of which they stopped. Connah saw the twisted snake and 'CLUBE SUCURI' and asked what *sucuri* meant.

"This is my cousin Fábio's place, the Club Anaconda."

"What kind of place is it?" Stone asked.

"Adult entertainment, many people work in the sex industry. In Brazil, prostitution is legal. There are no laws forbidding adults of age eighteen and older from being professional sex workers. Still, it is illegal to operate a brothel or employ sex workers in any other way."

"I don't understand," Connah said.

"It is legal for a man or woman to be a *puta*, but illegal for one to be a *cafetão*, what you call a pimp in *Inglês*."

"So, the hookers are legal, but someone who takes advantage of them is not?"

"*Sim.*"

"Your cousin is a pimp?" Stone inquired.

"No, his girls are all contractors. However," Correia replied, "it is best not to ask Fábio about his business dealings. I would think that the same is true of your profession."

Connah grinned. "That's no shit."

They entered the club, and Stone stopped, staring at the left wall, which was a huge glass tank. Coiled in the center of the enormous aquarium was the most giant snake he'd ever seen. Its head lay on the top coil, and its cold eyes seemed to be staring at him. Stone looked at Connah. "You see the size of that friggin' thing?"

"It is a *sucuri*, anaconda in *Inglês*," Correia said, "That is a small one about three meters long. Lara is a Tupi-Guarani name, which means lady of the waters, and is a green anaconda. They grow to be the largest."

As they walked away from the serpent's vivarium, Stone commented, "No way in hell do I ever want to meet one of them in the wild. How big do they get?"

"Using your measurements, the heaviest and longest anaconda ever recorded weighed 500 pounds and measured a monster 27.7 feet in length, with a diameter of 44 inches," Correia answered.

"Do they always look at you like you're on the menu?"

"That is because you are." Correia laughed and then led them across the empty performance area.

As they neared the back corner of the room, Connah saw two tables pushed together. A stocky man with a full mustache sat with an attractive younger woman on each side of him. Connah noticed that his feet barely touched the floor beneath the table. If the man's reputation for ruthlessness was not enough, his thick, black mustache made Fábio Correia Goncalves look like Josef Stalin. The resemblance was close enough that Goncalves could star in the title role if a movie were to be made based upon Stalin's life.

Correia stopped in front of the table and said, "Señhor Fábio Correia Goncalves, I am pleased to present Señhores Connah and Stone. Señhores Connah and Stone, Señhor Fábio Correia Goncalves."

"Please, gentlemen, take a seat," Goncalves said in accented English.

When everyone was seated, and drinks had been ordered, Goncalves asked, "How has my cousin been treating you?"

"Excellent, he has been an exceptional tour guide."

"That is good. Manaus has many fine places to see. Has he taken you to see our theater, the Teatro Amazonas, and the Palácio Rio Negros?"

"Yes," Connah said, "he has taken us everywhere."

"That is good. Now to business. Otávio has told me you seek one of your countrymen, a fat pig who is called Sandberg or possibly Sanders."

"That is correct, *señhor*. This man has something of mine."

"I have also heard this."

"*Señhor?*" Connah leaned forward and cast a stern look at the Brazilians. "How did you hear about our quest?"

"Come, Señhor Connah. Did you think that your quest to regain the three million American dollars that this pig stole from you would remain a secret?"

Connah sat back and waited for what was coming next, knowing he was about to be charged through the nose for any service Correia and Goncalves provided.

"The man you seek is not in Manaus. He was, but only for a short time. I have, however, learned where he has gone. He is west of Tefé."

"Where is Tefé?" Connah asked.

"On the Rio Solimões, west of Manaus, 525 kilometers if you fly, 595 by the river, about 375 of your miles," Correia added.

Goncalves said, "We have also learned that the first thing he did was hire many local *Indiano.* They are training them to use modern weapons."

"Mercenaries?" Connah asked.

"*Sim*," Goncalves added, "he has also bought a rubber plantation with a large fortified house."

"If we fly, is there a place where we can purchase weapons?" Stone asked.

"If you fly, your quarry will know you are there ten minutes after you land," Goncalves said. "Your best bet is the river. Boats travel the Rio Solimões all the time. I can get you any weapons you need."

"The Rio Solimões?" Connah asked.

"The upper Amazon River. I have a boat," Correia said. "It will take about *três dias*, three days, or maybe more, depending on weather, to reach Tefé. Then we must continue on. I don't know how long it will take to locate this *plantação de borracha*, a rubber plantation. You can use the time for planning."

"What will it cost?" Connah asked.

"If you are successful, we ask twenty-five percent of whatever you recover. In return, we will provide weapons, supplies, and transportation."

"How big a boat?" Stone asked. "I ain't spending six or more days in no dugout."

"My boat is a ten-meter fishing boat. I have sleeping quarters for six. I will throw in three of my friends who have certain skills you might need."

"Such as?" Connah said.

"Tracking, shooting, and, if needed, explosives."

Connah turned to Stone. "What do you think, Don?"

"Don't look at me. You're the one footing the bill."

Connah addressed Goncalves. "All right, you got a deal."

57

The rainforest pressed against the shores of the brown water as the *Princesa de Amazonas* struggled to make its way upstream. Connah stood on the stern and watched the propeller churn the water into a frothy trail. He wiped the sweat from his brow and began to have second thoughts about choosing to take the river to Tefé.

Stone came out of the boat's cabin carrying two frosty bottles of Cervejaria Wäls, a popular Brazilian beer. He handed one to Connah and took a pack of cigarettes from his shirt pocket.

"I thought you gave those up."

"I did, but when I found out that they only cost three *reais*, seventy-five centavos, I had to buy some."

Connah looked at the pack of Marlboro Red that Stone held. "Marlboro? They sell American cigarettes for a buck-twenty?"

"Actually, it's only sixty-seven cents, U.S."

"Either way, that's cheap for American cigarettes."

"Well, kinda, sorta," Stone said. He handed the pack to Connah. "See for yourself."

Connah inspected the box and saw 'PRODUTO DE PARAGUAI' printed on it. "I think this says 'product of Paraguay'? How do they taste?"

"I can't tell the difference." Stone leaned his arms on the railing that surrounded the deck. "Hotter than hell, ain't it? I don't think I ever been in heat and humidity like this."

"You better change your ways then. It's pretty hot in Hell too."

A sudden growling sound startled Connah. "That must be one big cat."

"Not cat," one of the men Correia had brought along said, "Howler monkey."

Correia appeared in the door to the cabin in time to hear Connah say, "A monkey sounds like that?"

"The howler monkey is thought to be the loudest animal on Earth," Correia said. "Their howl can be heard as far away as five kilometers."

"Damn," Connah said.

"You guys got all sorts of weird shit," Stone said. They broke out of a densely foliated part of the river, and Stone pointed at a pasture surrounded by a tall wire cyclone fence. "That to keep the cattle out of the river where piranhas can get them?"

"The Amazon is home to twenty varieties of piranha. Them eating cattle and people is a myth. They mostly feed on animals that are already dead. I don't think I've ever heard of them swarming and devouring a human."

"Well, I ain't plannin' on goin' in the water, so I won't be the first."

"The fence is more for keeping the cattle from wandering into the rainforest where predators, such as jaguars, will get them."

The growling howl of the monkey stopped, and they could once again hear the calls of tropical birds.

"We are making good time," Correia said. "At this rate, we should arrive in Tefé late this afternoon. Then we follow the river until we find a place to spend the night. Tomorrow we find your target."

"Why not spend the night ashore in Tefé?" Connah asked.

"Tefé is a river town, and the people there pay close attention to visitors, especially non-Brazilian visitors. You will stand out, and within an hour of our arrival, word of the *Ianque*, Yankee, visitors will have traveled for miles up and down the river."

"What's the plan, boss?" Stone asked Connah.

"We spend the night on the boat and recon the layout from the river. We'll know more once we see the place."

$ $ $ $ $

The sun dipped below the trees, and Connah enjoyed the sudden drop in temperature. Finally, he thought, relief from the blazing sun. Then the mosquitoes and other flying predators arrived. In a short time, they drove him inside the cabin. Correia handed him a local insect repellent and said, "Put this on. You won't be able to recover your money if you're down with Malaria or Yellow Fever. Then there are several types of encephalitis, of which, at least one is known to be 100% fatal."

Connah removed the cap from the repellent and smelled it. "Christ, that stuff is foul. What's it made from, animal guts or something?"

Correia laughed. "I have never had the nerve to ask the ingredients. All I know is that it works."

"How can anyone live in this place? There's more shit here that can kill you than there was in Al Capone's Chicago."

"It is like your winter. I would die in the cold and snow, but you grew up in it and know how to survive. It's like that for us. We know the dangers and how to either avoid or survive them."

Connah looked at the repellent and said, "You got enough of this stuff for me to take a bath in it?"

$ $ $ $ $

It was twilight when Connah got his first look at the rubber plantation—it was immense. Connah stood inside the boat's cabin, watching row after row of perfectly aligned pará rubber trees. Occasionally, he saw lights bobbing among the trees, and he asked Correia what they were.

The captain gave him a brief lesson in harvesting latex. "Each night, a rubber tapper removes a thin layer of bark along a downward half spiral on the tree trunk. If done carefully and with skill, this tapping panel will yield latex for up to five hours. Then the opposite side will be tapped, allowing the first side to heal over. The spiral allows the latex to run down to a collecting cup. The work is done at night or in the early morning before the day's temperature rises, so the latex will drip longer before coagulating and sealing the cut."

Connah watched the lights for several minutes and then turned and watched Correia navigate the river, paying intense attention to the river illuminated by the boat's roof-mounted spotlights. "Are you familiar with this location?" he asked.

"It has been some time since I was up here, but I am familiar with some of the history of this particular plantation. It was built in the 1840s by Julian Fernandes Santos. The Santos family became very, very wealthy during the rubber boom years. Before the late nineteenth century, when the British took seedlings to their colonies in Asia, South America was the only source of rubber. Today, we produce less than several Southeast Asian countries."

"Where is the main house located?"

"Twenty maybe thirty kilometers upstream," Correia replied.

"Twenty or thirty kilometers, how big is the plantation?"

"Ten million square meters."

"That large?" Connah asked.

"It is one of the smaller plantations."

Connah took out the insect repellent that he'd been given the previous night and covered his exposed skin with a liberal amount. "I'm going out on deck for a while."

"Be careful. Insects are not the only thing you should be wary of. There are the bats."

"Bats? They don't usually bother humans."

"There are three vampire bat species, the common vampire bat, the hairy-legged vampire bat, and the white-winged vampire bat. There have been reports of the white-winged bats feeding on humans."

"You're shitting me."

"I wish I was," Correia answered. "Remember, we are deep into the Amazon Basin rainforest, and there are many exotic—and potentially dangerous—species of animals. As for the vampire bats, there is little danger of them sucking enough blood to kill you, but they do carry hantavirus, which can be fatal to humans."

"Jesus, Otávio, is there anything in this jungle that can't kill you?"

"We haven't even discussed the deadliest inhabitant of all."

"Which is?" Connah asked.

"Man."

Connah left the cabin, walked to the stern, and looked at the sky. Even though the sun was down, the sky was still brighter than the ground. He wasn't sure if he saw a bat flying overhead or if his discussion with Correia had him spooked. He thought, Christ, it isn't enough that Sandberg is arming and training local Indians. There are snakes, spiders, bats, scorpions, and poisonous frogs. It almost made him empathize with how Harvey Westin felt in the Maine woods.

$ $ $ $ $

They rounded a bend in the river, and in the sky above the forest, he noticed an area of light. Connah saw the plantation house's location for the first time.

He saw movement from the corner of his eye and turned to see Don Stone resting against the rail.

"So," Stone said, "we finally arrive. What now?"

"There's no way we're going to wander around in that bush in the dark. We'll wait for Correia to find an eddy where he can moor for the night, and then we'll sit down with him and come up with a plan of attack."

They watched the lighted area of sky pass to their rear and then disappear as they traveled upriver.

58

At six a.m., Connah stood on the deck, drinking his morning coffee and studying the imposing flora of the rainforest. He heard the cabin door open, and he looked over his shoulder. Don Stone held a mug of coffee in one hand and lit the cigarette suspended from his lips with the other.

Stone looked at Connah and said, "I don't know how you feel, but I, for one, am not looking forward to a day in that dense bush. Before this day is half over, we'll be giving everything we have for a breeze."

The morning quiet was broken by the howl of a howler monkey. "Every time I hear that, the hair on my neck stands up," Connah said.

"I wonder how big they get? They sound as if they're the size of a gorilla."

Correia joined them on the forecastle. "I see the howlers are serenading us. They can be anywhere from four to six feet long, from nose to tail. In fact, half their length is tail."

"If that's a serenade, I don't want to hear him when he's pissed off."

"When do we go in?" Stone asked.

"Any time you want," Correia answered. "Take as much water as you can carry. As much as you may be tempted, do *not* drink the water in the streams. There are parasites in them that you can't see and to which your body has no resistance. If you're shitting and puking your guts out, you won't get anywhere."

Connah listened to the Brazilian and asked, "Is the bush inland as dense as it is along the river?"

"No, once you get inland a bit, the canopy starves everything below it of sunlight. Most of what you will encounter is deadfall and mosses, plants that thrive on little sun and water. The canopy here is as dense as any roof made by man."

Connah nodded to Stone. "Let's saddle up. We got some humping to do."

"Will you be needing any of my people?" Correia asked.

"I don't think so," Connah answered. "I believe that Stone and I can get closer if we're alone."

"That is your choice. Be careful. We may never find you if you get lost." Correia pointed at Connah's feet. "You should…" He made a motion as if he was tucking the cuffs of his trousers. "…I don't know what you call it, but in Portuguese, it is *dobrar*. It means to wrap your trouser bottoms around your legs so that leeches and other insects can't get on your legs."

"Ahh, we call it 'blousing' the trouser legs."

"*Sim*, leeches can live on land in the forest, then there are the *carrapatos*. I believe you call them ticks."

"Now ain't that wonderful," Stone commented.

The Americans raised the legs of their jungle pants to the top of their boots. They tightened the drawstrings to snug the cuffs against their legs.

"We'll follow the river," Connah said. "That'll keep us on course."

One of Correia's crew sat in a small dugout and held the small boat steady with one hand while Connah and Stone climbed over the side and sat in front.

"*Vá com Deus*," Correia said.

$ $ $ $ $

Veterans of the wars in Iraq and Afghanistan, neither Connah nor Stone had ever been in a rainforest. The sudden transition from the blazing heat and glare of the sun to the stifling heat, humidity, and dim light of the jungle startled them. The air was still, and, in a short time, sweat soaked their clothes, flowing from their heads and down their faces. They wrapped strips of camouflaged cloth around their foreheads to absorb the perspiration before it entered their eyes, stinging them. Ninety percent of the brilliant, tropical sun was blocked by the canopy above, leaving the interior a world that lived in perpetual twilight. The thing that impressed them the most, however, was the terrain. Unlike how the Tarzan movies of their youth depicted the rainforest, the jungle floor was not an impenetrable wall of vines, giant ferns, and overgrown vegetation. The result of the low-level light that filtered through the dense canopy was a world comprised of shadow and decay. Nevertheless, movement would not be easy. The forest floor was littered with rotting tree trunks and branches coated with yellow mold and white mushrooms.

Stone stood transfixed. "Can you imagine," he said to Connah, "fighting a guerrilla war in this shit?"

"It's been done for years," Connah replied. "In the Philippines and islands in World War II and again in Vietnam."

"Give me the desert any day. How in hell can you see the enemy in this?"

Connah studied the terrain. Beneath his boots, a slick mulch of decayed leaves threatened footing. Buttress roots supported the emergent trees and were spread under the carpet of leaves, waiting to break the ankle of any careless walker. The ground itself supported scant vegetation. The men were surrounded by a festoon of fan-tailed ferns, thorny bromeliads, graceful orchids, and slender palms, around which rope-like vines called lianas were draped.

Then there were the insects, flies, mosquitoes, and leeches. Connah recalled Correia's warning about leeches living out of water in the moist air. He also knew that one could not ignore the presence of predators such as snakes (both venomous and constrictors), vampire bats, and jaguars.

Connah recalled one of Shakespeare's sonnets: *How do I love thee? Let me count the ways.* He altered the sonnet to fit their current situation: *How can I kill thee? Let me count the ways...*

$ $ $ $ $

Connah thought about Stone's earlier comment, something about giving everything he had for a minute of breeze. Despite the lack of direct sunlight, the temperature was triple digits, and the humidity was oppressive. Connah's body was chafed raw from constant contact with clothes soaked through with perspiration, and the slightest movement brought pain and discomfort.

They stopped and squatted in the roots of a kapok tree, and Connah drank water from his canteen. Stone's face was flushed, and he looked as if he was suffering from heat exhaustion. Connah wondered if he looked as exhausted as Stone. "How you holding up?" he asked.

Stone lit a cigarette and shrugged. The smoke from his Marlboro hovered around his head. "Not even enough breeze to blow the smoke away," he said.

"You're getting hooked on those things, Don. Is getting your ass blown up worth it for a sixty-eight-cent pack of cigarettes? All it would take is for someone to see the smoke, smell it on you, or for you to cough at the wrong second."

Stone removed the cigarette from his mouth, looked at it, and ground it out on a rock. "Nah, no way." He took the pack out of his shirt pocket and threw it into the rainforest. "You know, Ian, I never really understood why I started smoking in the first place."

"Probably like the rest of us who started as teenagers. We were rebelling. We did it despite what we were told. Maybe, because we were told not to start." Connah rested the bolt action .308 caliber, Remington 700 rifle across his thighs. "It's amazing how a nine-pound rifle gets heavier when you carry it all day." Fábio Goncalves had equipped them with a Remington rifle and a nine-millimeter pistol, as well as canteens and some gear. The drug-runner explained that experience had taught him what they needed to travel through the rainforest.

"Tell me about it," Stone replied.

They stood and adjusted their gear to continue their trek. Stone wiped the sweat from his brow. "Give me the 'Stan any day."

"This terrain sure gives me an appreciation for the guys like my grandfather. He was on Guadalcanal and lived in this for months without a break." The mere mention of the tropical heat and humidity seemed to escalate it, and they felt their fatigue even more.

Stone asked, "How much farther do you think it is to the plantation compound?"

"It can't be very far." He pointed to the east. "Maybe a kilometer, two at the most."

$ $ $ $ $

Harry Sandberg had doubts about his decision to come to this pestilent-infested country. The only good thing he had to say about it was that there was no way in hell Ian Connah would find him here.

Sandberg flicked ash from his cigar into an ashtray and realized his clothing was saturated with perspiration. Questioning whether or not the air conditioning was operating, he checked the thermostat.

He wondered how anyone could live here before the invention of solar panels. There was no way he could power this plantation with generators. He would need a fleet of boats hauling gas tanks down the river to Tefé to keep them in fuel.

Sandberg walked out of the living room and entered his office. He picked up a two-way radio and spoke into it: "Miguel, come to the house."

Sandberg's security chief, Miguel Rodrigues Oliveiras walked into the office. "Yes, *señhor*?"

"Miguel, get someone to look at the air conditioning. It's hotter than hell in here."

"*Sim, señhor. Señhor,* several rubber harvesters reported seeing a boat on the river. They believe that it was headed this way."

"What is so important about this boat? Many boats go upriver."

"This one was going very slowly, and one of the workers said there was an American who seemed to be studying the area."

Sandberg's heart skipped a couple beats. "An American? Did they get a good look at him?"

"No, *señhor*, but they heard him speak. His accent was enough for them to think he was American. Do you want me to put the security guards on high alert?"

"Yes, do that."

"Very well, *señhor*. I will have the maintenance people check the air conditioning."

"And, tell Araujo I want the plane ready to leave at any moment. I may have to go to Manaus in a hurry."

Sandberg absentmindedly flipped his fingers at Oliveiras, dismissing him. He would have been even more upset if he could have read his security chief's mind. As Oliveiras walked out, he thought: There is nothing wrong with the air conditioning that losing fifty kilos wouldn't fix, you fat pig.

Sandberg opened the top drawer of his desk and took out a white paper packet, a mirror, and a razor blade. He unfolded the paper, rolled the quarter gram of cocaine onto the mirror, and processed it with the razor blade. Once the coke was finely chopped, Sandberg used the edge to align the dope into five straight rows. He took several Brazilian *reais* notes from his wallet, returned all but one, which he rolled into a tube, and snorted all five lines.

Despite minimizing the boat's presence to Oliveiras, he could not get it out of his mind. Had Connah located him? If he had found Rojas, it was entirely possible. If Sandberg had learned anything over the past few months, it was that you cannot trust anyone—no matter how much you paid them for their loyalty.

His heart rate increased, and he hoped that the speed used to cut the coca wouldn't give him a heart attack. He was under enough stress and strain as it was. He took a .32 semiautomatic pistol from the top right-hand drawer and checked to ensure it was loaded. Rather than return the weapon to the drawer, he slipped it into his pocket.

$ $ $ $ $

Connah squatted in the branches of a giant kapok tree and peered through the leaves, studying the wall that surrounded the plantation house. Outside the walls, the area had been cleared of trees for at least 100 meters. Connah quickly determined that this compound had been built with invaders in mind. A brief landscape survey convinced Connah that it would have to be a night op if they wanted to scale the wall and enter the house. He descended to where Stone was concealed in a coppice of dense bushes.

Stone said, "Ain't gonna be easy, is it?"

"Never is." Connah ignored the flies that were dive-bombing them and pulling away without biting. It was as if Correia's insect repellent had constructed an invisible wall around them. "We need to expand our recon. I'll circle the perimeter going left. You go right."

Stone stared at the lighted area. "You think they got dogs?"

"I don't know. Inside the walls, it's a definite possibility. I'm more concerned with the cameras and lookout posts on the walls. They may have motion detectors too. Seems to me that a dog would always be setting off alarms."

"Well," Stone replied, "that'd also be the case outside what with jaguars, and however many other animals must prowl around here. But, if a friggin' Great Dane takes my leg off, I'll remember what you said."

"You know," Connah said, "you've become cranky since you quit smoking."

Stone stared at the wide-open expanse surrounding the plantation house, then nodded once. "Well," he said, "this ain't gettin' it done." He gave Connah a thumbs up and disappeared into the early evening gloom.

Connah gave Stone five minutes and then headed in the opposite direction. The landscape was tall tropical grass, small brush, and wet boggy soil. As he moved through the rainforest, he watched the jungle floor closely. He paid close attention to the ground, alert for any of the various predators that stalked the jungle floor at night. There were deadly mammals and snakes and deadly arachnids like the Brazilian Wandering Spider, known to be one of the most venomous on Earth and sundry nocturnal hunters.

When Connah reached the first corner of the perimeter wall, the sun had dropped below the trees, and a pre-darkness gloom settled on the jungle. He took a few seconds to study the wall. Like the house, it was composed of smooth stucco. Atop the wall, glass shards had been embedded in the concrete. Razor wire was coiled above that. There was little chance that he and Stone would enter the compound by scaling the wall.

He continued creeping along the rampart. Suddenly, high-intensity spotlights turned on with the loud *clack* of electrical switches actuating. The sudden brilliance caused Connah to freeze in place and look around. He heard the howling and growling of dogs; it was impossible to know definitively how large they were—but, of one thing he was sure, they sounded big. He wondered if Stone had heard the raucous barks and growls and smiled.

The voices of several men speaking Portuguese were muffled but discernible. Connahs' knowledge of the Portuguese language was rudimentary, barely good enough to get his face slapped in a bar. However, years of experience led him to believe that they were responding to the dogs and the spotlights coming on. Connah ignored caution and darted across the open area toward the rainforest. As he reached the relative safety of the darkness, the loud SNAP of a bullet passing over his head, followed quickly by a rifle's boom, sent him diving to the jungle floor.

He heard more gunshots which he believed came from the opposite side of the grounds, and hoped that Stone was all right. So much for the element of surprise, he thought. Sandberg turned out to be smarter than Connah had previously given him credit for.

He suddenly thought of the night hunting spider and rose to his feet. Exercising great caution, he crept forward toward the planned rendezvous with Stone.

59

Harry Sandberg watched the monitors installed in the small security office near the manse's front. An intruder ran toward the rainforest, and he studied the form carefully, trying to identify him. When he zoomed in on his face, the features became blurred. Still, his heart skipped—it had to be Connah! His first thought was: How in the hell did he find me so quickly?

He walked out of the office and saw Miguel Rodrigues Oliveiras standing by the door. "I want you to take some of the men and find and kill the intruder—be careful, Miguel. If it's who I think it is, he's a very competent assassin."

"*Sim, senhor.*"

"I must emphasize, take no chances with this man. He's a highly-skilled, professional mercenary and assassin-for-hire."

$ $ $ $ $

Connah heard Stone before he saw him. Rather than approach his partner and risk being mistaken for an enemy, he stayed where he was. When Stone passed by his position, Connah whispered, "Stoney, over here."

Stone reached his side and said, "Are you okay?"

"Yeah, how about you?"

"Surprised the shit out of me when those lights came on. I was expecting some sort of lighting, but that place lit up like Fenway Park during a night game."

"What did you find out?" Connah asked.

"Only one thing of importance—Sandberg has an airplane."

"Did you see it?"

"Not exactly. But I did see that there's a windsock on the back wall. A large gate leads from the compound to a short road, big enough to be a taxiway. Did I mention the runway? All of which makes me believe either he has a plane or someone did at one time or another."

"I have to agree with you. We better pull back in the event the security people come after us," Connah said. "We can assume they know this terrain a helluva lot better than we do."

As if on cue, they heard the sound of pursuit.

Stone turned to Connah. "You probably heard that they have dogs."

"It won't matter if we don't get our asses in gear."

They turned into the rainforest.

$ $ $ $ $

Connah and Stone rested between the massive roots at the base of a kapok tree. The cacophony of windblown tree branches and forest denizens made it impossible for them to hear the sound of their pursuers.

"How far you figure it is to the boat?" Stone asked.

"Two, maybe three, kilometers."

"A bit more than a mile."

Connah wiped the sweat from his forehead. "That can be one hell of a rough mile in this heat and terrain."

"You think Correia will come help if we get into a firefight with these assholes?"

Connah shrugged his shoulders. "If he does, he's a fool. Nevertheless, if we do get into a shit sandwich, I hope he has the motor running when we reach the river."

Stone nodded.

"Well," Connah said, "time we hauled ass."

Stone looked up. "How high you figure this tree goes?"

"I don't know. It's kapok, and they've been known to grow as high as 200 feet." Connah chuckled. "Stoney, you come up with the damnedest things at the damnedest times."

Stone grinned, his face shiny with perspiration. "Hey man, inquisitive minds need to know."

Connah shook his head and crouched over as he stepped out of the tree's sheltering roots. He heard the baying and barking of dogs, and he turned to

Stone and said, "We better move out… those dogs sound close."

Stone struggled to his feet and placed his hands on his lower back. He arched, stretching the kinks and soreness away. He listened to the sounds of pursuit for several seconds and said, "You know, Ian, we're getting too old for this stuff."

Connah started walking away. "Well, if we don't get moving, you won't have to worry about that for long."

Stone rested his rifle in the crook of his arm and followed. "We better not get turned around. It's so dark I can't see my hand in front of my face."

"If we get lost, we'll be up to our butts in snapping alligators. The Amazon is about seven million square kilometers."

"That's reassuring… Until you told me that, I thought it was big."

$ $ $ $ $

Connah and Stone moved slowly but steadily through the night. They couldn't see more than a few feet ahead and, on many occasions, stumbled against tree roots and into branches. The baying of the hounds behind them made it useless to attempt to use stealth. They knew no matter how quiet they were, it wouldn't matter; the dogs were tracking scent, not sound.

Once again, Connah stopped and wiped the sweat from his face. "We'll never throw them off. This place is darker than the inside of a black cat's ass in a coal bin at midnight…"

"I love the way you always point out the obvious," Stone answered.

"We need to find some type of waterway."

Stone nodded. "There has to be something nearby. The river can't be that far from us."

The sound of baying seemed to get louder.

"They're closing the gap," Connah said.

They pushed forward, hoping that they would soon find a brook or stream that they could follow to the Amazon River. Twenty minutes later, they found it.

"Which way?" Stone asked.

"We follow the current. These streams probably feed into the Amazon. I'll be surprised if it's the other way."

"We ain't gonna cross it, are we?"

"We ain't got a choice," Connah replied.

"What about piranhas and them big goddamned crocodiles?"

"Caiman."

"What?"

"Those big crocs are caiman. I heard they can grow to be almost twenty feet long, maybe more."

"Wonderful."

"Then there is the candiru."

"What's that, some tropical disease?"

"No, it's a fish that's common here. People call it a toothpick or vampire fish. They're about two inches long, real skinny. They have a habit of swimming up the human urethra and lodging there."

"The what?"

"The urethra, the channel which passes urine and semen through the penis."

Stone pushed his face close to Connah's. "You telling me there's a fish that will swim up my...?"

"Yup. They spread their gills and block your bladder. Hurts like hell, and you'll die in about twenty-four hours." Connah gave Stone a rakish grin. "I've seen you in the shower. You ain't got to worry."

"Very funny, Connah. Why do you always tell me shit like this after the fact?"

Connah chuckled. "Well, the fish exist, but the rest is still unproven." He stepped off the bank and into the water. "What those dogs will do if they catch us is a known fact. We better cross here—and quick."

Connah looked through the narrow opening in the jungle canopy and saw the low-intensity gloom of impending daylight. They entered the stream and were submerged to the waist within a few feet. By the time they were halfway across, their legs ached from the exertion required to move through the water. Suddenly there were loud bellowing sounds. "Howler monkey," he said.

A different sound—the unmistakable baying of hounds—drowned out the howlers. "Looks as if they've caught up with us," Stone said.

Connah nodded in agreement. "Looks like the only option we got left is to make them regret it." He waded to the bank opposite the sounds of the pursuit. They quickly took cover behind some fallen trees parallel to the stream and watched the opposite shore. The early morning sun fought its way through the narrow opening in the canopy above the waterway, and an eerie mist rose from the ground.

Connah checked his weapon to ensure it hadn't picked up any foreign objects that may interfere with its operation. As he settled down to watch the opposite bank, he began to shiver. Even though they were in a tropical rainforest, the early morning air chilled him. He took a deep breath, hoping to get the shakes under control—it helped, but not a lot.

He glanced at Stone, who had removed his penis from his trousers and was shining a small penlight on it. He suppressed a laugh and said, "Everything pass inspection?"

"I guess."

"Believe me, if a candiru was in there, you'd know it. Now we got more urgent things to deal with, so put that away and get with it." He gave Stone a thumb-up signal. They'd been in situations like this before, and there was no one else in the world that he'd rather have covering his butt than Stone.

Movement caught Connah's eye, and he saw a hound break out of the bush on the far bank. His handler leaned back in a futile attempt to hold the canine back. Connah had no desire to kill the animal. It was only doing its job—however, the handler was another matter altogether. He sighted in on the man's chest.

Two other dogs and handlers appeared, with several armed men immediately behind. "I'll take the lead handler," he said in a voice so low it would not be inaudible more than a few feet away.

"I'll go for one of the others," Stone replied.

"Once we shoot, they'll be confused and taking cover while they try to locate us. That'll be our best chance to haul ass out of here."

Stone replied with a thumb up.

The lead hound came to an abrupt stop. Its head dropped to the ground, and it started to circle, dragging the handler with it. Connah followed the handler keeping his sight locked on the man's torso. He fired.

The handler dropped to the ground; the dog's leash still wrapped around his wrist. The dog howled, spun around, and ran into the rainforest, dragging the incapacitated handler behind him.

Connah heard Stone fire a shot, and the second handler went down.

The rest of the pursuing men scattered. Several made no attempt to hide the fact that they were running back the way they'd come. Obviously, whatever Sandberg was paying them wasn't enough for them to risk getting shot. Connah nodded to Stone, and they crept back into the jungle until they were out of sight and resumed their retreat to the river.

$ $ $ $ $

Correia heard the gunfire but was unable to tell where the source was. Of one thing he was sure, it was not local Indians. The natives indigenous to this area mainly were Yanomamo and Tikuna, neither of whom were armed with modern weapons. They used machetes, bow and arrows, spears, and poison darts fired via blowguns; all were traditional, ancient weapons. He began reassessing his situation, deciding whether or not he was being paid enough for this. However, of one thing he was sure—he wasn't being paid enough to die. Correia was loyal to anyone who paid for his services, especially those who paid as well as these Americans. However, possibly it was time to adopt a different strategy.

He turned the wheel and started edging the boat toward the opposite shore.

60

Connah stayed still, listening for the sounds of pursuit. After several minutes of hearing the breeze blow through the dense foliage, he set off to locate Stone. The Howlers had been quiet since the sounds of gunfire and men shouting at one another had started. Now, as the jungle returned to its normal state, they began their loud growling again.

Connah found Stone hidden between the exposed roots of a gigantic tree. When he dropped down beside him, Stone said, "Those damned monkeys will drive a man freakin' crazy."

When Connah grinned, his teeth seemed to glow when viewed against the dirt and grime that covered his face. "Careful. For you and me, that might be a mere trip down the block."

Stone gave him a quizzical look.

"*Driving* us crazy," Connah said. "A lot of people think we're already there."

"What's our plan?"

"We head for the river and find Correia. Then we return to Manaus and put a team together. If we don't have trained people, taking that place ain't gonna be easy."

Stone waved his hands, trying to shoo the cloud of flying insects that swarmed around his bush hat. He thought about the implication of what Connah said and replied, "I figured that. So, where does it leave us?"

"Before we can find out, we've got to find our way back to the boat." Connah stood up and said, "One thing is for sure, sitting on our asses here ain't gonna get it done."

Stone stood and then followed him into the bush.

61

Given that he had no idea how far behind Sandberg's people were, Connah was happy to see that the *Princesa de Amazonas* was cruising the river toward them. He stepped to the water line and waved his arms so Correia could see them.

Stone crouched down beneath the broad leaves of a tropical plant and watched their backtrail for any pursuers. It seemed like an eternity before Correia brought the *Princesa* as close to the shore as he dared. He idled the motor and dropped the anchor into the murky stream.

"I ain't too keen on this," Stone said.

"On what?"

"Wading out to that boat. There could be a caveman in the water."

It took several moments for Connah to realize what his partner was concerned about. "You mean caiman?"

"Yeah, the friggin' crocodiles."

"I'd be more worried about leeches and piranha."

"Ain't you just a picture of optimism. I think everything in this place can kill you."

"How does it feel to be on the bottom of the food chain?" Connah stepped into the water and started wading toward the boat. He turned and saw Stone standing beside the bank. "You coming or not?"

"If I see you make it safely, I'll follow, but not until then."

"Give me a break."

"I have been. I just don't want to hear you say: Oh, by the way, I forgot to mention."

Connah shook his head and turned to the boat. As he neared the vessel, he was submerged to his chest and held his rifle above his head. Correia appeared on deck and dropped a small Jacob's ladder over the side. Connah handed his weapon to the captain, gripped the ropes, and climbed the wooden steps to the deck. He turned to Stone and said, "See? It's a piece of cake."

Stone took a tentative step off the bank and began wading. He reached the ladder, and Connah grabbed his rifle while Correia pulled him on board.

"Why did you wait to come?" Correia asked.

"Figured it would be safer. It was no big deal," Stone said with a bravado he didn't feel.

Suddenly, the water behind him erupted. They saw the black scales and ridges on the back of a colossal body break the surface.

Correia leaned over the gunwale and stared at the water. "That," he said, "is the largest caiman I've ever seen, maybe over six meters long."

Stone looked at Connah and Correia. "It ain't gonna take much more to make me *really* hate this place."

"I'm surprised," Correia said, "you don't usually see them in the water during the day. They're like bathing beauties and spend the daylight hours laying on the banks, soaking up the sun." He paused, "Come to think of it, you don't usually see them at night either. At least, not until they got you in their jaws and are pulling you under."

Stone looked at Connah. "What was it you said earlier? *I'd be more worried about leeches and piranha.* That'll teach me to listen to you."

The afternoon calm was broken by the sounds of men shouting and hounds baying.

Turning to Connah, Correia said, "We'd better find a quieter part of the river, pull up the anchor, would you?" When he saw Connah drop the heavy metal mud hook on the deck, he entered the cabin, opened the throttle, and headed upstream.

$ $ $ $ $

The *Princesa de Amazonas* rode the rapid current of the Rio Solimões for three kilometers. They rounded a bend and came to a place where the river was a half-kilometer wide, and the current was slow. Correia stuck his head out of the cabin's side window. "I think maybe this is a good place to stop." He looked up at the clouds, which were thickening and had dropped almost to the level of the tallest trees. "It will be storming soon and too dark to continue on."

"You're the captain," Connah replied.

"Okay, then it's decided. When I reach the center, drop the anchor, please."

Connah waited until Correia maneuvered the *Princesa* to the middle of the waterway and cut the motor before throwing the heavy metal moor into the water. Lightning suddenly struck about fifty meters in front of them, a deafening BOOM, and a deluge of rain coincided. The bolt hit the river and created a tsunami that flowed under and around the boat. All that saved Connah from being thrown into the water was slamming into the gunwale. He shouted in pain and dropped to the deck.

Stone ran over and grabbed his partner. "Jesus, what was that?"

Correia had seen Connah go down and come out of the cabin. "Lightning hit the water. The storm is directly overhead, and we may be in for a wild ride."

As if nature wanted to emphasize the Brazilian's prediction, another brilliant flash of lightning, followed by another crash of thunder, split the air. The electric charge surging through the water raised the hair on Connah's arms like supercharged static. The boat was heaved up again, throwing the three men across the deck. When the hull settled back into the water, Correia said, "We better get inside, out of the rain and water before we get electrocuted."

Neither Connah nor Stone said anything as the three rushed out of the storm and into the cabin. Once inside, Connah eased himself onto an empty bunk and said, "Isn't anyone going to ask me if I'm alright?"

Stone asked, "Are you alright?"

"No, I'm not. I think I have cracked ribs, but thanks for asking."

$ $ $ $ $

Harry Sandberg looked up when Miguel Rodrigues Oliveiras walked into the office. "Did you get them?"

The look on Oliveiras's face was all the answer he needed.

"They got away, didn't they?"

"*Sim, señhor.*"

"I thought that the dogs were on their trail."

"They were, but these *estrangeiro* are very—how do you say?"

"Competent?"

"*Sim*, that is a perfect word."

"How many men did we lose?"

"*Dois treinadores de cães* were shot, with one killed."

"*Dois?*" Sandberg held up two fingers. "Two what? Speak English, damn it."

"In *Inglês*, you would say dog handlers."

"Two dog handlers were shot, and you turned back?"

"No, we continued to chase them, but they had a boat waiting and went up the river. We tried to follow along the bank, but a strong storm came in and forced us to turn back."

"Miguel, I want those men dead, all of them, and I want that boat to disappear."

"*Señhor*, I think that would not be wise."

"Sandberg bent forward and put his face close to Oliveiras's. "*Why* do *you* think that would not be wise?"

"The boat is the *Princesa de Amazonas*. It is owned by Otávio Rodrigues Correia."

"Is that supposed to mean something to me?"

"He is a cousin to Fábio Correia Goncalves."

"When are you going to get to the damned point?"

"Fábio Correia Goncalves is *chefe* of the largest drug-trafficking cartel in *Amazonas* State and connected to the PCC. The largest organized crime organization in all of Brazil. They may control all drug traffic from Colombia to Guyana, Suriname, and French Guiana. He is not a man you want to be your *inimigo*."

Sandberg gave his security chief a sharp look.

Oliveiras caught the look and said, "Your enemy. Correia is more than his cousin. He is also one of Goncalves' main traffickers. The *Princesa* moves more drugs than any other single boat on the Amazon. There is also the fact that Goncalves controls an army of trained *mercenários*. He is, as you *Americanos* say, not someone with whom you should fuck."

Sandberg thought for a few moments and then asked, "Is Goncalves a man willing to bargain?"

"Possibly, he only worships one god… *dinheiro*."

Sandberg needed no translation. Goncalves and he had at least one thing in common, a love of money.

Lightning flashed, thunder pealed outside the window behind Sandberg, and a sudden downpour hammered the glass. "How do I reach him?" he asked.

"He owns the Clube Sucuri—Club Anaconda—in Manaus."

"Have the plane ready first thing in the morning."

62

The cacophonous cries of howler monkeys woke Connah. He tried to roll over on the narrow bunk and felt pain like someone driving a knife into his side. He broke out in a sweat and settled on his back, allowing his head to rest on the pillow, and groaned in agony.

"Mornin', Sweet Pea."

Connah glanced out of the corner of his eyes and saw Stone standing beside the bed holding a steaming mug of coffee.

"How are you feeling?" Stone asked.

"Like I been shot at and missed and shit at and hit."

Stone grinned. "You sure slammed into that gunwale hard enough."

Connah made another attempt to roll over and sit up. The pain racked through him again, and he fell back. He looked at his best friend and asked, "You gonna help me, or are you just gonna stand there grinning like a hyena?"

"I'm not sure. You're awfully surly this morning. I may take this coffee outside and enjoy the ambiance of a beautiful tropical morning."

"Am I supposed to believe you're starting to like the Amazon?"

"Nope, but I am enjoying the fact that you hurt too bad to bust my butt."

"Stoney, you need to recall that old Chinese proverb."

"Which one might that be? Over the years, you've made up a shit-load of 'old Chinese proverbs'. I seem to recall one that you said: He who crosses the ocean twice without taking a bath is a dirty double-crosser."

"I was thinking more along the line of the one that says: Everyone likes a piece of ass, but nobody likes a smart ass."

Stone smiled. "Oh, that one. As strange as it seems, it does fit the situation, doesn't it?"

Connah moaned again. "Okay, I'll stop making fun of you. Now would you please help me get up?"

"*Please?* You must have hit your head, too! In all the years we've known one another, I don't recall you ever using that word." He placed the mug on the small table beside the bed and held out his hand. "C'mon, old man, time to rise and shine."

Connah smirked at Stone. "You seem to be enjoying my misery."

"I won't argue that. Because I am."

Stone grabbed Connah's hand and ignored his grunts of pain as he pulled him to his feet. While Connah struggled to maintain his balance, Stone retrieved the mug and handed it to him.

"I guess we won't be running off into Hell's half-acre for a few days. You sure as shit ain't up to it, that's for sure."

"I was looking for an excuse to act like a caiman and lounge in the sun all day."

When they left the cabin, they found Correia sitting in a chair on the fantail, holding a fishing rod. "Any luck?" Stone asked.

"I hooked something big—then something a hell of a lot bigger grabbed it, broke my line, and disappeared before I could see what it was." Correia looked at Stone and smiled. "It might have been your caiman. He may be hanging around, waiting for your next swim."

"He better not hold his breath waiting," Stone replied, "he'll be long dead before that happens."

"I see that you are up and around," Correia said to Connah.

"It surprised me, too." Connah looked toward Stone. "It was either that or lay there listening to Stoney bust my butt all day."

Connah saw the quizzical look on the Brazilian's face and realized that he was unfamiliar with the expression. "He was giving me a hard time," he explained.

Correia nodded his understanding. To Connah, he said, "You seem incapable of doing what we came here to do. What is your plan?"

"I guess we may as well return to Manaus until I heal."

"I believe," Correia said, "that may be what is best. I heard an *avião*, an airplane, flying east about an hour ago. Possibly, your quarry is on his way there, too." He reeled in his line, stood up, and placed the rod against the gunwale. "We might as well start back. The return trip to Manaus should be a few hours less with the current aiding us."

63

Harry Sandberg stood before the entrance to Clube Sucuri. He looked at the neighborhood where the club was located with more than a bit of trepidation. The buildings were not in the best shape, and many of the people lounging around them did not look like the sort he would like to meet in a dark alley. He looked at Miguel Rodrigues Oliveiras and was thankful that he had brought him along.

"This place looks unsavory," he said. When he saw the look on Oliveiras's face, he realized that the Brazilian did not know what unsavory meant. "This place looks unpleasant," he explained.

"It is not so bad as some places in Manaus."

"I find that hard to believe."

"You should be thankful that we don't have to go to any of Goncalves' other clubs. They are nothing more than cheap bordellos. This one is his most upscale."

Oliveiras opened the door for his boss.

"After you," Sandberg said.

Following Oliveiras's steps, Sandberg entered a narrow passage. But abruptly halted when confronted by a glass aquarium occupied by the largest snake he had ever seen. He turned sideways, stepped back, and sidled past the offensive exhibit.

Oliveiras noticed his discomfort and said, "It will not hurt you. It is sleeping. They have possibly fed it recently."

Sandberg felt the unhealthy sweat of fear dripping down his face and continued putting as much distance as possible between the serpent and him. The narrow corridor opened into the main floor of the club. The smoke-filled atmosphere seemed to descend on Sandberg like a dirty blanket. Even though his eyes were irritated by the smoke and tobacco fumes, he saw the room was populated by women, all in various stages of undress. "I thought you said this place was not a bordello?" he asked Oliveiras.

"It is not. Bordellos are illegal in Brazil. However, prostitution is legal."

"So, he's a pimp."

"*Señhor*, it is not wise to say such things in a man's place of business. These *prostitutas* are independent contractors. In return for having a place to work, other than on the streets, they pay a small fee to Goncalves."

"What's the difference?"

"The difference is easy. It is the difference between doing business or getting your throat cut."

Sandberg felt a chill run up his spine. He suddenly had reservations about attempting to deal with possibly the second most dangerous man he'd ever done business with. Given present circumstances, Ian Connah had a solid lock on being the first person in that line.

As he followed Oliveiras across the floor, several whores came close to him; a couple slid their hands up and down his arms and chest. One placed a long-nailed forefinger under his chin. He rebuffed their advances, kept his eyes straight ahead, and was relieved when he stopped before a double-wide table. On top of the tables were several plastic bags filled with an off-white, beige powder. He didn't need to be told what it was—uncut, pure cocaine.

The burly mustached man sitting behind the table looked at Sandberg, immediately dismissed him, and turned to Oliveiras. When he spoke, the drug lord said in Portuguese. "Who is this fat pig (*porco gordo* in Portuguese) that you bring, Oliveiras?"

Oliveiras replied in the local language. "This is the American that has hired me to keep him alive."

Sandberg became nervous when Goncalves grinned, exposing bad teeth. He picked up a burning cigar from the ashtray before him, stuck it into his mouth, and inhaled. The end of the stogie lit up as the Brazilian sucked in smoke. Goncalves removed the cheroot from his mouth and blew smoke at him.

Still speaking Portuguese, the hoodlum laughed and said to Oliveiras, "If this is your chief, you picked poorly. Look at the fat pig. He is having all he can do to keep from shitting in his pants."

Goncalves turned to Sandberg and, in heavily accented English, said, "What is it that you want?"

The drug lord intentionally refrained from using the customary respectful *señhor* when he spoke. However, Sandberg was too nervous to notice the slight. His knees felt weak, and he wished he had a chair to sit in before he fell down.

Oliveiras started to speak, but Goncalves raised his right hand, cutting him off. "I did not talk to you, Miguel. If this man is a *chefe,* he can speak for himself. One *chefe* to another *chefe, não?*"

Sandberg swallowed the lump in his throat and said, "My name is Sanders, and I have come to propose a business deal."

Goncalves sat back in his chair. "What is this business deal?"

Sandberg hesitated for a moment. "There is someone who is looking for me. He intends to harm me."

"Really? I believe that I have knowledge of the man of whom you speak. I also know that your name is not Sanders. It is Sandberg. I must say that if you had stolen three million dollars from me—" He leaned to one side and reached to the floor beside his chair. He brought up a miniature version of the snake in the aquarium and set it on the table. The constrictor curled itself around his arm, and he began petting it. "I would hold a gun to your head until you returned my money, and then I'd give you to my little darlings." He petted the anaconda and grinned again. "These are amazing creatures. They can swallow a calf, and one as large as that in my aquarium might even be able to swallow someone as big as you. Of course, before they do that, they must crush all of your bones to make you easier to swallow."

Sandberg felt sweat soaking through his shirt. "I am willing to pay a half-million dollars, American, for your assistance."

Goncalves laughed. In Portuguese again, he turned to Oliveiras and said, "Take this son of a bitch out of my club before I have my men kill him. If you ever bring him near me again, I will kill you, too."

Sandberg knew from the tone of the drug smuggler's voice that his offer was being refused. He looked at Oliveiras. Before he could say anything, Oliveiras said, "*Señhor*, we should leave… and we should do it *now.*"

Once they were out of the club and back in their car, Oliveiras gave quick instructions to the driver. When they were safely away, Sandberg said, "What the fuck happened in there? He refused a half-million dollars! Nobody refuses that much money."

Oliveiras replied, "Unless someone else is offering him more."

"You make it sound as if there's honor among thieves."

"In my country, family loyalty is a significant thing. A concept that I feel is lacking in your culture."

64

The *Princesa de Amazonas* arrived in Manaus shortly before sunset on the second day of their return from the upper Rio Solimões. Correia had radioed ahead, contacting a doctor to meet them at the pier to look at Connah's ribs.

The doctor was waiting on the dock when they moored. He was led into the cabin where his patient was sitting on a narrow bunk. Connah had refrained from exposing his ribs since the lightning-generated wave had slammed him into the gunwale. It was a struggle for him to remove his shirt, and when he did, his entire side was covered by a blue-black bruise. He flinched and involuntarily drew back when the physician gently explored the damage. However, his relief was apparent when the diagnosis was better than expected.

"Of course, I won't know anything for sure," the doctor said, "until we can get you x-rayed. However, my preliminary diagnosis is that you have severely bruised ribs, but I don't believe any are broken."

Connah exhaled and relaxed.

"If you'd like, I can make arrangements for someone to do the x-rays tonight. I would recommend going to the Fundaçao Hospital Adriano Jorge if this is critical. However, it is merely an x-ray, and the Hospital Adventista de Manaus is closer." He handed Connah a business card; the name printed on it was *FRANCISCO CORREIA*. "I will call Adventista. If you go someplace else, have them send the x-ray to me. You should call me tomorrow, in the afternoon."

Connah looked at Correia, who said, "Adventista will be fine, thank you, Francisco."

Connah took out his wallet and asked, "How much do I owe you, Doctor?"

"You owe me nothing, *señhor*. I could never ask a friend of my cousin for money."

The doctor waved and exited the cabin. When he was heard walking on the pier, Connah looked at Correia and asked, "Just how big *is* your family, anyway?

Correia smiled broadly, exposing a gold canine tooth. "It is part of our culture that one cannot have too much family."

$ $ $ $ $

The Beechcraft King Air 350I taxied into the hangar. The ground crew quickly approached the aircraft and began securing it.

Miguel Rodrigues Oliveiras exited the airplane before his boss and waited for him. When Sandberg stepped off the stairs, he wiped his forehead and flicked the sweat on his hand toward the concrete surface of the hangar. "I want the guards doubled until we know for certain that Ian Connah and his bunch are dead, and I want them to be on high alert twenty-four-seven."

Oliveiras nodded and walked away to do his *chefe's* bidding.

$ $ $ $ $

Oliveiras walked into the security office and found his second-in-command, Alexandre Mota, sitting at his desk. "How was the trip to Manaus?" Mota asked in Portuguese.

"Not well."

"So, what is Porco Gordo going to do now? This *Americano* does not strike me as one who gives up easily."

"To start, he wants the guards doubled and on alert twenty-four hours a day, seven days a week."

"That is not going to make the men happy. Since you and Porco Gordo left, ten have gone away. This news may reduce our numbers yet more."

"Whatever you do, Alexandre, do not let them know that the *merda estúpida* (dumb shit) has now added Fábio Correia Goncalves to our list of enemies."

Mota leapt to his feet. "If Goncalves joins forces with the *Americano* we will have no chance!"

"I know that. What I don't know is how do we get Porco Gordo to understand it?"

$ $ $ $ $

Once on his feet, Connah found the pain in his ribs tolerable. He stood on the fantail of the *Princesa de Amazonas,* studying the Manaus skyline and enjoying the warm tropical breeze that blew down the Rio Negro. The heat from the tropical sun felt good as it warmed his damaged side. He heard someone walking behind him and turned to see Stone approach. He held two beers, one he handed to Connah.

"Thanks," Connah said. He turned back to take in the view once again.

Stone stood beside him, watched the setting sun, and said, "I gotta admit, the daytime heat is brutal, but you can't complain about the nights here. What season is it here?"

"If you remember, I told you when we arrived here that we're about two hundred miles… three hundred twenty-two kilometers… south of the equator. As we know them, seasons don't exist close to the equator. It's pretty much the same year-round."

"That isn't entirely true," Correia said.

The Americans turned to acknowledge him.

"We do have two basic seasons. Summer and the monsoon."

"I have to admit," Connah said. "I thought it would be hotter."

"On average," Correia replied, "the temperature is around thirty-one degrees centigrade, about eighty of your degrees. What usually gets to visitors is the humidity. We get over eighty inches of rain a year. In fact, it can rain as many as two hundred days of the year. Our true problem is humidity."

Stone pointed along the river. "What are all those lights?"

"Manaus," Correia said, "is a modern city. However, most of the population lives in poverty. Those lights are floating slums, *favelas flutuantes,* in Portuguese. You may have noticed that the hills around the city are covered with slums also."

"Speaking of the hills, could you arrange for us to meet with your cousin Fábio?"

Correia shrugged, "I will contact him. Might I ask what you need from him?"

"Men who know their way around the jungle and aren't afraid of a firefight."

"I take it you are not giving up on your quest."

"That was never a possibility. I've come too far to leave without finishing what I've started."

Correia asked Stone, "How do you feel about this?"

"What the fuck—this is as good a place to die as any."

65

Fábio Correia Goncalves sat behind the same table as the first time Connah had met him. As they were in his last visit, scantily clad women stood on either side of him. He smoked his ever-present stogie and acted like a buffoon—an act Connah didn't believe for a second. He smiled a broad smile showing his extensive gold and silver-colored dental work. "Ahh, *señhor* Connah, I hope you are feeling better."

"I am doing fine, *Chefe*. I spoke with the doctor this morning. I have some bruised ribs. They should be fine in a few days."

"How is it that I can help you?"

"I need assistance. I need your organization's help. I need men. My enemy has a fortified plantation with a well-equipped mercenary army. I need men who know the area and are not afraid of a fight."

"What makes you think my men have these skills?"

Connah knew he was walking a narrow path and had to be careful. "You have men who know the trails and ways of the Amazon. I know that they must be tough men to survive in this place. Men who are willing to face danger daily."

"If I am to make this commitment, I will require more than what we have agreed upon."

Connah had been expecting this and was ready to make an offer. "I am willing to give the agreed-upon money. If you are willing to assist me in this, I will give you the fat one's plantation and all of the equipment on it."

It was an offer he believed Goncalves would jump at. The plantation would provide him with a staging area and an airplane and make him rich.

Goncalves placed his cigar in his ashtray. Connah visualized gears in the drug lord's head as he pondered the offer. "How large is this *plantação*?"

"About 2,500 acres... 1,000 hectares."

Goncalves smiled, stood up, and held out his hand. "I have always desired to be a *dono de plantação*."

Connah looked to Correia, who smiled and said, "*Dono de plantação* means plantation owner."

Connah gripped Goncalves's hand. "All we need now is a plan."

$ \$ \quad \$ \quad \$ \quad \$ \quad \$ $

Sandberg paced his office. Sweat covered him, making his clothes stick to his body. He'd had Oliveiras contact all of his sources in Manaus and offer R\$50,000, equal to \$9,350.38 U.S., which was \$3,706.72 more than the average annual salary, to anyone who killed Ian Connah. The results had been non-existent. He was considering offering more but wasn't sure that it would produce a different result.

He circled his desk and accessed the safe behind the portrait of Julian Fernandes Santos, the founder of the plantation. He removed several stacks of currency that amounted to \$50,000. He took out an account book and opened it to the last entry. After purchasing the plantation, he still had slightly more than \$2,000,000 remaining in the account in the Cayman Islands.

There was a knock on his door, and he closed the safe and spun the dial. Once the repository was secure, he said, "Come."

Oliveiras walked through the door. Despite his dislike of Sandberg, he used a respectful tone when he spoke. "*Señhor*, my people have found Connah. He is staying on a boat at the floating pier."

"Good. In the morning, I hope to hear that Connah is no longer a problem."

"*Sim, señhor*, the people I have hired are dependable. They will be making a move tonight."

$ \$ \quad \$ \quad \$ \quad \$ \quad \$ $

Connah was in a deep sleep when a hand closed over his mouth. He opened his eyes and found Stone bent over him, holding an index finger across his lips. He placed his face by Connah's ear and whispered. "We've been boarded." He straightened up and put a nine-millimeter pistol in Connah's hand.

When Connah rolled off the bed, he felt a sharp stabbing pain in his side.

Nevertheless, he was happy that it was nowhere near as bad as earlier in the day. He glanced at his watch and noted the time was just before midnight. He doubted that the boarders were guests of Correia. His thoughts were validated when the captain entered through a side door. He, too, carried a weapon. The sharp blade of a machete sparkled in the ambient light.

Connah joined the other two in the center of the room. Using hand signs, he told Stone to watch the window on their right and Correia to watch the left. He crept to the door and reached for the knob.

Suddenly, the door was pulled open, and a man wielding a machete stood on the threshold. Connah fired three shots and walked through the door. His two companions immediately followed. There were three more intruders on the deck. Stone shot one, and Correia slashed another across his neck with his sharp blade.

The third would-be assassin saw that he was alone and jumped over the side. Connah went to the gunwale where the man had disappeared and aimed his pistol at the water. In the dark, he heard splashing but could not see the swimmer.

The others joined him, and Stone said, "You see him?"

"No," Connah answered. "Let him go."

"That," Correia said, "is a wise decision. Before the dawn, word will be throughout the city that we are not people with whom they should mess around."

Sirens were heard in the night. "Sounds like we're going to have some more company," Stone said.

"*Policia*, when they arrive, I will speak with them," Correia said. "My cousin Fábio has more than a little influence with them."

66

Fábio Correia Goncalves took Stone, Correia, and Connah to a remote location in the rainforest north of Manaus. The drug smuggler had been secretive about the reason behind the trip, and the two Americans had no idea why they were there.

"*Señhor*," Connah asked, "I do not mean to offend, but why are we here?"

Goncalves replied, "You will need to approach your, shall we say, objective with a great amount of secrecy, no?"

"*Sim*," Connah answered using Goncalves' native language.

The Brazilian waved his arms, pointing to the perimeter of the small meadow. "This is a small clearing, do you agree?"

"It is."

In a loud voice, Goncalves called, "*Mostrem-se!*"

Suddenly, armed men appeared out of the knee-high grass, wearing camouflage clothing and their faces covered with camo paint. Connah and Stone looked around and saw that they were surrounded by armed men.

"These," Goncalves said, "are the best ten men that I have. They were born in Amazonas State and know the rainforest from Colombia to Belém, on the Atlantic coast, better than any other group in the country."

"They seem to be as good as any scout sniper trained by the Marine Corps," Stone said.

"*Esses Americanos*," Correia explained that Connah and Stone were trained as snipers by the U.S. Marines Corps in Portuguese, "*foram treinados como franco-atiradors pelo Corpo de Fuzileiros Navais dos Estados Unidos.*"

"Ahh, so they too are skilled at concealment?"

"Very much so," Switching back to English, Correia addressed Connah and said, "Will these men meet your needs?"

"If they fight as good as they conceal themselves, they're more than adequate."

221

"They, like you, are skilled in combat. These men protect Fábio's shipments from Ecuador, Peru, and, of course, Colombia. They have fought many battles with both the armies and police of those countries."

Connah turned to Goncalves. In Portuguese, he thanked him, *"Obrigado, señhor."*

Goncalves smiled. "All that remains," he said, "is to decide about what supplies you will need and the date."

"We've been here for a week waiting for me to heal," Connah said. "I would like to leave as soon as possible."

"Of course, let us return to Manaus. We have a lot of work to do. You will need transportation, and I need to know what sort of weapons and special equipment you need. I believe you should be ready to go in four days."

$ $ $ $ $

As each day passed with no word of Connah's death, Sandberg grew more and more paranoid. He began walking the wall perimeter around the house, known as the farmhouse, *casa de fazenda*, to the Brazilians.

Sandberg's constant complaining and whining irritated Miguel Rodrigues Oliveiras to no end.

"Do you have men stationed along the river?" Sandberg asked.

"Sim, señhor, the river is being watched."

"The guards on the walls have been doubled?"

"Sim, as you requested. Can I be frank?"

Sandberg looked Oliveiras in the eye and said, "Please do."

"I could put every man we have on guard duty, and it will do no good. We hired Indians from local tribes, the Amanayé, Munduruku, Tikuna, and Yanomamo. We have them on the walls and in the towers, but I must be honest, they don't know what you want them to do. These people are farmers, not soldiers. If I had two years to train them, I doubt it would do any good."

Sandberg gave Oliveiras a scathing look. "I pay them top dollar."

"We don't pay them with money. Tribespeople have no use for it. There are none of your country's shopping malls or supermarkets in Amazonia in which they can spend what you would pay them."

"What are you paying them?"

"Usually, we give them hand tools, shovels, hoes, things they can use in their villages. They'll work for days to earn a machete, weeks for a set of pots and pans. However, no amount of training will make these men professional soldiers. Many of them have never been one hundred kilometers from where they were born. Only a select few have any idea how to fire the modern weapons you've provided. I assure you that they will be lucky to hit anything they aim at. The only *wars* they have ever fought have been brief raids when another tribe attacks them, usually to steal tools, women, and children. They use knives, spears, blowguns, and bows and arrows. From day-to-day, I never know how many are actually here. They come and go between here and their homes at will."

"What do you mean they come and go at will?"

"They go home to tend their crops and hunt for food. They have families to provide for. They will get word from their wives. Usually, one of their children is dispatched to fetch them, and they drop anything and go."

Sandberg's eyes narrowed. "Are you telling me they will be of no use if we're attacked?"

"Some will, maybe ten to twenty percent, might be. However, I cannot give you a definite number. In the forest, they can be fierce warriors. All their lives, they have fought out there." Oliveiras waved his arms toward the rainforest outside of the perimeter. "Most of them come from villages without walls. Villages that have never been attacked by a modern trained army. As I said, there is only the occasional clash with another tribe as ancient as them. They have no idea how to fight from a fortified position—let alone against a group of trained *mercenários* using modern tactics and weapons."

"God-damn-it! You make them sound as useful as eyeglasses are to a blind man."

"We have only been here what… four months. It takes more than a year to fully train soldiers. You're lucky they can perform guard duty."

"So, take some of them and give them what you can."

"That is the dilemma. I can either train them, which I'm certain will take more time than we have, or I can maintain the watches as you've instructed. I cannot do both. It is you who needs to decide, which should I do?"

"Do what I paid you to do. Your job is to protect me and my property. Just do it, God damn it."

"Okay, I will reduce the guard by one-fourth. Those men I will try to train on using our modern weapons. They, in turn, will be tasked with passing that on."

Sandberg grunted and walked away at a fast pace.

Oliveiras was unable to keep from smiling. Maybe now, he thought, Porco Gordo would understand the situation. He turned away to select the men he wanted to be trained. An activity that was most likely to be an exercise in futility.

67

The small three-boat fleet moored near a narrow sand beach, disembarking the small expeditionary force. Connah and Stone exited the dugout that had brought them ashore, and Connah chuckled when Stone sprinted into the trees. Edward Gomes, head of the Brazilians, looked at him, and Connah saw the question on his face. "He's afraid of caiman," he said.

Gomes smiled. "Me, too," he said.

Once he was under cover of the bush, Connah surveyed their area. The terrain was similar to that near the plantation. Since arriving in the Amazon, he'd learned that trees in the rainforest are anchored in two ways: one, by surprisingly shallow roots, anchoring them to the ground, and second, high above the jungle floor, their branches intertwined creating the ceiling-like canopy that blocked the brutal tropical sun. The world below was populated by large tree trunks interspersed with hanging vines and lianas, countless seedlings and saplings, and a relatively small number of ground plants. It didn't take long for him to understand why Goncalves had told him that the deep darkness was created by perhaps thirty meters of canopy vegetation. A flashlight would be more valuable than a machete.

"I expected it to be wetter," Connah said to Gomes.

"Many people think that," Gomes answered. He looked upward and said, "Much of the plants live high in the trees. Between them and the thick canopy, it can be raining for hours before we feel it."

"How long before we reach our target?" Connah asked.

"It's sixteen kilometers, about ten of your miles. It will be dark in about an hour. At a normal pace, we should be able to cover about half of that before it's too dark to travel. If we start out as soon as it's light enough for us to see, we should arrive early in the morning."

$ $ $ $ $

The invaders set up camp and were huddled around three campfires. Stone, Gomes, and Connah quietly talked, establishing a tactical plan for the upcoming assault. A loud sound, similar to that made by a saw pulling through wood, broke the quiet of the night.

Stone's head snapped up. "What in hell was that?"

"A *saw*," Gomes answered.

"Who in hell would be cutting wood at this time of the night?"

Gomes eyes and teeth seemed to sparkle in the flickering firelight. "A saw is the call of a jaguar."

"You're talking about the cat?"

"I'm not talking about the car."

"Christ," Stone said. "This place is a frigging zoo for animals that can kill you."

"Don't worry," Gomes said, "man is not usually on their menu."

Stone began to cast nervous looks into the darkness. "Next, you'll tell me that there are black panthers here, too."

"Actually," Gomes answered, "the black panther is either a melanistic jaguar or leopard." He noticed the quizzical look on Stone's face. "Melanistic is like an albino. However, instead of being white, melanistic is entirely black. Like albinos, they are scarce. There have been sightings of them in Central and other South American countries, but as of today, none in Brazil."

"Oh," Stone said, "for a minute there, I thought we'd be in trouble."

"Stoney, settle down," Connah said. "We've got more important things to discuss than the local wildlife."

He turned to Gomes. "One of the first things we need to do is either secure or incapacitate the airplane. This mission aims to get Sandberg alive and retrieve my money. Once that is accomplished, I don't care if you tie him naked to an ant tree."

"*Now* you tell me that ants live in trees?" Stone interrupted.

"I just learned about it myself. Correia told me last night. It's also known as a *novice tree* because only one unfamiliar with it would be stupid enough to touch it. The slightest contact and you'll soon learn how aggressive and venomous the ants are," Connah said.

Again, Stone began to search the area around their camp.

"You're okay in the forest," Gomes said. "The tree usually grows in disturbed habitats, like places where the forest has been ravaged by fire or logging. If you see a mottled gray-colored tree with smooth bark and leaves that are oval to oblong, avoid it. The undersides of the leaves are sometimes woolly with brown fibers, don't touch them. Don't get close to them. The ant that lives in the tree feeds on substances produced by it and defends it against invaders—and they will consider you a threat."

Stone looked at Connah. "Ants and leeches living in trees, fish that will swim into your dick, wild cats, piranha, twenty-foot-long crocodiles, and who knows how many different types of snakes, all of which can kill you... Partner, when this is all over, you will owe me. *Big time.*"

68

Connah, Stone, and Gomes studied the fortifications around Sandberg's house. Connah pointed out the defensive fortifications that he had noted on his first survey. The cameras at each corner were active, sweeping left and right. They believed they could avoid them by timing the cycle of the sweeps. The spotlights on top of the guard towers were not a problem. They would be attacking in daylight.

"I don't see any guards," Stone said.

"That is strange," Connah said.

"Maybe," Gomes said, "there aren't enough of them to cover all areas, and they're either roving or think the cameras and these walls will force us to attack where there are perceived weak points."

"You may have something there. But, either way, it ain't gonna be easy scaling the walls," Connah commented.

"We'll use plastique to blow holes in it," Gomes said.

"What are you using, Semtex or C-4?" Stone asked.

"Not that it matters, but we got both."

"Remember, we need to capture or immobilize the aircraft before Sandberg can get on board and flee," Connah cautioned.

"*Chefe* has instructed me not to destroy it, if possible," Gomes said.

"I'll take care of it," Stone said.

"I will take three with me, and we'll secure the wall and all the outbuildings," Gomes said. He looked at Connah. "That leaves three to go with you."

"Fine with me, so long as they know that Sandberg is mine. Ensure that no one kills him before I get what I need to get my money."

Gomes nodded and then looked at his watch. "It is eight o'clock. Have everyone in position in fifteen minutes. When we blow the wall, that will be the signal to commence the attack."

"He has dogs," Connah said, "I haven't seen them, but they sound nasty as hell."

Gomes grinned, "I am also called *filho da puta*. I believe that translates to son of a bitch in *Inglês*. Dogs will be no problem. *Vá com Deus, señhores*."

$ $ $ $ $

Gomes and his team crouched beneath the broadleaf plants that dominated the periphery of the rainforest. Gomes motioned to his men. When they convened around him, he handed each of them a block of plastic explosive, some wide super-adhesive tape, and detonating cord. He pointed out where he wanted the charges placed and daisy-chained the plastique to the blasting caps with the det-cord. He studied the cameras and told his men that the cameras were aimed outward, creating a blind spot at the base of the wall, and they should stay as close to it as they could. He dispatched them one pair per sweep when the camera turned away from them.

Gomes placed the blasting caps and the receiver in one end of the daisy chain when the charges were in place and linked by the detonating cord. He used hand signals to order his men back to the rendezvous point he'd decided on. The men crept around the corner and stood with their backs against the wall.

As soon as the team was assembled, he pressed the button on the transmitter. The charges detonated with one simultaneous explosion that blew over one hundred feet of the wall into piles of crushed stone and razor wire.

Using the cloud of dust created by the massive explosion, Gomes and his men rushed around the corner and saw Stone and his team run through the opening ahead of them.

$ $ $ $ $

When Connah's team had finished placing their explosive charges, they too returned to the periphery of the jungle. When he heard Gomes's explosion, Connah set off his. Connah and his men charged through the rubble and dust, entering the compound as Gomes had done.

$ $ $ $ $

Stone and his men raced inside the hangar. The occupants were surprised by the sound of explosions, and they surrendered with minimal resistance. Only a single person moved. A man dressed in a uniform ran toward the aircraft and reached the boarding ladder. He had one foot on the bottom step when Stone shot him in the leg. He crumpled on the stairs, gripped his injured leg, and made no further attempt to board the plane.

Stone rushed forward, leaped over the wounded man, ran up the steps, and entered the plane. He turned toward the cockpit and saw someone in one of the pilot seats. "Don't move!" he shouted.

The pilot turned with raised hands. Stone was surprised when a female voice said, "*Por favor não atire.*"

"She begs you not to shoot."

Stone looked over his shoulder and saw a Brazilian standing behind him. He stepped back and turned his assault rifle until it was pointed at the man. "Tell her to come out here... then tell me who the hell you are."

The man raised his hands and said, "*Venha aqui.*"

The young woman came out of the cockpit and turned sideways, taking care to avoid touching Stone when she passed him. She stood beside the Brazilian, and her brown eyes were wide with fear when she made eye contact with the gunman.

"Now," Stone said, "who are you?"

"I am Araujo Bocaiúva. I am the pilot."

"Who was the guy I shot in the leg?"

"Another pilot," Bocaiúva looked at the woman. "Her father, Paulo Braga."

"And her name is?"

"Francisca."

"Same last name?"

"*Sim*, she is not married."

"And I shot her father?"

"*Sim.*"

"Well, I guess there's no use asking her for a date." Stone turned to the woman. "Do you speak English?"

She looked at Bocaiúva, who said, "*Ele pergunta se voce fala Ingles.*"

"I guess that answers my question, doesn't it?"

"What do you want with us?" Bocaiúva asked.

"We don't want anything of you except to keep this airplane on the ground… one way or another."

Bocaiúva's brow furrowed. "I don't understand."

"I'm going to keep you from flying anyone out of here, even if I have to blow up this plane with you in it."

69

Gomes and his team came under sporadic small arms fire but suffered no casualties. These have to be the worst marksmen I've ever come across, he thought. They maneuvered across the open ground toward the first building, which appeared to be some sort of garage.

Gomes kicked open a small door on the side of the building and heard the unmistakable sound of a blowgun dart pass by his head. He knew then the reason for the poor marksmanship... the majority of the defenders were local tribesmen. More likely than not, this was their first experience with modern firearms. He warned the members of his squad to watch for the poisoned darts, "*Eles são índios. Cuidado com os dardos e flechas envenenados.*"

Gomes reached around the door's threshold and sprayed the interior of the building with automatic gunfire, and then ordered them to rush inside. He followed and found two dead men lying on the floor. A quick recon of the building showed no one else inside.

The squad moved on, assaulting the following structure.

$ $ $ $ $

Connah and his contingent raced toward the main house and immediately drew rifle fire. He heard a grunt to his left and saw one of the Brazilians fall to the ground. He fired his weapon at the open window directly in front of his position and saw a rifle drop to the ground.

Connah reached the exterior wall to the left of a heavy wooden door. He tried to open it, but it was locked. Beside him, a rifle barrel appeared from a window. He fired a burst through the portal. The weapon tilted up and then dropped to the ground.

Connah continued on. He dove through the open portal, somersaulted as he hit the floor, and came up on one knee. A young man—a kid—sat with his back against the wall; two red splotches of blood on his chest painted his white shirt. A quick check of the kid's carotid artery revealed no pulse. Connah left him, unlocked the door, and opened it, allowing the two remaining Brazilians access.

Before entering, the second member of his squad turned and fired a bust before entering. A yelp followed, and Connah knew the threat of attack dogs was diminished, if not eliminated.

$ $ $ $ $

Sandberg heard the explosions and ran to the vault. His heart was hammering with fear, and he entered an incorrect combination. He cursed and tried again.

He heard gunshots from multiple directions and panicked, once again entering an incorrect combination. "God damn it!" He quickly reentered the sequence, this time, it opened. He reached inside and removed the $50,000 cash and the account books with the passcodes.

"They are inside."

Sandberg jumped with surprise. He spun around and saw Oliveiras standing by the door. "I know."

"No, I mean they are in the house. They control the hangar. Eliminating the airplane as a means of escape. They also control several other buildings, one of which is the armory."

"What about your people?"

"As I thought, they are useless…"

"What can we do?"

"Me, I can escape. I have the skill to survive in the jungle. You? I guess you're royally fucked."

Sandberg felt his knees go weak.

Oliveiras raised his right arm and aimed a nine-millimeter pistol at the man he called Porco Gordo. "All that remains is for you to give me that money and the account books with the passcodes."

Sandberg stiffened. All his planning and the months of running were about to come to nothing. His fear was overcome by anger. He reached into the vault and grabbed a pistol. When he turned and saw the smile on Oliveiras's face, he hesitated.

The first bullet from Oliveiras's weapon hit Sandberg in his expansive stomach, driving him back a step. The second hit him in the chest. Sandberg fell forward. His torso lay across his desk for several seconds before he fell to the floor.

Oliveiras grabbed the case filled with money and the passbooks, turned, and ran out of the room.

$ $ $ $ $

Connah left the front room and saw a figure carrying a suitcase run down a hall and disappear through a door. He knew the man was not Sandberg and turned in the direction from which the man had appeared. He saw an open door at the end of the corridor and smelled cordite. He walked toward the door.

$ $ $ $ $

Sandberg fumbled around until he found a pencil and tried to write something on a pad of paper. He heard a noise and looked up. Ian Connah walked into the room.

"You're too late," Sandberg said. "Oliveiras has the account books, passcodes, and what cash I had on hand."

"Oliveiras?"

"Like you, he's another killer. He just left. You may have seen him…" Sandberg suddenly exhaled and went still.

Connah checked for a pulse, there was none. He turned and ran out of the room.

$ $ $ $ $

Connah exited the house and looked for the man with the suitcase. He saw Gomes and his men walk out of a small building to his left.

"Did you see a man with a suitcase?" he asked the Brazilian.

"No."

Connah gave no explanation but began running around the open area, looking behind buildings, in bush coppices, and checking vehicles. He saw no sign of him. He ran to the holes blasted in the walls and looked along the edge of the rainforest. Again, there was no sign of the man. He heard the report of a handgun and looked in that direction. He saw a large barn-like building, the hangar, and ran toward it.

A man lay on the ground beside a twin-engine aircraft inside the hangar. Connah ran forward and saw Stone appear in the airplane's door. Relieved that the apparently dead man was not his partner, Connah stopped at the foot of the ladder.

"What's up?" Stone asked.

"Have you seen anyone running with a suitcase?"

"No."

The man at Connah's feet suddenly sat up, and Connah saw fear in his eyes. "Who's this?"

"That is one of the pilots, Paulo, his daughter Francisca is also one of the pilots. You find Sandberg?"

"Yeah, he's dead."

"Shit, man, how'd that happen? What about your money?"

"In the suitcase. Sandberg told me his name is Oliver or something like that."

Stone held up a hand and said, "Wait a minute." He turned and said something to someone inside. A Brazilian appeared beside Stone.

"This is Araujo Bocaiúva, one of the pilots," Stone said.

Bocaiúva said, "How can I help?"

"You know a guy named Oliver?"

The pilot looked uncertain for several seconds, then seemed to have an epiphany. "Oliver... I think you mean Oliveiras. That would be Miguel Rodrigues Oliveiras. He was in charge of security."

"Is he familiar with the area?"

"Not so much."

"So," Connah said, "he probably doesn't know his way around the jungle?"

"He may know the river. He keeps a boat nearby."

"What type of boat?"

"A swift boat. If you were to ask me, I'd say it's too fast for the river," Bocaiúva said. "However, we too have a fast boat. Which I assume you now own."

"I know the river," Gomes said.

"Your partner and I can use the plane to locate him," Bocaiúva said.

Connah looked at his companions. "Let's do it."

PART III

THE MANHUNT

70

Miguel Rodrigues Oliveiras stayed in the middle of the river. He kept the throttle fully opened, and the nose of the speedboat was raised so that the front half of the watercraft pointed up. The nose was so high that he could not see directly in front of the bow and was forced to look over the side to see where he was going. It resulted in his being blind about what was happening on the opposite side.

He did not see the submerged tree until his bow bounced off it and his outboard motor hit, destroying the propeller and the gearbox. The boat went airborne, and the aluminum hull slammed the water so hard that the steering wheel was yanked from Oliveiras' hands. The vessel turned sideways, and its momentum drove him toward the south bank.

When he'd slammed into the tree, he hit the steering wheel so hard that it broke. The steering column raked along his side, and his nose broke when his face and forehead bounced off the metal dashboard. Oliveiras rocked back in the seat and lost consciousness.

$ $ $ $ $

Gomes was at the wheel while Connah handled the two-way radio. The radio squawked, and Stone's voice came out of the speaker. "I have visual on him. This guy must have a death wish. Over."

"Say again? Over."

"He's driving like he's in the Daytona 500. Christ, he just hit something in the river!" Stone was so excited that he forgot radio discipline and procedure. "He pulled to the south bank."

"How far ahead of us is he?"

"I estimate five miles. No more than seven."

"Okay, we're on our way."

$ $ $ $ $

The impact with the sandy bank jarred Oliveiras back to consciousness. It took him a few moments to recall where he was. Before exiting the boat, he checked the beach on both sides for any sunbathing caiman. He got to his feet and turned around. He strapped a belt containing a holstered pistol and a sheathed knife with a keen foot-long blade around his waist, then grabbed the valise. Each movement sent waves of pain slashing through his damaged side and face. The hurt was so intense that he felt like vomiting.

He heard an airplane and looked to the sky. It took a few seconds for his vision to clear; when it did, he quickly identified the plane—it was Sander's Beechcraft. He got out of the boat carrying his newly gained fortune and entered the rainforest.

$ $ $ $ $

Connah and Gomes pulled alongside the wreck of Oliveiras' vessel. They checked it and then searched the area. Gomes followed tracks in the sandy loam to the edge of the rainforest. "He's gone this way."

Connah joined him, peered into the dim light of the interior for a second, and then returned to the boat he and Gomes used. He picked up his rifle and one of the packs they'd brought from the plantation.

Gomes watched him, shrugged, and then did likewise.

"You don't have to come with me," Connah said. "You and your people have gone above and beyond what we agreed."

"I'm with you to the end," Gomes said.

Connah nodded and walked into the trees.

It took a few seconds for Connah's eyes to make the transition from the brilliant sunshine to the gloom of the rainforest floor. Along with the difference in illumination, a drop of ten degrees actually felt cool. Connah wondered if he was becoming accustomed to the tropical heat.

Gomes crouched and studied the ground, looking for signs of Oliveiras. He rose to his feet and walked in a circle. He expanded the perimeter with every orbit, never taking his eyes from the ground. He stopped about five meters to the south of their entry point and pointed to the south. "He went that way."

Connah nodded and followed the Brazilian's trail.

Gomes studied the tree litter that covered the ground as he walked, looking for any disturbance caused by Oliveiras' passing. The tracks led them on a southerly course.

71

Oliveiras stopped near the roots of a large tree and set the valise on the ground. He straightened up and wiped his forehead. Whenever he touched either his nose, which he believed was broken or the open wound on his forehead, he hissed with pain. His arms and shoulders ached from carrying the grip.

He scanned the immediate area and saw what he was looking for. Climbing its way up a tree was the flexible vine known as the reptile vine. He took his knife and cut off two lengths to fashion a crude harness. He tied the valise handle to the saddle and slid it over his head. He felt the weight of the case as the harness pulled, digging into his shoulders. It would not be easy, but two million U.S. dollars would make the pain worth it. He continued on his trek, heading deeper into the wilderness.

$ $ $ $ $

Connah was exhausted. It seemed like forever since they had broken camp this morning to trek to the plantation—then there was the firefight, followed by the chase—all in all, it had been a full day. He was not unhappy when it became too dark to continue on.

They settled at the base of a tree. Too tired to carry on a conversation, the men ate cold beef jerky and drank tepid water. The saw-like call of a jaguar raised their heads.

"You think it's close?" Connah asked.

"*Não*. We have no worries."

"I hope you're right."

"They only attack humans if they're sick, hurt, or cornered. What we do have to worry about is the stuff that crawls or slides on its belly."

"I've heard that."

They laid back and listened to the night sounds of the rainforest for an undetermined period. Connah broke the silence asking, "Why did you decide to come with me, Edward?"

"I have my reasons."

"Such as?"

"I like you. You are a man I'd go to war with and feel like someone had my back."

"Thanks for that. You said reasons—plural. What are the other reasons?"

"I would hate to see you become another crazy American who disappeared in the Amazon Basin. However, my primary reason for coming is to help you recover your *dinheiro*. If we don't get it, you can't pay my *chefe* what you agreed upon. If he is not paid, I will not be paid."

Connah knew that Gomes couldn't see his smile in the primordial darkness, but when he spoke, he laughed. "Edward, I appreciate your honesty. I will make a point of telling Goncalves what a loyal man you are."

Connah heard the sincerity in the Brazilian's voice when he said, "*Obrigado.* Now I think that maybe we should get some sleep. There is another hard day ahead of us."

"Or more," Connah replied.

$ $ $ $ $

As exhausted as he was, Oliveiras was unable to sleep. His broken nose made it difficult to breathe, and the few times he did doze off, the throbbing pain woke him. Any movement caused spasms of pain. The jungle canopy held in the heat, preventing it from venting into the night sky. The high heat and humidity amplified the levels of his aches and pains. With no breeze to help, Oliveiras' body and clothes were soaked with sweat.

His load had created open, festering sores. The makeshift harness rubbed his shoulders and back, and every movement made agonizing waves of pain. He often considered hiding the money, but he quickly over-ruled that—the rainforest was in a continual state of change. Without a global positioning system, he had no means of determining the latitude and longitude he would need to find his way back. There was also the ever-present danger of loggers clear-cutting the area. There were many forest fires at any given moment, some of which were natural, but most were caused by man. Fatigue, dehydration, and sleep deprivation had made Oliveiras delirious. He leaned back against a tree. Stabbing pain tore into his back and shoulders, he rolled onto his side and fell into a trance-like state.

He muttered softly as his subconscious returned to his childhood, growing up in his grandfather's hovel in one of the worst ghettos in Rio de Janeiro. The old man was more than a little drunk. He was pontificating about the government allowing the systematic destruction of the Amazon Basin. *The fools in Brasilia seem determined to let people burn and ravage the rainforest! Don't they know they are doing damage that may never be undone?* João–Vítor Oliveiras had been a learned man, an environmental expert, and member of the environmental/ecology faculty at the Universidade Federal do Rio de Janeiro and was a highly respected member until he spoke out about the way peasant farmers were being allowed to slash and burn large pieces of the forest. Being the world's largest rainforest, the Amazon took significant amounts of carbon dioxide out of the atmosphere and injected oxygen into it. The old man's argument was that if the present levels of clear-cutting, logging, and fires were not controlled, the Amazon would soon be emitting more carbon dioxide than it was absorbing. If that were to happen, the end result could be a cataclysmic level of global warming. All the old man got for his efforts was the loss of his position and all pensions; he was forced to live his last days in abject poverty.

A sudden peal of thunder brought him out of his state of half-consciousness. He could hear the torrential rain hitting the canopy above, but very little water reached the ground.

72

Above the dense canopy, the sun had been out for almost an hour. Nevertheless, it was still barely twilight on the rainforest floor. Connah heard Gomes moving around and grunted as he struggled to his feet. Every muscle in his body was stiff and ached when he moved.

Gomes handed him a metal cup filled with instant coffee. The taste took Connah back to his days in the military when the powdered coffee had been a staple. As bad as it tasted at that time, it was like the nectar of the gods.

He thanked the Brazilian in his native language. "*Obrigado.* This really hits the spot."

Gomes replied, "*Você é bem vindo...* you are welcome."

There was an early morning chill to the air, and the not unpleasant scent of wood smoke from the small fire Gomes had used to heat water hung close to the ground. Connah glanced at his watch. It was 7:30 a.m. He finished the coffee, shook the remaining drops, and handed it to Gomes.

After the coffee cup was stored, Gomes threw the pack over his shoulders and picked up his weapon. "Time to move out."

Connah nodded.

"Are you okay?"

"Yeah," Connah replied, "I'm just not used to sleeping on the ground. It's been a while since I've had to do it. I'm just a bit stiff. Once we get going and my muscles warm-up, I'll be fine."

Gomes nodded. "Here, you should eat something." He handed Connah some beef jerky. "I found his trail earlier before you woke up. We go this way."

They started after Oliveiras.

$ $ $ $ $

Oliveiras weaved a path through the dead logs and broadleaf plants that thrived in the rainforest understory. Many ferns grew to heights higher than the average man, forcing a traveler to cut a path through them with machetes. The trees at this level were spaced farther away than those that grew skyward, forming the canopy.

Each and every step had become an act of strength. Overnight, Oliveiras's broken nose had swollen so much that his eyes were narrow slits. It was like steering a tank using the limited viewing ports in its armor. He had no peripheral vision, and his eyes were continually tearing. His nasal cavities were continuously draining, and he had made the mistake of wiping the discharge away with his wrist. The result was a stabbing pain that nearly brought him to his knees. Breathing through his mouth had not helped him gain sufficient oxygen to replenish the energy he was expending moving through the jungle.

He walked along, mindlessly placing one foot before another, not actually seeing anything in his surrounding lines of sight. He had been barely conscious of the incline that the ground had taken. The land had turned into a steep slope, and he was forced to pull his body upward using small bushes as an aid.

He suddenly became aware of an odor that sent tremors of fear running through him—smoke! It was not the smoke of a campfire, and when he looked around, he saw a cloud of smoke covering everything. He suddenly became aware of a crescendo of sound, the crackling and snapping of wood burning, and the unmistakable flickering light of an out-of-control forest fire.

Flames jumped from tree to tree in the canopy above. Fireballs, looking like incendiary burning meteorites, fell into the understory. There was a sudden updraft of wind as the raging inferno sucked life-giving air upward to feed the flames. Instantly, all thoughts of pain and discomfort left Oliveiras' mind. His immediate need was a refuge from the inferno.

He looked around in confusion, barely noticing the panicked wildlife that raced past him. Deer, tapir, and numerous other ground dwellers passed by, paying him no attention in their terror. Overhead, monkeys and birds dashed through the trees in a desperate flight to stay ahead of the deadly flames, fumes, and heat so intense that it would suck the air out of lungs and replace it with searing fire.

He saw what appeared to be the entrance to a cave to his left and ran toward it. The maw in the earth was no more than twenty meters away, but it seemed like twenty thousand kilometers to the terrified man. The opening was too low to enter upright, so he dropped onto hands and knees and crawled into the relatively cool interior. He heard something moving in the dark further in and fumbled his right hand along his side until he felt the handle of his sidearm. He slid sideways until he was against the wall and aimed the pistol into the black interior.

$ $ $ $ $

Connah and Gomes had been climbing a slope for most of an hour when Gomes raised his right hand in the international sign for a *halt*. He turned to Connah, who said, "Yeah, I smell it, too."

"We must find shelter and soon." Gomes did a quick search of the area and then said, "Come this way."

He turned left and ran down the slope with Connah jogging behind him. They broke through a coppice of tall ferns and came to a deep pool. Gomes began cutting reeds and ensuring they were hollow.

Connah knew what Gomes was doing and asked, "Is it wise for us to get in the water? We don't know what may be there."

Gomes handed him a couple of reeds. "Probably not. Who knows what *may* happen? However, if we stay out here, we know what *will* happen."

A tree near the water burst into flames with a deafening WHOOSH, and Connah stuck a reed in his mouth, entered the water, and grabbed onto an underwater tree root to keep from rising to the surface. He would submerge the reed every few seconds to keep it from catching fire. The water turned an undulating red-orange as the fire swept over and around the pond. Connah felt the water warming and wondered if he was about to be boiled to death.

It seemed an eternity before the bright color of the water tapered off, and he could see debris from the air floating on the water. He remained submerged until the water temperature began to cool, then he stood up in the chest-deep water.

There were pieces of black wood floating on the surface, and the smell of carbon and burnt wood permeated the air. He heard a sound to his right and sighed in relief when Gomes broke the surface.

"Are you alright?" Connah asked.

"*Sim*, how about you?"

"I have to admit, I got more than a little concerned when the water began heating."

They remained in the water for several minutes. The air they breathed was foul with the odor of burnt carbon and bits of ash that floated in the air. Smoke drifted up from the smoldering torched trees.

"You think it's cool enough for us to start walking?" Connah asked.

"We may want to wait a bit. Finding Oliveiras's trail after this is going to be a challenge," Gomes replied. "On the other hand, if he survived and we do find his trail again, it will be easy to follow in the ash and bare soil."

"Shit," Connah spat out the word. "If the fire got him, there won't be any of my money left."

"I had that same thought."

Gomes brought his rifle out of the water and, when Connah did likewise, said, "We should take some time to clean these. Who knows, we may need them soon. *Não?*"

"We need to find a place where we can sit... and that isn't here."

They left the pool, found a large rock, spent time ensuring their weapons were functional and then began searching for Oliveiras's trail.

$ $ $ $ $

Smoke filled the cave, forcing Oliveiras to use some of his precious drinking water to soak a handkerchief to cover his nose and mouth. The crude filter stopped most, but not all, of the ash and soot that drifted in through the opening. If it were not for the noise he'd heard further in the cavern, he would have ventured deeper in. He heard a loud snort and aimed his pistol in that direction.

From the darkness, a face appeared. The distinctive oatmeal-colored markings on its muzzle and the brown markings around the eyes identified the co-occupant as a Spectacled Bear. The bear was small compared to those found in North America and known to favor a vegetarian diet. They are non-territorial and non-aggressive, calm and submissive by nature. However, they will attack for self-defense and for protecting their young. Oliveiras's dilemma was that he was unsure if the animal felt cornered and threatened.

The cacophony of the wildfire had died down. Oliveiras slowly backed toward the cave opening. He kept his eyes locked on the bear as he crept, dragging the makeshift harness and valise in his left hand while wielding the nine-millimeter pistol with his right.

He passed through the cave's entrance, and the bear ran forward. Surprised by the sudden burst, Oliveiras rolled to one side and prepared to shoot the animal. The terrified bear raced past him and bounded down the mountain slope without looking in his direction.

Relieved that the impasse was resolved, Oliveiras holstered his handgun. He returned to the cave, fell facedown, and waited out the waves of pain that wracked his body.

He had no idea how long he lay semi-conscious before the agony eased to a level with which he could cope. He struggled to a sitting position, gingerly removed his sweat-laden shirt, and hissed when the saturated coarse material pulled away from the open, festering sores. Serpent vines had rubbed and torn through his skin, and he saw raw flesh on both of his shoulders. He could not see his back but knew without a doubt that it, too, had suffered similar wounds. He took his canteen out and took a sip of water. He thought: I would have never imagined that money could be so much trouble. He gently put his shirt on and picked up the crude harness. Rather than risk further damage from the improvised harness, he discarded it and carried the briefcase when he left the cave and continued climbing the slope.

73

Gomes and Connah continued hiking south, assuming that Oliveiras had continued in that direction. The terrain had started rising into a steep incline. Gomes suddenly pointed off to their left. "A cave," he announced.

"You think he waited out the fire there?"

"Can't hurt to check it."

Gomes led the way upward. As they climbed, their clothes, hands, and faces became coated with a layer of black soot. Small clouds of coal-black grime and ash burst from the burnt ground with every step they took.

Gomes stopped and pointed to the ground when they neared the cave's entrance. Connah joined him and saw where the soot layer in the soil had been disturbed and two sets of tracks—one of an animal, maybe a bear, and one human.

"Looks like he made it this far," Gomes said.

Connah visually searched the area. He pointed up the slope. "Looks like he went up. What's over there?"

"If he continues going straight south, Bolivia. If he heads west, Peru. However, I don't think he'll be headed for either of them. He'll likely meet some loggers or miners; the Amazon is full of them. If that happens, he could get a ride to who knows where."

"Sounds like we'd better pick up the pace," Connah said.

Gomes grinned. "You're the *chefe*. I'm just along to protect my *chefe's* interest."

"I think you got a lot more say in this than you think. I'd be lost without you. Besides, you know where we are. I sure as hell don't."

"My *chefe* said that you were a smart one. Let's get going. Oliveiras has a head start on us."

$ $ $ $ $

It was midday before Oliveiras left the burnt land and reentered virgin forest. The trip through the fire-blasted land had been unnerving. Never in his life had he been in the rainforest when it was barren of any wildlife. Nor were the numerous species of birds and monkeys heard. He had crossed the remnants of an abandoned farm and, when he passed a pile of burned deadfall, he was sure that he'd found the source of the wildfire. He thought of his grandfather's belief that peasants burning trees they'd cleared for worthless farmland and the fire getting out of control caused the majority of the Amazon's wildfires.

Oliveiras was not traveling fast. Nagging pain, along with fatigue and discomfort, kept him from maintaining anything above a slow walk. The weight and bulk of the briefcase further slowed him, and he constantly prayed that he would find assistance soon. It was unusual to travel as far as he had without coming across a single logging or mining crew. He began to believe that he was so deep into the forest that few if any humans had traveled this far. That made him think about the indigenous Indians who roamed the deep woods. There are parts of the Amazon still occupied by ancient tribes. There were numerous stories of loggers and miners being attacked by them. He believed that men equipped with stone-age weapons stood little if any chance in an engagement with men bearing modern weapons. However, he was alone and could be easily overwhelmed by numbers.

Now that he was out of the open created by the burnt land and back in the safety of the dense forest, he felt safe enough to give his aching body some rest. While he took another sip of his rapidly depleting water supply, he watched his back trail. Thus far, he had not seen any signs of pursuit, and then there was the fire. Still, he had no delusions about the American assassin coming for his money. Look at what he'd already done. The armed attack on the fortified plantation had to be expensive. There was no way the American could have done that alone. He had to have local backing, and he was sure where it had come from. That idiot he called Porco Gordo had made an enemy out of Fábio Correia Goncalves. The American must have offered the drug runner and crime boss a lot of money.

Oliveiras settled against a tree and took a cigarette from his shirt pocket. He looked at the Marlboro. The paper was stained brown from sweat, but it had dried. He took a lighter from his pocket and lit it.

As he smoked, Oliveiras considered his situation. It was evident that there was no place in Brazil where he'd be safe. Indeed, by now, Goncalves knew that he had the American's money. Even if the assassin had died in the wildfire, the Manaus crime boss would be looking for him. He had no doubt that if Goncalves knew it, so did the higher-ups in the PCC.

Oliveiras decided he would have to alter his plans. He might have to leave South America to be safe… be safe? He would have to do what Porco Gordo had done. Find a fortified location and hire a trained security team to ensure his safety. He began to wonder if two million dollars was going to be enough to keep him alive.

He glanced up at the sky and realized that he'd been sitting longer than he had intended. Time to get off his ass and start moving.

$ $ $ $ $

It was dusk when Connah and Gomes came to the source of the conflagration. "Jesus," Connah said, "I thought only the state governments in the United States were dumb enough to allow anyone to do this."

"In Brazil, most of this is done illegally. Nevertheless, it is the federal government's failure to, how is it you say *processar*?"

"I think the English word you are thinking of is prosecute."

"They do not pursue the people who do this. They expect to find good soil to farm. They soon realize that all this ground is good for is to be a rainforest and move on to do it again."

"In my home state of Maine, it is logging companies that do this. They hire people called lobbyists to bribe our politicians to pass laws protecting the big companies who do it."

"We have that here, we call them *lobista,* and they do the same thing. It is the crooked *político* who the authorities need to arrest."

"If your country is like mine," Connah said, "it will never happen."

Gomes looked at the sky and said, "It is late. We should get to the other side before we camp for the night."

74

A car was waiting at the dock when the *Princesa de Amazonas* docked in Manaus. Correia watched his deckhands tie down the vessel and then walked down the gangplank. He was not surprised to see Fábio Correia Goncalves get out of the vehicle. The drug lord called in Portuguese, "Why haven't I heard anything from you in three days?"

"Do not panic, cousin," Correia answered. "Things went pretty much as we expected."

"Pretty much? That sounds as if not everything went well. What happened?"

"We should talk someplace less public."

Goncalves did an abrupt one hundred-eighty-degree turn, opened the Mercedes Benz's back door, and motioned for Correia to join him before reentering. Once they were settled, Goncalves said, "Leave us, Raymundo."

The driver exited the car, closing the door behind him. Correia immediately felt the cool air from the air conditioning overwhelm the ninety-plus-degree outside heat and humidity. "You are now the proud owner of a plantation, complete with the airplane."

"Did Connah get the money?" Goncalves asked.

"That is the part that did not go so well. During the attack on the main house, Miguel Rodrigues Oliveiras shot his former boss. Then took what money was there, as well as the banking account books for the rest of it."

"And?"

"They chased him down the river with a boat."

"They? Who is this they?"

"Connah and Gomes."

"Edward is still with Connah?"

"Yes. Oliveiras crashed his boat and fled into the rainforest with the money and account books. Connah and Edward are pursuing him."

An evil leer covered Goncalves' face. "So, the American and Edward are in the rainforest together?"

"*Sim.*"

"Cousin, this could work out even better than we hoped."

$ $ $ $ $

Oliveiras was exhausted. He lay in the shade of a broadleaf fern, watching his back trail. He had come to the decision that there was no way he was going to outrun his pursuers, not while he had the burden of carrying the valise. His only hope was to wait, watch, and ambush whoever was on his trail.

When he'd first stopped and hunkered down, the denizens of the forest were silent. He had laid quiet for the past twenty minutes or so, and the wildlife had come alive. He heard the chatter of monkeys as they cavorted among the treetops. He'd even observed two tapirs rooting in the sediment littering the ground in search of food. A jaguar sawed, and the wild pigs darted off into the undergrowth.

He relaxed. The animals would be all the alarm he needed. They would go silent as soon as the trackers arrived. Until then, he would rest. In minutes, his eyes grew heavy, and he entered into a delirious half-sleep.

$ $ $ $ $

Connah and Gomes were relentless in their pursuit of Oliveiras. Connah had stopped aching and hurting as his body adjusted to the stress and strain of traveling through the rainforest on foot. He chuckled, unaware that he'd done so aloud. When he saw Gomes looking at him, he said, "I was thinking that it's kind of nice not having Stoney here complaining about the jungle and everything in it."

"He does seem to dislike it. How long have you been working together?"

"Oh, we go back over fifteen years. Stone and I met in Marine Corps Scout Sniper Training at Quantico, Virginia. After completing the training, we were assigned to the same platoon. We just naturally became a team."

"A team?"

"A Marine Corps Scout/Sniper team usually consists of two men, a shooter, and a spotter."

"You were the shooter?" Gomes asked.

"Actually, we took turns. Each team member has the same training."

"You see a lot of jungle combat?"

"Truthfully, no. We were in the middle east, Iraq, and later Afghanistan. Don and I were mostly in cities, desert, or mountains—depending on the mission."

Gomes raised his right arm, the universal infantry signal for stop. Connah froze for a second, dropped into a crouch, and scanned the area. "You see something?" he asked.

"Actually, it's more what I don't hear."

Connah listened as he continued scanning the area. "I don't hear anything."

"Exactly, something has scared the animals."

"You think it was us?"

"Maybe, but I'd rather check things out before we rush into an ambush. I have been through enough of them to know when things are not good."

$ $ $ $ $

Oliveiras's eyes snapped open. The jungle was once again quiet. He peered out of his place of concealment, paying close attention to the barely discernible animal trail he'd followed earlier.

He settled in a prone shooting position, inhaling deeply when his movement strained the open wounds on his shoulders and back. Once the pain subsided, he turned the safety on his pistol to the *off* position, peered through the sight, and waited.

75

Connah crawled forward and watched the barely visible trail ahead of him. He settled on his stomach, lying beneath a broad-leafed plant, and made a slow, visual search of the area. For fifteen minutes, nothing moved but his eyes. A gentle breeze passed through the understory, easing the discomfort of staying still in the oppressive heat while sweat dripped from the back of his neck and tickled as it ran down his sides. The bandana that he'd wrapped around his forehead became soaked, and the excess moisture dribbled down his face. The rainforest was so quiet that he heard the drops of sweat as they hit the dead leaves and centuries-old compost that littered the ground upon which he lay.

For the first time, he fully appreciated Gomes' skill in the bush. They had settled on a plan in which Connah was to be the shooter and the Brazilian, the bait. Still, Connah had yet to hear Gomes as he crept through the undergrowth in an attempt to draw Oliveiras out.

He remained motionless and quiet, thankful for the training he'd received as a Marine scout sniper, and as time passed, the forest came back to life. He heard a call above which sounded like a maniacal laugh that changed from a joyful to a sad sound and rendered as *ha-ha-ha har-her-her*. Moments later, a hawk-like bird pounced on some type of prey with an audible thud. It raised its head holding a six- or seven-foot snake in its beak—Connah was by no means a herpetologist. Still, he knew a venomous bushmaster when he saw one.

The bird bit just behind the head with enough force to sever the head.

He'd never seen a bird like it before. The bird turned and faced him as if seeking praise for its kill and then launched into the air holding the headless snake in its claws, much as an osprey does. It settled on a branch where it began to rip the snake apart while feeding.

While it ate, Connah had an opportunity to observe the bird. The broad black face mask stretched across the neck as a narrow collar, bordered white. The feather shafts were dark on the crown, giving it a somewhat streaked effect. The upper wings and back were blackish brown. The upper-tail coverts were whitish buff, and the tail feathers were barred black and whitish, ending in white. The underside was uniformly pale buff; there was a bit of dark speckling on the thighs. He made a mental note to ask Gomes if he knew what type of bird it was.

Connah turned his eyes back to his visual search of the area. Although he could not explain its source, he had a feeling that his quarry was nearby. It was just a matter of time and waiting. In the sniper business, he who lays silent and motionless for the longest time is more than likely to get the first shot. Usually, that was all it took. His being alive was all the proof he needed to prove that fact.

$ $ $ $ $

Gomes moved through the undergrowth like a wraith. As he moved, neither a plant nor a bush moved. It was as if a shadow had passed by. He checked out the area and saw nobody. Confident that he was alone and would not be overheard, he took a two-way radio out of his pack and whispered into it.

$ $ $ $ $

Oliveiras felt the cramp in his leg and fought with all his willpower to remain still. The pain was worse than being stabbed with a knife. He gritted his teeth and tried to ignore the increasing desire to stand up and straighten the offending leg. It was not working. The more he tried to keep his mind on something else, the more his leg sent messages to his brain. Finally, he could stand it no longer and leaped to his feet. He stretched the offending leg, and as the pain began to lessen, he saw a shaft of sunlight reflect off a telescopic sight.

Someone shouted his name. He looked up and raised his pistol.

$ $ $ $ $

Connah saw movement beneath a wide-leafed plant and concentrated on it. Suddenly, an armed man jumped out of the cover and kneaded his leg. Was this his man or some hunter? There was only one way to find out. He centered his sight on the man's head and shouted: "Give it up, Oliveiras!"

The man's head snapped up, and he began to raise his weapon.

Connah pulled the trigger.

Oliveiras' head snapped back, his bush hat flew into the air, and he fell backward.

$ $ $ $ $

Gomes heard Connah shout and then the shot. He immediately returned the radio to his pack and headed in the direction from which they'd come.

When Gomes came to the slight trail, he saw Connah standing over a prone man. He stepped out of the overgrowth, and the American spun toward him, rifle aimed at his chest. Gomes raised his hands. "Whoa… I'm on your side, remember?"

Connah lowered his weapon. "Sorry, you surprised me."

"Not as much as you surprised him. Is that Oliveiras?"

"It had better be."

Gomes walked to the body, bent over it, and searched it. He found a wallet, opened it, and found a Brazilian driver's license. He handed it to Connah. "It was a good kill," he said.

Connah inspected Oliveiras' hide and found the valise. He opened it to ensure his money was, in fact, in it. Satisfied that there was cash and passbook for an offshore bank in the case, he decided to do a count later. His first priority was to get back to the plantation and secure it.

He hooked his rifle's sling over his right shoulder, picked up the case, and walked out of the dense growth. Keeping his eyes down to avoid tripping over the numerous roots and vines, he stepped onto the trail. He heard Gomes say, "Nothing personal, man. But I got my orders."

Connah looked up, saw Gomes aiming his rifle at him, and dove to the side.

He felt something hit his head and lost consciousness.

$ $ $ $ $

Gomes kept his weapon steady as he approached Connah. He crouched over him and felt his neck—a strong pulse was detectable. He saw the open wound along the side of the comatose American's head and debated whether or not he should do the wise thing and finish the job.

He had not liked his *chefe's* order to kill Connah and bring the money to Manaus. Taking the money didn't bother him, but he did not want to kill Connah. He and the American had not known each other long enough for him to consider them friends; however, he had grown to respect the man. Still, he had fired his weapon intending to do what Goncalves had ordered. Connah's diving to the side resulted in a grazing wound, not a solid hit to the head.

Gomes decided on a course of action. He rummaged through Connah's backpack and left him his flashlight, the two-way radio he'd used to communicate with his partner in the airplane, and the means to make a fire. Gomes stood, gathered Connah's rifle, unloaded it, and grasped the barrel. He swung the rifle like a baseball or cricket bat and smashed the weapon against the trunk of a tree. The stock shattered, and Gomes sent the metallic parts spinning into the dense undergrowth.

He stood over Connah and said, "I know you cannot hear me, but I am giving you a chance, however small it is. Avoid contact with hostile Indians, poisonous snakes, and starving predators, and you might find your way back to the river. Then you'll be close enough to contact your friend by radio." He crouched down beside the unconscious man and reached for his gun. He stopped, shrugged his shoulders, and added. "I will leave you your pistol."

Retrieving his rifle and the money-filled case, he bade farewell to his former partner, "*passe bem, parceiro*," and left.

76

Connah woke up and noticed two things: one, his head throbbed with the most excruciating headache he'd ever had, and two, it was dark. He sat up and touched the left side of his forehead. He immediately winced with pain and felt sticky moisture. He knew that the wet substance was blood. He lifted the bottom of his camouflage shirt and ripped off a strip of his tee shirt. He made a crude bandana and tied it around his head. The shirt was damp with his salty sweat, and he hissed when it came in contact with the open wound.

He remained sitting and tried to recall exactly what had happened. He recalled seeing Gomes aim his rifle at him and then nothing. He recalled an old axiom: *You never hear the one that hits you.* Connah realized that he'd finally learned the truth—he had *not* heard the shot. He was still wearing his backpack, removed it from his shoulders, opened it, and felt its contents. His hands came in contact with his flashlight. He took it out and turned it on. The beam of light illuminated Oliveiras' corpse, and in the narrow beam, his face appeared to be pulsating. A closer look revealed that the dead man was covered with giant millipedes, ants, and other insect scavengers. He realized how close he'd come to being likewise, and an involuntary shudder raced through him.

A further search of the area showed that the valise was gone, as was his long gun. He felt his hip and was relieved to find his sidearm still in its holster. He was unsure if it was his imagination or not, but he heard a myriad of sounds. He imagined what other creatures and bugs would be attracted by the body, now in the early stages of decay, and wanted to spend the remaining hours of darkness in a spot free of scavengers. He struggled to his feet and shined the light in a circle until he located the trail he'd taken to get here. He staggered for several steps until he regained his balance and walked into the forest without so much as a final glance at the feast that had been Miguel Rodrigues Oliveiras.

He didn't go ten meters before nausea and dizziness overwhelmed him, and he dropped down, rolled over on his side, and passed out.

$ $ $ $ $

Now that Gomes was not encumbered by the American, he could cover more ground faster. He arrived at the burnt land in less than half the time it had taken with Connah. He had carried the valise in his left hand. He used his two-way radio to contact Fábio Correia Goncalves. He gave his boss a quick update on his situation. They discussed a likely place where Goncalves' people could rendezvous with him.

Gomes wondered if he'd made a mistake by omitting the fact that he had intentionally left Ian Connah alive. The thought that it could be a mortal mistake entered his mind. However, he decided that he'd deal with that when, and if, it happened. He knew that if Connah found his way out of the rainforest, he would undoubtedly come after him. If that were to happen, Gomes wouldn't be as compassionate next time.

$ $ $ $ $

The sound of something snapping woke Connah. He sat up and struggled to a sitting position. His head was pounding, his stomach nauseous, and he squinted as he tried to compensate for his blurry vision. From past experience, he knew that he was concussed. He heard a loud clacking noise and looked toward it. At first, he wasn't sure what he was seeing. There was an undulating gray mound on the trail about fifty meters away. He began blinking his eyes until they cleared enough for him to discern what it was. He was surprised when the featherless head and neck of a King Vulture popped out of the mound, followed by two more. The largest bird in the vulture family is common from southern Mexico to Argentina. Although among the ugliest birds on Earth, they are also one of the most colorful. The skin on their heads is wrinkled and folded, and they have shades of red and purple, vivid orange on the necks, and yellow on the throats. All have a highly noticeable irregular golden crest attached above their orange and black bills. The scavengers were tearing off bits and pieces of a dead animal.

It took several moments for his head to clear enough to recall the events of the previous day. It would be some time before his thought processes wholly recovered. He suddenly realized what or who was the main course at the vultures' banquet—it was Miguel Rodrigues Oliveiras. That knowledge, coupled with his queasy stomach state, caused his abdominal muscles to violently contract, and he barely turned his head away before he vomited.

The sound of his retching disturbed the vultures, and they launched into the air. Connah saw the red mound that they'd abandoned. He suffered a wave of intense dry heaves, which he believed would not stop until his very insides came out of his mouth. He took a deep breath, trying to stop the contractions, and staggered to his feet. He turned away from the carnage, wrapped his arms around his stomach, and staggered away. He heard the loud flapping of wings as the vultures returned to their meal.

77

Connah woke up. Unable to determine the time, he looked at his watch and saw that it was 2:45. The fact that some light could penetrate the canopy told him that it was afternoon. He grabbed a vine, pulled himself to his feet, and stood for a few moments trying to stabilize. His head still throbbed, but not as much as it had during his last period of consciousness. Experience with prior concussions had taught him that he should avoid strenuous activity... that was a laugh. There was no way in his current situation that he could do that. He wanted to curl up in a fetal position and sleep for days. However, his recent experiences with rainforest scavengers made him want to avoid doing anything that would make him look like food for insects and vultures.

He opened his backpack and took an inventory. Gomes had left his flashlight, two-way radio, and other items for some unfathomable reason. Each of them may turn out to be essential for his survival. The nine-millimeter H & K VP9 pistol and two seventeen-round magazines were the most critical things. There was no way that those items would have been left behind if Gomes thought he was dead or by accident. Connah was confused. If the situation had been reversed, he would have made sure his victim was dead or had no chance of surviving the rainforest alive. It was apparent that Gomes had done what someone else wanted him to do. Connah had no doubt that was Fábio Correia Goncalves.

Okay, Connah thought, Gomes was obviously following orders. I'm going to do whatever I have to do to make him regret not finishing me off.

He repacked his stuff and began backtracking his trail to the river.

$ $ $ $ $

Gomes reached civilization in a day and a half. Not having to continually follow the trail left by someone else cut the time required by more than a day. He chose to not return to the boat but traveled cross-country to Tefé. Not a large city by most standards, the river port was home to roughly 75,000 people. But most important to Gomes, there was an airport with commercial air transportation to Manaus. He arrived shortly after nightfall and walked through the dark streets along the river to one of the safe-houses that Goncalves maintained along the drug route from Columbia.

He rapped on the door, and it was opened only far enough for the old man to peer out. In Portuguese, he said, "Yes?"

"Hello, Carlo."

"Edward? What are you doing here?" The old man opened the door and leaned out. He checked the unpaved street in both directions. "You are alone?"

"Yes. Step aside for Christ's sake." Gomes pushed his way through the door, pushing the old man before him. "I need a place to stay until Fábio can arrange for me to get to Manaus."

"Of course, of course." Carlo Alves eyed Gomes' valise on the room's single table.

Gomes had never trusted the old man and, when he saw him peering at the case, said, "Which room, you old fool?"

Alves nodded and motioned for Gomes to follow.

Gomes followed the old man, whose back was bent forward ninety degrees with kyphosis. He had to angle his head back to see where he was going, down a narrow corridor and then up an equally narrow flight of stairs. Alves stopped before the first door, fumbled in his pocket until he found a key, and opened the door.

Gomes entered the room and then turned to Alves. He held out his hand. "The key. Give me the key."

Alves gave Gomes a hurt look and said, "This is the only key I have to this room. In fact, it is the only one for all of the rooms. It is a master key for all doors inside and out."

"That is even better. Give it to me."

"But—"

"If you don't give me the damned key, you will not have to worry about anything… ever."

Alves immediately got the message and handed him the key.

"It will only be for one, two days at the most," Gomes said.

78

Connah found his way back to the river as the sun was setting on the third day since Gomes had left him. He'd been drinking water from small streams and pools for three days and replenished his canteen from the river. Thus far, he'd been fortunate and had not been afflicted with diarrhea from the untreated water, a malady Marines called Montezuma's Revenge.

He'd been hearing a plane circling the area for the past hour and took a chance on using the two-way radio. He almost cried when he heard Stone's voice come out of the speaker.

"Is that you, Ian? Over."

"It is. I'm at the river where we left the boats. Over."

"Is one of the boats operational? Over."

"It might be, but I'm not in any shape to drive it. Over."

"Stay where you are, and someone will be there in the morning. Will you be all right to spend another night? Over."

"I don't think I have any other option. Over."

"Roger that. Did you find Oliveiras and the money?" Stone asked.

"Yes, but there's a lot more to it. Will you be coming tomorrow? Over."

"Just let someone try to stop me. Over."

"Okay, I need to find a campsite. See you in the morning. Out."

Connah broke the radio connection, saw the Beechcraft King Air 350I descend, and approach him. It passed by, no more than twenty feet above the muddy water of the Rio Solimões. As it flew past, he held up his right hand and waved. The pilot wagged the plane's wings and elevated. Connah stood in the evening gloom and watched as the aircraft flew away, and he could no longer hear the soothing sound of its motors.

$ $ $ $ $

Gomes walked through the terminal of Pref. Orlando Marinho Airport Aeroporto in Tefé. He checked the departure board and saw that Azul flight 4184 was scheduled to depart at 07:55 and arrive in Manaus at 09:00.

He found the departure gate and took a seat near the door. He studied the faces of the other passengers, assessing the level of danger each of them might present. He glanced at the clock over the door. It was 06:45—another hour before boarding. He went back to developing his threat assessment.

After fifteen minutes of studying his fellow passengers, he began to wonder if it was time for him to find another line of work. Drug smuggling and being armed muscle for Goncalves was making him paranoid. His thoughts shifted to Connah. Had he died, or had he survived? It wouldn't surprise him if the American assassin was alive and had found his way out of the rainforest. He decided that he'd better assume the worst and keep his eyes and ears open for any sign or word of him. Now, he surmised, that *is* paranoid.

$ $ $ $ $

Connah stood on the river's bank, keeping a close watch on the shoreline. The last thing he wanted was to come in contact with a caiman with a New York attitude. He held the H & K pistol in his right hand and placed his left one over his eyes like the visor of a ball cap to shield his eyes from the sun. He was still suffering the effects of the concussion and, among other things, was still light-sensitive. The sun reflecting off the river made him blink, and he felt as if he'd just visited an optometrist and had his eyes dilated. Considering how restricted his vision was, he realized that he should step back from the river's edge.

He was unsure how long he had been waiting before he heard the motor of a high-speed boat approaching. He knew how Robinson Crusoe must have felt when he saw the sails of the ship that rescued him. He saw Stone standing up beside the man at the controls and waving. Connah smiled a broad grin when the boat did a sharp right-hand turn and cut its motor. He resisted the urge to run into the water as the craft slowly drifted toward the shore.

The bow slid onto the sandy shore, and Stone vaulted out. He stopped short of Connah and said, "No offense, partner, but I've seen roadkill that was in better shape than you."

Although Connah did not have a mirror, he knew what his partner saw.

Connah's clothes were torn, covered with grime, and had white salt lines where sweat had dried. He had not shaved nor showered in almost a week and had a bloody strip of T-shirt wrapped around his head. "I look that bad, huh?"

"Well, let's put it this way," Stone said, "there's no way the Corps would want you on a recruiting poster—that's for sure."

Stone stepped forward, grabbed his arm, and led him to the boat Connah had left when he went after Oliveiras. "C'mon, let's get you to the plantation and clean you up. You can fill me in on your latest adventure." He paused and looked around. "Where's Gomes?"

"That's a story all by itself."

79

After a hot shower, change of clothes, and filling Stone in on his hunt for Oliveiras, Connah fell asleep. He woke up to find Stone, Araujo Bocaiúva, and a strange man standing beside his bed.

"How you feeling, partner?" Stone asked. He turned to the stranger. "This fellow is Rodrigo Cruz. I guess you might call him the chief of a tribe of indigenous Indians. I don't recall which tribe…"

"The Tikuna. We are the largest tribe by population. The Yanomami are the largest if you consider the land they populate."

Connah gave Stone a quizzical look.

"He's also a doctor. His tribe lives close by, so Araujo sent for him. He came to look you over and see if you're okay."

Cruz nodded, shook Connah's hand, and said, "Señhor Stone has told me that you have received a head wound."

"Ain't nothing, just a graze."

"Have you experienced a loss of balance, nausea, blurry vision, severe headaches?"

"All of the above."

Cruz nodded and spent fifteen minutes examining Connah. When finished, he closed his medical bag and said, "It appears that you have been severely concussed. Frankly, I'm amazed that you were able to find your way back to the river."

"It wasn't easy, that's for sure."

"Two of my tribesmen were hunting in the area where you were. I'm amazed they did not find you."

"To be truthful, Doctor, I'm as amazed as you are. I don't remember much about my return either."

Cruz looked at Connah and then said, "They did, however, find the skeletal remains of a human being. It seems as if the vultures and various scavengers had been at it for several days, and there were signs of one maybe two more people. You didn't come across that, did you?"

"Nope. As delirious as I was, I think I'd remember that."

"Okay. I was hoping you could shed some light on it. I have reported it to the authorities, but it could be a week or more before they arrive. You should take it easy until the symptoms lessen."

"Thanks, Doc. You're English is excellent."

"Duke University Medical School and I interned at Cook County Medical Center in Chicago."

"Cook County? I've heard that can be tough duty."

"It is," Cruz said, "but there is no better place to learn trauma medicine. It's a skill that I have found invaluable in my practice here. What do you have for medical supplies?"

"I don't know," Stone said.

"For the headaches, mild pain killers such as aspirin, acetaminophen, or ibuprofen are fine." He turned to Connah. "Normally, I would tell you to minimize all physical activity for the first few days. However, it's too late for that. Nevertheless, you should avoid physical activities, such as general physical exertion or any vigorous movements, until these activities no longer provoke your symptoms. Other than that, you should be fine. Get as much rest, both physical and mental as possible."

"What do we owe you, Doctor?" Stone asked.

"Well, money isn't all that useful out here. How about you airlift any of my people who need medical care above and beyond what I can provide?"

Connah looked at Bocaiúva. "That okay with you?"

"*Señhor*, it is your airplane. I will fly wherever I am told."

"You got a deal, doctor," Connah said.

$ $ $ $ $

The following two days were blanks to Connah. He got out of bed on the third day, and he, Bocaiúva, and Stone discussed their next move. "There's no way in hell that Gomes did this on his own. Goncalves gave him the order to kill me once we recovered my money," Connah said.

"So, what's our plan?"

"I intend to teach the sonuvabitch that if you screw with a bull, eventually you're going to get gored."

"I take it that if you find out he's behind this, all deals are off."

Connah looked around the grounds of the fortified plantation. "What do you know about running a place like this?"

"On a scale of one-to-ten? Zilch point shit."

"That much, huh?"

"Actually, less."

"We can deal with that later. Right now, we need to figure out a way to get into Manaus without Goncalves knowing about it."

"The only airport is in Manaus. Araujo, where is the next closest?"

Bocaiúva spread a map on the table and pointed. "Parintins, here, is the closest commercial airport. It is 370 kilometers, 230 of your miles, by air. The only other way is to take the ferry, about nine-and-a-half hours. However, the riverboat captains all know each other, and it won't be long before Otávio Rodrigues Correia knows of it. If he knows, then Goncalves knows."

"So, how do we get there?"

"Ah, *señhor*, I said the nearest commercial airport was 370 kilometers away. However, there are many smaller landing strips that the drug runners use. For instance, I know of one, less than ten kilometers by the Rio Negro Bridge." Bocaiúva touched the map with his right index finger. "Here, near Cacau Pirera. If you were to ask me, that is where I would land. I could drop you and then fly back. Some people could meet you there and help you get into Manaus, along with any weapons and equipment you may need."

Connah looked at Stone. "What do you think?"

"It's your show. You call the shots."

Bocaiúva grinned, "It so happens—I."

Connah said, "Let me guess, you have a cousin."

80

Connah sat in the co-pilot seat, peering out the windscreen at a black void. He glanced at Bocaiúva, who smiled, "Don't worry, *señhor*, I know this airfield. How is it, you Americans say? Like the back of my hand."

"As dark, as it is in this part of the world, I doubt that I'd be able to find the back of my hand once the sun goes down."

Bocaiúva pointed to their front. "There is our landing field."

Connah looked in the direction the pilot was pointing and saw what looked like the headlights of four vehicles, all aimed toward the west. "It still looks awfully dark between each pair of lights. Are you sure that it's safe? What about the wind direction? Isn't that a factor, too?"

"I have all the information I need to land safely. The two cars closest to us mark the beginning of the runway. The farthest away is at the end. The direction in which the lights are pointing indicates the wind direction."

As he watched, Connah saw the headlights of one of the vehicles turn on and off, then back on.

"That," Bocaiúva said, "tells me that the wind speed is one kilometer per hour or less. He will flash once for each kilometer of wind. This will be a routine landing."

They started their descent. While lining up with the airfield, Bocaiúva said, "While my cousin's men will help you and Señhor Stone unload your equipment, my cousin and I will refuel the plane."

"Are you staying overnight?"

"No, I will fly back to Tefé and wait for you there."

"That's over nine hundred miles."

"*Sim*, but this airplane will cruise at 360 miles per hour. Tefé will be no more than a three-hour flight. To remain here would guarantee that Goncalves would know that an airplane was here. I would also expect that his people who were at the plantation have given him a description of this plane."

The Beechcraft descended, and when Bocaiúva turned on the landing lights, Connah was surprised to see how close the ground was. Obviously, Bocaiúva was not a novice at landing in remote airfields after dark. His level of respect for the Brazilian's piloting skills tripled.

The landing gear touched down on the grass runway with nary a bump. Connah said, "It's evident that you're not new at this."

"Before entering into Señhor Sanders... excuse me, your service, I owned my own plane, not as nice as this one, and flew cargo for some people in Manaus. I never worked for Goncalves, but several of his competitors were good customers."

As they neared the end of the runway, Connah saw that the vehicles lighting the strip were trucks. The plane turned 180 degrees and taxied to the approach end of the runway with the trucks following.

Bocaiúva did another 180, pointing the plane's nose into the wind. "We have arrived," he announced.

They exited the cockpit, entered the cabin to find Stone outside, and opened the hatch. Connah de-boarded first and saw several Brazilians helping Stone unload the wing lockers. A man broke away from the rest of the crew and hugged Bocaiúva. He greeted him in Portuguese, "*Araujo, meu primo!*"

Bocaiúva returned the hug, patting the big man on his back. In English, he turned to Connah and said, "Ian Connah, this is my cousin, Guilherme Inacio Rocha. Guilherme, this is Ian Connah, who I spoke of with you."

Rocha gripped Connah's hand. He had a grip as firm as a vise. At first, Connah thought he may be involved in a conflict of egos, but then, when the grip loosened in a few seconds, he realized it was more a case of a man who had no idea of his strength.

"*Señhor* will come with me, please?"

Connah nodded and followed the giant to one of the trucks. Rocha jumped into the back and disappeared into the dark interior; his cat-like litheness belied his size. Connah heard the sounds of a heavy crate being moved and stood back when Rocha reappeared. He carried a large wooden box. Still holding the container, he jumped down and placed it on the ground. He grabbed a corner and pulled upward. The crate opened with the loud screech of nails being torn from wood. Rocha stood, holding the crate's cover, and grinned, reminding Connah of a child looking for praise after completing a difficult task. Out of the corner of his eye, he looked at Bocaiúva. The Brazilian pilot shrugged his shoulders to say: what can I say?

Rocha stepped away from the open crate and said, "*Por favor.*"

Connah stepped over to the crate and peered inside. With reverence usually reserved for an audience with the pope, he picked up the Barrett M95 .50 caliber sniper rifle. Someone whistled behind him, and he turned to see Stone standing over his shoulder.

"What you gonna do, pard, shoot holes in a cinderblock building?"

81

Rocha drove Connah and Stone in his SUV; they left the unofficial airfield and crossed the river via the two-miles-long *Rio Negro* bridge. "I had no idea there was such a bridge across the Amazon River," Connah said.

"The bridge's name is the Ponte Rio Negro—in *Inglês*, it is called the River Black Bridge."

"I've never heard of it."

"The river you call the Amazon begins east of Manaus. It is Manaus where the Rio Negro joins with the Rio Solimões that the river you call the Amazon begins."

They entered Manaus and turned away from the main thoroughfares, sticking to backstreets. Initially, Connah was alert for any sign that Rocha and his crew were not trustworthy. He was still stinging from how Harry Sandberg and Fábio Goncalves had betrayed his trust. He would never again place his trust in anyone or anything until it had proven itself trustworthy. If anything, the neighborhoods they were traveling through added to that uneasiness. From the corner of his eye, he looked at Rocha.

The gang leader must have picked up on Connah's mood. "We must travel with care in certain parts of Manaus," he said. "The situation here is rather complicated."

"Oh, in what way?"

"You most likely know that in 2014 the World Cup football championship was held in Brazil. Soccer teams from all over the world came to Brazil for the matches. Rather than play the contests on a single site, it was decided that the games would take place in multiple locations around Brazil. Manaus was chosen as one of those sites.

"The result was the most significant economic period for Manaus since the rubber boom of the late nineteenth century. The city wanted the world to see a thriving modern city and not some backwoods… how should I say it? Boomtown, yes, that's the word. There was a feeling that the world would view Manaus as one of the mining boomtowns that have become ghost towns in your American west.

"All was fine until the World Cup ended. Within a year, Manaus had reversed into a struggling economy. Crime was possibly the only growing business."

"That," Connah said, "is a story heard in many places."

"One year after the cup, shit had gotten worse in Manaus. Entire families were out of work. The price of most basic goods rose beyond the ability of those with jobs to pay for them. Government and corporate corruption and graft were out of control. Add to this a prolonged drought and heat as high as forty-five degrees, 113 degrees Fahrenheit, and the city was about to explode.

"In a short time, the prisons became overcrowded, prisoners were stacked like sardines, and contraband flowed. The prisons were run by a São Paulo-based prison management company, *Umanizzare*—to whom prisoners were a commodity, not human beings. This is not a major problem in the rest of the country. Nationally only three percent of Brazil's prisoners are in privately managed prisons. However, in Amazonas State, forty percent are private, supported by local, state, and federal politicians who accept *contributions* from the company and in effect become proponents of the company line."

Connah interrupted, "Excuse me for interrupting, but I have a question of a personal nature. If you don't mind."

Rocha smiled. "That depends. If your question is about my life, I may answer. If it is about what my wife and I do behind closed doors, I will not."

Connah laughed. "No, it's nothing like that. I have come to believe that you are an educated man."

"University of South Carolina, I have a degree in mechanical engineering."

"Then my question is this: why are you doing what you do for a living?"

"One does what one must to get ahead."

"Why not move to one of the more prosperous cities like Rio de Janeiro or São Paulo?"

"Manaus is my home. It is where I was born. My wife and children were also born here. Our parents have lived here all their lives. Now that they are elderly, they need my assistance. In Latin America, roots run deep, and family is essential above all else."

"I have been told that," Connah said. "I sure as hell don't understand it. In my country, there is a saying: you can pick your friends, but you can't pick your family. When our children reach the age where they can support themselves, we expect them to do so, even if it means they leave us."

"You have children?"

"No, but that's probably for the best."

"Wife?"

"Not currently."

"Ah, so you are a widower?"

"Divorced." Connah held up four fingers. "Four times."

Rocha's head snapped back, "*Quatro esposas...* four wives?"

"I'm not what you would call husband material."

"So, you are alone in life?"

"I guess I kind of like it that way. Getting back to what you were telling me."

"Ah, yes. To shorten the tale, it reached the point where the situation became untenable. The rampant crime led to increased prison populations, which led to riots in the prisons.

"A local gang leader became involved in a riot at a nearby prison. He was transferred to a federal prison in the south. While there, he met a long-time rival. As a result, sworn enemies were locked up beside leaders from Brazil's oldest and most organized criminal organizations—*Commando Vermelho* of Rio de Janeiro, commonly referred to as CV. *Primeiro Commando da Capital* of São Paulo, widely referred to as PCC. Over time, the gangsters from Manaus learned from the CV and PCC the benefits of being organized. They realized they were at the point where they had a choice. They could remain at war over the river or form an alliance that would rival the PCC. They allied, and the *familia do Norte*, or FDN, was born. Now we come to today. While cocaine use in the United States has declined, it has increased in Brazil. The PCC has realized that the FDN is taking in a lot of money they feel should be theirs.

"Your former colleague, Fábio Goncalves, has aligned his organization with the PCC. Therefore our current route is designed to ensure we travel through safe neighborhoods. Did I mention the third organization in this insane situation? The various police organizations, all of which are equally corrupt."

82

It was mid-morning when, holding a coffee mug, Connah exited the stilt-house and leaned on the railing along the plank walkway. The very air he breathed reeked of the sewage and waste that drifted in the water beneath his feet. He sipped from the mug and surveyed the houses clustered along the river bank. He felt a vibration caused by someone walking the planks and looked up to see Guilherme Inacio Rocha walking toward him.

"*Bom dia*," Rocha said.

"And good day to you also."

Rocha said, "I apologize for the accommodations, but if we put you in one of the better hotels, the PCC would know of it before we even got you checked in."

"Maybe," Connah said, "it would be best if they knew."

Rocha turned his head slightly. "I disagree."

"You're probably right. Although it may not hurt if the PCC knows that I'm not here to interfere with their business. I just want what is mine returned."

"You know that, and I know that. Nevertheless, Goncalves is their business. He is an excellent earner for them."

"I suppose." Connah returned his attention to the area around them. "This is a city of many faces."

Rocha joined him at the railing. "I believe that if a city can have human characteristics, Manaus would be diagnosed with dissociative personality disorder. Over the years, the city has become divided into four quadrants—the northern zone, the southern zone, the eastern zone, and the western zone. Each quadrant seems to have a different personality. We are in the western zone—the same zone as the Club Anaconda, which, as you know, is crime-ridden and belongs to Goncalves. There is only one law that governs the entire city. The law of gravity. Wastewater flows downhill into these small rivers, *igarapés* in Portuguese." Rocha took out his cell phone and scrolled through the screen. He found what he sought and handed the phone to Connah.

Connah saw a video of the creek over which he stood. The stream, which was now calm, placid even, was raging. Tires and appliances tumbled in the current, water swelled over the banks, and parts of houses were being swept away. However, what caught his attention was the green anacondas and speckled caiman that swam through the house's living room in which he was staying.

"That was last month." Rocha took the phone back, found what he sought, hit *play*, and handed the phone to Connah. "This was taken at the same time."

The video showed an electrical transformer in flames, as were the surrounding homes. Black plumes of heavy smoke filled the air.

Rocha pointed across the river. "That is São Jorge, where that happened." He stared at the far shore and then said, "Do you know that the Amazon Basin is the world's largest watershed? Yet, twenty-five percent of the homes in Manaus have no running water. The sewer system is old and serves less than ten percent of the population. The other ninety percent are susceptible to hepatitis, acute diarrhea, and intestinal parasites. These people have lived in this for so long they no longer notice the stench that surrounds them."

"Yet, you remain here."

"Someone needs to try and bring down the corrupt people—both criminal and political—that steal the funds the government sends to address these conditions. Those that live a life of luxury while the majority of my people live lives of misery."

"People like Fábio Goncalves."

"*Sim, lixo* like Fábio Goncalves. He saw Connah's confused look. "*Lixo* is garbage in our language."

Don Stone stepped out of the hut, inhaled, and said, "God, I love the smell of shit in the morning." He turned to Rocha and said, "You know what the worst thing about this place is?"

Rocha said nothing and remained stoic as if he were waiting for a nasty comment.

"The worst thing about this place is that it isn't the worst place Ian and I have ever stayed in. In fact, the really disgusting part of it all is that any country you go to, including the United States, has to deal with the same shit. I've yet to meet a politician that was worth the powder it would take to blow his head off. Even the ones who start out with good intentions end up part of the regime."

Connah grinned at Stone. "Don't hold back, Don. Tell us how you *really* feel."

Rocha smiled at them and then looked up at the tropical sky. "I think," he said, "this will be a perfect day to kill some human scavengers."

"Well," Connah said, "it sounds to me like we need a plan of attack."

$ $ $ $ $

Otávio Rodrigues Correia walked onto the fantail of the *Princesa de Amazonas*, leaned against the rail, and lit a cigarillo. The morning air was strong with the odor of the trash-filled river and already showing signs of the heat that would surely follow.

"Do you ever get accustomed to the stench?"

Correia's stomach sank, and his heart skipped a beat. Taking care not to appear threatening, he slowly turned and saw Ian Connah leaning against the corner of the boat's cabin. Hoping his fear was not evident, Correia greeted him in Portuguese, "*Bom dia, señhor.*"

"How much did you get?"

Correia opted to play dumb. "I don't understand."

"*Besteira.* Isn't that how you say bullshit in Portuguese?" Connah stepped away from the wall, revealing the nine-millimeter pistol he wore butt-forward in a holster on his left hip. "How much of my money did your asshole cousin offer you to rip me off?"

Correia stood mute.

"The American writer Mark Twain once said: *it is better to keep your mouth closed and let people think you are a fool than to open it and remove all doubt.* Perhaps you may have heard it too and are remaining silent?"

Correia shrugged his shoulders and turned his hands. Hence, the palms faced the American, which was as close to admitting he understood Connah as he was going to go.

Connah slowly approached the boat captain, keeping his eyes locked on the Brazilian. "I'm not going to kill you, Otávio, not unless you force the issue. I want you to go to Goncalves and tell him that if he sends me my money, less what we agreed upon, I will consider us even."

"We both know that even if he could do that, he will not," Correia replied.

"I figured that. You tell your fucking asshole of a cousin that if he does not do as I ask, it will be a declaration of war between us."

"He has business associates to answer to."

"You talking about the Brazilian mob in São Paulo? I believe they call themselves the *Primeiro Commando da Capital* or the PCC."

Correia nodded.

"Did I tell you that I've worked both for and against mobsters for most of my life? If not, I tell you now that I have. I know they are not smart people—if they were, they'd be doctors, lawyers, or engineers. I also know that they are like dogs. Brave, cruel, and lethal when in a pack. But, when confronted alone, they will tuck their tails between their hind legs and run. At their best, they are bullies—*valentões* in your language. When someone stands up to them, they are cowards. I will kill them all. Starting with Goncalves. Him I will cripple, then I will toss him to the *sucuris* he loves so much."

Correia felt his face warm as it flushed.

"You tell all of them that I'm coming." Connah started walking toward the gangplank, then paused and turned. "Also, tell Goncalves's number one dog, Gomes, that he fucked up. He should have finished the job in the rainforest. I learned a long time ago that you finish the job when you have your enemy down. *I* will not make that mistake, nor will I be forgiving—any of you. You cannot hide, nor will you know when I will strike. Nevertheless, I *will* hit you and hit you hard."

Correia watched the American depart and looked at his trousers. He was surprised to see that he had not pissed in them.

As soon as Connah was out of sight, Correia left the boat, mounted a motorbike, and drove away.

$ $ $ $ $

Fábio Correia Goncalves was eating lunch in his penthouse when his cousin, Otávio, was shown into the dining room. One look was all it took for him to detect the fear that he emitted like the odor of the offal that floated on the *igarapés*.

"The American assassin lives," Correia announced before Goncalves had an opportunity to greet him.

"And you know this, how?"

"He came to my boat, not more than an hour-and-a-half ago."

"This is why you act like a man who has just shit in his pants?"

"Fábio, this is not a man to take lightly. He is not like the one he came here to find."

Goncalves threw his napkin on the table and stood. "Come," he said as if he were ordering a slave rather than talking to a member of his family.

He led the way through the posh apartment with panoramic views of the vast river and the brilliant green landscape. While passing through the living room, he motioned for Edward Gomes. Gomes, who had been watching highlights of Team Brazil's most recent soccer victory on a multi-screen television that covered the entire wall, followed.

When they arrived at their destination, a windowless office in the center of the penthouse, Goncalves ordered Gomes, "Shut the door."

Once they were secure and alone, Goncalves turned on Gomes. "Did you or did you not tell me that the American was dead?"

Gomes looked at Goncalves's face and slowly said, "What I said was that he was no longer a problem."

Goncalves slammed his hand on the top of his desk. He closed his hands into clenched fists, placed them on the desk, and leaned forward. "Then please explain to me how it is that he visited the *Princesa de Amazonas* this morning?"

Gomes maintained his composure. "I left him lying on the jungle floor, three days walk into the bush, with a head wound. I thought that he was in no condition to find his way out."

"Edward, I pay you to do what I tell you to do—not to think. I have lawyers for that. You were instructed to take care of him once you had the money. Which I *thought* you understood to mean that you were to kill him. It appears that we both made a mistake by thinking! Now, you get your ass out on the street and find him. When you do, I want you to kill him this time! Now is there anything about this that you need to *think* about?"

"No, boss."

"Good. Now get out there and do what I told you to do, and this time I want assurance that Connah is dead—even if it means you have to bring me his head!"

Gomes nodded and left the room.

Goncalves turned his attention to his cousin. "Now, am I going to have to worry about you?"

"No."

"Fortunately, we have people to assist in this matter."

"Fábio, he knows much more than we thought. He knows about your alliance with the PCC."

"This knowledge did not seem to concern him?"

"Actually, I believe it had the opposite effect. Connah seemed to be looking forward to the challenge."

83

Don Stone, Guilherme Inacio Rocha, and Connah met at the stilt house.
"What have you learned?" Connah asked.

"Goncalves lives well. In a penthouse apartment in the center of the city."

"Security?"

"Up the ass. The building has its own security, and if that ain't enough, there's the police."

"So, we have to draw him out?" Rocha asked.

"Or we scare him out," Stone replied.

"How do we do that?" Rocha countered.

Connah reached behind the couch he sat on and brought out the Barrett M95 rifle. "This," he said. "In the 'Stan we shot holes through one-foot-thick walls with one just like it. Stoney, what are the other buildings in the area like, and how far away?"

Stone took out his cell phone and accessed the photo gallery. "All are relatively modern. When the World Cup was in Brazil in 2014, the central city was given a complete overhaul. The buildings were all updated. They are similar to what you'd see in any modern city." He handed the phone to Connah.

Connah touched a high-rise on the picture. "What's this one?" Connah spread his fingers, enlarging the top of the structure, and turned it so that Stone and Rocha could see it.

"It just happens to be Goncalves's home," Stone answered. He flipped the image to another and showed it to Connah. "This building is about eight hundred meters away and a couple of stories higher. It'll make a great place for a hide. It's west of the target, so the wind will most likely be aiding."

Rocha looked at the picture. "I know this building."

Connah couldn't suppress a smile. "Don't tell me that you have a cousin."

"As a matter of fact," Rocha said, "I do."

Connah looked at his watch. "It's a little past one. I'd like to see this building today." He turned to Rocha. "Can you get hold of your cousin?"

"Of course. My cousin has contracted the night cleaning of the offices in that building. There is no part of it that he does not have access to."

"He'll be willing to help us do this?"

"Why not? He helped unload your airplane the other night."

$ $ $ $ $

Rocha, Stone, and Connah met with João Silva Inacio at nine o'clock in the evening. The subcontractor was short, stocky, and looked every bit the manager of a cleaning crew. His belt was lined with several dangling keyrings, and he seemed to know every key so well that when they moved through the building, he did not have to search for the one he wanted. He removed the appropriate ring from his belt and immediately found the correct key.

They accessed the roof via a service elevator, ensuring they were not disturbed by using the proper key to turn it off at the top. The sun had been down for over two hours. However, when they stepped out of the elevator, the surface was still sticky from being superheated by the equatorial sun. "This place must be like a pizza oven during the afternoon," Stone commented.

"Lying in a prone position would be a major problem. We'd better bring a tarp, so we don't get stuck to the roof," Connah added.

"You ain't planning on being up here in the afternoon, are you?" Stone asked.

"No. Our target is a creature of the night. I doubt he gets home until the wee hours of the morning."

Connah used a rangefinder scope to check the distance. He lowered the device and said, "Eight hundred meters. A shot this long won't allow the use of a suppressor. Which rules out a daytime shot... too many people around. If I'm going to give Goncalves a message, it'll have to be a night shot. Before the tenants of this building start their working hours. I'll take the shot after he gets home, which I believe will be sometime after two or three in the morning. This brings up another problem, the Barrett. It's forty-five inches long and weighs twenty-three and a half pounds. No way in hell will I be able to walk through the lobby with it."

"I will get your rifle up here," Inacio said. "My people always bring in cleaning supplies and equipment through the service entrance. We do it so often that the security guards no longer check us upon entry."

"*Obrigado,*" Connah said.

"When do you want to do this?" Inacio asked.

Connah checked his watch. "It's 9:30. I'd like to get here in about three hours?"

Inacio nodded. "Be at the service dock no later than one o'clock. Come, I will show you the location of the dock."

$ $ $ $ $

Since midnight, Stone and Rocha had been positioned on the roof of a vacant building not far from the Clube Sucuri. They took excellent care to remain undetected while watching Fábio Correia Goncalves depart the club.

Their patience was rewarded at 3:10 a.m., when the drug kingpin exited via the front door. A black Mercedes pulled up in front of the door, and the driver ran around to the passenger side rear, opened the back door, and waited. Goncalves dashed across the sidewalk and dove into the back seat.

Stone almost laughed out loud when he heard the gangster screaming at the driver to get his ass in the car and go. It won't take much to scare this piece of shit, Stone thought. He nodded at Rocha, who handed him a cell phone.

Stone sent a text: *The bird has left the coop and is headed for the nest.*

$ $ $ $ $

It was 3:30 a.m. when the lights went on in the penthouse. Connah settled down, peered through the telescopic sight, saw a shadowy figure walk to the window that overlooked the city, and fired.

$ $ $ $ $

Goncalves dismissed the security guard. He closed the door and walked to the bar. He poured a glass of whiskey and silently cursed Gomes for putting him in this position. If he'd only done what he was told, he wouldn't be in this situation. He walked to the window and stared out at the lights of central Manaus—then the window exploded, showering him with glass.

84

When his cell phone rang, Antônio Melo Cavalcanti was sleeping with his mistress in her São Paulo luxury apartment. He fumbled in the dark until he located his phone and then sat up in the bed. He put on his eyeglasses and read the screen. Why in hell is Goncalves calling me at four in the morning? It damn well better be crucial.

Cavalcanti was the boss of bosses in the *Primeiro Commando da Capital.* He had started out as a tough young guy living in the slums of São Paulo, Brazil's largest and most populous city. His criminal career started on the lowest rung of the ladder. He'd grown up making a living as a pickpocket and petty thief; tourists and visiting businessmen were his primary targets. Even now, in his sixties and the head of one of Brazil's most prominent criminal organizations, he'd never forgotten his roots. Ensuring that his people did much of their recruitment in the country's most poverty-stricken areas—and there was no shortage of candidates. His climb to the top had been anything but astronomical. He climbed to the summit of the PCC over the bodies of anyone who was in his way. It was known throughout the organization that he did not suffer fools. Fábio Correia Goncalves didn't realize that Cavalcanti thought he was the biggest fool in the PCC. He would have had a wonderful funeral years ago if he had not been a successful mule stationed in Manaus.

Cavalcanti turned on the light and admired his lean, trim nude body in a full-length mirror. Not bad, he thought, for a man of seventy-six years. He looked at the naked body of thirty-three-year-old Adriana Silva. He felt her body was exquisite. She excited him so much that he could still achieve an erection without the assistance of chemicals.

Adriana stirred. She opened her eyes and turned onto her back, revealing her beautiful body. "Is something wrong, Antônio?"

"Business, go back to sleep, my darling. I'll only be a moment."

He walked into the living room and answered the still ringing phone. "For your sake, I hope this is fucking important," he said in Portuguese.

"We have a problem," Goncalves said. He spent five minutes explaining the situation in Manaus.

"Why is this *our* problem? It sounds to me as if it's *your* problem."

Goncalves did not answer the question.

"Are you still there, Goncalves?"

"Yes."

"Why are you calling me at four in the morning to tell me that a fuck-up you created is *our* problem? You are the one who caused this. Fix it!"

"There are extenuating circumstances."

"What *extenuating circumstances*?"

"The two Americans are highly skilled assassins—"

"Two? Two? You have how many people in your organization?"

"About seventy-five."

"Listen to me, Goncalves, and listen closely." Cavalcanti waited for a few seconds and then continued. "Did you have a father, or were you the result of a night of pleasure gone horribly wrong?"

Goncalves sounded meek when he said, "I had a father."

"Did he ever get angry with you? Maybe you were doing something you weren't supposed to be doing."

"Yes."

"Do you recall him ever saying: Don't make me come in there because you'll be sorry if I do?"

"I don't remember."

"Well, stupid, let me say it. Don't make me send people up there to bail your ass out of this mess you created. Do you understand what I am saying?"

"Yes."

"Fix this and fix it fast. If I have to get involved, it will not be a good thing—especially for you."

Cavalcanti closed the call, returned to the bedroom, and slid into the bed beside his woman, who turned over and offered herself to him.

85

Fábio Correia Goncalves and Edward Gomes stood off to the side as workers finished replacing the picture window. "What have you learned?" Goncalves asked.

"They are not staying at any of the better hotels."

Goncalves gave Gomes a scathing look. "I could have saved you some time. I had already figured that out. Sometimes, Edward, I look into your eyes and want to ask: *is anyone in there?*"

Gomes stared back at his boss, and not for the first time did he see beneath the surface to the real person. Goncalves was a brutal, cruel person when he was in control and surrounded by his henchmen. However, when he was directly threatened and alone, he was softer than bird shit. Nevertheless, Gomes always told people *my father raised a fool, not a babbling idiot.* What he did say was, "Boss, when it comes to your safety, I leave nothing to chance. What if Connah, too, thought that we'd think that way and we overlooked them? You'd have my hide nailed to a tree."

Goncalves stared through the newly installed glass. "Where do you think he was?"

Gomes turned his attention to the panoramic view. "Most likely one of the taller buildings."

Goncalves pointed at the tallest building. "That one there. How far do you think it is?"

Gomes thought for a moment and said, "I would estimate just under a kilometer."

"Could this Connah hit something that far away?"

"Connah and his partner, Stone, made a living hitting objects over a kilometer away. For example, the Barrett M95 has a maximum range of almost seven kilometers. Its effective range is two kilometers."

Goncalves paled. "With such a weapon, he could be anyplace in the city and have a chance of hitting his target."

"Easily. He was trained by the best. And with his experience, I would say that he's only gotten better. I'd say that if he gets you in his sights, there's a one hundred percent probability he could put a bullet through your left eye."

"That doesn't make one feel comfortable, does it."

"Considering," Gomes said, "that I'm on his list too, it scares the shit out of me."

$ $ $ $ $

As well as being the best hitman in the PCC, Cristiano Melo Cavalcanti was Antônio Melo Cavalcanti's eldest and favorite grandson. He was so good that he was only called in when the job was beyond the abilities of the mainstream assassins. As soon as he hung up from his conversation with Goncalves, Cavalcanti knew this was a job for him, and he sent word for Cristiano to meet him at his office that afternoon.

Cavalcanti handed him a glass of scotch whiskey and then sat on the opposite end of the plush leather sofa. "You do understand what needs to be done, Cristiano?"

"*Sim, Vô.* You want me to go to Manaus and deal with the Goncalves situation."

"Contact these Americans and ask what it will take to make them go away. If they will not meet with you, find them and take care of them. They must be getting help from someone local. Find them also."

"And Goncalves?"

"That fool's fate is already decided. Take as many men as you need, but put an end to this. It is bad for business."

"For a task as important as this, I will handle it personally, alone. I will be on the next flight to Manaus."

$ $ $ $ $

"So," Rocha asked, "what is next?"

"We send Goncalves a couple messages. One personally and one at his club."

"How will you send him a personal message?"

"I have just the messenger."

$ $ $ $ $

When Ian Connah, Don Stone, and another man stepped off the dock and onto the deck of the *Princesa de Amazonas*, Otávio Rodrigues Correia knew that he should have run sooner. However, he was prepared for the worst and silently prayed *Hail, Mary* over and over. After several tense moments, he said, "Good afternoon, gentlemen."

Stone looked over his shoulder, then to Connah. "Is he speaking to us? I sure as hell don't see any officers here, just a couple of pissed-off grunts."

"Be nice, Stoney," Connah said. "Can't you see that Captain Correia is having a hard time controlling his bowels? I imagine that right about now, he's come to realize that he has, on a scale of one in ten, a zilch-point-nothing chance of coming out of this shit sandwich in one piece. If we don't get my money back, I'll kill him. If I do get my money back, his piece of crap cousin will feed him to the snakes."

Sweat began to run down the side of Correia's face, dripping onto his T-shirt. "I have done nothing to you. It was Fábio who double-crossed you, not me."

"That may be so. However, you did nothing to stop it either. More than anyone, you should know that when you lay down with snakes, sooner or later you're going to get bit—or in your case, crushed is a better way of saying it."

"What is it you want from me? I have none of your money. After Gomes took it, he ran straight to Fábio, who has kept all of it."

"Well," Connah said, "that makes it easy, doesn't it? If you consider Gomes' part in this, we only have to deal with one, possibly two people."

"Relax, Otávio. You look like you're about to shit a double-edged razor blade. Nothing is going to happen to you. However, understand that only you can ensure that. For the time being, I need you to do something."

"What is this thing you want me to do?"

"I need a courier, someone who can carry messages to your cousin while we negotiate. You be straight with me, and I'll see that no harm comes to you—not from us anyway. You screw me over, and you're a dead man. I'll be frank with you. I'm getting more than a little sick and tired of people thinking I'll just sit back and let them take what's mine."

Correia leaned against the railing. "What is this message?"

"I want you to tell him that tomorrow night is his deadline. If he doesn't come up with what's mine, I'll take everything that means anything to him, namely his family. I understand that he primarily only gives a shit about himself. Still, there must be others, a sister or brother, nieces, and nephews? Tell him if I don't have my assets in hand by 9:00 p.m., twenty-one hundred hours if you prefer, I'm coming for him, and there's no way in hell he can stop me. I can get him anyplace and anytime I want."

"He will not comply."

"Then you better convince him. Don't let him make a bad decision, one that could fuck-up the rest of his life—as short as it will be. I'm all done playing games with him. He may think that he can deal with me, but he can't. I will rain down on him a shit-storm like he's never seen. Finally, you may want to remind him that you never hear the one that gets you."

Connah motioned to Stone and the stranger, and they left the boat.

$ $ $ $ $

When they stepped off the pier, Stone turned to Connah. "You're bluffing, right?"

"About what?"

"About killing Goncalves' family... including women and kids."

"Yeah. But when you're dealing with shitheads like these guys, people who would do that very thing, you have to use language they understand."

"Whew. You had me worried for a minute there."

"Let's hope that I have them worried too."

$ $ $ $ $

Correia slid down the railing and sat on the deck. He considered doing what he'd intended and running upriver to Colombia or east to Belém. He got up and studied the area around the dock, hoping to detect if Connah had someone watching him. He saw no one but was too scared of what might happen if he were wrong. He sighed in resignation. It was time to visit Fábio, and he was not looking forward to it.

86

Cristiano Melo Cavalcanti arrived at Eduardo Gomes International Airport in Manaus at 1:30 a.m. on GOL flight 1650. He was picked up by a local member of the PCC who took him directly to the Clube Sucuri.

Entering the club, he passed the anaconda in the glass cage without so much as a glance. There were four or five 'hostesses,' a bartender, and no more than nine or ten customers in the club. Cavalcanti walked directly to Goncalves, who sat in his usual seat. "We must talk. In private."

Goncalves, one of the leading crime bosses in north Brazil, was not accustomed to being told what to do. With a stern look, he said, "We close in half an hour."

Cavalcanti reached inside his jacket, brought out a nine-millimeter SIG-Sauer P320 semi-automatic pistol, and placed it on the table. Goncalves' eyes widened and were locked on the handgun that the PCC hitman still gripped with the barrel pointed at him. "Close this fucking place—*now*." Without raising his voice, he got his message across.

Goncalves motioned to the bartender, who was watching the confrontation with interest. He made a slashing motion across his throat, and the bartender summoned the hostesses and bouncers. In ten minutes, there were no customers left in the club.

Cavalcanti lifted the pistol off the table and slid it into his holster. He bent forward, pushing his face within an inch of Goncalves' face. "Private means you and me—everyone else gets the fuck out." He stood up, turned around, and shouted, "Everyone, get the fuck out!"

In less than three minutes, the only living things in the club were Goncalves, Cristiano Cavalcanti, and the caged snake. Cavalcanti grabbed a chair from one of the tables, placed it in front of Goncalves, and sat.

"Do you know how much shit you are in? Are you aware that I could put a bullet in your goddamned head, and the *chefe* would reward me? Who knows, he might even be so happy he will let me fuck his mistress. You have an entire organization at your fingertips. You let two—two!—not even three, assassins from America scare you so much that you call *meu vô*, crying like a schoolboy who has had his ass kicked by the playground bully. Well, are you just going to sit there?"

Goncalves knew that for Cavalcanti to send his grandson to deal with the mess he'd created was not a small thing. If he was not careful in what he said, he'd have a better chance of escaping from a pit of aroused vipers than he would have of getting through this alive. Still, he was not entirely successful at keeping his emotions in check, and he said, "What would you have me do? If I agree with you, I'm fucked. If I disagree with you, I'm still fucked. Say what you will. These are not your normal hitmen. If they decide to hit Chefe Cavalcanti, they will hit Chefe Cavalcanti. Not me, nor you, or anything will stop them."

Cristiano had an epiphany. He sat back and studied Goncalves. "I believe that you are more afraid of them than you are of us."

"Not more than, but *just as* scared."

"Suppose, as a starter, you tell me about them. Everything you know. Leave nothing out."

Goncalves talked nonstop for the next hour.

$ $ $ $ $

Stone and Connah were in position atop a building a kilometer away. Their line of fire was clear all the way to the door of the Clube Sucuri. Shortly before 4:00 a.m. Stone's cell phone vibrated. He listened for almost a half-minute, then broke the connection. "There's been a complication," he told Connah.

"Tell me what it is, and then we'll decide how to uncomplicate things."

$ $ $ $ $

Goncalves was relieved when Cristiano stood up, checked his watch, and said, "I am tired. We will meet again at noon. We have to put together a plan.

Goncalves did not look happy at the prospect of meeting with this disrespectful ass again. Still, he knew he had no other option and avoided showing his inner feelings when he nodded.

He remained seated as Cristiano walked to the door, opened it, and turned as if he had something more to say. Suddenly, the vivarium exploded with a deafening SNAP, immediately followed by the BOOM of the biggest weapon he had ever heard.

$ $ $ $ $

Cristiano heard a loud snap and glass hitting the floor. He dove to the floor and crawled back from the door. As he pushed himself past the anaconda cage, he saw that the huge snake lay half out, and its body was torn in multiple places by flying glass and shrapnel. It twisted and thrashed its way toward death.

87

Edward Gomes was summoned to Clube Sucuri and arrived shortly after five o'clock a.m. The door was open, and when he entered, he slid on the broken glass spread across the floor. The foyer looked like the site of a gunfight. The anaconda cage was smashed, the limp body of the ten-foot-long snake hanging out of its den. Half of its body trailed down the wall. Its head lay on the floor.

He heard a chair slide on the floor and saw his boss sitting in his usual seat. His face was ashen in the light of the early morning. "*Chefe*, what in the hell happened?"

"What happened, you ask? The man you did not kill happened!"

Gomes looked to the man sitting beside his boss. "Who is he?"

"He is Cristiano Melo Cavalcanti, Chefe Antônio Melo Cavalcanti's number one assistant. Do I have to tell you who Cavalcanti is?"

"No, I know he is *chefe* of the PCC. How did they get involved?"

"That is none of your concern," Cristiano said. "Your concern is to make that mess in the entrance disappear. Once that is done, you and I will find this Connah and finish what you should have done in the rainforest."

"I'll have a clean-up team here within the hour," Gomes said. "In the interim, I would suggest that we at least close the door."

Goncalves' face told Gomes that there was no way in hell he was going anywhere near the door. "I don't think Connah is still around. From the looks of the damage, I'd say he used a heavy piece, something along the line of a Barrett M95. I doubt he was close by. He took his shot and then left." He turned his attention to Cristiano and added, "He knew what he was shooting at, and I can assure you that it was not you. He's sent you a message. He can take you out anytime, anyplace, and any way he wants."

Cristiano remained stoic; his eyes locked with Gomes's. Beside him,

Goncalves's face was a portrait of fear.

Gomes broke contact with Cavalcanti and spoke to his boss. "You're right about my making a mistake by not killing him when I had the chance. However, you deciding to double-cross him was the dumbest fucking thing you've ever done. So, I guess that we each signed our own death warrant in our own way. So, we'd better get our shit together, and we need to do it fast."

Gomes turned to Cristiano. "What do you want to know?"

"What's he like?"

Gomes raised his right hand with the thumb extended and aimed it over his shoulder toward the wreckage of the snake's den. "He's a lot more deadly than that snake ever was."

$ $ $ $ $

Gomes drove from the club to the riverfront. He boarded the *Princesa de Amazonas* and banged on the cabin door until Otávio Rodrigues Correia opened the door. It was apparent that the boat captain had been asleep. His hair was uncombed, his face was puffy, and he squinted against the rising tropical sun. He looked at Gomes and said, "What do you want?"

"You know what I fuckin' want. We got to talk."

Correia stepped back, opening the door wide. "Shit, I'm up now. Come in."

Gomes entered and sat at the small table along the portside wall without waiting for an invitation. "You got coffee?" Gomes asked. "I've had a long night, and the day ahead looks even longer."

"I'll make some."

When Correia walked to the stove, Gomes said, "Connah made his move last night."

Correia slowly turned his head and asked, "He kill Fábio?"

"No, but I have no doubt that he could have if he wanted. As it is, he may have killed him in another way."

Correia filled a small percolator with water from a drinking water jar, added coffee to the strainer, and turned on the gas stove. He turned to the table. "You talk in riddles. Explain to me what you mean."

"The PCC sent their best enforcer from São Paulo to look into the matter."

"Who'd Cavalcanti send, his grandson?"

"You're familiar with these people?"

"You don't run coca as long as I have and not learn who's who in the PCC."

"*Sim*, he did."

"So, it was Cristiano who Connah killed."

"No, Connah killed nobody."

"I wonder why didn't he kill Fábio?"

Gomes slapped his hand on the table. "You know goddamned well that Fábio is worth over two million dollars to Connah. There is no way Connah will do anything but scare him until he gets his money. You've been carrying messages between the two, haven't you?"

"What is Fábio going to do, run?"

"No, he's either too scared or too stupid to do that. He has told me to work with Cavalcanti to kill Connah, and you're going to help us do it."

"Good luck with that," Correia replied. "You and I both know that killing him won't be easy. Shit, if I heard right, you had the chance and didn't do it."

"That is my problem. Yours is to contact Connah and set up a meeting."

"I got no way to contact him. I never know when he will show up here."

"Then do the obvious…wait for him."

88

When Connah walked out of the cabin where he and Stone were staying, Guilherme Inacio Rocha sat in a chair on the roofed porch watching the sun rising through the treetops. "One of my people found out who was with Goncalves last night."

Connah dropped into a chair and said, "It must be imperative to bring you out so early."

"I think it is."

Stone walked out and leaned against one of the posts holding the roof. "Something tells me that the plot is about to thicken."

"His name is Cristiano Melo Cavalcanti."

"Who is he?" Connah queried.

"The grandson of Antônio Melo Cavalcanti."

"Now, that name I've heard," Connah said. "Isn't he some big-time hoodlum?"

"You might say that. Cavalcanti is the PCC's equivalent of the Italian *capo de capo*, their boss of bosses. His grandson, Christiano, is number one in line to take over when the old man steps down."

"Now *that* is truly interesting."

"It should be," Rocha replied. "He's every bit as ruthless and blood-thirsty as the old man."

Stone had been studying Connah for the last few minutes. He saw Connah's countenance suddenly brighten, and his eyes widened.

Without saying a word, Connah got up and walked into the yard. He stood still, staring into the forest.

"What did I say?" Rocha asked.

Stone raised a hand and nodded. "Nothing. He has a brainstorm. I've seen him like this several times. Give him a few minutes, and he'll have a plan for some hair-brained scheme or another."

Several moments later, Connah turned around and returned to the porch. Stone asked, "What did you come up with?"

Connah addressed Rocha. "You say this hitman is the PCC boss's son?"

"Grandson, yes."

A lascivious smile spread across his face. "What we have to do is so obvious."

"Really?" Stone said. "Why don't you share this obvious course of action with us?"

"We're going after *chefe* junior."

Rocha was silent for a few seconds and then turned to Stone. "Has he always been suicidal?"

"From time to time," Stone replied.

Rocha turned back to Connah. "Do you have any idea what will happen if you kill Cavalcanti's kid?"

"Yeah. The biggest shit-storm to ever hit North and South America. That's why we ain't gonna kill Junior. We're goin' to kidnap him. Then we'll tell grandpa that if he wants his grandson back, all he has to do is tell Goncalves to return my money. He must forfeit all claim to the money I agreed to pay him, as well as ownership of the plantation up-river. I'm giving that to Cavalcanti as a recompense for all the trouble I've caused him."

"Have you," Rocha asked, "ever read *The Ransom of Red Chief* by the American writer, O. Henry?"

Connah's brow dropped as he thought about the question. "I don't think so. What does it have to do with what I want to do?"

"The story is about a rich man whose son is kidnapped. The kidnappers ransom the kid for $2,000. In the meantime, to keep the kid amused, they play his favorite game where the kid is an Indian named Red Chief. The kid is their worst nightmare, so bad they lower the ransom to $1,500. The father sends back word that he'll only take the kid back if they pay him $250.00. The kid is so bad that they try to release him for nothing, but he is having so much fun that he refuses to leave. The kidnappers pay the $250 and promise to leave town and never return.

"I hope," Rocha continued, "that Cristiano Cavalcanti won't turn out to be our Red Chief."

$ $ $ $ $

They had everything planned at two o'clock that afternoon except for one item. Who would deliver the ransom demand to Antônio Melo Cavalcanti?

Stone held his hands up and said, "Don't look at me. Getting my head chopped off is where I draw the line. Get Correia to do it."

"Cavalcanti will not speak to an Amazon Riverboat captain," Rocha said.

"I know someone who may do it. I'm certain that Cavalcanti will listen to him. Right now, our first priority is to get our hands on junior."

89

The mini-convoy drove up BR 174, the only road between Manaus, Venezuela, and Guyana. The city of Presidente Figueiredo, population less than 40,000, is roughly sixty-seven miles north of Manaus. Due to road conditions, it took two-and-a-half hours for Rocha, Stone, and Connah to make the drive.

"Our rendezvous isn't until tomorrow morning," Stone said. "So, why are we driving there this morning instead of tomorrow?"

"After the sun goes down," Rocha explained, "the road is closed to vehicles. There were too many collisions with wild animals on the road. It's impossible to restrict the wildlife but easy to keep cars and trucks off the road during hours of darkness.

"Many tourists visit the Presidente Figueiredo Sanctuary Waterfalls near the city. It is very popular."

"Where are we meeting Gomes and Cavalcanti?" Connah asked.

"At the waterfall," Rocha answered.

"Is that wise?" Stone asked. "You just said it's a popular place for tourists to visit."

"At the time of our meeting, I do not think there will be many tourists about."

"Sounds like as good a place as any," Connah said.

$ $ $ $ $

The three kidnappers were in Connah's hotel room, putting the final touches on their plan. Connah spread a tourist map of the sanctuary in front of Rocha.

"The agreed-upon meeting will take place here." Rocha pointed to a particular spot on the map. "The falls are on the Rio Urubui, which discharges into the Amazon via the Rio Preto da Eva and the Rio Uatumã. Our meeting is at 06:00 tomorrow morning, so there shouldn't be any tourists at that hour. If we arrive two hours before that, we should have sufficient time to check out the area. Once we verify that we are alone, we will decide where Stone should position himself."

"Let's hope that Cavalcanti and Gomes will be willing to refrain from trying anything with people around," Connah said. "The PCC has a reputation for causing a lot of collateral damage when they act."

"That is always a consideration when one interacts with the PCC."

Connah directed his next question to Stone: "Don, do you have any input?"

"Do you have any idea what the effective range is when a suppressor is on a Barrett M95?"

"I don't think that's going to be an issue. A suppressor becomes an issue at 400 meters. You'll be two hundred at most. If you think that's a problem, we can use the 7.62 millimeter I brought along."

"I'd prefer that. At two hundred meters, the M95 would be like shooting a squirrel with a .44 magnum—basically, I think it's overkill," Stone said. "I think we can do away with the sound suppressor too. The sound won't be the issue if I have to shoot anyone. People seeing the target being blown away will be."

"So," Connah concluded, "if we're all in agreement, let's get some sleep."

90

They arrived on-site a few minutes past four in the morning. The river was narrow and ran over a series of small waterfalls that cascaded down a series of stones that resembled a staircase. They scouted the area and decided on a position from which Stone would have an unobstructed line of fire to the spot where they'd decided they would await Gomes and Cavalcanti. They agreed that if there were bystanders in the vicinity, they would fire their weapons only if they had no other recourse.

They spent an hour checking out the area to ensure Gomes and Cavalcanti had not beaten them to the site. Once they were satisfied that they had arrived first, Connah said, "Now all we have to do is take our positions and wait."

$ $ $ $ $

Stone settled in his shooting position and remained silent and immobile, skills he'd learned from years as a sniper. At half-past five, he heard a noise off to his right and, rather than act prematurely, waited. He heard a scraping sound and slid his K-Bar knife from its sheath. In a short time, he detected movement in the tall grass and undergrowth. He slid back and concealed himself beneath a broad-leafed fern.

In a matter of minutes, he saw a man appear out of the grass. He low-crawled to the spot Stone had vacated and hesitated when he noticed that the vegetation in the place was matted down as if someone had laid there. He stopped his crawl, and his head moved from right to left as he tried to see if he had company.

When the sniper's head returned to the front, Stone made his move. He placed his rifle on the ground beside him, rose to his hands and knees, and propelled himself forward. He jumped on the shooter's back, pushed his face into the ground, and drove the knife through the back of his neck. The man suddenly relaxed and expelled a breath. Stone held his head in place and pressed down. He remained that way for a full minute before he was satisfied the man was dead or, if not paralyzed with a severed spinal cord.

He had a microphone poised before his lips and clicked the transmit button two times.

$ $ $ $ $

Connah heard Stone activate his microphone in the earbuds he wore.

To Rocha, Connah said, "They're here."

Gomes and a tall, slender man appeared on the footbridge that crossed the river to the swimming area. Connah and Rocha remained in place and watched them approach.

"The one wearing cammies is Gomes," Connah said.

"The tall one in the suit is Cristiano Melo Cavalcanti. You must have really shaken things up for Antônio to send his best enforcer, not to mention favorite grandson and heir."

"So, we have a positive identification?"

"That we do."

As the distance between Connah and Gomes shortened, Connah felt anger build. Above all attributes, the one he valued in a friend was loyalty, and Gomes had shown his stripes in the rainforest. Connah kept his poker face and hid his desire to kill the drug runner.

Gomes and Cavalcanti stopped about ten feet away. "I was glad to hear you found your way back, Ian."

"If I were you," Connah replied, "I'd have the opposite feeling. This isn't the time, Edward, but you and I aren't finished."

"I'm sorry you feel that way. It was business, nothing personal."

"Oh? Then you'll be surprised to learn that I take being shot and left to roam through the jungle until I died, very fucking personal."

Cavalcanti had been patiently listening to the discourse.

"You, I assume are Cristiano Melo Cavalcanti," Connah said.

"I am."

"I want to be clear on one thing," Connah said. "What is happening in Manaus has nothing to do with the PCC."

"Unfortunately, we feel that a threat to one of our people has a lot to do with us."

"Be that as it is, what is the purpose of this meeting?"

"To show you the folly of taking us on," Cavalcanti said.

"I want nothing from the PCC. I want what is mine." Connah gave Gomes a stern look. "That which this man stole from me under orders from the cowardly piece of shit he works for. Return what is mine, and I will leave Brazil within forty-eight hours of receiving it."

"My instructions are to end this...no matter what it takes," Cavalcanti replied.

Gomes suddenly started looking around. "Where is Stone?"

"Unless I'm wrong," Connah said, "he's looking at one of your heads through a rifle scope."

Gomes and Cavalcanti bent forward, their hands moved toward their hips, where they must have weapons.

"I'd think twice about reaching for any weapons," Connah said.

He maintained eye contact with his adversaries and called out, "Stoney, send the package." In his peripheral vision, he saw a body tumble into the river. "Right about now, I'm fairly sure you may have someone watching over us. I know that Stone has eliminated one of your people. In the event there are more, I assure you that I may die here, but so will you...both of you."

Cavalcanti straightened up and said, "So we are at an impasse. How do we resolve it?"

"We can start by having you place your weapons at your feet."

"If we don't?"

"Then Stone will say 'eeny-meany-miny-moe' and shoot whichever one of you is the loser."

Gomes also relaxed. "You surprise me, Ian. I thought you were a man of honor."

"There was a time when I believed that of you. I was wrong then, and you are now. Are you about to tell me that you came here alone, without backup?"

"A mistake I will never again repeat," Gomes replied.

"You expect me to believe that?" Connah asked.

"How can we convince you?" Cavalcanti said.

"Disarm yourselves."

"If we don't."

Connah raised his voice. "Start the count, Don!"

Cavalcanti spoke up. "Wait." He shed his suit coat; he made a slow turn with great control until his back was to Connah, exposing a pistol in a holster. "I am going to remove my weapon." He removed the gun, dropped it to the ground, and raised the legs of his trousers, revealing there was no hideaway there.

"Edward," Connah said. "Your turn."

"If I don't?"

Connah took his pistol from the holster at his back. "Then we'll see if I can shoot you as accurately as you did me. Then again, I may decide to just blow your head off. Your choice, which will it be?"

Gomes shrugged. "If I return without resolution to this, I'm dead anyway." He reached for his handgun.

"Don't be stupid, Edward."

Gomes dropped his pistol to the ground.

Cavalcanti did not look at their backup man's body as it drifted over a waterfall and disappeared from sight. "Impressive. I don't think even I could have done this better. Now what?"

Connah said, "You come with us. Edward, you take off. Let your boss know what happened." He paused. "You guys really came with only one man?"

"That was my fault. I was sure that we could handle things alone. It's obvious that, like Gomes, I underestimated you. I, too, was wrong," Cavalcanti said.

Connah said to Rocha, who had stood silent throughout the meet. "Let Stone know it's over, and then call your cousin and tell him to have the plane ready. I have a feeling that Manaus is going to be too hot for us for a while."

91

Antônio Melo Cavalcanti answered the phone, and a voice he hadn't heard in many years said in Portuguese, "Tônio?"

There was only one person who ever called him that. "Rodolfo?"

"How are you, my old friend."

"Things are good here. How is your life in New York?"

"Business is good here. I'm afraid that this is not a personal call."

"What can I do for you?"

Rodolfo Barrios Ribeiro said, "It is not what you can do for me. It is what I can do for you."

"I don't understand what you are talking about."

"I am calling about the situation you have in Manaus."

Cavalcanti was surprised. "What do you know about a situation in Manaus?"

"I received a call from a man who has assisted me in dealing with several difficult situations up here."

"Does this man have a name?"

"Connah, Ian Connah."

"You know this man?"

"Yes, I know him well."

"Tell me about him."

"He is a man of honor. He has always done anything I have asked of him."

"Really? Why has he called you?"

"He feels that you would not speak with him."

"About what?"

"This morning, he met with three men about a problem he is having in Manaus. One of them is now dead."

Cavalcanti felt fear for the first time in several decades. "Cristiano?"

"Alive and is being held by Connah."

"What does he want?"

"From you, he wants nothing. Only to get back that which was taken from him."

"And I should do what?"

"Convince Goncalves to return what he stole."

"If I don't?"

"Tônio, be reasonable. Do not force his hand. It will cost you nothing to do what he asks. However, it will result in great grief for you if you refuse. As a father who has lost a child, I would not like to have you go through that experience."

"Thank you, Rodolfo. I will consider your advice and do what I must to close this matter."

$ $ $ $ $

"You are certain of this?" Antônio Melo Cavalcanti listened to the answer from the informer in Manaus. He took care not to show his anger by resisting the urge to slam the phone when he placed it in its cradle.

He sat at the head of a long rectangular conference table, and before speaking, he made direct eye contact with each of the twelve men that sat six on each side. "It seems that I made a miscalculation about the situation there. As you know, I sent Cristiano there to take care of the situation I told you about. That call was from one of our people in Manaus. Cristiano has been taken prisoner."

There was a brief period during which Cavalcanti allowed them to voice their levels of indignation and anger over the abduction of a high-level member of the organization. When their outrage had run its course and the assembled crime bosses' adrenalin levels lowered, the *chefe* for Cuiabá City in Mato Grosso State stood up. "We must find out who is behind this and deal with them!" he cried out.

"I'm afraid that one of our own has created this problem. Fábio Correia Goncalves, *chefe* of our operation in Manaus, has put us in this position."

"How will we deal with him?" asked another of the *chefes*.

"After this meet, *I* will be flying to Manaus. I will meet Goncalves and make a decision. Our problem is not getting revenge. It is how we minimize the destruction Goncalves has caused. At the minimum, he has started a war with

American mercenaries, who can create havoc along the routes we transport products from Columbia and Peru. We could lose millions in revenue."

"Then let us send people to deal with these Americans."

The room was filled with the boisterous agreement.

Cavalcanti held up his hands, quieting the irate *chefes*. "I do not think that we want to take on people who seem capable of disappearing into the rainforest and striking us at will. Nevertheless, I will consider all options once I discuss this with Goncalves."

"What has he done to these *Americanos*?" the Mato Grosso *chefe* asked.

"What would you do, Sergio, if someone stole two million U.S. dollars from you?"

"I would kill him, not just anyone."

"Ah, so tell me, if you killed this thief, how would you recoup your money?"

The *chefe* called Sergio nodded. "I see."

"I believe this *Americano*, who is called Connah, wanted to convince Goncalves that he was serious. It was, I believe, unfortunate that Cristiano was in the wrong place at the wrong time. I can guarantee you that Goncalves got the message."

"The problem as I see it," Sergio said, "is that our credo says: Brother does not kill brother. Brother does not exploit brother."

"Yes, it does. That is why I will look into the matter personally. Then I will return, and we, as the supreme council, will decide what to do with Goncalves. Do I have your consent?"

The entire body nodded their heads, affirming his plan.

$ $ $ $ $

Fábio Correia Goncalves could not believe what he saw when two PCC enforcers walked into the club. They checked the room, paying considerable attention to what remained of the glass cage near the entrance. One of them stood against the wall, his hand inside his jacket. It was evident to everyone in the room what he held there. The other man Goncalves knew, he was Martin Rossi, Antônio Melo Cavalcanti's personal bodyguard.

Rossi exited the club and returned with Cavalcanti in less than a minute. Having grown up on the streets of Manaus, Goncalves had little education. However, he did not need a diploma to know that the appearance of the PCC *chefe dos chefes* did not bode well for his longevity. Leaping from his seat, Goncalves greeted him with the subservience of a sharecropper before the owner of his land.

"*Chefe*, it is a pleasure to see you in my humble club."

Cavalcanti stopped in front of him. "Stop your ridiculous pandering. Where is my grandson? I will speak to him."

"He and two of my best men went to Presidente Figueiredo yesterday. I expect them back soon."

Cavalcanti walked around Goncalves and sat at a table directly in front of the bar. A server scrambled to the table and asked, "Can I get you anything, *señhor*?"

The PCC overlord glanced at his watch. "*Sim, café.*"

The young woman almost ran to fill the order. When she returned with the coffee, Cavalcanti turned in his chair, looked at Goncalves, and summoned him with a crooked finger.

As he rushed to comply, Goncalves nearly ran over two servers who were carrying trays filled with drinks. When he reached the table, Cavalcanti said, "Sit." He pointed to the chair opposite his. "Over there, where I can keep an eye on you."

When Goncalves was settled, the top mobster in Brazil leaned toward him and said, "Close this place."

"Close?"

"Which part of close do you not understand? If you are afraid to do so, my men will do it for you."

"*Chefe*, it is just past three-thirty in the afternoon. I will lose almost a full day's business."

"If you don't want to close, we can talk in my car. I warn you, if you walk through that door with me, you will not walk back in—ever."

Goncalves stood and beckoned to the bartender. "Close," he said, "then you and all of the staff take the rest of the day off, with pay."

There was a lot of complaining from the customers. Still, in fifteen minutes, the only occupants of the club were Goncalves and the three PCC members.

Cavalcanti sipped from his cup, placed it back in its saucer, and said, "You said Cristiano is due back shortly?"

"That is my understanding."

"Please, tell me, Fábio, how have you stayed alive as long as you have? I believe that you have no idea about what is happening in your own organization."

312

"Has something happened that I don't know about?"

"Not much, only that one of your men who accompanied my grandson to Presidente Figueiredo is dead, and Cristiano is now a prisoner of Connah."

Goncalves' stomach sank, and his knees went so weak that if he were standing, he would have fallen on his face.

"What can I do, *Chefe*?"

Cavalcanti slapped the surface of the table so hard that his coffee cup bounced off the saucer and spilled coffee. "I think you have done quite enough. However, I will tell you what you are going to do. The first thing you will do is give me everything you took from Connah, all the cash and the papers, whatever gives access to the bank in the Caymans. Second, you will forfeit any claim to whatever money you and he had agreed upon. I mean every single real of it. Third, you had better beg me not to have my people kill you. If you don't do this quickly, or anything happens to my grandson, I will personally kill you, and it will be a slow and painful death. You have until six o'clock tomorrow evening to complete these requirements." He once again glanced at his watch. "I will be leaving Pedro to accompany you. He will stay with you every minute until you have done these things."

Cavalcanti stood and rechecked his watch. "Six o'clock tomorrow, just over twenty-six hours from now. You better not be so much as a minute late."

When Cavalcanti and the other man left, Goncalves looked at Pedro, who smiled and said, "Hello there."

92

Correia guided the *Princesa de Amazonas* toward the dock in the small village on the outskirts of Tefé. He smoked a cigar and watched the sun coming up over the confluence of the Tefé and Amazon Rivers.

Edward Gomes stood beside him, watching the mate tie the boat to a cleat on the dock. "What time is the product scheduled to arrive?"

"Tonight, at the earliest. Don't be surprised if it's late. The river has a nasty habit of springing surprises on anyone traveling it."

"What do we do in the meantime?"

"We relax, have a few drinks, and sleep. Once we transfer the cargo, we depart for Manaus, and there will be no sleep for anyone. It will require the full attention of everyone on board to watch for obstacles in the river."

Gomes threw the remains of his cigarette into the swirling brown water of the eddy.

$ $ $ $ $

Connah, Stone, and Rocha departed the Beechcraft King Air 350I at the general aviation hangar at Aeropuerto Internacional Alfredo Vásquez Cobo in Tabatinga, Brazil. Rocha deboarded first and met a man at the bottom of the ladder. They spoke in a strange mixture of Spanish intermixed with Portuguese. After several moments, Rocha motioned for the others to join them.

"We must hurry," Rocha said. "The shipment will be coming through within the next three-and-a-half hours, and it will take us half that time to reach our place of ambush."

In a short time, the airplane was unloaded, and Connah gave Bocaiúva his orders: "Remain here. If you don't hear from us in four, five hours at the most, get out of here. The plane is yours."

$ $ $ $ $

The ambush crew arrived by truck with an hour to spare. The men clustered together, and Rocha briefed them on the area. "We are near the place where the borders of Peru and Brazil meet. Less than twenty miles that way is Colombia. We must ensure that we do not trigger a war between the three countries. It is here that Peruvian and Colombian products are combined and then sent to Manaus for distribution throughout Amazonia. From Manaus, the majority of the products are shipped to Belem. From there, it is shipped to the rest of the world."

"So," Connah said, "it's a big shipment."

"Worth millions on the U.S. market. If we are successful, the PCC will want our scalps. Taken while we are still alive, if possible."

"Well," Connah said, "Let's get set up."

$ $ $ $ $

The barge pushed through the coffee-brown tinted water. Armed guards stood on each of the four corners, and two were centered on the sides. The day was overcast and the water-laden clouds obscured the tops of the taller trees. The day was uncomfortable, a mid-ninety degrees Fahrenheit temperature, and the humidity was eighty-five percent. Everyone's clothing was soaked from sweat and stuck to their bodies like fly-paper.

Connah watched the drug barge approach and wriggled his body as he settled into a firing position. He checked the locations of the other members of the ambush, ensuring that no one was directly behind him. Satisfied that the area was clear, he pulled back on the arming trigger handle. Connah positioned the M-72 Light Anti-tank Weapon on his right shoulder and poised his fingers above the triggering bar. A slight touch and the LAW would launch a sixty-six-millimeter rocket that traveled at over one-hundred-forty-five meters per second. Connah waited patiently. The projectile was deadly, able to penetrate an eleven-inch-thick armor plate. Still, its effective range was only three hundred meters.

Stone lay beside Connah, peering through a range-finder and counting down the distance. "Three-seventy-five."

Connah replied, "Tell me when they get inside two-fifty."

"You're the man."

The two-man team lay in wait for what seemed like hours but was, in reality, only minutes.

"Two-forty," Stone announced.

Connah pressed the trigger bar. The weapon fired, the rocket ignited, sending a blast of air and debris behind that was so strong it would have blown apart a wood crate. The rocket, as designed, burned all of its propellants before it left the tube and flew true to course. The high-explosive projectile flew across the barge's bow, slammed into the far bank, and exploded. The explosion was so large that it created a geyser that hit the boat's bow, pushing the barge onto the river's opposite bank.

The bewildered crew scanned the trees and bushes in a vain attempt to see where the rocket had come from.

Connah stepped out of his hiding place and fired several bullets into the side of the barge.

In Portuguese, Rocha hollered at the crew to drop their weapons, or the next rocket would hit the barge. The guards on the barge dropped their weapons and raised their hands. "What now?" Rocha asked Connah.

"I want to speak to the boat's captain."

A burly man in a dirty T-shirt appeared from the cabin with his arms in the air. Rocha ordered him to come ashore.

The drug runner was soaked with sweat when he reached the attackers.

Connah handed him an envelope, and Rocha said, "Give this to your *chefe*."

The captain looked at him with disbelief, then snatched the envelope and ran back to his vessel.

When the barge was back in the middle of the river, Connah said, "I think, if they didn't already get the message, they have it now."

Rocha walked out of the brush and studied the carnage on the river. "A strong message. The street value of what is on that barge will be many times more than what they took from you."

Stone smiled. "That's my boy, Ian. As subtle as a kick in the groin."

$ $ $ $ $

Six hours after the forced stop, the barge reached Tefé. Gomes jumped aboard and shouted at the boat captain, chastising him for being late.

The Colombian thrust the envelope into Gomes' chest and told him of the forced landing. He turned to his crew and began shouting at them to move the cargo to the *Princesa de Amazonas*.

Gomes opened the envelope and read the brief letter inside. He was still laughing when he boarded the boat.

"What is so funny?" Correia asked.

Gomes told him the story he'd heard from the barge captain and said, "If Fábio thought he was going to keep Connah's money, this would surely change his mind. Connah has promised that if he doesn't get what is his, Cristiano will be killed. His body dumped in the jungle for the vultures to feast on, and no more shipments will arrive via the river." He handed the letter to Correia.

"When Cavalcanti hears about this, the shit is going to hit the fan."

"I hope you have already said your goodbyes to Fábio."

"He has made his bed, and now he must sleep in it. His fate has been decided. It's his family that I am worried about."

93

Antônio Melo Cavalcanti was sitting in the living room of the penthouse suite of his hotel when there was a knock on the door. "Come," he called.

Martin Rossi entered the room and took as much time as possible approaching his boss.

"Why are you acting like a child who has broken his mother's favorite vase?"

"Pedro called me."

"Is Goncalves doing what he was told?"

"Yes, but there is this." He handed a crinkled sheet of paper to his boss.

Cavalcanti read the letter, and the look on Rossi's face told him all he needed to know. "Get me Goncalves...and I want him here an hour ago!"

Rossi nodded and then bowed to the *chefe* before he darted out the door.

$ $ $ $ $

Fábio Correia Goncalves looked like a freshman who'd been called to the principal's office for the first time. He stood with a valise in hand at the threshold of the living room door, uncertain what to do next.

Cavalcanti's back was turned toward the local drug lord. He finally turned, and his red-faced anger showed his level of outrage. "Do you know what your stupid action has done? For a mere two million U.S. dollars, you could have cost us a shipment of coca with over ten million U. S. dollars street value. If you can't do the math, I'll do it for you, that's about fifty-six-million, seven-hundred-thousand *reais*—and for what? Twelve and a half million *reais* and a rubber plantation that has not produced a single cup of usable latex in fifty years!"

Goncalves knew that he stood on the brink of a very high cliff and could be pushed off at any second. He had no idea what he could say, so he placed the valise near the *chefe's* feet, stepped back, and remained silent.

Cavalcanti looked at the briefcase and appeared to calm down. "Is it *all* there?"

"*Sim.*"

Cavalcanti walked over to his bar and poured himself a glass of *cachaça*. He picked up a satellite phone and dialed a number that Rodolfo Barrios Ribeiro had given him. "I have your merchandise," he said in English. "I assume my payment will soon be released?"

Cavalcanti broke the connection and motioned to his under lord. "Well, don't stand there like a dummy. Come, let's drink and celebrate. This mess will be over in a few hours."

Once Goncalves had poured a drink, the *chefe* of the PCC said, "Let's go onto the balcony. We can get some fresh air, take in the scenery, and possibly come up with a plan." He turned to Martin Rossi and added, "Martin, why don't you join us?"

Rossi nodded and followed them through the sliding glass portal leading to an expansive patio that overlooked Manaus and the Rio Negro. He stood two paces behind Goncalves and his boss. They leaned against the balcony's railing and looked like two old friends having an early evening cocktail while taking in the sights.

Cavalcanti turned to Goncalves and asked, "Have you learned anything from this business?"

"*Sim, Chefe.*"

"That is good." Cavalcanti looked at Rossi, who nodded. "Now," Cavalcanti said in a calm, almost friendly manner, "let me ask you if you have heard about the shipment that was coming downriver from Tabatinga?"

"I have heard that there was a shipment due, that's all."

"Well, it did not arrive in Tefé on time. We have reason to think that this American, Connah, may be the reason."

Goncalves's head snapped around. "Connah?"

"*Sim*, Connah…who, I'm told, if you had not fucked with, would have taken what was stolen from him, paid you as agreed, and now be on his way back to the United States."

Cavalcanti nodded to Rossi.

The assassin stepped forward, placed the sound suppressor of a nine-millimeter pistol against the back of Goncalves's head, and pulled the trigger.

For a second, Goncalves stood as if nothing had happened. Then he stumbled forward one step and fell across the railing. Rossi picked up the dead man's feet and threw him over the balustrade.

Cavalcanti turned from the barrier and entered the penthouse before the body hit the paved tennis court thirty stories below.

94

Stone stood near the hangar when the Beechcraft taxied inside, and Araujo Bocaiúva shut down the engines. Connah exited the aircraft, and Stone asked, "I see you're still alive. It must have gone okay."

"It went fine. Cavalcanti gave me the cash, and I have the passcode book to get my money in the account in the Caymans, and in turn, he got his grandson back."

"You know," Stone said, "once I got to know Cristiano, I grew to like him."

"I had a friend once who had a pet snake. Like you, he grew to like that snake. 'But,' he told me that he was always careful with it, 'because when all is said and done, a snake is still a snake.' I always remembered that."

"Did you deal with Gomes and Correia?"

"Cavalcanti told me that they were no longer my problem. I believe him."

"He going to have them whacked?"

"Worse, he hired them. He reminded me that one should always keep their friends close, but their enemies should be kept closer. I interpreted that as telling me that if either of them crosses the line, no matter how little, they'll be taken care of."

Stone pondered that and said, "That sort of reminds me of a story I heard years ago."

Connah smiled. "I'm surprised. It is usually me who has all the stories."

Stone grinned. "And this time, you have to listen to me. You ever hear about the sword of Damocles?"

"I've heard the expression but never thought much about it."

"The famed 'Sword of Damocles' dates back to the moral of an ancient parable. The tale centers on Dionysius II, a tyrannical king who once ruled over the Sicilian city of Syracuse. Though wealthy and powerful, Dionysius was supremely unhappy. His iron-fisted rule had made him many enemies.

Tormented by assassination fears, he slept in a bed chamber surrounded by a moat. He trusted no one but his daughters to shave his beard with a razor.

"One day, the king got mad when a court flatterer named Damocles kissed his ass with compliments and remarked how blissful his life must be. 'Since this life delights you,' the pissed-off king replied, 'do you wish to taste it yourself and make a trial of my good fortune?' When Damocles agreed, Dionysius seated him on a golden couch and ordered a bunch of servants to wait on him. He was treated to the best cuts of meat and lavished with scented perfumes and ointments. Damocles couldn't believe his luck. But just when he was starting to enjoy the life of a king, he noticed that Dionysius had also hung a razor-sharp sword pointing down from the ceiling. It was positioned over Damocles' head, suspended only by a single strand of horsehair. From then on, the courtier's fear for his life made it impossible for him to savor his good luck. After casting several nervous glances at the blade dangling above him, he asked to be excused, saying he no longer wished to be so fortunate."

Connah chuckled. "That about sums up what life for Gomes and Correia is going to be like."

They exited the hangar, and Stone said, "This came together good—almost too good."

"Yeah, I know. When I offered Cavalcanti this place, he thanked me but said he had no use for it. You and I both know that is a bunch of bull. It would be a great depot for bringing his boatloads of shit, if nothing else. The plane would have been handy too."

"So, you keeping the place?"

"I decided to give it to Araujo Bocaiúva and Guilherme Inacio Rocha."

"That's really nice of you."

"Well, Cavalcanti also told me to get the fuck out of his country, and if I ever come back, he'll have me skinned alive and hung from the roof of his cabana."

"Ouch. What are you going to do about that?"

"Araujo will fly us to Rio tomorrow. We have two first-class tickets on a flight out of Rio the day after. Like I've always said, 'my father raised a fool, not a babbling idiot.'"

Epilogue

Union Oyster House, Boston, Massachusetts

Connah was sitting with his brother Tom, Amanda, and Stone. They were drinking beer and enjoying raw oysters on a half-shell when Billie O'Reilly and Bobbi Spinelli arrived. Connah was shocked to see the two former antagonists acting like best friends forever. He was even more surprised when the three women hugged and air-kissed as if they had been childhood cronies.

When they were seated, he said, "I must admit I never expected to see this day. You two have been after one another's scalp for twenty-plus years."

"Unlike you," Billie said, "people do change."

"Yeah," Bobbi said. "Nothing unites people like a common enemy."

"I hope," Connah said, "that you aren't alluding to me."

"Don't be a narcissist," Billie said. "We're talking about Jiggs."

A server appeared, and they ordered drinks. When the waiter left, Bobbi turned to Connah. "So fill us in on the latest. What's the situation in Ecuador?"

"Brazil," Connah corrected her.

"Brazil, Ecuador, what's the diff?"

"Yeah," Stone said. "What have you heard?"

"Well, the last I heard, Correia is still running drugs and anything he can to make a buck. Cavalcanti has turned the Manaus operation over to Gomes."

"He got promoted?" Stone seemed astonished.

"It might look that way. Running an operation for the PCC can be like walking through a minefield wearing lead boots and a blindfold. It's only a matter of time before you screw up and end up dead." He took a drink of beer and asked Billie, "You ever hear what happened to Tegan Hale?"

"I can answer that," Bobbi said. "She's on death row in the federal prison in Muncy, Pennsylvania."

"For killing Diaz?" Connah asked.

"Don't know if they got her for him or not. I do know when they ran a background check on her, it came back like a who's who in the world of terrorism. I believe if they could have, they would have put her in that prison in Afghanistan where they tortured the prisoners."

"Bagram," Stone said.

"Bless you," Bobbi said.

"The prison is Bagram. It's gone now."

"And you two?" Connah asked.

"We're working things out," Billie said. "It's gonna take time, but at least we're talking."

Billie turned to Amanda. "How you doing, Hon?"

"Better. My doctor has me on meds that don't make me feel like a zombie."

"I'm happy for you," Billie replied.

"I don't know how you live with your condition," Bobbi said. "I know I couldn't do it. I'm not as strong as you."

"What have you been up to, Tom?" Billie queried.

Tom looked at Connah and hesitated.

"Go on, tell them," Connah said.

"Connah wouldn't train us to be snipers," Tom said, "However, he's financed us. We own a gun shop in New Hampshire. We're doing okay." He chuckled.

"What?" Billie asked.

"Yeah, fess up." Bobbi toned in.

"Well, I handle the books and run the store. Amanda talks about the guns, gives shooting classes, and handles all the technical stuff."

In unison, they turned to Connah and Stone. "What about you guys?" Billie asked. "You going back to Brazil anytime soon?"

"How about never," Connah said. "When the top man in the PCC says if you return, he'll have you skinned and make a beach umbrella from your hide, you better listen. I'm happy sitting on my deck."

"I'm back in my trout stream," Stone said. "Ain't no cavemen there."

Other than Connah, everyone seemed befuddled by his comment. "He means caiman," Connah said, "It's a big, nasty crocodile that lives in the Amazon River."

"Oh," Amanda said.

"What about the future, Connah. You just gonna sit by your lake?"

"I don't know," he said. "I've been thinking of getting married…"

Stone snapped back so hard his chair toppled over backward.

Tom shook his head and said, "He'll never learn, will he?"

"Hasn't since we were in junior high school," Billie said.

"I think," Bobbi said, "he got hit in the head with a hockey puck one too many times."

Author's Note

I had the wonderful experience of visiting São Paulo, Brazil, in 1999. The Brazilian people were terrific hosts and made my trip memorable. However, one aspect left an impression that has remained with me.

The flight took me over the Amazon Basin. I was astonished to see the smoke from numerous fires throughout the area. Today we continuously hear about global warming and its repercussions. I don't argue that industrial pollution and carbon emissions are part of the problem because they are. Nevertheless, all we ever hear about is the industrial causes in the media. I believe that deforestation of Earth's tropical rainforests is a more severe and urgent problem.

Since 1978 about one million square kilometers of Amazon rainforest across Brazil, Peru, Colombia, Bolivia, Venezuela, Suriname, Guyana, and French Guiana have been destroyed. Why is Earth's largest rainforest being destroyed? Before the arrival of Europeans, deforestation in the Amazon was primarily the product of subsistence farmers who cut down trees to produce crops for their families and local consumption. But in the latter part of the 20th century, that began to change, with an increasing proportion of deforestation driven by industrial activities and large-scale agriculture. By the 2000s, more than three-quarters of the forest clearing in the Amazon was for cattle-ranching.

It is common knowledge that plants, trees included, absorb carbon dioxide (CO_2) during the daylight hours and emit oxygen during the night hours. I've heard it said that the tropical rainforests are where Earth sweats. Combine the decrease in oxygen with a corresponding loss of rainforest, and you have a recipe for disaster. In 1973 an ecological thriller entitled *Soylent Green* was released. It portrayed a dystopian world where, by 2022, the cumulative effects of overpopulation, pollution, and an apparent climate catastrophe have caused severe worldwide shortages of food, water, and housing. By my calendar, I was writing this in November 2021, and I see the movie in the same vein as I see Orwell's *1984*. Orwell envisioned many things that have happened, and I see *Soylent Green* as equally prophetic.

It is time for us to wake up. It is not just the industrialized countries that are causing the problem. If climate control is to happen, every country on Earth needs to start taking this seriously. In 2021, the United Nations Climate Change Conference was held in Glasgow, Scotland. Notable absent nations were some of the leading countries emitting greenhouse gas. The prime ministers or heads of state from China, South Africa, Russia, Saudi Arabia, Iran, Mexico, Brazil, Turkey, Malaysia, and Vatican City did not attend the meeting. If global warming is a great danger, as we are being told, something must be done to bring all causes and producing countries to the table.

I live in Maine, a state where logging is a major proponent of the economy. I, however, do not see how it helps anyone to turn this:

into this:

Stockholm, ME
December, 2021

Acknowledgments

A tip of the hat to the gang at Encircle Publications weekly Happy Hour and the Thursday afternoon writer group meeting via Zoom.

Edwin (Jay) Bullard for all the help he's given these past years.

Heidi Carter of Bogan Books in Fort Kent, Maine, supports and assists.

Thanks are owed to Jill Sutherland and Matt Cost, my Beta Readers. Their feedback was invaluable.

To my late sister-in-law, Shirley Bokun (1936–2019), a terrific source of support for many years.

As always, I owe more than I can ever repay to Jane Hartley for her support.

And to the Readers who make all of this possible.

About the Author

Vaughn C. Hardacker is the author of six published novels. His short stories have appeared in several anthologies. He is a member of Mystery Writers of America, International Thriller Writers, and the Maine Writers & Publishers Alliance. Three of his novels, *Sniper* (2015), *The Fisherman* (2016), and *Wendigo* (2018) were finalists in the Maine Writers and Publishers Alliance Maine Literary Awards. *Ripped Off* is his second novel for Encircle Publications; *The Exchange* (September, 2020) was his first.

Vaughn served as a U. S. Marine from 1966 to 1970 and from 1972 to 1974. He is now on inactive status and is a member of The Marine Corps League. He lives in Stockholm, Maine, which he says is "two miles from the end of civilization as we know it." He is working on his next crime thriller.

If you enjoyed reading this book,
please consider writing your honest review
and sharing it with other readers.

Many of our Authors are happy to participate in
Book Club and Reader Group discussions.
For more information, contact us at info@encirclepub.com.

Thank you,
Encircle Publications

For news about more exciting new fiction, join us at:

Facebook: www.facebook.com/encirclepub

Instagram: www.instagram.com/encirclepublications

Twitter: twitter.com/encirclepub

Sign up for the Encircle Publications newsletter:
eepurl.com/cs8taP